I0545293

THE LAST BLADE OF GRASS
ROBERT BROWN

SEVERED PRESS
HOBART TASMANIA

THE LAST BLADE OF GRASS

Copyright © 2015 by Robert Brown
Copyright © 2015 by Severed Press

www.severedpress.com

All rights reserved. No part of this book may be
reproduced or transmitted in any form or by any
electronic or mechanical means, including
photocopying, recording or by any information and
retrieval system, without the written permission of
the publisher and author, except where permitted by law.
This novel is a work of fiction. Names,
characters, places and incidents are the product of
the author's imagination, or are used fictitiously.
Any resemblance to actual events, locales or persons,
living or dead, is purely coincidental.

ISBN: 978-1-925342-01-7

All rights reserved.

CHAPTER ONE
THE JOURNEY HOME

June

Be careful what you wish for. I always knew the saying had meaning, but never imagined my wishes for a global re-start would be caused by zombies. Well, I guess I shouldn't say I never imagined it. I was a big fan of zombie books and movies before the world fell apart. What I mean is that I am a realist and a skeptic, so while thoughts of zombies once were entertaining, I knew the odds of some type of disease taking hold that could be considered a zombie illness was extremely remote.

To humanity's good fortune, the zombie-like infected population is like the old school movies in the way they move. They creep up on you slowly and silently, only sometimes giving themselves away with a raspy breath or a scraping shoe. Their shuffling pace is nothing faster than a regular walk. This slow movement has helped those groups of survivors such as us overcome the sheer volume of actual infected people that are out there.

Another fortunate thing for us is the infected aren't actually the risen or walking dead. It's just a disease, an infection that was spread intentionally, but with the unintentional consequences of turning the population into zombie like cannibals. But that's not so important right now.

Based on what we have been able to learn from other survivors around the world with Ham radios, it seems that like here, most of the human population in urban centers became infected in the first week of the diseases' arrival.

The primary reason for the high level of infection was an inability of people to effectively defend themselves against the diseased. The only way to fight back without fear of infection is using firearms from a distance, because any physical interaction with a diseased person exposes you to the infected blood or saliva.

Unfortunately for humanity, most countries had low gun ownership rates and high restrictions for the general populace, so those nations and the U.S. states and cities with the lowest firearm ownership saw the highest infection rates. Even with firearms the fighting was difficult, because any noise, especially the loud report of gunfire, attracts the infected.

Now, eight months into this situation, the numbers of humans both infected and un-infected have dropped sharply. The severe winter we just made it through in the U.S. and other nations in the northern hemisphere killed off many of the people that had managed to survive the infected. People just aren't used to living without the comforts of electricity or oil or natural gas heat. The die off was particularly severe, because for sustained periods the temperatures around the world dropped well below zero degrees Fahrenheit. Here in Oregon, the temperatures were more like what we had when we lived in South Dakota, in the range of -10 to -15 °F for weeks at a time. Even now in June, the weather is unusually cold.

So here I am eight months after the first reports of "rioting" began, crouched down and hiding in an abandoned store with my family. My wife and our five kids have been on a supply and training mission of sorts. Since the numbers of infected have dropped off and the weather started to turn better we've been looking for other groups of people, news, supplies and any unusual concentrations of remaining infected, that we should be concerned about. We are heading back to our property where there are several other families waiting for us to get back.

We didn't have much luck with finding other survivors this trip. Yesterday we ran into a man named Jim Margrove in a small town on the outskirts of Medford, Oregon. He was dying from an infected cut. He told us he had been scraped up pretty bad in a fight a week earlier, that's where he got his infection. His broken leg prevented him from freely searching for medicine, and you could see blackish spider veins over nearly his entire right thigh and abdomen. The blood poisoning had spread too far for antibiotics to help at this point. We both exchanged our incredulity that one could survive the zombie apocalypse for eight months, only to die by what was once considered a minor infection from being cut.

The worst part of the situation for Jim is that it wasn't a fight with an infected that did him in. He happened to cross paths with what sounded by his description like one of the druggers of the past. Druggies are the current and former users of illegal drugs, but that definition didn't fit the new threat we had to deal with. We started calling the formerly medicated population "druggers." This is to distinguish them from those individuals that just went bat-shit crazy from dealing with all the fighting and dying since the end times arrived. The druggers are the people that were on meds to allow them to properly function in society. You know the ones, the severe paranoids, schizophrenics, manic depressives, and others.

Not that we have many problems from the depressives, if they survived the initial attacks, even their meds couldn't help them deal with the psychological impact of seeing people they know get run down and chewed up. Hell, it hasn't been easy for any of us, but when you throw in a medical tendency to get depressed when things are good. Your life expectancy isn't very long when the world literally turns to shit, and you no longer have modern medicines to help regulate your moods.

The schizophrenics are the ones we really have to worry about, and one of them is probably what happened to Jim. If anything will help you survive a zombie-like pandemic apocalypse, it is being paranoid about everything. The schizophrenics have the market cornered for that realm. I mean a lot of them died in the early days of the infection, because they were medicated and thought the bloodied up corpse-like looking people coming toward them were illusions. So unfortunately, many of them died as a result of learning to ignore things that they felt shouldn't be real.

I shouldn't say unfortunately though, because it is truly fortunate for us that there aren't more of them out there. The schizophrenics are amazing survivalists. It seems that their deep down instincts to hide, distrust, scavenge, and kill have truly blossomed in this world. And once they were no longer assisted by the hallucination blocking drugs they were used to, every human became an infected to them.

So I'm going off on a tirade against people that were once considered mentally diseased, and I could never have gotten away with bashing them like this when times were good, but then I also didn't have a cause to. Now I'm just pissed that it isn't just a plague of infected cannibalistic humans that I have to worry about, or the gangs of criminals and violent opportunists. It is also those that are just plain crazy that will walk up to you like it is a wonderful morning, happy as a clam to see another human being, and they will pull out a knife or a club and try to kill you.

My anger over the situation runs a little deeper since I can imagine the pain he was going through before his death. Jim didn't just break his leg and get cut up in his encounter. His wife was killed in the fight as well. Jim and his wife were heading through the town of Central Point and into Medford for the same basic purposes as us; to try and find supplies, people, and maybe some information.

3

The two of them encountered a young man sitting on the steps outside a house. After they said hello to the man, he started crying, and asked them if they were real. What should seem to be a light bulb going off type of question was actually a common one now with most people isolated and displaced, surviving on their own for months with no non-infected human contact. So when a normal person approaches another survivor, each of them often think the other person they are seeing is just wishful thinking, or at worst, a minor hallucination.

When this guy asked Jim and his wife if they were real, started crying and walking toward them, they weren't thinking danger as he approached, they were thinking lets comfort this kindred spirit. Not so kindred of a spirit though, because when he reached them, as quick as a flash, he pulled out a blade and cut Susan's throat. Jim told us the fight with the guy wasn't long, twenty seconds, maybe thirty from the first swing at Susan to Jim killing their attacker. Jim got cut and broke his leg in an awkward fall while struggling with the guy, and still managed to pull out his own blade to kill his attacker. But it was all too late.

I'm pissed because I keep reliving Jim's story whenever we rest and I have a moment to think. I can feel his loss as if I was him and it was my wife Simone that was killed by the stranger. Part of my anger, though, is guilt. I think most anger contains some form of guilt, but my guilt is because I have been doing so well. My whole family has survived this disaster for humanity. Of course I was a prepper, but the odds of us all surviving this long were not high at all, even with our preparations.

There are seven of us, and since the winter hopefully ended and encounters with the infected have dropped off, we all travel together. My wife and I figure any day could be the last one, and we want to be together if it happens. So either we all go at once or at least we will know what happens to our loved ones if they die.

I'm sure it sounds insane to take small children out into an infected world, but this is the reality we live in, and they have to grow up knowing what they must do to survive. This makes me think back to a movie I saw with my wife before the collapse. The movie was good, but it still pissed us both off, because the kid in the movie was so unprepared for the world he lived in. At the time we watched it, our kids were already more prepared to deal with a disaster, and weren't born into it the way the kid in the movie was.

Because we did consider the negative possibilities in life and prepared for them, it just made the movie that much more unbelievable that a kid born after the end of the world wouldn't have been toughened up by their parents' to learn to survive in that new and dangerous environment.

Once upon a time, before this world descended into hell, our children were not only learning how to save money and find out which store had the best deal on milk. Those were the necessary survival skills of the modern age. But we also taught them things like knowing how to be quiet with approaching danger, how to hide effectively, and of course, how to shoot and how to fight.

Even if the world never fell apart, there were murderers and rapists in the world, as well as rabid animals or mountain lions when out hiking. My wife and I figured the children that were raised on the plains of Africa around lions, elephants, and hippos already knew the skills we were teaching our own kids. It's too bad more people didn't raise their children with a proper understanding of the dangers in the world, as opposed to trying to shield them from all mention of harm.

Looking back at the faces of my family around me in the store, I hope my five kids will live to be the start of a new human society. I've done what I can to give them the right start. Now I just have to keep them alive so they can grow into well-rounded adults. Well-rounded in this current version of the world, of course, means being able to scavenge, kill, and survive.

Our kids are young. They are Hannah, age 12; Olivia, age 10; William, age 7; Amelia, age 5; and Benjamin, age 1. Benjamin was born just four months before this disease started to hit. Normally I would say that the eldest children have the best chance of surviving in a disaster situation, but in this world I'm not so sure.

Our four oldest kids can remember, like Simone and I do, the fun and easy world of America. A world where we spoiled our kids with tons of toys, took them to the lake and the beach, went on hikes, played games on the computer, or just sat and watched movies at the theatre.

We still have a good amount of food stored, so we don't starve, but there are no longer the visits to Subway for sandwiches or IHOP for some pancakes and eggs. And no more trips to the toy store to pick up the latest plastic toy made in China. The world we were accustomed to changed, and we are constantly struggling to deal with it.

Our youngest, Benjamin, however, will only know this world. We will do our best to teach him what things used to be like, but he will never have the longing for what he once had as the rest of us do. I think that will make him stronger. All of us have the *here and now* to deal with and for our kids, the brief moments of entertainment, like reading or singing songs, are small parts of their day if we can fit them in, rather than being the rule of the day in the world for us before the collapse.

*

The infected with their steady lumbering pace are finally shuffling past where we are hiding. They were probably trying to follow us but didn't see us hide, because Benjamin saw them before they got too close and told us the infected were coming, in his own way. Benjamin is our one year old, and when he sees an infected, he gives a growl. So when we heard him say, "GRRRR," in his baby tone, we all turned to see where he was looking. Far off down the road shambled two infected. We would normally be able to outpace them, but are moving slower due to the supplies we are carrying on our bikes and trailers. Fortunately it is just two, so it's better to kill them now than have to deal with them later.

Back to our present situation, the two infected have finally walked by the front door of the store we are hiding in, and it is time to deal with them. My job is to walk out behind them and kill them before they have a chance to turn to kill me. It is a basic ambush tactic we successfully use regularly when we are out. We would use our guns, but I'd rather not attract other infected, or other survivors for that matter, with us moving so slowly and loaded with these supplies.

"I love you, Simone! I love you kids. You know what to do if I don't make it?" I ask.

"We know what to do, Eddie," my wife replies. "Just be careful and quick. We are right here watching."

So I glance one more time at my wife and kids, a few of them give me little smiles, and I step out the door. I normally use my mini-sword for close up ambushes like this. It is actually a sixteen inch blade machete. It is great for hacking, and I ground the tip into a point so it can also do some stabbing. I take four quick strides to catch up to the slower infected and give a good swing with the long blade. I strike him perfectly, right on the back of the head, just at the bottom of the ear, chopping through his cerebellum and spinal cord, and sending him on his way down.

The infected in front, a woman, starts turning to face me, but her slow shuffling movements prevent her from even getting her arms up in an attempt to grab at me before I start my swing. My movements are much less fluid after drawing back from my hit on the man. Fortunately for me, she is turning around to her left, presenting the back of her neck to my right handed swing.

While swinging the blade I hear my wife yell, "No," from inside the store, and it causes me to flinch enough that I don't give a straight swing. My angle changes so my blade gets stuck in her neck instead of cutting through. It's lodged in her vertebrae, and judging by her downward motion, it did do enough damage to at least paralyze her legs, if nothing else. Whichever one of my kids is making Simone yell 'no' and distracting me during an infected cull is going to be in huge trouble when I get finished.

The infected lady hits the ground and is facing away from the store, with my machete sticking up from her neck. I start to step over her so I can put my right foot on her back to use the leverage to yank out my blade. That's when I get hit.

I heard some more yelling from the store a split second before the impact, but even if I had the chance to glance up at my attacker, I'm stepping over a body, and wouldn't have any balanced movement for escape or defense. I have been tackled by a large man. He's probably 230 pounds, and of course, is athletic. He blindsided me from close to the same direction the two infected came, hitting me on my left side. He came from an angle north of the store, so he was out of the view of the store window until it was too late.

Even under normal circumstances, a standing attacker can cover 20 feet of distance and get to you before you can draw a weapon for defensive fire. There just wasn't enough time for my family to adjust their aim to shoot the man, who was running at full speed, before he slammed into me.

This guy might be a drugger, maybe a schizophrenic. I can't think of any other reason someone would run full hilt into me while I am killing two people who are obviously infected. The crazy people are never former fat slobs or cubicle dwellers. They always seem to be athletic, high school or college aged, and they suck. I mean I'm 45 years old, almost 46, and I have to wrestle with a psychotic idiot that is younger and easily 50 pounds heavier than me.

It's just dumb luck that my body position when I get hit causes my left arm to wedge at his neck under his chin. His impact into me dislodged my machete from the spine of my former ambush victim, but I can't hold onto it when I hit the ground so it flies from my hand. I can barely breathe from the impact, with the ground, and from the weight of this guy on top of me.

He is already snapping his jaws, trying to bite at my face. "Wait what?" Looking at his expression, I can see that this is no psycho or druggie. This guy is infected. But it can't be. This guy was moving fast! I mean running full speed when he hit me. At least that's what it felt like. He hit me hard, and I don't think the impact was just from his size.

I start reaching wildly with my right arm trying to grab my smaller blade kept by my leg, while he is snapping above me, and grabbing at my face with his hands. I pull my knife out, and I stab it up through the center of this infected's mouth. The handle of my blade wags obscenely out between his lips, like some kind of new designer metal tongue, and he keeps snapping his teeth at me, chomping down on the knife's handle. I can only stare at him while I'm still trying to hold him off and catch my breath from the impact of landing.

The biggest problem with the infected so far, besides the fact that they exist, has been their numbers. We all learned early on that with this disease, it is either kill them, or they will eat you. Or they'll infect you, and you will turn if you manage to escape after being bitten. Dealing with the infected has already been difficult for most, impossible for some. But a decent defense can be made against a slow moving group of the infected, even when dealing with hundreds or thousands if situated properly.

The slow infected are the only kind that we have encountered so far. They are the only type anyone has seen anywhere in the world. I mean, we haven't spoken with everyone out there of course, and haven't heard much at all these last two months, but no one has mentioned the infected running.

The problem we have now is that they are changing. Either the parasite has mutated or the infected are adapting. The tables had turned against us humans that day when the infection was first spread. And right now in front of me, sitting on my stomach, I am seeing the latest evolutionary step of the infected kind. The knife sticking out of this infected man's mouth would not be noticed by any other infected that I have encountered. I have seen them stuck or have stabbed them in many places, and unless there is blunt force trauma to the head or severing the spine at the neck, they just don't acknowledge any injury.

This infected man knows the knife is in its mouth and can't bite with it there. Like other infected, it didn't flinch or blink when I shoved the knife in, but this infected has stopped its grasping of my face and head, is sitting back up from leaning over me, and is now pulling the knife out of its mouth. It understands what is wrong and knows how to fix it.

This is not supposed to happen. These things have never moved quickly once infected, and they're not supposed to regain their reasoning skills once they have the fever. We have tested people to see what happens when they get infected, and the parasite causes severe body tremors and a fever that usually runs in the 108 to 109 °F degree range. It burns just long enough to fry most normal cognitive function and fine motor skills. So, manipulating your wrist, hand, and fingers to grab onto a knife and pull it out and away from your mouth should be impossible.

A loud *crack* sounds out above me as Simone bounces her baseball bat off the head of this infected bastard, causing him to collapse on top of me. "Did you just see that!" we both yell to each other. Our second lines are not identical but are each equally disturbing. While I am yelling, "It just pulled the knife out of its mouth!" She is yelling, "That thing just ran!" We both just blindly stare at each other for a second, absorbing this new information.

Finally, I start to lift my back off the sidewalk so I can drag the rest of my body out from under my avid admirer. He apparently has decided that he just doesn't want to see me go without a goodbye kiss. In this case, a goodbye bite. So he clamps down on my left forearm right below the elbow, through the shirt sleeve, and into the meat. It hurts like a motherfucker, and the blood that is around his lips and on my sleeve shows that he is piercing my skin.

Two more successive *cracks* from Simone's bat cave in my attackers head, but the damage is already done and plain to see. I pull up my sleeve. My arm has a distinctive bleeding bite mark and also some torn flesh where the teeth pulled back when the infected's head was slammed with the bat. So I am bitten, and my kids are gathering behind my wife. Hannah and Olivia are standing with shocked wide eyes. William is on the verge, like Simone, with tears welling up. Benjamin says, "Uh-oh, owie." And points to my bleeding arm. Only Amelia stands stoically, and says, "You'll be all right, Daddy. You always are."

"Simone! Kids! Check for more infected," I say, realizing we were all out in front of the store now, and made quite a commotion with the fighting. "My being bitten doesn't change a thing. You all have to keep watching out for more of them, okay?"

The infected female that I hit is paralyzed from the neck down, but her mouth is still snapping and her eyes are darting from person to person wishing to get a bite on one of us. Simone uses her bat to collapse the skull of the chomping head. You can see the fear and anger in Simone's face as she repeatedly brings down the bat. It is a terrifying sight that I never want to be on the bad side of.

Getting out from under this idiot that bit me is difficult. Getting up is painful and not just because of the bite on my arm. My back is killing me from the fall, and I'm sure I have some friction burns on it from sliding a little when I impacted. Hannah is first to say that nothing else is out here, and Simone shortly agrees.

"Okay," I tell them. "Everyone get back in the store. It has almost been a minute since my bite. I could change anytime. Just stay in there for five minutes and watch me."

Five minutes come and go as I am sitting outside waiting for the change. I don't turn, so I get up and head into the store to figure out our next step, and get my arm cleaned up.

I have a small medical kit with disinfectant, bandages, and stitching supplies. So while Simone is cleaning my wound and preparing to stitch up my arm, I am going over what we should do next with everybody. "I've been bitten, and we are about four hours away from our place at a slow walk. I didn't become infected immediately, so we should have the six hours before the fever hits me. If nothing has changed, this will give us plenty of time to make it back home to the ranch. It also looks like it is just about noon, so we have plenty of light left in the day to get there without issue as well."

"We could leave the bikes and trailers here and head back at a quicker pace. If we hurry, we might make it in two hours if we want," Olivia offers.

"I'm not going to leave all of these archery supplies here. This is the future of your defense. Rushing home would be a good plan if my injury required getting help more quickly," I reply. "But we have cleaned it as well as we could at home, and your mom is stitching it up right now. We have a good amount of time to make it there with everything we gathered. Also, I am concerned that increasing my activity level by rushing home may quicken the spread of the parasite, and I would rather just stay as calm as I can to make sure that you all make it home safely."

"So *we* all make it home safely," my wife adds.

"Let's just get ourselves pulled together and ready to finish our trip home in one piece, okay?" I smile while saying it, but inside I am worried and you can see in Simone's eyes that she is as well. To distract from the mood, I add, "We should remember where this shoe store is so on our next trip this way, we can get some extra shoes for everybody, and stock up on everything as a possible trade or barter item in the future."

While I would normally suggest that we look through everything now and see what we can find, I can't risk not getting them back to the house and other families before the fever hits. We also have our bikes and trailers loaded down to the extreme with the stuff we picked up, so shoe boxes will definitely not fit without leaving something else behind.

As we leave the store and the three lifeless infected bodies, my mind starts to wander through the happier thoughts in life. One big positive that has come from the apocalypse is a healthier eating lifestyle. I mean, I miss fast food and chocolate donuts, and my wife misses ice cream, but because we were already prepared for some type of disaster, we had food stockpiled and are doing quite well. We have buckets and buckets of sealed rice, beans, and dehydrated potatoes. Thousands of cans and jars of beef, chicken, fish and the same amount, if not more, of vegetables and fruits. Most importantly, we have an abundance of seasonings of various types to make sure we aren't eating plain rice and bland chicken.

I know that thousands of people, if not millions right now, are not just trying to hide from the infected and survive this end of the world scenario, but they are starving while they are doing it. I feel for them. I do. And when good people have come our way, we helped them the best we could, and tried to get them started in the right direction if they were unable or unwilling to stay with us on our ranch. Even with my sympathy for those suffering out there, a less compassionate part of me always wanted things to fall apart from what they were. Not to this extent, but enough to remind people how precious life is, and to appreciate what they have.

Thinking of food makes me chuckle to myself, and say, "Simone, when we get back, after my fever is done, I would like a nice steak."

"Cow I hope," she replies. Insinuating I might want people steak after my fever.

We both have a good chuckle over it, but the kids are still oblivious to many of the strange things we find funny.

The final length of the trip home was largely uneventful according to the current state of the world. We saw no other survivors and only had one more of the infected to put down. I was on point and managed the kill cleanly with Hannah's spike. She has a long tire iron and the non-curved edge was sharpened into a point. That point went right through the face to the left of its nose and out the back of its skull. It was a female, only about 5' 6" and 120 pounds, so I decided to keep our group moving and just end it when the thing was within reach. No search of the body was necessary, as this infected must have been attacked while she was relaxing at home, due to the tattered remains of pajama pants and top.

Over the four hour trip, my mind keeps replaying the events of the last five days away from the house, mainly repeating today's events. We've lost a lot of people at the ranch already, and a huge portion of the human population has been infected or killed off by this thing. But no matter how bad it has gotten so far, there was always a hope of wiping this thing out, and rebuilding. I don't know anymore what hope there is if the infected can run and use their hands for more than just basic grabbing. Will they know how to open gates and fences? Could they possibly use tools to smash or cut through defenses? How many runners are out there? Too many questions and not enough answers.

It took quite a while for Simone and me to come to terms with these things no longer being human. For us, there was and still is the remorseful thought that after the fever hits, these are technically just brain damaged people. Brain damage with extremely violent tendencies, but still the type of thing that in our former life would have been treated as a deadly disease or illness. The people who contracted it being afforded all the rights and protections as every other citizen of these former United States. Perhaps if it didn't spread so fast and kill so many, that is exactly as it would have been. A bunch of brain fried violent individuals locked up in special medical facilities, and family members visiting them occasionally.

Coming to terms with things doesn't seem to be the case for our kids. They are far more elastic since they are still learning about and processing the new information of life. Something seemed to click in our older kids and just made them deal with it. There should have been a great extent of screaming and crying, and while there was some, there wasn't as much of it as even I would have suspected.

As a *responsible* father, before things fell apart, I had already exposed my children to scary movies. I told them about the zombie books I read, and they saw me play great video games with visually gory gun blasts and regular beheadings. I didn't try to shelter them from violence the way some misguided people do. I exposed them to it and explained what they were seeing if explanation was needed. Knowledge truly is power, and not knowing truths about the world, such as how violent it can be, is a handicap to survival.

Once the world fell apart and we knew what we were dealing with, I didn't lie and tell my family everything was going to be okay. I said we were going to have to fight to survive, and I directly explained to Hannah, Olivia, and William that if they yell or cry when they see an infected, the infected person will find us and kill us. From then on they made sure not to make noise when we told them to be quiet.

For Amelia and Benjamin, I'm mainly just concerned with keeping them alive. They watch and copy their older siblings like any young child does. These days, what they are copying is stealth and stillness rather than mimicking a phone call. This is the only world they will know, so they are being raised without the run free and yell when you feel like it mentality of the rest of our childhoods.

CHAPTER TWO
DEATH AND GOODBYE

Now that we are near enough to see the fence line, there is another obstacle facing us.

We made it to our property in just ten minutes over the four hour mark. Before we bought the land, it was originally part of an equestrian ranch with riding stables. Our land is a 120 acre parcel that we chose as our retreat location in case things fell apart the way we feared it might. It is far enough away from the Medford area not only in distance but with winding roads and turns to make it hard to find by car. And the hills and woods make it difficult to reach without concerted effort on foot. But it is still close enough that we weren't too far away from the town to make regular or daily trips impractical. Even though it would have worked for us as our main residence, it was more practical to have this as our retreat home. We also used the location as a training facility for people, to teach, and learn about outdoor living and survival.

The house where we actually lived before this disease started was right at the edge of Medford. I built a storefront on to it, so I could technically work from home, and have the kids nearby.

We had to abandon that house at the start of the outbreak because it was too close to the city. Looking back, I doubt that we could have made it out of Medford and to our retreat property safely if we had stayed for even a day longer than we did. Things fell apart incredibly quick that first day. I'm thankful we had another place to escape to, but especially that it was our own stocked survival training center.

There are multiple buildings and outbuildings on our property, but the main house now sits about one hundred yards from the fence. We chose to move the fence away from the buildings after a large attack by the infected hit us. We have a chain link fence surrounding about 30 acres of the property. This encloses the main house, the bunkhouse, two mobile homes, barn, stable, riding stable, storage buildings, and various smaller structures we put up to house extra survivors that came along.

Around that fence, and twenty yards out from it, is another hodge-podge of fencing and obstacles that we put together to funnel any persons or infected interested in entering our property toward the front gate area. There are fruit trees and gardens on both the inside and outside of the fences, but we cleared the larger trees to about twenty-five yards beyond the fence line to prevent an easily concealed approach. There are some trenches, trees, and large rock piles on the inside of the fence to allow for defensive positions, in case someone was attacking our home.

It is a decent setup as a prepper defending their homestead against a band of intruders or wandering infected. It is not so ideal when returning from a foraging outing to see someone you don't recognize standing guard on the inside of the fence and no one you know in sight. And that is the obstacle and potential problem we are now faced with.

"Simone, I don't see Arthur, Greg, or anyone else on the property. Hannah, do you see anyone through your binoculars?"

"No, Dad. I don't see anyone but that man, and nothing is going on in the house either that I can see."

I decide to huddle with everyone and discuss our options. "The situation obviously isn't perfect, but it isn't necessarily a disaster either. The man we don't recognize is pacing back and forth more than guarding, and seems rather distracted. There aren't any signs of a fight or battle on this side of the house, and this is the easiest approach, so here's what I think we should do. One person in each direction will hug the woods and circle the property to see if there are any signs of bodies or a gunfight. That guy is definitely not infected by how he looks and acts, so we know the place wasn't overrun by the diseased. If this was a hostile takeover, there should be some sign of a firefight from our people. So that's what we'll be looking for, signs of a fight. Sound good?" I watch as they respond. "You're all nodding so who wants to go?"

Everyone offers to go except for Benjamin.

"Simone and Olivia, you two should go. Simone, take William with you. It will be good practice for his stealth and observation skills. Olivia, you go the opposite way and when you two meet on the other side, continue around to check if the other group might have missed anything.

"Hannah, you stay here with me. If there is any trouble from people on our property, I can hold off any advance. You will take Amelia and Benjamin east to our first fallback location, and everyone will meet there. And Hannah, if there are any problems with me, you protect your brother and sister and get them to the fallback location as well, does everyone understand?"

"There won't be any problems, Eddie!" Simone offers a bit too anxiously.

"Simone, I am over four hours into a bite by an infected that had dexterity and could run. We don't know if the six hour limit is certain or if there will definitely be a fever this time. I trust you to take care of the kids, and I trust Hannah to take care of me if she needs to, that's why she is staying here. Simone, I love you. I'm sure you are right, but we already don't have much time. Let's get moving."

I can see the hurt and sadness in her eyes, but she knows the truth as much as I do. Our home means survival for our family. Even after we lost so many people when we were overrun, it has continued to be the place of safety for us.

We have little caches and fallback points around the extended property, but nothing beyond it. The odds of our family surviving intact were already slim and beyond the scope of odds in our favor. Without me in the picture, they won't all survive without the house and its supplies, especially without the other families we have shared our survival experiences and supplies with. And to put it bluntly, I am already bitten and running on less than two hours' time to get them in there before the fever hits. If a fever will still hit, that is.

Simone and William move off to the right, and Olivia to the left, disappearing into the trees from our view, within twenty yards. While they move off, Hannah steps back from me about ten feet and puts Benjamin and Amelia into a smaller pull cart that we have attached to the bike trailers. She unhooks the cart and sits down next to it, with her Ruger 10/22.

"Thank you, Hannah. Your mom is probably right as usual, but keep an eye on me anyway, okay? Even if we get into the fence line, you keep track of me while your mom and I deal with whoever is there, all right?"

Her face tightens up into a stern expression and she nods.

She was always a smart girl, all of our kids are smart for that matter, but I feel this huge regret that she can't just keep being the girl that would get frustrated and cry because she couldn't figure out how to read a new word, or how a game worked. Now she is playing an adult role in a world of everlasting horrors. She might have to shoot and kill me to protect herself and her brothers and sisters from this damn disease. And stoically, like a battle hardened veteran, instead of complaining or whining that she can't and I mean too much to her, she simply accepts what is given to her, and recognizes her responsibility in this new life. I couldn't be more proud of her. If she survives this mess, she and the other survivors will make much sturdier stock than the current devastated generation did.

The man behind the fence is definitely acting strangely. I'm watching him while I wait for the others to finish circling the property, and this guy is pacing erratically. It seems like he is supposed to be keeping watch out here, but he keeps looking back to the house and acting like those expectant fathers' on television, nervously walking around outside a hospital delivery room. Still, I don't hear anything unusual, and don't see any activity on the property other than him.

At least when I approach the fence to speak with him, I know there won't be any other roving patrols to contend with. If there were, I would have seen them by now. The area inside the fence just isn't that large to hide anyone moving, at least not if they were watching specific areas near the front. And anyone else walking the perimeter of the yard would have made it around by now. So it will be him and me, having a simple discussion of who he is, why he is on my land, and where everyone else is.

"Marco?" a voice calls from the woods.

"Polo," I reply.

Olivia walks out of the trees from the right, and Simone and William should be back shortly as well. We use the simple Marco Polo game to identify ourselves on the rare occasion we split up like this. We figure it's a decent phrase that will help us identify normal human from infected, as well as let us know when someone from our group is returning.

The infected can't speak, at least currently, and I hope they never regain that skill. All they do is issue this horrible slurping groan. It is a mixture of a growl and a gargle—deep, wet, and rumbling. It's an extremely disturbing sound that no human body should issue. They make it whenever they find prey that they can't reach. It is another hunting instinct of theirs, I guess.

If they feel they can reach one of us non-infected humans, or an animal for that matter, they will remain silent. They'll creep along slowly hoping to pounce on us, in an unsuspecting manner. If we are behind a wall or other obstacle, the infected can't maneuver over or around. They make that sound, which I guess is more of a call, to their fellow infected that there is food nearby and they need help. Other infected always show up when that call is made.

"Did you see anything, Olivia?" I ask

"Yes, there is a small cart around the back of the house with some supplies on it. It doesn't look familiar, so it probably belongs to that man. The usual scavenger survivor stuff is on it but also a sheet on the back with blood on it."

"Marco?" we hear from off to our right.

"Polo," I call to Simone.

"Anything else, Olivia?"

"No Dad, no signs of a fight. No brass on the ground. No marks on the house or holes in the fence. Everything seems mostly left alone."

Simone walks up with William, "Hi sweetie, I'm glad to see you're still here." She has a sly but bittersweet smile.

"Tell me about it. I'm in no hurry to...." I start to joke about my condition but can't say it. Not even in trying to keep the mood a little lighter.

I don't like being bitten at all, and I know what I have to look forward to thanks to our experiences over the last few months. Simone was working as a nurse in one of the local hospitals, when management warned all of the staff to look out for anyone coming in exhibiting certain kinds of fevers or wounds consistent with human bite marks. Everyone was told that the CDC considered this a real threat for our area, and once they finished the briefing, Simone called me. After a short conversation where she told me about the threat, I made her promise to come home immediately. I'm not sure what excuse she gave, but she told them she might be gone for a few weeks.

As unlikely as the scenario was, she knew what a supposed zombie outbreak would sound like from the books that I read, and what I told her about them. The news reports of riots, random violence, and starvation in other countries due to the collapse of the world's economies, already had everyone on edge. Fortunately for me, she was quicker to convince of the coming apocalypse than I was. When she called me at home and told me that the hospital reports were about zombies, I thought she was trying to play a joke on me. That is until she described what the hospital officials told her and everyone else.

The CDC warning mentioned violence, fevers, tremors, and they warned that symptoms are similar to rabies in that the people they have observed are all attempting to bite and eat other people. The worst part was, the hospital administrators lost contact with the CDC official they were speaking with after hearing screaming on the other end of the line, and were no longer able to contact other hospitals in that area.

So I'm not looking forward to the fever, the shivers, or especially the change and new hunger associated with being bitten. All I want right now is to get my family into our house.

"This is my idea, guys," I say, getting everyone's attention. "Hannah, you be ready with the laser on your 10/22. Turn it on if the man seems to get aggressive, or if I point my gun at him. Just point it at his chest so he can see the dot. All of you will stay here out of sight. I will walk up and call out to him. We should know pretty quickly by his reaction to me if he will get aggressive. If he doesn't, I will slowly walk to the fence to make contact with him. I will explain who I am, unlock the gate and enter, or shoot him and then unlock the gate to enter. If I have to shoot at any point, be prepared to offer either supporting fire or retreat, depending on what happens."

"Is everyone following me so far? Any questions... No? Okay. Remember I am already bitten, so if an army pours out of the house or outbuildings, I want no heroics to try and rescue me." I give a stern look to everyone.

"Simone and Olivia, have your rifles handy, and be ready to run up to the house when or if I give the all clear. William, you stay on the binoculars, and keep an eye on everything but me and this guy. You need to see any potential surprises, all right? And tell Mom or Olivia if you see anything or anyone."

"Hannah, you use your best judgment as to whether you should shoot the man or not. He is still human, but as you know, not all people are friendly. Just remember the story Mr. Margrove told us about his encounter and the men that tried to kill us all. Do you think you can do this, or should Mom do it?"

She gives me a serious and stern reply that shouldn't come from a twelve year old. "I've got it, Dad. Just don't block my shot."

I still get a little shocked when I hear one of my kids say something like that. I keep telling myself that I have to start giving these kids more credit—to be able to handle life in this world. Before this war for survival broke out, some kids that were 12 to 14 years old were already doing horribly adult things, doing hard drugs and raping and killing each other. Kids and teenagers are capable of some extremely violent actions. It is just that my kids didn't live in a city with regular violence, and they didn't hang out with the kinds of people that committed crimes, none of us did. So this change in them to being serious and about getting the job done, even relating to killing another person, is jarring. So the saying is true, innocence is always the first casualty in a war.

"Hannah, Olivia, William? I want you to know how proud I am of you three. Your mom and I have asked you to do things and be responsible for things that we didn't have to take care of at your ages. I know that once you are back inside our house I don't have to worry about what will happen to any of you, because you stick up for each other, and work so well together. If I could give you one piece of final advice before I head out, you need to express your concerns and hesitations to each other going forward, all right? Ask more questions and don't always trust the first plan given.

"My plans aren't always the best. I often leave things out that I should have thought of. So if you ever have concerns or suggestions, make sure you make yourself heard, because your idea could save someone's life. Now, does anyone have any questions or ideas before we start?"

Hannah replies, "I think I should go instead of you, Dad. I don't think you or Mom use us enough as approaches to strangers. We are less threatening, and in this case, I might be able to approach the house without that guy freaking out, where another adult is especially a threat."

I give a small smile to Simone and think briefly how to let Hannah know the reasons for my going instead of one of them. "You are right that you would be less threatening, Hannah, but in this case, it is not his property. He is the intruder, and I want him to feel threatened to a certain degree. I need my presence and your laser dot on his chest to help convince him that he should put his gun on the ground without fighting back. If you are there with him, it's like threatening someone with a tiny gun. It may be just as deadly as a larger gun, but bigger things often feel like greater threats. Like the difference between a big fat infected guy and an infected little kid, size matters in how we see things."

She nods, but I can tell she isn't completely convinced.

"The other reason I'm going is that I am already bitten. The threat or potential threat inside our house could be so immense that no one that is at that gate makes it out alive. I will only send you to speak with strangers after we have had a great deal of time to observe them and find out how they react to outsiders. Ultimately, your life is just more valuable than mine." I pause, then add, "But if you were bitten instead of me, then I'd probably let you go, okay?"

That seems to have satisfied all of the questions and after a round of quick *I love yous*, *be carefuls*, and *goodbyes*.

I start walking toward the gate, and call out, "Hello, you inside the fence."

To our good fortune, the man lifts his hand over his eyes to peer out at the woods where I called from, rather than ready his weapon for a fight.

"I am coming out of the woods and approaching the fence now," I call as I casually walk forward and let him know what his position actually is. "My name is Eddie Keeper, and I am the owner of the property you are now in. I am not alone, and I need you to remain calm and not make any aggressive movement or actions toward me, do you understand?"

He nods his head, and says, "Yes," but then stupidly pulls his rifle off of his shoulder by the strap, and aims it at me when I am halfway between the woods and the fence. He then bizarrely says, "That's far enough. Now, tell me who you are?"

Great! I think. *Someone is in my yard that can't remember the last two seconds of conversation.* But I stop, and tell him, "I told you who I am. I am Eddie Keeper, and this is my property. I told you not to make any aggressive moves, but you have, so now you need to look at your own chest."

The red dot is easily visible on his blue shirt, even though it is not dark outside yet. As he looks down and sees it, I can't help but smile. I guess my fighting lessons to the girls are paying off. The laser started at his chest and lowered itself to hover over the man's crotch. His rifle lowered with the movement of the dot.

"Okay, now," I yell, bringing the man's attention back to me and my now raised rifle. "I tried to be civil with you, but apparently you are either unable, or unwilling to follow instructions. You will now slowly place your rifle on the ground, and then step over it leaving it behind you. Do it now." This part at least he is listening to. I continue to move forward after he has placed his gun on the ground and it is behind him. "Who are you, what are you doing on my property, and where are the other families that live here?" I say as I reach the fence.

"My wife got hurt, and we came here for medical care. My son, Mike, was looking for help last night when he ran into some people, a Samantha and her group. She told him where your place was, and there is a nurse that lives here that might be able to help my wife, but the nurse isn't here."

I step in between this guy and Hannah's laser, and give a thumb-up sign with my left hand since he is starting to get hysterical while telling me this. I don't want Hannah to mistake his animated discussion style for aggravation, since I don't believe they can hear him from where they are.

"I get it that you seem worried about your wife, but I still don't know who you are. I want to get myself and my family back inside our home. Now I am going to hang my rifle on my back, draw my pistol, and get my keys out to unlock the gate. I need you to stay very still, and I mean statue still, because I will shoot you if you move this time. Do you understand me?"

He nods, but I better be quick, because this guy is definitely on the edge. His jerky, almost jittery demeanor indicates he is not functioning on all cylinders. I step to the right, giving Hannah back her line of sight to him. While I'm unlocking the gate, he tells me his name is Carl, and he is an accountant from Grants Pass and something about them being in

Rogue River for a while and needing to move on. He is speaking super-fast, and his focus just isn't on this situation. So I stop him and bring him back to the present.

"Look Carl," I say and then lift the gate handle, re-insert the lock, and lock it with the handle up, then push the gate open, keeping my Glock 27 at waist level but pointed at him. "Your wife is hurt, and my wife is the nurse that lives here. The quicker I can safely get my family in this fence, the sooner my wife can start helping your wife, okay?"

All right, I think. *I'm inside the fence now, and the gate is open. If anything happens, he won't be able to close the gate, especially while he is under fire.*

He finally seems to be calming down somewhat. I see him taking deeper breaths, and his eyes actually look like they are starting to focus more instead of just dart around. This man is undeniably acting like someone that is missing his normal medications.

"Carl, someone else is inside, right? I'm going to call out to them, okay?"

"Greg," he says. "Greg is in there."

I'm not normally a believer in Murphy's Law. I mean, with the luck I've had in keeping my family safe to this point, I couldn't seriously believe bad luck was on my side, but this particular encounter is just not working out very well at all. I call out to Greg, who I think should already be out here with all the yelling I was doing. "Hey Greg, get out here. It's Eddie Keeper. We're back."

At the same time I see Carl's eyes focus on the bandage on my left arm. His eyes go wide, and you can see his face change from compliance to anger, and I mean a hate filled anger that makes him look like he will explode from it.

He starts mouthing, '*You've been bitten! You've been bitten!*' And on the third time round he gets his voice back, and the hateful accusatory sound that flows forth again doesn't sound like the same man I have been dealing with. "You've been bitten, haven't you? You're trying to sneak in here and kill us all!"

Now, I know with all of his various behaviors and reactions that this man is a drugger. I just have to hope that his symptoms or issues are mild and he can still use reason, and see logic. I don't want to have to shoot a man that has a son and sick wife inside. *Please let this work.*

"Carl, calm down. Yes, I've been bitten, but that was five hours ago. I didn't turn when I was bitten, that means I have an hour left before the fever hits. I just need to get my family home, none of them are bitten."

"What?" he yells.

He is finally being coherent, only this isn't the kind of cognizant reaction I would like him to have.

"You're full of shit. You probably don't even live here, you bastard."

I have to raise my pistol to his chest as he tries to take a step toward me.

"Carl, I used a key to unlock the gate. I wouldn't have the key if I didn't live here." I think I lost him. My last hope of bringing him back to his senses is gone.

"You're full of it!" he yells. "You think just like the rest of them. You think you can pull one over on me just because I can't always think straight. But I got you now. I understand this deal plenty well. You've been bitten, and no one with you is coming in here."

This is just bullshit. I go on a long scavenging run with my family for supplies, and hopefully news about the world, and have to return with a fresh bite from an infected to face off with some damned mixed up, possible drugger, just to get back to my own home. For all of Carl's erratic behavior up to this point, I do understand his fear of someone with a bite. But whatever Carl's issue is, he is letting me know in no uncertain terms that our goals and desires are completely opposite, and after he is secured and my family is safely in the yard, he must leave as soon as humanly possible. I move the finger on my gun from the ready to the trigger.

Greg, whom I will later find out was in the basement and couldn't hear me, decides it is finally time to emerge from the house, and sees me with Carl and calls my name.

I turn my head to the right to look at Greg, and while my head turns, Carl steps forward, grabs my gun, and tries to wrench it out of my hand. I pull the trigger while my eyes are darting back away from Greg and shoot Carl in the chest, on the right side, right about where his nipple would be. Hannah shoots Carl in his right side about six inches down from the armpit before Carl is able to release his hold on my Glock. Finally, Carl registers a look of shock and surprise on his face as his body starts to fall backward, with a slight clockwise spin to his left.

Time was in slow motion for me for a while, and now I realize I also lost a few seconds in the aftermath, because Greg is now next to Carl on the ground checking on him. I didn't even notice him dash over from the house. I finally re-focus and turn my anger on Greg.

"Greg! Where the hell were you? Is everything okay here at the house? Why the fuck did you let this guy in here? He was obviously a drugger! What the fuck is going on?"

Greg is jolted a bit by my yelling and more so by seeing me shoot Carl, but is still able to reply a stuttering, "Yes, everyone here is okay. I think, except for Carl. Why did you shoot him?"

"Are you serious? He grabbed my gun and was acting like he was missing some major medications. All mixed up and unable to focus."

Looking down at Carl, I can see he is dead. Not dead yet, but dead in the next few seconds, his body is shutting down. He is staring up into space, with blood coming out of his mouth, and only a slight gurgling sound as the air leaves his lungs. His shirt and chest are covered in blood. Even if it was just my shot, in normal times, with functioning hospitals, there would be a slim chance he would survive from a pointblank shot to the right lung with a .40 caliber bullet. It's the kind of wound that would have had mixed success in treatment if addressed quickly. But adding in the .22 shot through in his side that probably made it to his heart, there is nothing we could do for him, even if we were all surgeons.

I know I should feel remorse or sadness over this dead man in my yard, but right now, I need to get my family inside the second fence line, especially since we fired two shots out here. There usually isn't infected activity in this area, and it has decreased everywhere else which allowed us to expand our searches, but that doesn't mean there are none out here. I would almost like to say that regular people are once again the greatest threat to our survival, but then I remember the runner.

"Greg, I know this is a lot to take in right now, but we need to get moving. Simone and the kids are out by the trees. We have supplies on the bikes and trailers, and above all else, I have been bitten!" I show him my arm, and he slightly lowers and shakes his head. "We need to get them in here, and I need to be tied down in the shed. We are coming up on five and a half hours after the bite. It's too close to six hours for me to be out here with everyone." I step back to the gate, and say, "Greg, are you coming?"

"I, well, yes. I'm... no, I'm not coming, Eddie. I think I better explain what's going on to everyone. You get Simone and the kids back in here."

I turn to him and follow his gaze to the house where Jessica is standing by the entry wall with her rifle and a sad and concerned look on her face, and Lilly is looking out from behind her with a look of fear. I briefly forgot just how complicated this episode made things.

I turn back away from the house to get the driveway gate swung open. Now my mind is reeling again. How do I put the pieces of this screw-up together? What needs to be done before I get tied down in the shed? There is a son with his sick mom inside, and I just killed their husband/father.

Jessica and Lilly are totally unaware of what happened and will have things explained to them by Greg, who only got the last few seconds of the exchange and my yelling. I am bitten and only have about 30 minutes before I black out into a fever. What can I figure out first? I'm not sure what Greg, Jessica, and Lilly must think of me right now, but I guess it doesn't really matter at the moment. You don't stop and cry over the body of a fallen soldier during combat, you move on, and keep yourself or your team alive.

I need to get my family inside and safe, and then the chips will fall where they must. It is important to have Simone explain or try to explain what happened to Mike, Carl's son. I don't need him flipping out and trying to exact revenge on my family for the loss of his dad. Hopefully, the son doesn't have the same medical issues that the father seemed to have.

I yell to everyone while nearing the woods, "Everything is secure at the house, let's get everyone and everything up there—and quick. Those shots could still attract an infected or someone else." I grab my loaded bike with its trailer and give Simone a look and shake my head over the situation.

"Hannah?"

"Yes, Dad?"

"I'm sorry you had to shoot him, but thank you for doing it. You helped get your mom, brothers, and sisters back home. You helped save their lives, okay? That man would not have let you into our yard if he had his way." She is silent, but I know she understands. I hope she understands.

Simone walks up next to me while we head toward the yard, and I fill her in on everything I think she needs to do.

There is a young man, who must be Mike, kneeling and leaning over his father's body, crying. He doesn't sit up or turn to look at us as we walk in behind him. He seems more absorbed in his own grief at the moment than in seeking answers for his loss, and I am grateful for that. I don't have time for questions or answers. I just walk right up to the house and around the left side, to the back where our medical shed is.

This was a nice sized garden shed once upon a time, but we retrofitted it into an emergency operating room so we wouldn't have to carry the injured or wounded into one of the houses. Fortunately, it is something we haven't had to use very often.

There's a sturdy metal topped table in the center that has wide tie-down straps to hold arms and legs in place if a particularly painful surgery was to be performed. Or for the current task at hand, securing someone that has been bitten for the change. There is also a head box that gets clamped to the table. The box secures around the head to keep it from being able to move side to side and a strap over the forehead prevents upward movement. A wood gag is set into the mouth to prevent biting. There are also a good set of metal cabinets holding some medical supplies. I tiled the walls and floor in order to make it easier to clean. A regular woodshed would have been unusable after the first major surgery soaked it in blood. I have fond memories of building this shed.

I wish time would slow down, but no wishes will be fulfilled for me right now. At least I got my family home. I am mostly undressed and laying on the table as Simone is strapping me in. Her tears are falling onto me, a little drip here, and a little drip there. Each one of my kids comes in and grabs my hand and tells me they love me. I can't turn my head to look at them though or let them know what I feel, I can only see the lights hovering over my eyes, blurring through my own tears.

Greg, Jessica, and Lilly don't come in, and I don't blame them, I don't think I would either. Simone kisses my forehead through the strap and lingers there so I can feel her breath in my hair. She grabs my hand, gives it a squeeze, and I hear her sit down next to me.

"I love you Eddie. I'll stay here with you until the end."

I can't reply. My mind starts swimming as the fever takes hold.

CHAPTER THREE
THE BEGINNING

October/ 8 months earlier
U.S. Outbreak Day 1
Military Base U.S.

"All right, listen up. You know the routine. We have a new set of shots for you guys that just came in. It's supposed to turn you into some unbeatable soldier before you get re-deployed," the sergeant shouts addressing a fifty-eight man platoon that just returned from overseas. "This stuff isn't going to turn you ladies into a badass soldier like myself, but it will help prevent you from bleeding out when you get your dick ripped off, and handed to you by some ninety pound senior citizen."

The platoon's company captain walks up and starts addressing the men. "As you know, the situation here at home is bad. Many of our families are struggling, and I know a lot of your wives and children have had to house together to make things work since the cutbacks."

A grumbling emerges from the lines of assembled soldiers. The military received another set of cuts to enlisted pay to try to make up for shortfalls with the interest payments on the national debt.

The Captain continues, "You all knew when you enlisted that this wasn't going to be a cakewalk or that you'd get rich joining up, but I am with you, and the General is with you too when you say you aren't being treated fairly. We know your families are hurting, but we all have a job to do.

"The good news is your deployment is right here in the good old U.S. of A." Heads start turning to look at each other with questioning looks. "The bad news is your deployment is right here in the good old U.S. of A. The word coming from the top is that there will be massive unrest here unlike anything this nation has seen before. The bottom is about to fall out here at home, that is why most of our troops have been brought back. We will be dealing with our fellow citizens and most likely enforcing martial law." That part gets everyone's heads turning. "Yes you heard me right, I said martial law. The President is expecting he will have to declare martial law after the economic numbers come out in two days. Whether he does or doesn't, our job is to be ready."

"Captain, I don't want to go up against our own," a soldier from the middle of the formation calls.

The sergeant yells back as he steps toward the men, "Keep your hole shut, soldier!"

The captain stops the sergeant and looks around at his men for a while before continuing. "I want you all to listen to me very carefully. I swore an oath to protect and defend the nation and the constitution of the United States. We all did, and I am here today as your captain, and have not received a promotion in five years because I hold true to that oath. Many of my commanding officers have been forced out or retired over their expressed rejection to engage the American public should it be deemed necessary. I will not ask you to betray our people or your oath. What I will ask you to do is to help save their lives.

"Like I said before, the bottom is about to drop out. Our economy, as bad as it has been, is about to get worse—ten-fold—maybe more. We have an armed populace that will have few resources, and many will hit the streets to take what they need by force. Our job, should martial law be declared, will be to distribute food supplies and maintain law and order. We will not be searching for hostiles or dealing with enemy combatants. We will be the force behind local police to ensure the men and women of our country don't all kill each other, and these injections will make sure we don't get killed while we are doing that job.

"What I have been told about this drug is this. You are supposed to develop a fever in six hours when your body is saturated with the drug, so be prepared for a difficult afternoon. Also, we are supposed to get the whole base inoculated today. You are the first group getting it, so go through quickly, and then you'll get situated in your barracks."

*

This particular military base houses a battalion of six hundred forty-three men and women split into three companies and twelve platoons. The efficient med techs at the base clinic are able to inject ninety-three people with Zeus in the minutes before any symptoms occur. The first of the symptoms are extreme twitching tremors which start hitting five minutes after injection. They are similar to epileptic fits, but the body goes more rigid than flailing.

Private Hernandez was the first man through the line for injections this morning. He was happy to be stateside again. His wife gave birth to their new baby girl three weeks ago and this re-deployment means he gets to be with them and his two year old son. He sits down on his cot in the barracks to go through his duffle bag when the dizziness hits. He can feel his muscles start to tense and lies down quickly to try to stop the room from spinning. It starts out feeling like a night of too much drinking and the onset of a leg cramp, but the cramps move all over his body. It quickly turns into seething pain, and he starts to convulse, with his eyes open, and a painful grimace etched on his face.

Several of the other men with Hernandez notice something is wrong with him when his tremors make him fall off his cot onto the floor. They see what is happening with him, but with each person realizing that something is wrong, that person too soon drops due to their own dizziness and start of tremors. Several of the soldiers make it outside of the barracks to try for help, but they also drop from dizziness and convulsions before they can get a warning out.

In the ten minutes after the first injection was given, and after the first groups came and went, the med techs inject another one hundred twenty-four soldiers with Zeus.

Nine minutes and forty-two seconds after his injection of Zeus, Hernandez gets up from the floor, and looks around the room, in a jerky and dazed manner. There are shaking bodies on the ground everywhere. What is left of him sniffs the air, listens, and walks toward the open door. He pauses every few feet to sniff the air near one of the shaking bodies but moves on to the exit without completely stopping.

As Private Hernandez reaches the door, just outside the barracks are two civilian contractors that are on break. They have just run over to several soldiers that are collapsed on the ground.

Lucinda Thompson and Charlie Brand are two hardworking people with families of their own. Lucinda is trying to dial the base clinic on her cell phone and Charlie is bent over one of the men with the most severe convulsions trying to keep him from thrashing against the concrete.

Neither one of them notice Hernandez until he grabs Lucinda, bites into her shoulder, and she screams. Lucinda struggles to get away from Hernandez, and while she easily breaks free from his weak grasping arms, his teeth and jaw are set firmly in her flesh, so he gets pulled off balance as his head is attached to her shoulder. Hernandez falls to the ground ripping the chunk of meat from her shoulder, and she passes out from shock.

Charlie is frozen on the ground for a few seconds, watching Lucinda fall. His mind jumps right to his wife and kids and that he will never see them again. The thoughts, *Nerve gas, Bio-Weapon*, flash in his mind as he sees more soldiers start stumbling out of the barracks. When Charlie grabs Lucinda under the arms to pull her away, Hernandez bites her on the knee and grabs her legs causing her to wake up and scream.

The onslaught is just too great. Charlie thinks for a moment about dropping Lucinda and running, but it is too late. Charlie is grabbed from behind by one of the collapsed soldiers from the ground that has gotten back up. While he is pulled to the ground, the other men from the barracks reach him as well.

Due to the governments coordinated efforts in inoculating all military personnel before the release of the economic numbers, the same scene plays out at every major military installation and base in the U.S.

U.S. Outbreak Day 2
The Krenshaw's House 5:30 a.m.

"Susan, I'm telling you there's something different about this violence. Why would there be riots at the military bases? I mean, soldiers don't exactly have the same rights as we do. So, if they were starting a protest or act up, they would get rounded up, and immediately put in lockdown. They wouldn't let it get out of hand like this."

"So you think this is something different? Fine, I trust your judgment. I just don't like where this might take us. You've worked so hard. We all sacrificed so much to get your company off the ground, and now finally when things are going great for us, you think things are about to fall apart. I just don't like how it feels."

"I don't like it anymore than you do, and I hope I'm wrong. Just promise me you will call Eddie at his store after he opens to see what he thinks about it. That should settle things one way or the other."

"How does he get his information anyway?" Samantha asks her husband Conner. "I mean, I like spending time with him and Simone, and it was fun doing some of those classes at their ranch, but they do seem a bit overly paranoid to me."

"I'm not really sure, maybe the police or maybe the hospital where his wife works. But the last two times I thought things were going bad, he's the one who calmed me down and let me know the whispers he was hearing, and nothing ended up happening here in Medford. Besides, it is his business to know what problems are out there, with his store, you know.

"One other thing you should know about him, Sam, he's the one that kept my head in the game when we lost all of those contracts a year ago and I thought I would have to shut down. I stopped by his shop one morning to browse, talk, and just complain about the week I was having. We were talking about the poor economy when I brought up that I thought I might have to close the business.

"He's the one that told me Jim Franklin was going to close *his* trucking business. He told me Jim was selling off his gun collection and that people like Jim only sell their guns when things are rock bottom. A month later Franklin Trucking was closed, and we picked up all of his contracts and the work with the state."

"Not exactly what I would call insider information," she shoots back slightly sarcastically.

"No, but Eddie made the introduction between Jim and I. Once Jim got to know me, he spoke with his former clients, and suggested his contracts should sign up with me once he closes up shop. That is why things moved so quickly for us after the bottom seemed to drop out. Eddie isn't just a paranoid prepper. He seems to see the details through the bullshit. Just listen to what he says, hopefully, he'll say don't worry like the last two times."

"Okay. I think his shop opens at eight, so I'll call him after I get Jake to school."

*

<u>At the store</u>

"Hannah, can you get the phone? I'm up on the ladder."

The best part about having my own store is being able to have my kids with me all the time. I don't have unlimited time with them like if I was at home, but it is far more time together than if I was off at an eight hour job five days a week. It's nice having them around.

"Dad, you better take the phone, it's mom," Hannah says. She holds it out to me.

"Hi Simone, is everything all right?"

"Eddie, there's something going on at the military bases and in some of the larger cities. We were just told by the hospital administrators that the CDC put out a warning regarding some type of infection that we should watch out for," she says frantically but in a whisper.

"Simone, calm down. Is anything happening at the hospital?"

"No, not yet, but they gave us a warning of what to look for. Eddie, it sounds like your books, the zombie books!" she says forcefully to emphasize the point

Simone is a nurse practitioner at a hospital in Medford. As a result of being married to me, she hears about many of the zombie books that I read as I describe what I consider key events to her. She doesn't like horror movies or stories, but doesn't mind my limited descriptions of some of the things that I read. She is also a very practical minded person. Meaning as much as she may want to, she would never be able to pull off this conversation as a gotcha type of joke, so I know she is being serious.

"Simone, what do you mean? What exactly did they say?"

"They said there is a nationwide outbreak of some plague originating at U.S. military bases. They said it began yesterday and is causing the soldiers to attack each other. We are supposed to look out for people acting aggressively, people with extreme fevers, and anyone with bite marks or trying to bite. They want us to watch out for *people* that are trying to bite! Turn on your computer, there must be something in the news about it."

I briefly turn away from the phone, and call out, "Hannah, turn on the computer and check out the news sites. See if there is anything about violence on military bases. Simone, leave work and come here now."

"I can't, Eddie. I'm only two hours into my shift."

"Damn it, Simone, you called me for a reason. Don't get all professional on me now. You tell them whatever you have to. Tell them I died if you need to, but you get out of that hospital and get home now. I mean right now! I'm going to call Conner and see about getting a truck. We're going to go to the ranch. Simone, I love you. Just drive safe, okay?"

"Okay Eddie, I'll leave now. I love you. I'll call you when I'm actually in the car and leaving. Bye"

Simone and I are both preppers. That is the nature of my store; 2nd AMENDMENT GUNS and SURVIVAL PRODUCTS. So you could say I have an excessively developed sense of paranoia. It doesn't prevent me from living and enjoying life, but if there is a potential threat, it is literally my business to be prepared for it. I would much rather have the luxury of being alive and embarrassed that I jumped into action when there was no real threat, than to be embarrassed that I am dying from something I could have prepared for.

When we lived in South Dakota, I just had the gun store, but I had to close it. I started it with a limited inventory and based the model on being able to order in guns from distributors, but the gun market soared and instant availability dried up. The manufacturers couldn't keep up with the demand. The distributors' stock dried up, and I had to close when I couldn't order any guns or ammo to re-stock my shelves.

This new store I started with much more inventory than the last, and with prepper items like the ones that Simone and I both got for our family, and thought other people would want as well. It is essentially a gun store with survival foods, clothing, and other gear as well.

Shortly after we opened, there was a woman that came in and hit it off with Simone. That is Samantha. She is another prepper and was excited to have a store move into the area as a potential hot spot to meet other like-minded people. She had gotten her husband into prepping after they went through some floods in Oregon a few years back. Their town was cut off for over a week due to washed out roads, and she started wanting to have extras on hand. Samantha and her husband aren't into the collapse scenarios like we are, but they know the importance of having certain supplies on hand because of their own experiences.

"Dad," Hannah calls over to me from the computer. "It says all military bases are on lockdown, and there is some spillover rioting going on around some of the larger bases. There's a CDC warning about a possible outbreak and to stay away from the rioters as they may be infected. What's going on, Dad?"

"Your mom was warned at the hospital to look out for people with bite marks and trying to bite."

"You mean zombies? You're kidding, right?"

Unlike my wife, I am a great practical joker. I try not to be mean about it, but I love playing jokes on Simone and especially the kids. This is exactly the type of thing I would joke about, and then maybe get into a discussion with everyone about what they would, should, or could do if it was real.

"Hannah, I'm sorry sweetie, but I'm not joking this time. Your mom was told to look out for people that are aggressive and trying to bite. I told her to come home. I want you to keep checking the internet for anything you can find. Type in *plague, military, riots,* anything you can think of and find something, okay? I'm going back into the house to check on your brothers and sisters."

"Dad, there are people outside, are you going to open the store?"

"It's not eight yet, so no. I need to check on everyone and make a call before I open up, *if* I open up today," I say as I head out the rear door into the house we built the storefront onto.

Our household consists of my wife, Simone, me, of course, and our five kids. We have three girls and two boys. I guess you could say we were bucking the trend of concern on overpopulation and just enjoyed having kids. Not just making them, which is fun in and of itself, but our kids are smart, good looking, and healthy. We genuinely enjoy having them around, so we wanted to have more of them.

What is really odd in a way about our choice to have more kids is that we are *preppers*. Deep down we believed that the world was going to have a major upheaval of some sort, and we arrogantly thought we could have as many kids as we wanted and still make it safely through life with them. So far we have done a pretty good job, even though the current economic collapse isn't as bad as we expected. We thought we would be dealing with just a major global financial collapse, or worse still, an electric grid collapse due to an electromagnetic pulse attack (EMP) or solar event.

We figured correctly for the financial collapse, that there would be mass inflation and job losses, followed by increased crime and some starvation due to prices shooting up and making almost everything unaffordable. That has happened, but on a more controlled time scale than we thought it would occur. The country has been in continuous decline or stagnation for almost ten years and has increased its decline over the last two.

What we imagined would happen was a quick collapse. With our dollar as the world's reserve currency, our government has been able to print up an endless money supply to help artificially keep things afloat. We figured our reserve currency status would eventually end and the delayed inflation from all that printing would hit, making essential items like food and fuel unaffordable. The stock markets would collapse as well, and the banks would try to call in all outstanding debts to try and stay afloat.

All of those things happening are supposed to cause mass chaos and society would quickly crumble. Then everyone fights and takes whatever they need to feed their starving families. So we stockpiled lots of food and water, ammo, reloading supplies, and guns and opened this store in order to try and help others do the same. Everything has happened, but on a gradual scale that causes people to react like a frog in water that is slowly heating to a boil. People can tell something is wrong with the state of things, but most can't see the end result, so they don't bother getting prepared.

The EMP scenario had us moving in a slightly different direction with us buying tools and equipment that could be used without electricity; saws, hammers, hand drills, manual blade grinders, as well as lots of paper books, cards, games, candles, oil and oil lamps. Finally, the EMP scenario had us stockpile a ton more food and ammo than just for the economy scenario. We figured with the loss of all power and electronics, the same lawlessness would occur as with the economic scenario, only worse.

With an economic collapse, there is always the knowledge that things will turn around eventually, and not everyone would be affected to the same degree. We are prime examples of people that did well during the downturn while many others were suffering. With a lights out case, everything would come to a crashing halt for everyone, us included.

There would be no ray of sunshine, no hope that some other person, government, or country will save everyone. It would be an instant case of take care of yourself and your family and survive or don't.

Some communities would pull together initially, but without electricity there is no gas, without gas there is no food, without food there is no hope. With no hope, most people would go feral, and we would have to hunker down and stay hidden for a long period of time, maybe a few years until it was safe to be out farming the land to grow our own food without risk of attack.

So we are as prepared as we can be for everything electronic to just stop working and/or for the country's money to become worthless, and the chaos that would ensue. We even stockpiled medical supplies for whatever the latest possible pandemic was running through the grapevine at the time; SARS, MERS, H1N1, or Ebola. We are far more prepared than most in end of civilization scenarios, but we didn't figure into our vision of the future the imaginary monster scenario of a zombie disease taking out the world.

As I look in on Olivia, William, Amelia, and Benjamin playing, I hope that the violence and riots on bases they are talking about is nothing more than the same chaos and destruction that has plagued our larger cities for the last few months. Military personnel are having the same issues with low or delayed pay and degraded services as everyone else. Perhaps it is just their turn to riot and it seems worse to everyone because they have more guns than the rest of us. But if that were true, there would be no warnings about bites. How are we going to protect our kids from zombies?

"Olivia. How are you doing?"

"I'm fine, Dad. We're just playing with Scooby Doo." There is an assortment of Scooby Doo figures set up by a small castle.

"I see that. Amelia, William, are you two okay?" They both say *yes* at the same time.

"Thank you for playing quiet. Let me know when Benjamin wakes up, okay? Hannah is in the store with me, so if you need anything, just come in there."

I dial Samantha's number on my cell and wait for her to answer as I walk back into the store.

"Hello? Eddie, is that you? I was going to call you after I dropped off Jake," Samantha says a bit nervously.

"Samantha, have you heard what's going on at the bases?"

"Yes, Conner and I were talking about it earlier this morning, but at the time, I didn't think it was such a big deal. Eddie, have you seen what's on the news? They just started showing someone's cell phone footage from one of the bases in Arkansas. Everyone is going crazy. I mean, they seem insane and are just attacking each other. Do you think this is some kind of terrorist attack?"

"I don't know. I guess it could be an attack, but it seems a bit of a stretch to think terrorists could hit so many bases all at once. Listen Samantha, Simone is coming home from the hospital, and I think you should get Conner back home as well. When Simone called, she said they were warned to look out for people becoming violent and trying to bite each other. The CDC is telling the hospitals it is some kind of plague. They just aren't alerting the general public directly yet, but I imagine that will hit the news soon." I pause for a moment to let that info sink in, then say, "Samantha, I am moving everything to the ranch." There is a short silence on the other end.

"Do you think it's that serious?"

"Yes, Samantha, I do. And apparently a lot of other people do as well. I have a small crowd outside the store right now, and I'm supposed to open in ten minutes."

"What are you going to do?"

"I'm not going to open up. I'll have to tell the people out there to go back home. It's only me here with the kids, and I'm not about to let thirty desperate people come into the store and start fighting over what I have on the shelves."

"You have that many people out there? Eddie, do you need us to come by and help?"

"Thanks, but not yet. You get Conner and yourself ready to head out to the Ranch. Be prepared to take everything, Samantha. If this is what it sounds like, then we won't be coming back to the city anytime soon. Oh, one thing I do need you to do, have Conner arrange for a semi to come by the store so we can load everything that's here and take it with us. Tell him I'll pay the driver four times the rate if they can show up in the next few hours. And I'll need someone to help load the truck. Whoever it is should be trustworthy. They'll know where we are and all of the supplies."

"Okay, I'll let him know."

"Dad, Mom's on the phone," Hannah says, offering the store phone to me.

"Samantha, I have to go, Simone's on the phone. Get Conner home and get us a truck okay?"

"Okay, Eddie. Goodbye."

"I'll take it Hannah, thanks. Simone, where are you?"

"I'm in the car and leaving right now."

"Okay, come on home and drive carefully. I'll see you in about twenty minutes. I love you"

"I love you too. See you soon," Simone says and hangs up.

The Krenshaw Household

"Hi honey, did you call Eddie already?"

"No, he called me. Conner, he says he is moving his family to the ranch, and we should do the same."

"Did he tell you anything specific?"

"The CDC is warning the hospitals that there is a possible plague outbreak. His wife was told to watch out for people coming into the hospital with bite marks and acting aggressively."

"What? You mean like an animal attack? This is something to do with rabies?"

"No! Conner, they were told to watch out for people biting each other. People! Not animal bites. Conner, I believe him. You need to come home. There was something in the way he told me what was happening. It sent shivers down my spine, and it let me know he was absolutely telling the truth."

"Was he that dramatic?"

"That's just it. He was calm, firm, and direct. It made me feel like I was on a ship and the captain was telling me we were sinking."

"Okay, honey. If he is taking it this seriously, then we should as well. I'll leave work in the next half hour. First, I have to tell my people what I know, and give them a chance as well."

"Conner? Eddie wants you to send a driver with a truck that can haul all of the stuff he has in his store, and someone to help load. He said he would pay four times the rate if the driver can be there in the next two hours."

"Samantha, you need to call Emily, and get her back here from Portland."

"Oh Conner, she's not going to like this. She has that scientist from Germany with her right now."

"Who is with her?" he asks, clearly confused by what his wife is saying.

"Her biology group is getting to work with him because of that research paper that she was telling us about. Don't you remember?"

"Samantha, you need to get her to come home. It doesn't matter who she is with if things are serious enough to move to Eddie's ranch. I'll call her after you do if I have too, but she'll come home if you explain everything to her, okay?"

The Store

I turn to Hannah with a great deal of concern on my face. "Hannah, I'm not going to open the store today, and I have to go and tell those people out there. They might get angry and try to force their way in, but most likely they won't. Just in case they do, take this Ruger and be ready to shoot anyone that comes through the door without me. If they knock me down to get in, they could hurt you and your brothers and sisters. Do you understand?"

Hannah's eyes go wide but she nods.

"Good girl, Hannah. This is just like the riots we have looked at on the news, but it is coming here now. This is just like when we practiced for someone trying to rob the store."

I have a concealed gun under my shirt, but put an exposed Kydex holster on my belt and put my five-seven into it. In this situation, I want my ability and willingness to use force to be plainly visible to the people outside. I walk to the door, unlock and slide the security gate open, and some of the people outside start crowding in and pressing against the glass, so I yell through the door for them to back up. They don't back up right away so I draw my gun and tap it on the glass at face level. This has them backing out quickly into the parking lot, with a few of them falling down as they stumble backward in their haste. I open the door and step outside to speak with the crowd, sliding the security door closed behind me.

There is grumbling in the crowd, and you can tell these people are agitated—and not just from me pointing my weapon at them. There is a desperation etched in their faces, and I can't let this get out of control. At least there are a couple of faces out here that I recognize that seem calm. They are standing off to the sides and scanning the crowd like I am, rather than staring at me with angry or fearful eyes.

Addressing the small crowd, I keep my gun at the ready in my hands in front of me pointing down. "I am sure all of you are frightened of the news and want to rush in here to get something to make yourselves feel more safe and secure. The time to prepare for potential problems is not today however, the time to prepare was yesterday. I am not opening the store. All of the supplies inside have been requisitioned by the government to assist the local populace if things get out of hand. There will be military forces here within the next few hours to collect everything inside and take it to a holding facility where it will be distributed to you, if and when you need it. Please go home and keep yourselves safe and secure, and if things get out of hand, the government will let all of you know what you should do."

"We just need a few supplies," one guy yells, and a chorus of *yeahs* erupt from the crowd.

"I understand what you believe you need at this moment, but these supplies are no longer available for sale. I and those inside have been ordered to protect them for government collection using any means necessary. There are about thirty of you out here, and my gun holds thirty rounds. Do not make me use it, but understand that I will if you do not leave."

"This isn't right," one lady yells.

"We need to take care of our families too," another says, but most of the crowd starts to head back to their cars.

I try to give an extra reassurance to those who are lingering instead of going back to their vehicles. "The local government is prepared for problems such as this and has stepped up preparations since the riots in the larger cities began. Your local leaders will tell you what steps you must take, if any. Just return to your homes and everything will be all right. You have put your faith in the government to protect you up until now, and you should continue your faith in those leaders that you elected to see you through any troubles that might occur.

"There are four of you here that have special orders you were supposed to pick up today. I will ask that you stay so you can pick up your already purchased items," and I point out four individuals that I recognize as customers of mine.

The four of them, and one other man that I recognize, remain. We all watch the other people as they get into their cars and drive off, one by one.

I shake hands with the four I pointed out. "Billy, Matt, Katherine, and...Jessie. Good to see you. Is everything okay with you?"

Katherine says, "I was hoping to pick up a few extra things and got worried about what you would have left when I saw the crowd. How can the government take all of your stuff?"

"They didn't," I reply. "They can of course, based on executive orders, but they haven't. At least not that I have heard."

"I knew it," the fifth person waiting nearby says. "You lied to all of those people. How can you do that? They just wanted to get some things because of what's going on."

"Everyone, I would like you to meet the worm," I mention with contempt. "If any of you remember the crappy article a guy wrote about me and this store a few months after I opened, this is the loser that wrote it. Meet, Chad Hansen."

I turn and face Chad directly. "I remember your uninformed article which deliberately left out the critical information of *why* people should be prepared. Do you, Chad, remember what my reply to your article said?"

"Fuck you!" he replies.

"Very articulate, Mr. Moron. This idiot left out my mention that the government has recommended for the last few years that everyone should have at least a month's worth of supplies on hand. A month's worth of food and water, and at least three months accumulated funds to help pay bills and cover regular expenses in case of emergency.

"This sorry sack of left-winged drivel wrote that I was fear mongering, and how did you put it...? My 'Biblical end of the world conspiracies should go back to the Bible-belt in South Dakota from whence I came.' That's it, right, Chad? That and my ultra religious-right mentality is not welcome in Oregon. What a wonderful welcome you provided to me, my family, and my new local business." I just stare at him in disgust.

"I thought you were an Atheist," Matt says.

"That I am, Matt. I am and have always been an Atheist. This idiot didn't bother doing his research. He had no intention of writing a fair article about me or my store. He is just an anti-gun hoplophobe who wanted my store shut down. He doesn't, or should I say he didn't, see any reason for my store to exist." I turn back to Chad, step up less than a foot away from him, and say, "So what is it? Why are you here right now? I doubt you are here for another article about my store."

"I'm here for some supplies. And yes, I remember your reply to my article. The editor published it right next to my own piece in the paper, and it nearly cost me my job, you asshole," Chad says angrily, pointing his finger at me.

"Listen, Chad, even if I liked you, which I obviously do not, you aren't one of my regular customers, which these four people are. I am going to let them in and buy a few things. I will not let you have anything, and you can write whatever you want about it in your little column section of the paper. You had your chance to get ready for what is coming, and you chose to ridicule and harass me and people like these folks. You should have been more open-minded about the possibility that your government might not have all of the answers for you. And just to put things in better perspective, even if I let you have everything inside of this store, you wouldn't know what to do with most of it, and would still probably die if you ever had to protect yourself.

"And as for my article, it did nothing to your credibility or job standing. My article was filled with non-vindictive truth that told people why they should prepare, and that while I am right wing, I am an Atheist and not the religious extremist that your whole piece made me out to be. It was your own article that nearly got you fired, and it is your own attitude and actions that are sending you away from here empty handed. Now, get out of here."

"I'm not going anywhere. You're not going to do anything to me. I'm a reporter," Chad says desperately, with a little spittle flying from his mouth.

I rack the slide of my gun loading a round into the chamber and point it at his head. "I'm sure you've seen the news, Chad. You work for the paper so you might even have more information than we have on what's going on at the bases, that's why you're here. I'll just tell the sheriff that you tried to bite me. They'll have you bagged up and cremated before the sun is down. Make your choice."

Chad's face goes white with fear, and he stumbles a bit as he turns and quickly walks away. He gets into his car and drives off, giving me the bird as he goes.

"What a worm," I say. "Okay, let's get you four inside. Hannah, I'm coming in and bringing four with me, you can put the gun down." We enter the store, and I lock the door and the security gate behind us.

"You have your daughter working security?" Jessie asks.

"Come on guys, this is a gun store, not just survival supplies, and we are uncomfortably close to anti-gun California for my liking. I have all of my kids trained on what to do if anyone gets violent and tries to rob the store for things they can't get where they live. If anyone made it past me outside, they wouldn't have made it past Hannah, or any of my kids that can hold a gun."

"Damn," Jessie replies.

Hannah innocently smiles and waves at him while nodding.

"So this is serious, isn't it?" Matt asks.

"That's why you and all of those other people were here." I tell them about what Simone heard from the hospital administrators and how she thinks it sounds like zombies.

"I think this is it, the end game. The only people that can make it through a disaster of plague ridden violent cannibals are those who are already prepared like us. Unfortunately, there are many people out there who I'm sure wanted to be part of the prepping community, but just couldn't put things together because of the economy."

"Hopefully those people still developed skills they can trade to survive with," Matt adds.

"I'm packing everything up and taking it to my ranch, so if any of you need a place to stay, you are welcome with your families and trusted friends. Before you go, I'll give you all directions to my place. As for what is here in the store, your money won't be worth anything in a few days, so just tell me what you want or need, and I'll see if I can part with it. Billy?"

"I'm pretty well set up on my own land. I just came here for information, and I guess I found it," he replies.

"Well, Billy, you know where my ranch is, so if these infected people overrun your place, you can come to mine."

"Matt? What about you?"

"I'm in a different situation. My place is pretty well stocked for a regular grid down scenario, and I think I could have even defended my place for a while if the rioting made it here to Medford. However, I'm right in the heart of town, and not set up to defend against an infected zombie horde."

I shake my head in disbelief, and say, "I guess that is what it sounds like then, isn't it. When Simone said it sounded like zombies on the phone from the hospital, I couldn't believe it. I'm having a hard time dealing with the books I read coming to life."

Matt continues, "I was hoping you could help me out with a possible future place to stay and relocation of my supplies. My wife, Rachel, is visiting her parents in Idaho with our two kids, Lindsey and Paul. I am planning on heading there. They have a small farm and live away from any big towns, so we might just hold up there until things get back to normal. I was hoping you could take my stuff and store it at your place."

"I don't know, Matt. I don't think this is going to be some easy fix where you can just come back and pick up your stuff in a few months. If this is some kind of virus and it's all over the country already, then the whole of society is probably going to get wiped out. You might not even be able to make it back for a couple of years. Think about it, there will be the infected to deal with, the desperate, the criminals, and the crazies that can't get their meds. All of the infrastructure might be gone, and you can forget about motorized transportation if the roads get clogged."

Katherine adds, "There's sure to be a mass exodus out of all cities when they hear about a plague, and with the gasoline shortages we've been having, cars and trucks will fill the roadways with people unable to get fuel. If you go to Idaho, you should take all of your stuff with you. Get a rental truck or something, but don't plan on making an easy trip back. This is just the type of thing we've all been preparing for."

"I would, trust me, I would take my stuff, but I need to get there quick. Any long road trip with a truck full of supplies is just an invitation to disaster. I know you're both right, that things will really crumble because of this disease. Things were already bad enough without throwing a pandemic in the mix. But my main priority now is getting to Rachel and the kids. The supplies are secondary. I know I'll probably never see those supplies again. I just don't want them raided or destroyed by staying at my place. Please, pick them up."

"All right, I will if I can get to them with a truck. When are you leaving?"

"When I leave here I'm heading back home to pick up my guns and ammo. Everything else in the house that you can grab, take to your place. Save them for as long as you can, but use anything that you need. I have a detailed list of everything, in a binder on the kitchen table, and here is a key to the house. I know where your ranch is, so if I can make it back, I'll stop in to say hello someday." Matt has a somber look and an attempted smile on his face.

"I'll get the stuff, Matt, but I'm clearing out this place first. I'm assuming you don't have a big sign advertising survival supplies on the outside of your house," I say with a grin.

"That is a definite *no*. I'm glad you had this place, though. I didn't want to order most of my stuff through the internet or on the phone and have the NSA and other government types knowing what I have purchased and stored," he replies while heading over to the door.

I unlock it to let him out. "Goodbye, Matt. Be safe on the road."

Everyone shakes Matt's hand, and he leaves.

Hannah calls over from the computer. "Dad, the news is getting worse. Whatever this thing is seems to be spreading quickly. I mean, it's everywhere. Not just here in the U.S. either. It's all over the world according to bloggers reports. And it says something about martial law."

"Martial Law? Did they say it has been declared?"

"No, some bloggers and a few news sites are saying there is a document from some general talking about martial law and this illness. I'm trying to find the letter right now, but every link that is supposed to take me to it is blank."

"It sounds like someone in the government is trying to cover up their tracks," Jessie offers.

"Dad, Benjamin is awake," Olivia calls from the door to the house.

"Hannah, can you take care of Benjamin? Mom is almost home, and then she will take him. I need to finish up here, okay?"

"I can take him, Dad," Olivia says.

"Thanks, Olivia. Still, I want Hannah to go with you and tell you what's going on. I'm going to need you Hannah and William to pack up all of your toys and books. We're going to take everything to the ranch, okay?"

Hannah jumps up and goes over to Olivia. "We like the ranch," they both say almost in unison.

"Katherine? How about you? Need anything? How are you and yours set up?"

"We're okay, Eddie. I do need a solar charger, a back-up water filter, and maybe a few more guns."

"Go and grab the supplies you need and put them on the counter. As for the guns, get what you need off the shelves or out of the counters, and I'll see if I can part with them. Okay?"

"That's fair. I'll get it now." And she heads to the shelves.

"I guess that leaves me," says Jessie

"How are you set up?" I ask.

"Not too good. I haven't been prepping long, and I was only preparing for a short term economic collapse. I mean, I have two guns, some ammo, and some food stored up, but nothing for long term. And definitely nothing for a long term siege of violent attackers. I have been putting most of my money into silver, gold, and barter items like coffee and alcohol. I didn't think things would go completely south and thought I just needed a few months to half a year of food to get by initially and maybe some things to bribe corrupt officials once things started turning around."

"You've got skills though, right?" Billy asks.

"I can weld and do all kinds of odd jobs," Jessie says hopefully.

I nod, and say, "Well, I have a caretaker at my ranch. He is good, but it never hurts to have someone extra around. Especially with more armed patrols needed. How are you set up Billy? Could you use someone with Jessie's skills?"

Billy nods. "Honestly, yes. Skilled manpower I could definitely use. My wife and I were thinking the economy would collapse further as well, and were planning on bringing in some of our neighbors. They are all older folks, and we have already been helping some of them. A few of them have canned food storage and a few hunting guns, but not really a prepared mindset and I'm not sure how well they would do on scheduled round the clock watches. You can come to my place if you want Jessie. Is there anyone with you?"

"I'm not sure. I have a girlfriend, but she went to visit her parents in San Francisco." Billy frowns.

"I'm sorry, Jessie," I say while I shake my head. "That could be Mars now considering the distance and population between her and us."

"I know, I tried calling her, but they must be out somewhere, because none of them are picking up."

"It's up to you, Jessie. You can come to either of our places."

"I don't live too far from Billy, so I think that will be my best bet to be able to check if Emily or any family and friends show up at my place."

Billy and I look at each other, and Billy says to Jessie. "Just keep trying her and get back to your place to pack stuff up. You can bring it all to my house and let her know where to come when you get in touch with her, okay?"

"Yeah, that sounds good," Jessie replies.

Katherine sets another gun on the counter next to her items and says she's done.

"Katherine, give me a minute, okay?" I say. "I need to make a sign to put out front so people don't keep trying to get in." I grab a can of spray paint and head out the door after Jessie who is leaving.

I keep sheets of plywood in a shed at the side of the house and grab two, dragging them to the front of the store, and lean them up on each side of the door. On one I paint STORE CLOSED INDEFINITELY. On the other I write, ALL ITEMS SOLD OUT.

One car pulls into the parking lot as I'm finishing up with the second sign. They read the signs, turn around, and speed away. I'm sure they're off to the next location they hope has something.

Once back inside, Billy and Katherine are sitting at the counter. Billy asks, "Is it right to turn people away like this, Eddie? It isn't really the Christian thing to do."

I almost smile at the ridiculousness of his statement, but just shake my head before I speak. "Billy, I know you believe in a God, but try to remember that I don't. But since you brought it up, let's see what I'm faced with. I have my five young kids in here and had about thirty very nervous people outside wanting to get in. You saw the looks on their faces, how they all pressed up against the door to get in.

"Those people were all discovering for the first time that our society might be more fragile than they once believed. I know from what you told me about your time in Venezuela a few years ago, you experienced the absolute chaos that occurs just trying to get groceries. And we have all seen the panicked riots that have been happening all over the country, hell, all over the world.

"Do you think any of those people would have just walked in here in a civil manner and politely offered to give up the packet of survival seeds or the hunting knife they had their hands on if someone else wanted it? No, they wouldn't and you should know better."

Billy cuts in, and says, "Look, as preppers, we all think a little irrationally at times. If you stop for a second and think about what you are doing, I think you'll realize turning people away isn't right."

I'm starting to talk louder as I get more frustrated with each word I have to utter. "I believe I AM acting rationally in not letting those people in here. I won't jeopardize the safety of my family just to calm a stranger's nerves by giving them things they can't use. So aside from being rational, how are my actions in any way un-Christian in your point of view, Billy?"

I'm angry now, so I continue without letting him answer. "I have had my store open here for over two years trying to provide for the people of this area. I have given workshops and training seminars, most for free, to have people taught how to use the things that we sell here. I have done my part to make sure the people who I can reach are as prepared as they are capable of making themselves.

"I even provided food and supplies for your group to use when giving meals to the homeless! If I was Bill Gates I could have done more for those that weren't able to afford supplies, but I'm not. As for those that chose to ignore the proverbial writing on the wall, they will now have to face your God's ultimate punishment for non-preparation."

Billy, bristling at my accusation, loudly responds, "Now don't you put this situation on God. I know you have been good for the community. I just don't feel right being offered the chance at things you have when others are turned away. Others that I know don't stand a chance without at least some of the things you have here."

"Don't put it on God? Billy, if your God exists, he is the only one responsible for the end of the world. You've said it many times in our discussions that you feel, 'God is everywhere, sees everything and is the ultimate decider on when people are born and die.' You don't get to divorce your God of responsibility for actions when they happen to be bad rather than good! As to your continued assertion that I should have let those people have some of these supplies, they don't stand a chance with or without the things I have here. That is the essential problem with helping any of them. You know full well that they can't just drop seeds in the dirt and have a crop of edible food jump out of the ground. Most of the products here require practice and trial and error to perfect using. When rabid man-eating cannibals are knocking down your door it is not the best time to think about getting ready."

I pause for a bit but Billy is still shaking his head and is upset, so I continue, a bit more calmly, "Okay, Billy. Let me put it to you this way. You believe in the Bible and God, so let's come at it from a Biblical standpoint. How many people did Noah let on his Ark after it started raining?"

Billy and Katherine, just stare with questioning looks on their faces.

"Just think about that for a while. Think about the scene if it happened as it is written in the Bible. People were begging to join him. They were begging Noah to get one precious spot on his huge boat that could hold two of every animal. And don't picture a bunch of able bodied men begging to get on the boat. Picture it the way it would have been. There were women with their children and holding on to their babies. They were all in the crowd begging for their lives. I can picture women pleading with Noah to just take their babies or children so that they may survive, and Noah took no one.

"Now I'm not claiming to be some type of Noah, and I think the whole story is made up to illustrate a point, but the point is something that I get and you need to get straight in your head if you are going to survive this. You can try to be a *good Christian* to everyone that you meet and have all of your supplies stolen, and probably get yourself killed in the process. Or, you can be the kind of person that chooses to survive, and keep your family and those that have prepared alive as well.

"The rain is coming down now, Billy, and you have to choose wisely who is going to get on your boat."

Billy nods and lowers his head a bit. "I know you're right, Eddie. I just feel ashamed, and I shouldn't place my shame on you. You did right by the community and your family, and are even doing more for us right now. I just feel ashamed that I didn't do the same thing that you have. I haven't helped anyone to get ready but my family. I'm sorry."

I nod to Billy, and turn my gaze to Katherine, who is clearly uncomfortable at the exchange we just had. "Sorry Katherine, I'm sure you just want to get out of here and get all of your stuff together. Let me look at what you have." She has the water filter and solar charger, a case of survival butter, two Glock 17's, a Remington 870, and a Marlin Model 60. So I say, "I'm fine with what you've got here, how are you on ammo for these?"

"We have enough 9mm and 12ga, or at least what I think is enough since George has been reloading. I could use another case of 22lr ammo, though," she says hopefully.

I smile, and nod. "I can do that too. I'm amazed that I have been able to get my hands on as much 22lr ammo as I have. I mean, the supply never really recovered from the first shortage, so technically we are having a shortage on the shortage. I was surprised to say the least when two months ago I got two pallets of it. Most of it was my delayed personal stock orders from the last few years for the training camp, so it went right to the ranch for everyone to practice with."

"Thank you, Eddie," Katherine says with a sad smile.

"It's all right," I smile in return. "Just remember, I'll be expecting full payment and a background check if things don't end up collapsing. Now go out and drive your car to the back of the house. We'll bring your stuff out that way."

Billy, Katherine, and I are saying our goodbyes in the backyard when Simone drives up. Before Simone is able to get out of her car, Hannah calls out to us from the backdoor of the house, and says, "Dad, You need to see this paper online!" All four of us go back in and Hannah shows us the document she finally snagged that keeps disappearing from websites.

The document is a copy of a letter to a General Francis, U.S. Army, unknown base of operations and his commentary about the letter.

*

"I verified that the Zeus drug was administered to The Tiger Squadron and to General Taggart as well without incidence. It is assumed that the current batch was contaminated somehow, as most of the men who were inoculated started showing tremors and violent behavior from ten to twenty-five minutes after injection. By the time we realized the reactions of the men weren't fitting the guidelines, we had already managed to inoculate over three hundred men. Those men with immediate symptoms were able to attack and infect the remaining base personnel, and the infection spread exponentially. Those personnel who received the infection from attack, usually in the form of a bite, started showing tremors or violent action from one to five minutes time. I am currently trapped in my office with a small group of surviving soldiers under my command, and this is the only way left for me to get the information on this drug out.

I am sending this letter to the non-classified accounts at the CDC due to my inability to contact Washington and Homeland Security through my secure-line. I fear that all major branches of government may be in the same state of infection that my base is, and need to get this information out in the hopes that someone may be able to stop this infection from spreading. The following letter I received from my colleague, General Taggart. Something must have changed with this drug to be causing the violence we are experiencing."

"General Francis,

In response to your query regarding the safety and efficacy of the Zeus drug.

Due to the deteriorating condition of law and order within the Continental United States and abroad, nationwide martial law has been planned for and it is expected that the President will give the declaration for enacting it next week. The continuing societal unrest is expected to be compounded on Wednesday when the World Bank is set to announce an end to the dollar as the world's reserve currency. This will cause massive inflation and dollar devaluation to our already crumbling economy.

The troops under your command will be required to ensure the safety of the citizenry, as well as the prevention of violence, and property destruction. As such, you and all of your troops are ordered to take inoculations of the Zeus drug. This injection has been shown to minimize blood loss, reduce fear and anxiety, and remove pain detection. The combination of which will ensure a minimal amount of casualties with our soldiers in violent interactions with a rioting populace.

This drug has been tested safely on the Tiger Squadron of German soldiers working in Moldova for the last six months. There is a side effect of a high fever which takes place on the sixth hour after inoculation and lasts one to five hours after initial administration. As such, only one third of all troops are to be inoculated at any given time, to ensure all soldiers are not inoperative due to the fever at the same time. The time frame for the drug's effectiveness is two to three weeks, depending on the individual. All troops will be re-inoculated with the drug at such time as it becomes ineffective and as long as the order for martial law due to societal unrest is necessary.

I appreciate your concern for the welfare of your men, and I have the same concern for mine. This is why I have written more than the required "follow your orders or be relieved" reply. I have observed the Zeus drug being administered to the German soldiers and have had it administered to myself while in Moldova with the Tiger Battalion. I can personally certify its effectiveness. I will also mention that the reduction in fatalities to your troops resulting from armed conflict will help to prevent your troops from building grudges and animosity against the populace they must keep under control. Anything we can do to reduce casualties in the expected upheaval must be done.

Inoculations are expected to begin with the arrival of Zeus on Monday. In coordination with the military the CDC will be distributing inoculations nationwide to select first responders in high value areas.

Sincerely,
General Arthur C. Taggart"

*

"Well that couldn't have painted a bleaker picture," Simone says. "Do you think this letter's the real thing?"

"It's being scrubbed from the internet, and no one in the regular news is talking about it, so it must be the real thing," I reply. "It makes sense in a way to explain how this thing could spread across the country so fast. Nothing else fits why the military bases were all having riots. I mean, things are bad everywhere, but for all the bases to be having riots at the same time would have required massive coordination if it was to fight for benefits. The NSA is keeping tabs on everyone, but they are especially watching everyone in the military, so there is no way these attacks could have been some coordinated event.

"In any case, this letter doesn't change our immediate situation, other than to let us know this is probably the worst case scenario. If major branches of the government all received this drug and it is set to be given to first responders nationwide, then it could spread quickly even in areas without large military bases. Hannah, could you please print out several copies of that letter, actually print about thirty of them? I don't trust that it will stay available online."

We all just stand in an uncomfortable silence, staring at the computer, before Katherine and Billy say quick goodbyes and leave.

"Simone, I think you should get the kids and whatever they put together in their bags, and head up to the ranch now. I'm going to gather everything that's left in the house and have it set for when the truck gets here. Also, call your family. I'll be doing the same."

"So you did manage to get a truck?" Simone asks.

I nod.

"Good."

"Right, I guess I haven't filled you in on what's been happening. I did call Samantha right after you and told her to get Conner and head up to the ranch. I have to call them back and find out if there actually is a truck on its way, but I'm sure there will be. I want you and the kids out of here, because I don't know when things are going to start getting really bad, and not just because of people going crazy trying to hoard stuff at the last minute. When people with this disease actually start showing up in the area I don't want any of us to be around, but especially not you and the kids."

"Let's hope none of the hospitals or police in this area were among the *select first responders* chosen to receive that Zeus drug," Simone says nervously and walks away to get the kids ready.

I pick up the phone and dial Samantha again.

"Hello?"

"Hi, Samantha. It's Eddie again. Did Conner make it home yet?"

"No, not yet. He was going to let the truckers and workers know what was going on before he came back. I did tell him about getting you a truck, but don't know if he has anyone for you yet. Why don't I give you his cell number?"

"That would be great, Samantha. I also have a bit more information for you and him about what's going on. Apparently, there is some drug they are giving to the soldiers that is spreading the plague. Some drug called Zeus."

"What? Did you say Zeus? How do you know?" Samantha yells into the phone.

"Yes, a drug called Zeus. Hannah found a letter online that was being erased from all the sites it got posted to. Have you heard of it?"

"Emily…my daughter Emily in Portland. Oh my God. Eddie, can you send me that letter? Please send me that letter," she says frantically.

"Yes, yes. I'll e-mail it right now." I sit at the computer and e-mail the letter to her. "I'm sending it now, Samantha. What does this have to do with your daughter?"

"I just spoke with her, trying to get her to come home. She's getting her Masters in Biology, and her group is hosting a German scientist that developed the Zeus drug! I have to go, Eddie. I have to get this letter to Samantha. Maybe that will get her to come home." And she hangs up the phone in a panic.

I start looking up the number to Conner's trucking company when Simone calls out that a semi-truck is pulling up to the store. I guess it's time to start loading things up.

*

A few hours later I arrive at the ranch riding shotgun, literally, in a truck that was sent by Conner. The driver is named Donald, and his son, Joshua, came along to help with the loading and unloading. I wave to Simone and Arthur as we drive by and head past the main house and bunkhouse, to a storage building behind a barn. After we get the pallets quickly unloaded, we all discuss our next move.

"I've told Donald and Joshua what I know about this thing so far. They have helped us out and have some hunting skills with firearms, so I have offered them a chance to stay with us. Donald here," I say pointing to him, "already contacted his wife on the CB, and she is getting their stuff ready to be picked up. His son, Joshua, has been trying to get his girlfriend on the phone, but it seems the cell lines are already overwhelmed. So that's two reasons to head back out there, and I have to pick up Matt Soderberg's supplies at his house. He is heading to Idaho to his wife's parents farm, where she and their kids are visiting. He told me we can use what we need and store the rest. Anyway, I know he is set up pretty good, and if he isn't able to make it back, any extra supplies we have on hand will let us help extra people."

"How much stuff do you think it is?" Donald asks

"I would think a third as much as we took out of my store, maybe more. Matt was a med tech too, so I know he stocked up on a lot of medical supplies as well."

"Another thing I want to get is fencing supplies. I'd like to run by the hardware store and buy whatever they have in fence posts and chain-link. We're going to have to set up some type of fenced in perimeter to slow these infected people down if they wander out this way. In that storage building I have rolls and rolls of surplus razor wire that I got cheap from one of my suppliers, but I never got around to buying any fencing material. That's what I need. Let's hear what you guys need or if you have any ideas."

Joshua speaks up first. "I just need to get my girlfriend, like I said before. Well, she's my ex-girlfriend now, but I still love her. Anyway, I'd like her to be here with me."

"Like I told you in the truck, I need to get Karen and Katy, my wife and daughter," Donald says. "My folks don't live in this state and hers aren't alive anymore, so we won't need to bring anyone else."

"How about you, Arthur? You got any ideas or anything you specifically need?"

"Well, I think Donald should get back to his wife on the CB and tell her to head here now. You three can get the stuff from his place without her being at risk by packing their belongings. Joshua should go into the house and try his girlfriend on the landline. Maybe he'll have better luck with that."

Donald and Joshua both offer their thanks and head off in opposite directions.

"I'll show Joshua where the phone is in the house," Simone says as she walks off after him.

"I also think it may be better to leave this Matt person's supplies where they are. It wouldn't be bad to have another supply cache somewhere," Arthur offers.

"I agree, but his place is right downtown, and it's a nice house. There's a good chance that it could get hit with early looting because of where it's at, and scavengers would definitely try the place later on to find supplies if there are enough people left to do that. If it was off on a farm somewhere that fewer people could find, I'd agree, but he has too much quality stuff to let it just sit there. Besides, I already told him I'd get it in case he is able to make it back here with his family.

"One thing I would like you to do, could you take a bunch of cash from the safe and go to the hardware store in Rogue River right now to buy the fencing material?"

"I don't think I'll need to," he says and follows with a curious smile. "I never told you this before, but my brother Randy is the owner of that hardware store, and the construction supply store next to it. We don't always get along too well and haven't spoken for a few years. A year after I retired from the service, my Ginny died, and I took to drinking. I turned foul on the whole world without something worthwhile to do, and my behavior caused a serious falling out between him and me."

"I didn't stop the heavy drinking until about a month after I started living here on the ranch. Randy hasn't seen me since I got cleaned up. I've been too embarrassed about the things I've said and done to apologize. I think with this situation, if I can make amends with him, we could have whatever we want. It just might add more to the number of people we get here on the ranch."

"Arthur, you get whatever family you have on this ranch regardless of what they bring with them, okay? You've done right by me these last two years, and your family is mine now as well. You might also want to stop by the café and see what Eleanor is doing. I know you don't stop there every day for coffee or to admire their fine china. The end of the world might as well be the start of a new one for all of us."

"I appreciate the offer to bring my family in, but I know we can't really bring them in."

"What do you mean, Arthur? I'm serious, get your family here…unless you think they are troublemakers or something."

"No, I mean all of the discussions you've had with me about the ranch and supplies not being limitless."

"Right, I think this situation is a bit different than what I was planning for. A fast moving pandemic should leave a lot of supplies scattered around as opposed to an EMP or financial collapse. What we're going to need are bodies. Guard duty, scavenging, and eventually farming.

"We will need to limit who we let stay on the ranch at some point, but right now, we should take in any trustworthy people we can find until we know exactly how this thing plays out. Thank you for double checking with me, Arthur. I know I laid down certain rules for the ranch and haven't been here often to see things carried out. You'll find out now that we are here every day, that I am much more flexible than I made myself out to be while I was away."

"So the rules for the ranch are changing?"

"You'll be helping us figure them out, Arthur. I trust your judgment and how you ran the place these last couple of years. You also know a lot of the people from this area, so I'll need your input into who can and can't be trusted, those types of things."

"I like that," Arthur says as he nods. "I'll head out now."

"Arthur, the fence is secondary to Eleanor or your family, okay?"

"Thank you, Eddie. I'm actually more nervous about seeing my brother than about all this other nonsense going on, can you believe that?"

"I believe it. I'm still having a hard time wrapping my head around this whole thing. Be careful out there. People will start to panic, and they'll be acting like bigger idiots than normal, especially on the road. Take a gun with you and make sure you grab the cash. I don't want your brother thinking you are trying to pull one over on him. Take about eight grand with you. That amount should cover the cost of most of the fencing he has and help let him know you are being honest with him. Also take one of the letters we printed out from the General. Simone has them, I think."

Simone walks up with Joshua as I'm heading back to the truck. "Eddie, the internet has been shut down. You need to be quick out there, be careful, but be quick."

"You mean our service has been shut off?" I ask.

"No. I can still get online, but the only thing that comes up is a government message citing some security act signed into law authorizing the shut-down of the internet. The page tells people to turn to their televisions and radios for information. It looks like they were losing the public relations battle and had to block everyone's access. The TV and radio only have the emergency broadcast alert message, and all it's telling people to do is stay indoors and avoid people behaving strangely."

"Damn. This is happening too quickly. If the alert system has been activated, that means people are going to go really bat-shit crazy now. Everyone will be acting *strangely*. Is the phone in the house still working?"

"Yes, and Joshua did get through to his girlfriend, although I'm not sure if she will be coming here."

"Simone, hang on," I say as Arthur is driving up with the truck to leave. I wave him down, "Arthur, you need to get in the house and call your brother before you drive down there. The emergency alert system has been activated, so you know what that will do to people. Your brother might not even be there. He might be heading home."

"If it's just the same to you, I'll head straight there anyway. I know him, and he won't be leaving his store right away. I can't say what I need to say to him on the phone, and if the sickness is spreading this fast, we'll need that fence."

"All right, Arthur, go, but be careful. You've got a gun, right?"

"I've got two of them, actually. I'll be careful. Bye."

Simone and I keep talking as we walk the last few yards to the truck. "Okay, Simone. This changes a few things. You get the girls their target guns and have William ready as well. Start carrying your gun all the time now, load a few of the rifles from one of the safes, and put them around the house. We're out of the way here but not out of the way enough. I have been inviting more people to come here that we don't know, like Arthur's family and the like."

"More people, Eddie? Do they have specific skills we can use?"

"Honestly, I don't know. Some of Arthur's family own the hardware and lumber stores, so they should have building experience. Maybe some farmers as well. I know it isn't the controlled entry we planned for, but with a pandemic, I think we'll need numbers at first and can train people as we go."

"How many people do you think we'll have?"

"I'm not sure. I don't know how many people will take the offer or who they'll bring along. There's also the very real possibility that some of the people that took survival courses here might come by looking for a place to stay. It could end up being a lot of people, and at this point, I don't want to turn anyone away, especially anyone that has survival skills. Of course, even though lots of people might want to get here, some just may not make it, so I don't really know how many, but prepare for a bunch. We're probably going to have all three houses and maybe even the bunkhouse filled up, but we'll need the extra manpower to have effective round the clock watches."

"Eddie, don't go out there. We don't need his supplies, and we can give him some of our stuff if he returns."

"I know what you mean, Simone, I do. But we still need to get Donald's wife and maybe Joshua's girlfriend. I need to go because they need someone that can defensively use a gun and an extra set of eyes to watch for trouble. I won't go anywhere that I think is dangerous. We may not even get a chance to load anything in the truck if I don't think it's safe to get to Matt's place."

She gives me a stern but worried look.

"I'll be careful, Simone. I don't plan on dying on the first day of a zombie apocalypse. We'll be back as soon as we can, but it may be after dark, since it is already close to two."

She gives me a hug and kiss, ending with a sad half-smile. I climb into the truck after Joshua to begin my journey into the new American landscape.

CHAPTER FOUR
FIRST CONTACT

The drive into Medford feels strange. I expected there to be more chaos on the roads but there aren't that many cars out here yet. There are people walking everywhere though, far more than usual. The warning is out now, and you can see by the behavior of the folks on the sidewalks and gathered in front of stores that there is a nervous edge to them, like you see in videos of gazelle in African plains popping their heads up constantly to look for danger. If this sickness is real, we are going to be the prey, but those hunting us will be men, women, and children.

Joshua's voice snaps me out of my thoughts as we leave the business district and start heading into the housing area where his girlfriend lives. "What are they doing?"

I look back out to see what he is talking about, and the sidewalks and yards are packed with groups of people just like at the business'. To me it just looks like neighbors all out talking with each other. "Everything is out, Joshua. Think about it, there is no internet, radio, TV, or phone service now. Everyone out there is probably just trying to get a little more information. Hoping someone else has heard something that they haven't."

Donald adds, "It's sad that this seems a bit strange to us, but I bet to some of those older folks out there getting together with the neighbors is the long lost normal that they remember. A distant time before smart phones and the internet kept us secluded in our own homes."

"Hey Dad, that's it on the left up there," Joshua says as we approach his girlfriend's place. "It looks like she's out there with her mom."

Donald pulls the truck over across the street from her.

"Joshua. When we get out, try and make amends with your girlfriend, but don't leave the sidewalk and don't go in the house. The people that live here are already moving in our direction. I'm guessing to see if we have some information since they aren't carrying weapons. Just be prepared to leave quickly if we need too, okay? I don't think the disease has made it to Medford yet, and a lot of these people probably have no idea there is anything other than rioting going on in the country."

"How can they not know?" asks Donald, with derision.

"Most of the news channels, even the news websites, were talking about this like it was another case of violent rioting before it got taken down. Hannah was searching for news related to bites because of what Simone had heard at the hospital. If someone wasn't searching for bite information, there is a good chance they wouldn't have heard anything about infection either, since the CDC info never made it to the TV news. On top of that, think about how few people even bother to listen to the news, Donald."

"Hey, this is great and all, but can I get out of the truck?" Joshua says, waiting for me to get out of his way.

"Sorry," I say while opening the door and climbing out. "Just stay near the truck, Joshua. I'm going to talk with the people out there and see what they know."

In less than five minutes we are back in the truck and on our way to Donald's house. Joshua has a red spot on his cheek from getting slapped, and I have a growing sense of unease filling me. Not an anxiety of what might happen in the future, but what might not.

Donald's question pulls on exactly what I am thinking. "So what did you find out from those people? What have they heard?"

"Not a damn thing," I reply. "It's just as bad as I thought it might be. Maybe it's worse. Those people haven't heard anything with any substance about what's happening. They just think it is big city rioting and are pissed that the phones and internet have been cut off because of it. Most of them didn't even know that there are problems at the military bases. Honestly, it is making me start to think I got this wrong."

Donald looks over at me and back at the road before asking, "Do you know the sheriff?"

"I don't know him too well, just a bit as a customer from my store."

"Well, he doesn't live too far from us, and is on the same road. We'll be driving by his place before we get to mine, and we can see if his wife knows anything about what might be happening."

"That sounds like a plan. I don't want to be charged with spreading a panic about an outbreak if this really is just massive rioting in cities."

Donald has a small house on a few acres Northeast of Medford on the outskirts of town. He said it's a nice place to park his rig, and it has a decent workshop according to his brief description. I haven't yet found out what type of workshop it is and am thinking to ask him as we top a small hill.

Donald exclaims, "Uh-oh. Looks like something bad may be going on after all. Sheriff Barns is at home and looks to be loading a trailer and his truck."

"Good. Let's see what he knows."

When we stop I grab one of the printouts of the General's letter and climb out of the truck to talk to the sheriff. He acknowledges me approaching but doesn't stop loading stuff into his truck. "Hi, Sheriff Barns. I'd like to pick your brain, see what you might know."

"Hello, Mr. Keeper. You got that truck loaded with stuff from your store?" He stops and smiles at me.

"Just call me Eddie, Sheriff. Actually, that has already been moved. We're going after Donald's wife right now. He lives down the street from you a bit. I see you're packing up, so it's safe to assume this is the real deal, and I'm not just being a paranoid prepper, right?"

"You've heard the alert like everyone else, I'm sure. I don't trust what the feds are saying, and I don't like that they are taking charge, so I'm getting my wife ready to go. She'll be meeting our kids at my son's place near Klamath Falls."

"The feds are taking over?"

"Homeland Security is running the show now. They say it's some kind of executive order for states of emergency. They had some people here at the beginning of the week like they knew this was coming, and this morning, they were heading out to the state police headquarters. Are you going to be staying at your ranch?"

"Yeah, I plan too. Hopefully the hordes of infected zombies don't rush into the hills in a big wave and find my place," I say with a little nervous sarcasm.

The Sheriff chuckles, and asks, "Is that what they call the rioters these days? Zombies?"

"Um, no..." I hesitate. "I mean, the diseased, Sheriff." Sheriff Barns just stares at me, and I can tell he doesn't know, so I hand him one of the letters. While he reads it, I tell him what Simone heard from the hospital, and how Hannah got this letter printed out before the internet went down.

When he gets about halfway through reading it he runs to his patrol car, cursing the whole way.

Donald and Joshua get out of the truck and stand over by me. We wait and listen to the sheriff trying to get in touch with his men and various police officers and agencies on his police radio. We listen to him speak with the chief of the Medford police department.

"Charlie, you can't let those Homeland Security guys give any of your men those injections they brought for first responders. I've got a letter here from a General Francis that says it may be contaminated, and the people that get the Zeus drug become infected and violent. Zeus is what those guys called that drug, right?"

"Carl, give me a second. I've got men at the hospital with the DHS guys right now. I'll call you back on the direct channel."

Sheriff Barns stands up and looks at me with anger etched in every feature. "You got this letter on the internet? God damn it all." He doesn't give me a chance to answer. He just goes on to explain, "We have DHS guys that have been speaking with us about getting this injection. They say it is necessary to protect us from the violence that is spreading everywhere. That is one of the reasons I'm getting my wife to leave. Why would they do this? How could they spread an infection like this?"

"They might not know," says Joshua plainly, and we all turn and look at him. "It is the government after all. They aren't exactly known for great coordination or organized responses right?" He pauses and we all just stare at him to continue his thoughts. "I mean, it says in the letter they were preparing for martial law, and that the drug was being distributed. The DHS guys could just be following orders not realizing the drug they are carrying is causing the violence. I mean, they wouldn't hang around while it's given if they know what will happen, right?"

"That makes sense I guess," replies the Sheriff. "Every part of the military or government that gets the injection would shortly be overrun with the infected, and no one would be able to get a warning out. Everyone down the line would just keep giving the shots, especially as news of violence approaches their area."

"Carl, this is Charlie, are you there?"

"Yeah Charlie, this is Carl. What do you got for me?"

"We're too late. Some of my men and the hospital staff were supposed to be given the injection about thirty minutes ago by the DHS people. I can't reach anyone, not the DHS guys, not my guys or the hospital. I also can't reach the men I sent down there a short while ago to check on reports of violence. You said it's some kind of contamination in this Zeus drug that's causing an infection?"

"Charlie, it's a letter someone I know brought me. It basically follows the line the DHS guys have given us. It says that the drug is safe and is being administered to the military. Except there is a note from this General Francis that he is stuck in his office. His men are outside killing each other and trying to get in to kill him. He blames the drug and says after people get the shot they get violent and spread the disease by biting people. Bitten people then show the same violent symptoms within one to five minutes."

"Carl, I have to go. The regular channel is filling up with officers asking for back-up. I need tell my men what is going on."

"Charlie, if this is an illness spread through the bite of infected people, your men aren't equipped to deal with anything like that on a massive scale. They can't try apprehending these individuals or they risk infection themselves. And if the military is already out of the game, we can't expect help from the National Guard. You're going to have to tell your men to act defensively, and you know what that means."

"Carl? I have three groups of my officers that were supposed to get this injection today. I know some of the fire department guys were supposed to get it as well. If your men haven't been exposed, get them out! Carl, don't come in to help us, use emergency protocol for extreme outbreak or nuclear attack. I'll talk to you later."

"Good luck, Charlie."

"So I guess that's it, isn't it? The infection is here now," I say to Sheriff Barns.

"Eddie. Thank you for bringing this to me. If the damn phones and internet weren't down we could warn a lot more people about what is going on."

"Sherriff Barns, what is the emergency protocol you're supposed to follow?"

"To avoid having all emergency personnel wiped out by a terrorist attack or outbreak of some type, unexposed or uninfected personnel are required to evacuate the city instead of render assistance. We are supposed to form a perimeter around the city guarding all major roads leaving the area and set up a minimal quarantine zone to check for and prevent any exposed people from leaving. The problem is, we are supposed to coordinate with the National Guard on quarantine procedures. I haven't heard hide nor hair from the governor or the guard commander. I guess now I know why.

"I don't have the manpower to do anything without the guard, but at least I can get my people to safety. Eddie, you need to watch out for that newspaper guy Hansen. He stopped by my office this morning after he was at your place, saying I should go arrest you, and confiscate all of your goods for the *community*, but I could tell he meant for him. He knows where your ranch is, so he might be a threat if he survives this cluster fuck."

"Thanks for the heads up. We should be going. Oh, Sheriff Barns, if you need anything, you know where I am as well. I'm taking people in right now, and we'll be trying to set up a defensive perimeter around some of my land. If your son's place isn't safe or doesn't stay that way, you and your family can head to mine."

We say quick goodbyes and get back in the truck. When we start moving I see the Sheriff drop his head, turn and slowly go back toward his car, presumably to call his men and tell them what he knows and figure out what he should do next.

*

Pulling into Donald's driveway, I see his wife Karen is still at the house, and has a few travel bags set up in a stack out front. As he stops the truck, Katy, his daughter, runs out of the house followed by her mom.

Donald turns and tells me, "I had to sell my truck, and her car isn't running so well. It was better for her to wait for us here than her possibly breaking down on the road somewhere."

I nod my understanding, and we all head out of the truck.

Joshua and I carry the bags to the trucks trailer, while Donald tells his wife what we know so far.

"Is there anything else to load up?" I ask as I walk up to Donald and Karen. "Hello, I'm Eddie Keeper," I say to Karen shaking her hand.

"Hello, Mr. Keeper. I'm Karen. No, there isn't anything else to take right now. Donald told me on the CB earlier that you would be in a hurry to get some supplies out of the center of town. We do have a lot of things I would like to take with us, but nothing I would consider survival supplies." She turns to Donald, and asks, "Are you sure we'll be able to come back to get more things?"

"If things get really bad inside Medford, we can still skirt the city to get here from my ranch when we want to come back," I offer. "But if there is nothing else to take then we need to get going. It's already four thirty, so it might be dark before we finish loading up. If we can do it safely, that is."

"How far is this guy's place from the hospital the Chief was talking about on the radio?" Donald asks.

"Not far enough, I'm sure. I really don't know. We're just going to have to watch what the people in the area are doing, and listen for screams, gunshots, or anything else approaching us. Hopefully with the alert system telling people to stay indoors and keep secure, it will keep people from clogging the streets. We haven't seen too much traffic on the roads yet, but we've stayed off the highways for the most part." I'm about to get in the truck but turn back to Donald, and say, "I didn't see any guns with the stuff we loaded, so you should run in and grab what you have."

"Oh, Damn! I knew I was forgetting something important," Karen says

"That's all right, honey. Joshua and I will get our guns, and you can get Katy situated in the cab."

"Do you need any help getting them?" I ask.

"No, we don't have very many. It's just a couple of rifles and shotguns. My handgun I keep in the truck."

"Okay, I'll be in the truck as well then," I say and turn to follow Karen and Katy.

*

Some of the streets are starting to get backed up with cars. There are plenty of vehicles loaded with belongings heading out of the city to some unknown destination but not enough to completely clog the roads, and not nearly as many as I would have assumed. If I was living in any city, I would be getting my ass out. I'm guessing most people just don't have anywhere to go.

There is rioting nationwide, so the prospect of escaping one city for another isn't an option. It may also be a general lack of initiative, however, and that would be a truly sad scenario. And then with the economy in shambles for the last ten years, and the most recent downturn, many probably don't have the means to escape. They either have no vehicle or no gas.

Katy occasionally chats with her mom from the back of the cab, other than that, we are mainly in our own worlds. We are quiet and transfixed by this slowly increasing American exodus going on before us. Car after car filing by, headed toward the highway, and we can only stare in disbelief as if we are watching some movie in silence. The radio is still on the emergency broadcast. All stations telling people to remain at home and to be on the lookout for people acting strangely. Strangely! There is a stupid non-descriptive phrase if ever there was one. Do they bother telling people that there is an infection? No. Do they say the infection comes from a bite? No.

"Damn it!" I say out loud, jolting everyone from the muted, and eerie scene out the windshield. "Sorry," I offer. "I was just thinking about the alert system message and how it offers these people no help whatsoever. Millions of people, actually probably hundreds of millions, are going to die because of this thing. The government couldn't be bothered to give the people a fighting chance. No honest explanation of what is going on or at least what specifically people need to avoid. It just pisses me off to no end."

We drive on for a few more blocks before Karen asks from the back, "Do you really think that many people will die?"

"I'm sorry for the doom and gloom, but yes, I do, at least in this country. If this thing is truly global then we'll probably lose billions. I mean, imagine what we're looking at. An infection or disease of some type that takes just one to five minutes for a person bitten to become violent, and that is assuming it isn't quicker. Then you have a public that has basically no information about avoiding bites. Add to that the first responders being a main source of outbreak for this disease.

"During an emergency where do people go? They'll either go to the police station, fire department, or the hospital which in many places would be the epicenters of the illness. I mean, this is the perfect scenario for population reduction, except there is a very good chance of extinction."

"Come on," Donald says with disdain. "Now I know you run a survival type store, but I think your imagination is running wild here. I mean, we haven't seen any panicked people or any violent ones attacking each other. People that are driving by may be cutting each other off on the roads, but we haven't even seen any accidents yet, and there are a lot of people crowding the roads now. Maybe it will get bad but extinction of the human race? Really? There are seven billion of us. We're on every continent. We have the knowledge and technology to survive whatever is thrown at us. Even this thing, whatever it is."

"Maybe you're right, Donald. I'm basing my assumptions on this thing keeping the same transmission time or speeding up, but it could just as easily slow down and taper out. It could mutate away quickly if it is a viral outbreak."

"Even if it speeds up, I can't see the people in the labs, the scientists not looking for a cure or antidote or something," Donald says confidently.

"What people in labs?" Joshua questions.

"What now, you too?" he asks his son. "The CDC, the WHO, all of the disease studies labs and the scientists that work there."

"That sounds like essential personnel and first responders to me," Joshua says quietly referring to the internet letter.

Joshua's right, "Even if the people in those agencies don't take the drug and get sick, they will still be subject to fighting off those that are violent. And I bet they have military personnel guarding those facilities that will take the drug. Let's give it the best possible outlook. The buildings are secure, and the people inside and out remain uninfected. What kind of research will they do when the power goes out?"

"Why would the power go out?" Karen asks, a bit concerned.

"Power plants and utility companies are run by people. When things get really bad do you think the electricity producers will stay on the job, or will they go home to protect their families? And what if the plant comes under attack by the infected? Best case scenario is that all the power plants get manually shut down and the nation goes black. Only those places with generators or some alternative power source like we have at the ranch will get any electricity, and that is minimal compared to normal usage amounts."

"How is that the best case?" Karen asks. "All the power going out would be devastating."

"My wife and I moved here to Oregon because there are basically no nuclear power plants in the Northwest area. Only one in Washington, none in Idaho, Montana, Utah, or Oregon. The California plants are all far away. If someone at a nuclear power plant gets infected before the plant is shut down then it could be worse than Fukushima and Chernobyl. Just one nuclear facility going into meltdown would be a disaster when everyone is already dealing with a rapidly moving outbreak. There are a lot of nuclear power plants out there, especially on the East coast. There could be dozens of total meltdowns from a disease that spreads this quickly. Let's just hope DHS didn't send any of this Zeus drug to power plant security forces."

A car swerves in front of us from the passenger side, squealing its tires, and tries to drive down the road to our left, but the turn was too fast and too wide. Donald had to slam on the brakes and stop the truck. We watch as the car bounces on the curb, hits the street sign, and crashes into the concrete wall just beyond the sidewalk.

"Donald, get the truck moving," I say urgently.

"I can't, that car just had—"

"Get it moving now, Donald!" I yell, cutting him off. "They are either running from something we don't want to deal with right now or running because they've done something wrong."

Donald looks at me with anger as if he is ready to throw me out of the truck, but I point past him at the scene to redirect his attention to what is going on. The driver of the car has gotten out and is grabbing a duffle bag stuffed with some small boxes. A few fall out and look to be some type of smart phone or I-phone packaging. The passenger climbs out through the driver's door holding his head and tries to stagger away before the drivers duffle bag is thrown around his neck.

"Can we go now, Donald?" I say as the car's driver reaches back into the vehicle for some other probably stolen items. "The looting has started, and you have your family in the truck with you. If we run into a situation where I think we can help people without risking our lives, I won't tell you to leave, but I am asking you to trust my judgment until we get back to my place. Good Samaritans get killed during normal rioting, and we have to watch out for an infection as well."

He doesn't respond, just starts the truck rolling again to drive the final thirteen blocks.

"At least this place seems quiet," Joshua says. "There are only a few cars going by here."

"Let me go out and check the house. I'll make sure I can open it up and that no one is around," I say and hop down out of the truck and walk up to Matt's front door. It's locked and the key he gave me works, so I unlock and open it, then turn back to the truck, and say, "I'm going to walk around the house to make sure no one has broken in from the back or sides."

"You don't need to bother," a voice calls from my left. "Matt left this morning, and no one else has come or gone." It's one of Matt's next door neighbors.

"Hello," I say casually to the man walking up.

"Matt said someone would be by to pick up some of his things. I was amazed to find out he is one of those conspiracy people who thinks the world is going to end. I feel bad for you people having to move his stuff for no reason, but I guess moving companies have to make money too, right?"

"What's your name sir?" I ask

"John. John Matthews."

"Well, Mr. Matthews—"

"Just, John."

"Okay, John. We aren't a moving company. I'm a friend of Matt's, and unfortunately even the local sheriff is packing up and moving his family out of town. The Metro police chief told Sheriff Barns that he can't get some of his men on their radios, and the phone-line into the station was jammed with calls. Are you a person that is avoiding dealing with reality, or are you just unaware of what is going on?" I ask.

"Well, I um... Matt said it was serious and said it might be some type of illness, but he didn't have any information other than the rioting that's taking place. We haven't had rioting problems here in Medford, and I just thought... well, I don't have any idea what is going on. The alert said to stay home and didn't say anything like what Matt mentioned. I just figured he was overreacting."

"Give me a second Mr. ... I mean John. Donald, you and Joshua go ahead and start loading up the truck. Matt said there would be a list of the supplies he has on the kitchen counter or table, and it should also say where it is stored. Hopefully most of it will be in a room on the first floor. Load and bring your shotguns with you and leave them in the house while you're getting things loaded into the truck. I will be in to help as soon as I let John here know what's going on. "Karen, you get the rifles loaded and be ready to shoot to back us all up if things get bad."

"Do you want your shotgun?" Donald asks

"I'll actually take both the rifle and shotgun please, and one of the letters I brought." Donald passes down my FAL, my shotgun, and the letter which I hand off to Mr. Matthews.

"That is what we know so far Mr. Matthews," I say as I maneuver the rifle strap over my head and across my chest, and sling the shotgun over my shoulder. "Please read the letter, and I will answer any questions that I can," I say, redirecting the neighbors gaze from my guns to the paper he is holding.

After just over a minute of reading, John says, "This can't be real, right? I mean, is this a joke? It has to be."

"I was beginning to think the letter was a fake as well because everything in Medford has been so quiet. When we were at Sheriff Barns' house just under an hour ago, he was packing up to get his wife out of town, and I showed him the letter. He got really pissed and called the Metro Police Chief on his cruiser radio, so we heard them talk. Zeus, the drug mentioned in the letter, is what the local DHS people were distributing to first responders. The hospitals and local police were supposed to get it. The chief lost contact with his men who went with the DHS guys to give injections at the hospital. Only problem is we don't know which hospital, or if it was only one, but this infection is here now, and it is spreading."

John looks at me, and stammers, "I...I don't know what to do. How can the sheriff just leave if things are falling apart? Aren't they supposed to be in charge of situations like this?"

"Normally yes, but in times of national emergencies, the feds take over, and in this case it's Homeland Security, but their solution to this problem is giving injections of the drug, which is what is spreading the disease. On top of that, according to the sheriff, government protocol for this type of emergency is for unexposed first-responders to leave the immediate area so they can coordinate some type of quarantine. He says he doesn't have the manpower for it, and the National Guard isn't answering their phone."

Mr. Matthews' face blanches white a little, and I can see he has no idea what to do. "John, do you have a place where you can go to get out of town? Somewhere that has a lower population than Medford?"

"Yes. I can go to my sister's place. She lives East of Klamath Falls. I'll go there." And he turns back to his house to begin his attempt to evacuate.

"Hey, John?" I call. "What do you do for a living?"

"I'm a CPA," he replies. "Why do you ask?"

"I was just wondering," I say. *Just wondering if you might have useful skills,* I think to myself. But an accountant who thinks people who prepare are conspiracy people won't have anything to offer or he would have mentioned it. He probably has never prepared for anything uncivilized in his life. *Good luck, Mr. Matthews.*

I'm about to go into the house when I stop and look to the east, toward a distant sound of an explosion. There are several columns of smoke rising up from that direction. I walk in and find Donald and his son coming out of a room, with boxes.

"We found his main store room," Donald says.

"Okay, change of plans. There's smoke off to the east, and I just heard an explosion. We have to get this loading done quickly, but we shouldn't leave your wife and daughter out there alone, so we will all rotate. One person will always stay out there with the truck, to help keep watch for anyone approaching on foot."

*

With about half of the room emptied, Joshua and I hear Donald yell for us from outside. We both grab our shotguns and run out to see what he needs, and find he is looking in the distance behind the truck. A lone figure is walking and stumbling up the road toward us from the direction the explosion came from earlier. In the lower light of dusk it is harder to see them walking up, but whoever it is has on white. There are several more columns of smoke in the distance that seem illuminated from below, but they are just being lit up by the last light of sunset.

"I think it's time to go, Donald. I would love to get everything in the truck, but if we stay here too long we risk everything anyway. It's not safe to load anymore with it getting so dark."

Just then, the street lights pop on. Not really helping yet because it isn't dark enough, but giving us all a little extra courage against the approaching night and its hidden demons.

"I think we can get more," Donald says. "But you stay out here and watch the roads. Joshua and I will keep packing until you think we absolutely can't stay any longer."

"Okay, fine, but can you get the truck started so we can just hop in and go?" I ask.

Donald tells Karen to start up the truck and heads back into the house with Joshua, to get more supplies. I keep my eyes on the approaching person, back up to the cab of the truck, and tell Karen, "Turn the headlights on high beam so you can keep an eye on the road up ahead. There is one person coming up the road behind us that I may have to deal with shortly. If you see anyone up front, you yell, or honk the horn, okay?"

The person walking up looks infected. It is a woman, and she is one street light away from the back of the truck now. She is heading toward me in an awkward drunken type stagger, and I am moving slowly toward her. If this was any day but today, I would think she was the victim of some kind of assault, and would run up and ask if she needs help. She is wearing a white top and khaki pants and looks like she would have been a manager or employee at any typical retail store. Her white shirt is ripped open at the shoulder, and blood is running down that arm making the whole sleeve look black in the darkness.

"Are you okay, ma'am?" I say out of habit. *Of course she isn't okay, you idiot*, I think to myself. She doesn't respond to my question but just keeps coming toward me in her staggered walk.

She's twenty feet away now. "It's time to learn what I can." I say quietly to myself as I lower the shotgun, draw my handgun out, and aim it at her. "Ma'am, you need to respond. Are you okay?" Fifteen feet and I still get no response. "If you keep approaching I will shoot you ma'am. Stay away." She is now ten feet away and no response. "Ma'am, stop or I will shoot!" I yell loudly. A flash of light and mini explosion as I pull the trigger and my gun goes off. The first shot I aimed at the ground near her, but just to the side, so it wouldn't ricochet and hit her. She doesn't stop, run, or even flinch at the shot. With the second shot, I aim at her.

I hit the woman in the right shoulder, and I start backing up. She keeps advancing and has shown no hint that I shot her. Again, no facial flinch, no anger, or fear at being shot. Her face remains blank, emotionless, and she keeps walking toward me. There is a small spot of blood where my round hit, but not what should occur with a fresh bullet hole. I am keeping the ten foot distance between us, and I take my next shot. Flash—*crack*, another bullet shakes my hand as it leaves my gun. This round enters the woman's left leg above the knee.

The woman still doesn't respond to the bullet impact and it tearing through her skin and bone. She does fall down on the next step as the leg crumbles under her weight. She falls face down and disturbingly doesn't try to block or slow her downward motion. Her face smacks onto the pavement. I cringe at the thought of the pain it would cause and can clearly hear the wet crack of impact, even though my ears are ringing slightly from the report of the gun. She lifts her head to look up at me and has broken her nose. As she starts to crawl toward me I put a final round in her head and end my first terrifying lesson in what we are facing.

Donald and Joshua are standing at the sidewalk staring at me, and I'm sure Karen is looking at me from the cab as well. My skin is cold and sweaty, and I realize I am shaking slightly. "I had to kill her. She was bitten and kept coming."

"We saw it," Donald says. "I didn't want to believe it. I still don't want to believe this is happening. How can someone just keep coming after they are shot like that?"

Now that I see how an infected person reacts I know we are in serious trouble. This was the perfect setting to find out with no other infected around to chase me. I look at Donald and Joshua still just standing there, and say, "You guys need to keep loading stuff, or we should get in the truck and leave." The loading continues.

I didn't notice it before, but I can distinctly hear the crackle of gun fire now. It is going off in the distance here and there in various places in the direction we came from, and sometimes off to either side. The side noise is what worries me. This section of town we are in is residential, but I believe there are some strip malls to the north. I know the downtown shopping area is to the south. People were told to stay at home and inside, but it is human nature to seek out news and information. Many people would head to the local markets and shops that still exist to find out what they can. This would make a great buffet for the infected as well as provide a way for us to be surrounded at this house. I assume the infected would head to where they see the most people or hear the most noise, although I'm not sure how well they hear or see. I know they use sight because that woman lifted her head and seemed to look right at me before I shot her.

"We're almost finished," Donald announces from behind me, making me jump slightly. I had tuned out the sounds of them moving the boxes and totes of supplies, and didn't expect the human voice to call out.

She didn't make any noise, I think to myself. The whole time she was approaching me, I didn't hear anything but her footsteps. She didn't yell or cry when I shot her. She didn't growl or moan like they do in movies. Just silence, stealth. That must be how they can get people. She was moving slowly. I could keep away from her walking backward, so they must use silence to keep from being detected.

This thought makes my hair stand on end, and just in time to coincide with another stomach churning realization, I hear another uneven footfall in the distant darkness that sends a chill down my spine. Mingled into the night are the sounds of continuing sporadic gunfire and the occasional scream carried through the air.

The maker of the footsteps appears under a streetlight from a side street up ahead. He is limping very slowly but not staggering like the woman. He looks like he is just injured or freshly attacked and not yet turned.

"Help! Is there someone there? Help me," the man yells as he starts toward me and the truck.

"Have you been bitten?" I yell, but the answer starts playing itself out in front of me. Another person runs out of the same side street and tries to help the man over to me, but the injured man collapses on the road about fifty yards away, right below the streetlight.

I hear the man that is trying to help say, "Dad, get back up. You've got to get up."

But the man that was his father won't be getting back up. His body starts twisting around on the ground and for a few seconds it looks like he is having a seizure. The twisting and shaking stops, and the man's fallen father starts slowly getting back up.

I yell to him as I start advancing on the pair, "Get away from him. Your father's infected, you need to move."

He looks at me approaching with my gun raised, and says, "Hey, put the gun down. What are you doing? He's okay. Look he's getting back up."

It's too late at this point. The man is standing right next to his father. They are facing each other when the father grabs his son and bites him on the neck. I stop my advance but am already close enough to see a bloody wound appear, and thick pulses of blood spurt out as his father pulls his head away.

I want to pull my trigger and end the attack, but I can't get a clean shot with the son standing between me and his father. I know he is already infected because of the bite, but I'm not ready to start shooting people that aren't showing signs of infection yet. As I start backing up the two men collapse on the ground. The son falls on his own, probably passed out from the immense loss of blood, and the father drops down to him and continues his meal.

I return to the back of the truck keeping an eye on the scene of the attack as I retreat. It seems the infected people will continue assaulting their victim instead of moving on to a new one if the victim can't get away. I don't think the son will be getting back up. His father is just doing too much damage to his son's neck. Unless this disease can cause the dead to rise, which it better not. I just have to keep an eye on the father and look out for any other infected people approaching.

The dad eventually gets up from his meal. I can only assume it is because his victim has finally died. This guy is moving much faster than the woman did. He's moving at a walking pace but with a limp because of the wound on his leg. I don't like the idea of them moving fast like that. The faster they move, the more dangerous it is for us.

With them moving at these speeds, we don't have time to be doing any more loading tonight. I raise my shotgun and shoot the approaching man in the head when he is about twelve yards away from me. Another infected person soon appears from the same side street that father and son did, and heads in my direction immediately. I still don't know how their hearing is. This thing could have turned toward me because he just chose to or because of the sound of my shot. I don't think I'll bother to ask.

The horn on the truck blares, and I look to the front of it and see about four people run across the road, again north to south. These people were moving fast and didn't care that we were here, so they aren't infected, or at least aren't turned. It does mean that the infection is in front of us as well, and moving toward us from the strip mall portion of town.

Donald and Joshua come out of the house with their guns. "We need to go now, Donald," I say. "There is another one coming up slowly behind us, make that two. And some people were running up ahead so these things are almost here."

"I think we've gotten everything anyway," he says and heads to the trailer to close it.

I look at the progress of the two infected people coming from behind and go lock the house. A stupid habit, but there might be more supplies inside somewhere, and I don't want to give up anything that may help us all survive. I walk around the back of the truck, shoot the two closest infected. Four more have come from around the same corner behind the other two, but I turn and jog up to the cab, and climb in.

Infected people are starting to walk out from the road in front of us. There are six spread out and moving in our direction, but the truck doesn't move.

"You're going to have to run them over," I say, but Donald just sits there staring out at the people in front of us.

"Donald, there are more of them coming out from that street now," I say, almost yelling. Being in this closed cab with infected people surrounding the truck is making me feel like I'm in a coffin, and if he doesn't get the truck moving that's exactly what it will end up being.

I yell at him, "We are either going to stay here or you will have to run them down! They aren't going to move for us!"

Karen puts her hand over her mouth and gasps. I look out the windshield, and coming out of the side street, I see there is a young girl about the size of my five year-old dragging a doll by the leg. Karen begins to cry, and my stomach twists into a knot of fear. The infected people have reached the truck and are clawing at it attempting to get at us, their food prize locked in the cab. The collective sadness in the truck turns to a bone chilling fear when we hear our first moan. The sound is part scream and part gurgle, and the infected people outside seem frustrated that they can't get to us.

So they do make a noise when they can't get to their prey, I think.

The little girl with the doll finally makes it closer to the truck and walks into the light of the headlamps. The girl is missing a part of her face, it is just a bloody pulp, and we can see now that it isn't a doll that she is dragging by the leg.

"Donald! We need to go!" Karen screams, and the truck starts moving forward. The feel and sound of crunching as the truck drives over these people is sickening. Joshua actually throws up in the back, and I know we will all feel like that at some point in our journey out of town.

So this is our immediate future. In order to survive, we need to turn against every civilized instinct we have tried to ingrain into modern society. We must revert back to our tribal roots and begin killing other groups of people in order to survive. No more caring for the sick among us to help spread humanities warmth.

We didn't just run over a disease or infected monsters out there, they were people. No more caring for and protecting the smallest and weakest amongst us regardless of their situation in life. Every life, even a child's life, will have to be weighed against our own survival. We will have to kill children just as we had to run over that little girl. That little girl and the dead baby she was dragging behind her.

The next few blocks I sort of tune out. I am here, of course, but just floating in the moment like a bad dream. Every person has their point, their button. Sometimes it is a breaking point, sometimes an epiphany, but there is a point for everyone in which something happens and nothing will ever be the same again. Seeing that little girl was my moment.

I always wanted to have a family. I wanted to be happily married and have kids and truly be with my family. I wanted to actually be in their lives not just a side-note of a man who shows up in-between his working hours to eat and sleep. That was my ultimate goal, and I achieved it. Every moment from the point that I got married and on was doing what I thought would first keep us safe, and second, allow us to spend as much time together as possible.

My own childhood was not bad. While I can call my upbringing indifferent and not particularly close or caring in an emotional way, I wasn't abused or neglected. My experience growing up was like spending time with friends or acquaintances rather than a close bond of family. So because of the indifference I knew while maturing, I wanted to give to my wife and kids a loving family with a devoted husband and father, to which I believe I have been largely successful.

To keep us safe I actively pursued training in firearms for my wife, myself, and my kids, and got into the prepping side of life to ensure that no matter what happens in life, my family will stay safe, secure, and have enough food to eat.

Seeing that little girl in the road is a new moment for me. Even with all that I have done to make sure we had as much quality time together as possible, we aren't together now. I know that I shouldn't be out here alone. My wife and I should be here together with our kids, and I should not have left her at the ranch. As terrible as this moment is, it is something that we should be going through as a family, not as individuals in our own segment of the world's destruction.

The visions of what is happening outside the windows of this compartment can be described, but must be experienced to wholly comprehend. I will tell her about this trip, but she will never be a part of this experience that I have shared with Donald, Joshua, Karen, and Katy. In this moment, I am an outsider in their shared family experience.

"I think we're clear of the bad part," Donald says as he points to the clear road ahead. "It looks like we were just seeing the leading edge of this thing where we were. We are only five blocks from that guy Matt's house."

"Five blocks?" I ask. In my mind it feels like we have been driving for hours. "Okay. Donald, I want to get out of town as fast as we can, but we need to make one more stop now that we are clear of the current infection zone."

A chorus erupts at my statement, of, "What? What are you talking about?" and, "We aren't going to stop anywhere else."

"Look, I'm sorry but we have to search the truck. Donald, you need to get us to a good sized parking lot or area where you can pull over. Find someplace where we can see if anyone is approaching the truck from any side. I need to get out and check if any of the infected people are hanging on or stuck to the truck somewhere. All of the supplies in the world won't help us if we give an infected person a ride to my ranch tonight."

"That looks like a shopping center up ahead. They might have an area, but with so many cars driving in and out, I doubt it's clear."

Donald slows the truck because people are running around, and the people in cars are driving like idiots.

"Do you think these people are infected?" Karen asks, and we are all wondering as well.

"They aren't walking like the people back at the street we came from. They look like people that are just panicked."

There is a grocery store in this shopping center that is being rampaged. People are running out the front door with carts full of stuff. These look like regular people, and they are taking regular things. There are some people out there with your typical riot issue stolen TV or armful of clothes, but most of the carts look like they're full of canned goods and food.

"It looks like people are finally in full panic mode. Is there anything different on the radio?" I ask and switch it on myself.

It's just the same emergency broadcast warning to stay indoors and watch for people acting strangely. Joshua starts scanning through all of the stations and hits one of the smaller ones which is no longer issuing the emergency broadcast.

"Folks, I am getting reports of massive rioting going on here in the Medford area. Right now it seems to be centered in the northeast area but is spreading to the south and west quickly. I'm getting reports on my HAM radio that people are just attacking one another in the streets. It doesn't seem to be any type of organized riot..."

"Does anyone know the phone number to this station?" I ask. "If we can call him and tell him what we know, we might be able to save some people."

"I have a phone book in the glove compartment," Donald says. I reach in and grab it but give Donald a strange look for having it there. "I haul stuff for people all over the southern area and don't always trust the phone numbers on invoices when I'm making a delivery," he explains.

"Damn it! I still have no service with my phone. Are any of yours connecting?" I ask in frustrated anger.

They all shake their heads *no,* and I scratch mine in thoughtful frustration. This morning, most people could have let anyone around the planet know exactly what they were doing and also provided an instant video of it as well. Right now, we can't even call the local radio station to let them know what is going on.

"Hey, Dad? I think this station is on the side of town we're heading to. Since we are already moving away from the infection, we could run in there, and tell the guy in person."

"Tell me the address, son," Donald says, and Karen puts an approving hand on Joshua's shoulder. Katy is sitting on Karen's lap.

The whole scene is touching, and the sentiment is just and noble. I agree that we should tell as many people as we can about what is really going on, but a selfish part of me doesn't want to delay getting back to Simone and my kids any longer than I have to. This situation is easier for them to bear because they are all together. No matter what takes place tonight, whether we make it back home alive or not, they are already together, and won't have to wonder what happened to the people they love. I don't know what's occurring back at the ranch. I can only assume and speculate that everyone is okay.

I don't say what I am thinking, but I am a terrible poker player, and I know my displeasure is visible. I guess my look causes Donald to worry, because he asks, "Do you think it's too dangerous to stop there?"

"No, actually, I think it is the right thing to do. I'm just having a hard time not being with Simone and my kids right now. Especially, since we saw that little girl on the road.

"The look you see on my face is one hundred percent selfish, and I know if we can safely stop at that station and warn people, then it is what we have to do. Humanity's sake aside, every person that we can warn and save from this thing is someone we won't have to fight in the future. I mean, we won't have to fight them as an infected person, anyway."

Our survival luck seems to be continuing. The radio station is situated at the edge of the industrial area of town, and there is plenty of room for Donald to park his rig and for me to get out and check it. The Illness or disease is somewhere a couple miles back, and we have the space to get the truck clear so we can safely make it back to my ranch. However, now that Donald has stopped the truck, I am a little hesitant to open the door. I am ready to see almost every type of carnage that may be hanging, swinging, or grasping to stay attached to this truck. What I am not ready to see is that little girl again.

"Eddie, we'll go together, okay?" Donald says. He must have mistaken my hesitation and look of apprehension with a general fear of getting out of the truck, and he starts opening his door to show his support that we would go together.

"No, No, No. Stop! Damn it! Keep the door closed!" I yell at him. Fortunately, he isn't quick at opening it, and has just unlatched it. He froze at my first yell of, 'No,' and remains frozen as if he has stepped on a landmine pressure plate and can't move without setting it off.

"Donald, roll down your window first, and look out to see if anything is hanging onto your door or the door-step, and look all around as well. If no one is out there then open your door enough so you can close it so it latches."

Donald looks up, down and around and opens his door a bit them slams it closed.

"Look, Donald, I appreciate the solidarity of you coming with me, but everyone in life has certain levels of importance. I can't drive this truck, so I am less important than you in getting us home. You need to stay in the cab and let me check the truck. Then I'll go in and speak with the guy on the radio, you stay here with your family. We need you to get us home."

I look out my window, and then roll it down to check for anyone hanging on and waiting to grab me. I pull out my handgun, and get ready to go. "Joshua, close the door behind me, okay? I'm going to jump away from the truck in case anything is hanging on underneath."

I open the door, jump out, and turn to look at the truck. There is some blood sprayed on the side a bit by the tires, but as I walk crouched along the front looking at its underside, I don't see any bodies, either whole or in pieces. I make it all the way around and see nothing more than the red spray and splatter by the tires, and some on the grill. So I call up to the door where Joshua is sitting. "Do you think you can get up on the top of the truck from the cab so you can keep a lookout?"

He nods.

"Take a gun with you, Joshua. Donald, blow the horn if you need me to get out of there. I shouldn't be too long, I'll just give him one of these letters and tell him what we've seen and heard." And I turn and go into the radio station.

*

The final stretch of the drive home is filled with more silence. I know I am in a slight state of shock and disbelief over what we have seen. The worst part of the horror we witnessed tonight is that we only saw a small portion, a little snippet of the carnage that is playing out in streets around the world right now. I just hope I chose our ranch's location wisely, and that it is set in the hills and woods far enough from Medford and Grants Pass to avoid any major activity.

We'll be home soon enough so at least I can hold Simone and the kids. I lean over in my seat, rest my head against the window, and gaze out at the pavement, brush, and trees that float by in the trucks headlights.

CHAPTER FIVE
BUILDING A NEW HOME

There is trouble at the ranch. I can see the sky lit up at the ranch's location. It looks like a large fire being reflected off a pillar of smoke in the sky. My heart is thumping out of my chest, and I hold my breath while we pull into the property. The main house is in flames and people are standing across the yard watching as it burns. I can see Simone and the kids all next to each other in the crowd.

I don't expect the fire department to show up for this while the world is falling apart. Not that they would know there is a fire here anyway with the phones being down. Donald stops the truck and I jump from the cab and run over to everyone standing in the yard. I need to get to Simone and the kids, and find out what happened.

They are all so transfixed on the flaming house that they don't even see me walk up until I am right next to them. I just grab Simone and pull her to me in a tight hug.

"You left us here alone," she says in a sobbing voice into my shoulder. I can feel her tears on my neck.

"I'm sorry, Simone. I know I shouldn't have gone. What happened to the house? How did the fire start?"

"You left us here alone," she says again and looks up at me. Her face is stained with blood, the blood that was dripping on my neck, and I thought was tears. But I really didn't think they were tears. Tears don't keep flowing in a thick stream the way this liquid was. I guess I knew even as I ran up that my family was dead the way they were just standing there staring at the fire. I ran into my wife's arms knowing that it would be my death and knowing that it was the only place I wanted to be.

"I shouldn't have left you alone. I'm sorry."

"You didn't leave us alone," Donald says from behind the wheel. "Are you all right?"

I look left and see Donald behind the wheel of the truck. "Yeah, just daydreaming, and a horrible dream, too."

"Well, we're here, so you can tell me where you want me to put the truck," Donald says as we drive up to the gate.

"Just drive back toward the barn over there where you parked earlier today. We'll leave it there and figure out where to put everything over the next few days."

Arthur, the caretaker is at the main gate, and opens it up to let us drive in. Simone, Conner, and Samantha all come out of the house as we drive by. I'm happy to see Simone carrying a gun. I'll need to make sure everyone starts carrying wherever they go.

*

Finally back at the house, we have time to discuss what is going on. Arthur got most of his family to come, and Conner made it with his wife, Samantha, and their son, Jake. Arthur and Conner have decided to take watch and walk the perimeter of the immediate yard circling the buildings, while I speak with the group. Our dogs are out as well. They growled at the truck when they first smelled it, so we know they don't like the odor that the infected put off. We are assuming at this point that they will at least bark at anything that smells similar to the infected.

I don't relish the idea of going into a house full of strangers and telling them the world has just ended. It was one thing owning the shop and prepping for disasters with like-minded people, but telling people that aren't part of the prepping community about the end of the world doesn't usually end well. Hopefully, these people will accept what is happening in Medford from my descriptions. I don't know what I would be willing to accept without seeing it for myself.

I guess now that it is here, I can honestly say even I am shocked. I prepared for the ultimate disaster, but always thought we would see a six month, or at most, a two year event where things eventually go back to normal. A global pandemic on this scale takes decades, maybe even centuries, to bounce back from.

The house is packed with people and kids. There looks to be about 50 plus either standing around and chatting with each other or sitting and waiting for information. Arthur told me on the way in that he gave everyone a basic idea of what might be happening, but none of these people had been in Medford, and nothing happened yet in Grants Pass, so they don't know how bad it is. It's nice despite current circumstances, seeing everyone happily chatting with friends and relatives they don't often see together. It helps to counter the horror I've just witnessed while on the road.

This is the job that I asked for when I invited people to come here. I guess it's time for me to ruin the mood and bring everyone up to speed.

"Hello," I announce, getting everyone's attention. "For those of you that don't know me, I am Eddie Keeper, and I own this land. For many of you, what I am going to tell you will sound crazy or like some kind of wild story meant to scare you and your kids, but I just returned from Medford with Donald here," pointing to Donald standing next to me. "He and his family will attest to what we all saw happening there and what we've heard is happening all over the country right now."

I speak to the group for the better part of an hour, telling them everything from the start of the news this morning, to the blood soaked people walking the streets of Medford. The looks from people as I spoke were an assortment of fear and disgust, to outright disbelief and anger. What I told them was a shock to all they believed was possible. I can't blame them for not wanting to accept the things I say I saw. No one wants to think that the world can change so drastically in such a short amount of time, but this is the world we live in now. The faces of anger and skepticism fade as I finally tell them about the little girl that we thought was dragging a doll. Now, fear and shock are worn on all the faces. Many people are holding each other and crying.

"I know many of you don't want to believe that this is happening. I don't want to believe it either. Even after we saw the people running and the man being bitten by his father, I didn't want to accept that this was anything other than people just acting crazy, or maybe some more bath salts addicts, but that isn't what this is. Once we saw the little girl, we all knew that the threads of information we grabbed throughout the day were true. You all need to understand what you and your families are up against.

"I've been told that some of you only came here tonight to hear what I had to say, and you plan on staying at your own homes and properties to try and survive this. I welcome all of you to stay here with us and encourage you to do so. The more people we have together, the better chance we all have to survive."

"What about our friends or relatives? The ones that aren't here, will you let them join us?" Randy Langford, Arthur's brother, asks.

"For right now, every decent person that you know is welcome. Friends and family or people that you've worked with and know are good people. The difficulty will be contacting them, since all forms of communication are down, including telephone land lines."

"For right now?" another voice asks from the crowd.

"We won't be able to let just anyone in on an unlimited basis. There are only so many resources to go around, and when supplies grow thin, we will limit entry to those that have specific skills we can use here on the ranch. I'm not sure how long we have before we start limiting people coming in."

"What about my husband?" Beth Murphy asks. "I tried calling him earlier, but I didn't get him before the phones all died." She begins to cry.

Patricia Langford hugs her, and says, "I know, honey. Our son Matthew is in Washington, and we can't reach him either."

"We will still be letting people in over the next week at least, and missing family members will be welcomed if they show up. Again, providing they are decent people. I can't give you an exact timeframe, because I haven't planned for anything of this scope. At least not something that also took out the government and military at the outset like this thing has. All of our plans were for survival until the government was able to re-establish control and some form of safety for the citizens."

There are a few more random questions from the group, but mostly aimed at each other and specific people they know rather than anything I can answer, so I step off to the side to talk with Simone.

As the gathering breaks up people are hugging and crying. Many are talking about loved ones that are missing and what might be going on. I am thankful that I have my immediate family with me, but my relatives are spread throughout the U.S. My mother is here with us. She's sixty-seven and was living near the ranch. During most days she would come here to play with the animals and grow vegetables. It's nice to have her here and know she isn't alone somewhere wondering if any of her kids are going to survive this outbreak.

I have a sister in Hawaii who I couldn't reach before the phones went down. I called my dad in Louisiana. I was able to get him a warning about what's going on, but it was basically a quick goodbye for both of us. He lives in New Orleans, and his wife is on oxygen and can't travel. He told me he loved me and to keep my kids safe. I told him I loved him as well and hoped he could make it up here, but knew it wasn't possible. When I called my sister in Portland, her husband wasn't home. She was going to try to reach him and head down here. Out of my extended family, only my sister in Portland has a chance to make it here to safety. Of course, that is presuming that we have a chance here at the ranch.

Simone called her Mom and two brothers in Washington, but with things falling apart so quickly everywhere, they might as well have been in Louisiana with my dad instead of just one state over. Unless this thing burns out quickly or the infected die right away, travelling is going to be too dangerous for a long period of time. Hell, staying in one place is going to be too dangerous as well. I guess I'll see if having these supplies will mean anything.

I walk into the kitchen and grab a glass of water from the sink. I hate water. I've never liked the empty taste of it, but I guess it's time for me to start appreciating it. There won't be any sports drinks manufactured anymore.

"Eddie?"

I turn and see Randy standing in the doorway, with his wife. I'm exhausted and don't want to say anything more, so I just nod at him with a sad smile, and sit at the table.

"When Arthur came by today after not seeing him for so long and told me what was going on, I thought he was drunk again. This is real though, isn't it?"

"I'm afraid it is."

"I appreciate you offering to take us all in. I know there are a lot of mouths to feed between all of us, do you have the supplies for this kind of thing?"

"Honestly, Randy, I don't know. I've been putting quite a bit of stuff away for the last four years. I started before we moved here and opened my store. It will all run out eventually though, faster with more people, and we will need to start growing our own food and raising our own livestock if we can manage to live long enough for that. I had Arthur in charge of the inventory, so I just don't know."

"I thought all survival types like you knew exactly what they had. That's part of being ready, right, knowing when you've got enough?"

"When we moved here we had enough long term food stored for my wife and kids, and ten other people, to last two years. I thought at the time if things get bad my extended family might be able to make it here, and we would ride out whatever storm there was together. Since then, I just continued storing more supplies. With every order I placed for the store or for a customer, I would order extra for the ranch, or just to get a better discount and bring it here. Even without it, Randy, Arthur is my family now, and I won't turn his people away."

"Thank you," Randy's wife, Patricia, says.

"What about that poor woman Bethany's husband? Is there some way we can pick him up from his job? Beth's husband is working in North Dakota. She says he moved there to work in the oil industry. He was in construction, and I'm sure you're aware how those jobs completely dried up after the last downturn. He was saving up and was going to send for

THE LAST BLADE OF GRASS

her and their two daughters in the spring. We should do something for her if we can."

"I don't even know a way to safely get my own sister from Portland, let alone get someone here from North Dakota. I truly wish there was, Patricia, but I'm afraid not."

I shake my head silently and they turn to leave.

"Oh Randy, I almost forgot. Sorry to bring it up now, but I don't know what time we have left for things. What about the fencing supplies? Did any of that stuff make it here today?"

"Our big truck was already loaded and out delivering when Arthur came by. We loaded what we could on the two smaller flatbeds but still have a bunch to bring up here."

"If you are willing, and it's safe, I would like to bring everything you have from your yard up here to the ranch. We're going to need a lot of building materials beyond the fencing as time goes on."

"Whatever we can get up here we will," he says and leaves the kitchen.

Simone sits down at the table while holding Benjamin, and asks, "Should we tell people to stay here tonight?"

"We probably should," I say and nod. "At least I'll let them know it's okay if they want to. I don't really know what is best, though. Should they stay tonight and be too late to help their friends and family tomorrow? Or should they go now and possibly get caught by the infection somewhere?"

I don't stay to get an answer. I just go outside and leave it to the people to decide for themselves what they should do.

*

Grants Pass

Eleven hours and forty three minutes after the first injection of Zeus in Medford, Oregon, the biting sickness reaches Grants Pass, Oregon.

A man named George Romero managed to bring his sick wife to the hospital in Grants Pass. He had been trapped for three hours in his bedroom as his wife clawed and banged against the door trying to get in at him. He finally managed the courage to open the door and quickly subdue her with a heavy comforter. He tied her as securely as possible and placed her in their car in an attempt to get her help at one of the local hospitals.

His attempts to reach the hospitals were blocked by mad rioters and other people that seemed to have the same sickness she had. *Probably some extreme form of rabies*, he thought to himself, as he madly weaved through the wrecked and abandoned cars on the road.

Twice he hit people with his car who walked out in front of him, as he tried to escape the city, and get his wife to a hospital somewhere else. He stopped and wanted to help, but couldn't get himself to exit the car to check on the injured. With each event, when he tried to open the door to check on the people, they grabbed onto the car and tried to get at him. He saw they had the illness, the same thing his wife has, and he couldn't do anything for them. His wife was much smaller than the two people he hit, it took everything he had to keep her under control, and that was with a comforter.

He looked for police through his cars windows and kept hitting the keys on his phone, amazed that it still wasn't working. He finally decided to move on seeking help for his wife outside of Medford.

When he finally makes it to Three Rivers Community Hospital in Grants Pass, he is overwhelmed with joy that he has made it to safety. He can finally get his wife help. As he drives up, however, he sees the entrance is blocked off by the police, and they are checking the cars and drivers. *They must have heard about me hitting those two people in Medford and just driving off.*

It doesn't matter what happens to me, I have to get her help, he thinks as he pulls up to the checkpoint and rolls down the window. The police see the damage and blood on the car, and Mr. Romero yells to them, "It was an accident, but I need help with my wife, she's in the back."

"Sir, you hit someone?" the police officer asks, pointing at the hood of the car.

"Yes, but there were no police around, and my phone isn't working, I came straight here after it happened."

"All right, sir, you drive up to the emergency entrance there." And the officer points the way to let the illness in.

The police had received word from Sheriff Barns of Medford that the illness was spreading and deadly. They managed to block off access to the hospital and were screening everyone arriving to look for signs of bites or the disease. They didn't find anyone yet. Mr. Romero is the first person to escape Medford with an infected loved one. No one that gets infected is able to make it to Grants Pass for help on their own, they turn too quickly. So Mr. Romero is the first bringing a case through the line, and this isn't what they are expecting or prepared to look for.

"This guy can go through—he has a car accident victim in his car," the officer tells the others at the roadblock behind him. Mr. Romero doesn't bother correcting the police officer. His only concern is getting his wife the help she needs. He doesn't know what the officers are looking for and has no idea what this sickness is. All he knows is she was bitten and went wild, and the people at the hospital must know what to do.

When he drives up to the doors of the emergency room, two people come out and stop at his car's bloody and dented hood. "It was an accident. I hit somebody. My wife is in the back," he says as he gets out and walks them over to the door. When he opens the car, the doctor and nurse from emergency stare at each other for a second in surprise.

Working in the emergency room for many years, they have seen quite a few things. What this image shows them isn't a car accident victim, it is an attempted murder. The look the doctor and nurse exchange with each other says the same thing. This man tried to kill his wife. No one wraps a blanket over the head and body of an accident victim and ties them up with curtains.

The nurse heads back to the hospital door to get an officer to arrest Mr. Romero, while the doctor works at untying Mrs. Romero in the back seat, so he can get an idea how bad her injuries are. *She isn't yelling or crying out in pain, so she might be drugged and disoriented*, he thinks as he unties her.

The police officer walks up and sees the body being untied in the back seat, as the nurse described and grabs Mr. Romero, telling him, "You're under arrest."

"Yes, I know, I'm sorry," he says, thinking he is being arrested for the hit and runs.

Doctor Jackson, the physician on the scene, has been a doctor for twelve years. He has been in emergency work his whole career. He has been married for eight years to another doctor at this same hospital. He enjoys bicycling and dancing. His wife is three months pregnant with their first child.

Mrs. Romero bites into Dr. Jackson's neck once he lifts the comforter off of her head. He falls back out of the car and hits the ground. Only a gurgling sound comes from the hole in his throat. Mrs. Romero steps over the dying doctor and starts to spread the disease.

CHAPTER SIX
FALL ISOLATION

I wake up in a strange yet familiar room. I'll have to get used to living at the ranch now. I guess that is true for everyone. Most of the people that were at the meeting last night chose to stay here. It was too big of a risk for most of them to head out into the darkness to try and find people they know, especially those that had their immediate families here with them already.

The morning is filled with chaotic buzzing movement of many more people than I am used to interacting with. The kids are having a great time playing with each other and are busy running in and out of the house, presumably to play with some of the animals. Simone spots the concern on my face as I watch them running out the door, and says, "There are people standing guard. The kids are feeding the goats and chickens."

"We'll have to do a good job explaining to everyone that no children should go off on their own. In fact, even adults should travel in pairs. If just one person gets bitten walking alone on the ranch, then we're all dead."

"I'll speak to everyone. You need to eat something quick and meet Arthur by the trucks."

I'm not feeling hungry, so I just grab two pieces of toast off the table in the kitchen, and walk out the door. Stepping out into the morning air, I see that the Earth is still unconcerned with the troubles of man. Cool air tingles the hair on my neck, and a bright sun in the clear blue sky kisses my face with warmth.

I guess it is ego or arrogance that makes me think the world should care what happens to us. I never stop to consider the enduring nature of things when a cat catches a bird, and I doubt other birds consider their smallness in the scheme of things when they see each other getting eaten. Still, I am surprised that the morning seems like just another morning after witnessing the horrors of yesterday.

Today will be a day of running for supplies and checking for friends and relatives. If luck stands with us, then we will either get most of the building supplies today, or we will be able to safely retrieve things for at least the next few days.

What I would love more than anything would be for everyone to run up to me, start laughing, and call me Chicken Little. Even seeing what I saw in Medford last night, I want nothing more than to be told that I'm an overreacting fear monger, and the worst is over. For now though, it seems our interpretation of the events is true at least in that everything is still off: television, phones, and radio. Electricity is still working, so that isn't an issue for the modes of communication that are out.

We'll all head out to our respective destinations, guns loaded and ready, hoping to find people we love and items we'll need to survive.

*

It's the third day after moving to the ranch. The best news came the first day when Randy Langford returned with his son, Matthew, and Matthew's family. They had arrived the night of the collapse at Randy's house for a surprise visit, unaware of everything going on, or where his parents were. The reunion of their family was the only heartfelt highlight over the last few days. No other family members for anyone have arrived since that first day, and we just discovered it is now too dangerous for us to leave the compound and venture into the towns. The disease has spread everywhere that we can easily reach by car or truck.

We did have a few more arrivals of friends and strangers. The first day when Matthew Langford arrived, we also welcomed Brian and Melissa Carpenter. The Carpenter's were finishing their vacation by staying on the property next to mine, which belongs to Brian's father, Clyde.

Clyde is also a prepper and did some combat training with a group at my property. He told Brian to come to his land or mine if there were any type of upheaval, so it was an easy decision for them to join us until his father gets back. They drove over to our place with their truck pulling a beautiful new fifth-wheel trailer they had been breaking in over the summer. Unfortunately, Clyde and Brian's mom, Barbara, are on the road in an R.V. somewhere in the U.S., and Melissa's parents, brother, and sister are in central California.

The second day was another good day for additions to our ranch. A couple, Timothy Weyland and Dianne Blount from Iowa, were found and rescued from a minor car accident on the highway. They had been camping by the ocean near Crescent City in California, and drove up Redwood Highway to Grants Pass, initially hoping to go up to Portland, but Grants Pass was in chaos already, and there were wrecks and abandoned vehicles blocking I-5 North.

They had to head east toward Medford and got in an accident just east of Rogue River, when a man walked onto the highway in front of them, causing Timothy to brake and swerve into an abandoned vehicle. They only hit the other car slightly, but the airbag deployment killed the car, and then they were trapped in it by a group of infected, until Randy, Matthew, and Joshua happened by on a supply run. Seven infected were killed to remove the couple from their car, and it was the first killing that any of those people had to do or see.

The other new arrivals came that morning while I was out picking up more supplies from the Langford lumber yard. Daniel Palmer, a Jackson County Sheriff's Deputy, showed up with five other people; his girlfriend, Jessica Dixon, and her sister, Ashley; his father, Michael, mother, Jennifer, and his sister, Megan. He was sent here by Sheriff Carl Barns after things had completely collapsed and the Sheriff's office was overrun.

Daniel spent the rest of the day after having to abandon the sheriff's office getting to his girlfriend, and her sister, and taking them to temporary safety at his parents place. They left in the early morning while it was still dark to head here to the ranch.

Today, the third day out isn't turning out to be a good day. The disease has made its way into our closest town, Rogue River, so we are now going to be locked down on the ranch once we get back. We were driving into town but have stopped on the road just on the outskirt. There is smoke coming up from different parts of Rogue River, and we know what it means. After talking it over we have decided to head in and drive around if we can, hoping things might not be so bad yet, or that we might drive through and rescue some survivors.

We have a convoy of three vehicles; two pickups and a flatbed, and we're turning the vehicles around to drive in on a small dirt road called Laurel Street that turns into 3rd Street. If there are any survivors that can make it to us, they can jump into the back of any of the trucks without any of us inside the cabs being at great risk.

I personally doubt that we will be able to do much for anyone here, but I understand the need to at least try. This is a smaller community and most of the people know each other, if not personally, then by acquaintance in shopping at a store or gassing up at the gas station. But with smoke from several fires visible in parts of the town, I know it is lost. None of the people with this group were in Medford with me three days ago, so they really don't know what might be out there. I think it's better that they see for themselves.

The paved portion of 3rd Street is just ahead, and I can already see the infected. They are everywhere, just wandering around in the streets. The scene doesn't look like fresh carnage though, so the infection must have arrived here yesterday. Maybe sometime after our last supply run at 2 p.m., or maybe even while we were still here. I'll never know.

Our group has stopped, and some of the people from the back two trucks have stepped out of the cabs to look ahead. The noise from our vehicles is already starting to attract the infected this way. I open my door, and yell back to everyone, "Get back in the trucks, we're going to have to turn around and head back to the ranch"

The trucks start backing up to turn when we hear a woman screaming. She is running at us from the backdoor of a house on Nugget Drive, just off of 3rd, about 100 to 150 yards away. She is screaming, "Help me," at us and is attracting a much larger group of the infected to stumble after her and toward us. It is easy to see she is injured and most likely bitten. Her blouse is soaked with blood on the left side from some kind of shoulder wound, and she looks pale white, either from terror, or blood loss.

Our three trucks are all too close to easily maneuver, especially the large flatbed at the back. I feel like an idiot for letting ourselves get jammed up in such a way, but I am at least thankful we weren't next to the houses yet. Those tight neighborhood roads would have made getting the trucks turned around a very slow action. As it is, the injured woman manages to reach the lead truck I'm in and jump on the hood before we can turn the truck around.

Samantha is behind the wheel and screams when the woman jumps on the hood. Conner and I both flinch back, as if she might continue her motion, and come through the windshield at us.

The woman on the hood grabs hold of the windshield wipers, and yells, "Go, go, go! Get me out of here!"

So I know now she isn't infected.

I can tell Samantha is ready to floor the accelerator and make the lady fall off, so I reach across Conner, grab Samantha's arm, and yell, "She isn't infected! Let's just get out of here."

I don't actually know if the woman isn't infected, but she isn't acting infected. She was running, and she is yelling for us to help her and not to stop. She doesn't look right, though. She must have lost a tremendous amount of blood. Looking at her through the window you can see that some of the blood on her is dried, and more is still coming out.

Samantha drives us back down the road a bit, and we stop long enough for the woman to get off of the hood and climb into the pickup bed. All of the vehicles backtrack east on Wards Creek Road a couple miles, and we pulled over to speak with the woman and check on her wound.

"Kim. My name is Kim," she says through a weak exhaustion.

"What happened?" Jason Anderson asks, walking up with a first aid kit.

Kim starts sobbing, and through the weeping, says, "My husband attacked me. Yesterday evening the rioting started in Rogue River. Neither of us understood what was happening. This is a small town, we all know each other, but people started attacking each other in the streets when we were at the store. We went home quickly. We still thought it was just rioting until this morning at five. We heard someone trying to break into our garage. My husband, Jim, went out with his revolver to scare them off, but he got attacked. He came back in with blood on his arm and a scratch on his face, and slammed the front door behind him."

"I got bit, that guy bit me," was all he kept saying, and he made it into the bathroom before he collapsed. I was right there with him, and he started convulsing. I thought he was having a heart attack or something, and I grabbed him to keep him from shaking worse, but then he stopped and bit me."

Jason is applying pressure to the hole in her shoulder, with a bandage, but when she says she was bitten, we all step back.

"How long ago did he bite you?" I ask from a few feet away, with my right hand gripping my sidearm in its holster.

"It was 5:14 a.m. I remember looking at the clock after trying to call 911. The phone lines were still down, but I didn't remember right away why I couldn't get through. I was thinking maybe 911 was closed and looked at the phone.

I look at the time on my watch. "So he bit you almost five hours ago?" I ask.

She is able to reply, *Yes*, but then passes out. I'm not sure what to think. Is she immune? Will she still turn violent and try to attack? Is she contagious and just a carrier?

"What do we do with her?" someone asks.

"Let's tie her up and take her back to the ranch," I say. "I don't really know what her situation is, so be careful," I add and draw my gun aiming it at her head while they secure her arms and legs. "I remember the letter from the internet saying there was a six hour time frame from injection of that Zeus Drug to the fever. We need to watch her and see if she turns violent like everyone else that is bitten. Gag her too."

"Eddie, should we risk taking her back?" Conner asks.

"Absolutely!" his wife Samantha exclaims. "This woman could be immune! We need Simone to look at her. We should get her wound dressed before we head back to stop the bleeding."

I'm not so thrilled at the prospect of this woman being immune. I like the idea that maybe not everyone will get violent when infected, but we aren't doctors, or disease specialists. There isn't anything we can do with someone that has immunity but congratulate them and hope that we are all immune if we ever get bitten.

*

"Kim has died," Simone tells us as she walks into the house with Michael Palmer, one of our new arrivals from yesterday. Michael was an EMT with the fire department until two days ago, so he and Simone are our resident medical experts.

"Did she turn?" I ask.

"No. At least we don't know. The fever hit right at the six hour mark, but she died before the fever was finished. She was just too weak from her extensive blood loss to make it through such a severe temperature. Her pulse was extremely weak when you brought her here."

"I'm sorry she died," I say. Unfortunately, no one on the ranch knew this woman. We only know her as Kim.

While we were waiting to find out Kim's prognosis, most of us were in the living room discussing what we saw. Now we are all facing each other in silence. I hate feeling defeated like this, so I offer, "Should we try another trip into Rogue River?" I ask the question with sincerity but receive very shocked faces in return.

"I guess that means we are locking down now," I frown and nod. "We have a lot of supplies on hand and have plenty to do to make this property and the houses more secure. Let's find Arthur and ask him to split us into work groups to start the fencing and reinforcing projects, then."

"Arthur's in the woodshed you built," Simone replies as everyone gets up and starts heading outside. She grabs my hand as we walk out together, and continues, "Michael and I asked him to pick one of the buildings that we could remodel into a medical room. As time goes on, we'll have other people that get bitten or seriously injured, so we are going to need a building where we can do minor surgeries."

*

Even with the addition of the people who arrived in the last three days, we are at a net loss. Of the over fifty people that were here the first night to hear what was happening, almost all left the next morning in hopes of finding people or belongings they needed. About half of them did not return. I want to think that they found a better place to remain safe, but know that we will likely face them at some point in the future as infected and have to kill them.

So as we stand now, we have 44 people on the ranch. Thirteen age 12 and under, four in their teens, and twenty-seven people age 20 and up. I'm not sure what real bearing age will have in our future. Children won't get to have the childhoods that we all knew. I guess everything will be determined by ability and maturity level rather than age. I know I will expect a lot from my own kids, especially Hannah and Olivia.

*

It is the middle of November now. It has been a month and a half since the infection first arrived. The winter hit early again this year. No snow yet, but very low temperatures for this part of the country in October and November. We haven't had any more people arrive to the ranch since the first two days and fortune has prevented us from losing any. We have been completely isolated so far. The phones and internet never came back on. Electric service stopped just over a week after the collapse, and we had to switch to all of our alternatives and reduce overall usage.

We have used our time wisely, I think. We put up a chain link fence around a good portion of the land to stop or slow down any wandering infected. There are small bells from Christmas decorations, and used soup cans with coins inside attached all over the fence line as well, to sound off if someone or something touches the fence. There is also razor wire at the top to prevent anyone, healthy or sick, from climbing over to get us.

Everyone that can hold a firearm has trained extensively with them or with the airsoft training guns here at the ranch. We all rotate through various twenty-four hour patrols and lookouts. The cold temperatures have made the moving patrols favored over the lookout positions, even with heavy blankets.

Until just after noon today, we haven't seen any infected at the ranch. I thought at some point we would have had a straggling infected person come through the woods and get hung up on the fence somewhere, but it never happened. Then today we had a slow but continuous showing of the infected arrive at the south fence line. They wandered up several at a time through the woods and directly at us. We shot forty-nine of them and that is probably all that was with this group. We haven't seen any more for two hours now.

We were planning on waiting another week and then head into Rogue River or the outskirts of Medford to scout out what things were like, until the events of today. If these things are moving around in groups like this, then it won't be safe to travel anywhere by car. Anyone could get easily blocked in by twenty to fifty of these things walking on the road. Tomorrow, if we don't get hit by another group, we'll gather the bodies to burn and scout out the forest to the south, to make sure there are no more wandering infected are out there.

*

It's December ninth, and we had another attack yesterday. The recent group of infected was much larger than the first one. We counted 276 bodies during the cleanup today. We were more prepared for this attack than the last one since we suspected they were coming. Ashley and Megan were on patrol and said they heard music playing in the woods to the south. We thought the cold was getting to the girls' heads when they told us, but we all heard it when we made it to the fence.

The fact that this group came from the same direction as the last could have been contributed to some random geography that is making the infected funnel toward my ranch, but Daniel and I don't think so. With the addition of the music before the attack, and the behavior of the infected in Rogue River, we think someone might be driving them this way. We haven't seen any infected grouping together in herds except for the ones approaching the ranch.

When we took a trip into Rogue River a week ago, the infected were still there. They were staggered all over town and not bunched up or traveling any particular direction like the groups that have attacked our place twice now.

Several of the infected broke through the fence this time when they bunched up on it. No one was hurt, and we were able to take out all the infected, but it was a closer call than any of us would have liked. We decided to organize a specific response routine that we will practice over the next several weeks, so we will be prepared if another even larger group of infected show up. I am so thankful we have the airsoft replicas of most of our guns, so that everyone can continue target practice safely indoors with these cold temperatures.

At least the cold weather is slowing these things down even more than they normally move. I just wish they would finally die off so we could think about retaking the world. I expected most of them to have starved or dehydrated by now since they aren't the walking dead, but they seem to manage somehow. I wish we had a doctor or scientist and a lab to tell us what is going on with this disease.

CHAPTER SEVEN
OVERRUN

January

There are some things in life that none of us should see. None of us should, but all of us do, at some point. There is always death around us. Every step of the way it's always like this. Death and destruction are Nature's way. To me, the blatant horror of how people are dying now is what is so disturbing. In our previous pampered lives we didn't have to witness the kind of destruction that the infected now commit. Even the history books do nothing to express the horrors that direct physical contact in battle causes.

Stories of knights and villagers fighting their foes on distant battlefields are always looked upon with honor or reverence. The sacrifice that those people made in order to survive were incredible, and the suffering during and after a battle must have been just as difficult as their sacrifices. The vicious bloodiness of a battlefield full of swords and axes had to have been overwhelming for those involved, and yet, survival always seems a better path to attempt when faced with such destruction.

We have all been sheltered in modern times. Before this plague hit us, we lived lives that were far removed from the horrors that our ancestors experienced. Today it seems that the past is revisiting us. Something drove the infected from the city, and they are headed right at us. They will be at the ranch within the next half hour, and I don't know that we can survive the numbers we will be facing.

Hannah and Steven saw them while they were riding the horses in the hills, trying to find the music we've been hearing. They said they saw just a few at first, stiffly wandering up through the trees, and then more and more stumbled out into the open. They said the infected just kept slowly creeping into view and estimated the numbers as at least a thousand, maybe more.

The road exiting the ranch to the South is a lower elevation and flatter grade than we are at here, so if it is a random horde, it has probably already covered those roads. All of the roads are also covered in snow now and most of our vehicles wouldn't make it. We could try plowing our way through with the tractor, but that just makes us a bunch of sardines in our cars waiting for the infected to stumble upon us. So all we can do is prepare for battle. If the numbers they think they saw hit us all at once like this, this will truly be a fight for our lives, and not just a shooting gallery like the last two attacks. If the plan we put in place and practiced for doesn't work flawlessly, then I'm not sure we can survive. Too many *ifs* for my liking.

There are thirty-four of us able to fight. Beth, who is already injured, is staying with her two kids in one bunker, with Geraldine's daughter. There are two other bunkers where we have split the groups to defend and fall back too if they get overrun. The hope is that everyone will survive. The fear, of course, is that none of us will.

I would love for us to be able to just hide in what we dub as our underground shelters until this crowd passes, but with the numbers of animals we have on site, the infected are almost guaranteed to want to stay for a longer period than the shelters are capable of keeping us alive. Also, there is the very real probability that the infected would just smash their way through the doors of the shelters, and get us with the numbers that are headed this way.

With all of the preparations my wife and I accomplished in the time we owned this property, we never got around to making survivable bunkers. They were just too expensive for us to buy at the time and not necessary for the training academy. So, what we are using as our shelters are nothing more than simple root cellars, shipping containers that we had buried below ground level to store survival goods. There are no air-filtration delivery systems installed in the containers, and with large groups of people entering the shelters, we have no idea how many hours of air they'll have before having to crack open the doors to let more air in.

Because of the numbers we think we are facing, we decided to let most of the large animals loose. If we leave them locked up, the number of infected coming at us would be able to tear through the barn and stable walls, and eat the cows and horses we keep there. I'm hoping we will be able to find most of them when this is over. For now, we herded them all out through the gate at the north fence. Our goats and chickens we put into the stacked containers we have in the field.

We are all staggered in a line between our respective shelters and the fence, so we can kill as many as possible, before being forced underground or onto the stacked storage containers. Simone and I are together by one of the bunkers with eleven other shooters, including Hannah and Olivia. William, Amelia, and Benjamin are already inside with Christine, my mom.

The bunkers are on the east section of the property, which was a training field before things fell apart. Once spring hits, we are planning on plowing down the practice defensive hills around the stacked containers and turning the whole area into planted fields.

We only have the shipping containers out in this area of the property, the rest of the storage buildings and living areas are to our west. If the infected continue to swarm at us, our bodies as bait should draw them away from the houses, so those structures hopefully don't get destroyed.

Now that we are all set up, I am feeling confident and that our chances are pretty good. Everyone here has been practicing non-stop with the airsoft replicas of our rifles and even a bunch of live fire training. Our shots are true. Most of us are even able to make headshots two out of three times. Hannah and Steven also said the infected are moving much slower than they normally do, most likely due to the continuing bitter cold weather. If they are really as slow as described, we should be able to take on a thousand of these things without even having to go to the stacked containers. I hope their estimate is accurate.

I grab Simone's hand and squeeze it tightly before walking toward the fence from our position. Fourteen of us with scoped rifles are spread along the fence, looking out into the trees beyond. I'm waiting to get the first glimpse of the infected heading toward us. The rest of the group at the rear, are ready with carbines and rifles that we will all grab and fire once the forward group has to back away from the fence. But until they have to join in the fight, they are all frantically loading as many magazines for the AR-15s as possible.

Crack. The sound of the first shot goes off to my left and makes me jump. I reset my eye to my scope and start searching the woods again. The first shot I have is a withered looking man, he is shirtless and dirty. Covered in a smeared blackness that is probably his own dried blood, and his head is cocked to the left side, leaning on his shoulder as if his neck is frozen in place. My shot is true, and he falls.

Just over nine minutes have gone by, and I have emptied three twenty round magazines, and I'm halfway through number four when I hear, *click.* My rifle has jammed. "Fuck," I yell and drop down to my knee to clear the jam. The gunfire going on around me sounds like simple target practice at any outdoor range in the U.S. prior to this mess. The feeling in my gut is nothing that I've had before, however. The slow sound of steady shots as the shooters acquire their targets is speeding up as well. More bodies are emerging from the woods giving us more and more to shoot at.

I am a mixture of fear, anger, and sorrow all bundled together with the frustration at having my gun jam when I need it the most. "Just the bullet," I say to myself as I clear the dud round from the chamber. The infected are close enough now that I don't have to stand to get a clear shot over the bushes beyond the fence, and I resume shooting from my kneeling position.

*

Seven more minutes of shooting and most of us are backing away from our positions at the fence, with the rest of our people moving forward to start backing us up in mowing down this diseased onslaught. I am down to the last two loaded magazines for my FAL, so I know I shot one hundred forty rounds so far. The fear I am feeling is starting to build in my mind at the numbers we are facing. Between the fourteen of us that were at the wall shooting, we should have killed at least twelve hundred infected with the rounds shot and our bullet placement.

We've already shot far more than we thought we would have to deal with today and their numbers are increasing. I see at least as many ahead of us as we already put down, maybe more. Looking in the distance toward the main gate where we expect more might come from the road, at least there is good news from there, as none have made it from that direction yet.

The sound of shooting multiplies again as the remaining shooters join the firing line. The shooting goes on and on. I sling my empty FAL over my shoulder, grab one of the M4s, and continue firing. I'm glad I started with the .308 and switched to this thing instead of trying the other way around. The kick was really starting to wear on my shoulder. Hopefully, my sore shoulder will be the only thing that concerns me when this swarm is over.

Yells and screams emerge from the distance and in my own group as fear and anger grips us all. The ones close by are our screams of rage, exploding from the frustration of the continuing and growing attack that is wearing on us all. Some of these things are starting to move toward us faster, but perhaps it only seems that way because they are now so close. Some of the screams I am hearing don't sound like battle cries, but there are too many infected at our location to go to anyone else's aid.

The snow covered ground in front of us is littered with bodies, with pools of darkness oozing out from where they lay. Some of the infected who have been shot are still crawling their way toward us, and hundreds more are stumbling and walking over them. I yell over the shooting, and shouts of anger and defiance, to watch the ground for crawlers.

*

Twenty-one minutes after the first shot and we have been pushed nearly back to the ramp down to the storage container doors. I glance toward the front of the property, and see the infected are starting to pile up at the gate there, attempting to push through. It won't hold much longer, and we will be facing the threat from two sides since we are the closest group to the front of the property.

Hannah looks at me, and yells, "We have to go now!"

I nod and tell Simone to grab Olivia and head into the bunker, and then yell to everyone else by us, "Head into the bunker now!" I make it to the door and continue shooting at the growing numbers of infected that are shuffling their way onto my land.

"Simone, you get in there, and take care of the kids. We're going to climb the containers now."

Simone kisses me fiercely and quickly, and gives me a look and a nod that says everything we want to say but have no time for. I turn to continue shooting. She shoves a radio into my pocket right before she walks down the ramp into the container and pulls the door closed.

Daniel and I run to one set of the stacked shipping containers, followed by Donald and his son Joshua. We have about thirty yards to cover from the buried container we were at and have to climb over the five foot defensive hill that encircles the containers. Daniel climbs up the ladder last, and we both pull it up to the top while the others start shooting down into the crowd below. There are two of these stacked storage containers on the property, which were used as lookouts and defensive forts of a sort, when the property was still used for survival training. I look in the distance and see three people climb onto the other stacked set.

Our final stand begins here, in the cold winter air surrounded by the infected and snow. Our job is to shoot every infected body that walks up to us until they stop coming or we run out of ammo.

When we put the ammo up here after the second group of infected came to the ranch, I thought we would have plenty to finish the job, but now I'm not so sure. Looking around at the property and at how many we have already put down, I know there must be at least two thousand infected that are already dead, maybe closer to three thousand, with thirty-four shooters on the line. I shot over three hundred rounds so far, and while they weren't all headshots, many of them were.

They don't have to be headshots to kill when you have a safe place to retreat to. These infected people aren't the walking dead; they are just diseased with extremely slow metabolisms and burnt out brains. If you make a good shot to one in the chest, it will die in five to ten minutes from the shot. Five to ten minutes is still plenty of time for it to reach you though, so headshots are always the rule of the day. Put it down with one shot so you don't worry about it hobbling or crawling up to you and taking a bite.

Looking around at what's on my land, what we have already shot looks like nothing compared to what we are facing. The yard looks like the stadium at a big concert. It is packed with bodies, and they are swarming around our container fortresses trying to get at us, the tasty meals that we are. The overwhelming sight causes me to freeze for a few seconds. I try to calculate what our odds are, which is probably a mistake that will overwhelm me even more.

We have six cases of .223 for the M4's, which totals 3000 rounds. 200 slug rounds for the shotguns that we left up here. One 120 round battle bag of South African .308 for my FAL. One 500 round case of 40 S+W for the Glock and Taurus pistols we have, and two cases of 22lr for the Ruger 10/22's. The two cases of 22lr are the only thing that gives me hope, and even that is slim. Each of those cases has 5000 rounds, giving us 14,800 rounds that we can fire into the crowd.

The people on the other stacked containers have about the same amount of ammo, except for the .308 rounds, and they have 9mm instead of 40 S+W. The problem I'm having while looking out into the crowd below is that I have no way to gauge how many infected there are, but it looks like far more than the nearly 30,000 rounds that we have available. So even if we make every shot count, we could still be at a deficit.

"Make sure you shoot away from us, out into the crowd!" Daniel yells to correct everyone's aim. "Don't shoot at the ones near the container, or we will build a ramp of bodies for them to climb up and get us."

Fortunately they have completely surrounded the containers now and are pushing from all directions. The bottom two containers are filled with heavy goods, and are set four feet into the ground, so there isn't a great chance of them moving it to begin with, but anything is possible when you get enough bodies or mass on one side of an object and continue to push. It almost seems that just the squelching wet moans coming from so many of these things could knock down the containers. And if it wasn't for the false moat created by the hill circling the containers, the numbers of bodies pressed directly against the container sides would probably cause them to cave in, toppling the top containers and us into the crowd.

*

Seven hours have passed since the first shot was fired. We have been shooting just 22lr for the last hour, and the rate at which we can shoot has been cut way down. We are taking turns loading magazines while two of us shoot. All four of us are shivering from the cold, and I can barely feel my fingers as I load the rounds. I seem to drop one bullet for every five I get in the mag. At least it seems the numbers of infected are dropping off. Of course I'm just seeing what I wish would happen instead of what is actually out there.

We have about 7000 rounds left, and the sea of these things just keeps surging around. There is a huge wall of bodies completely around our container now, about fifteen yards out. It seems to be about ten feet high at its highest point, and I can't see the earthen hill underneath it at any point. If not for that hill or the cold, I know we would already be dead. Every little thing helps in a way. These things have to slowly climb over the bodies of the dead to make their way to us. It makes our shooting easier while the cold and weariness makes it more difficult. I can only shudder as I imagine the numbers of bodies that are piled there to make such a disgusting wall possible.

*

Nine hours in and it's too dark to continue shooting. I'm not sure what type of moon we're supposed to have tonight, but it doesn't matter with the heavy cloud cover. All we can do is eat and load the magazines. We have to try to get some sleep. Sleeping, of course, seems like it should be next to impossible since I can barely even think over the noise of the moans. In reality, I'm having a hard time staying awake with the exhaustion I'm feeling. The overwhelming fear of the numbers we are dealing with apparently kept my adrenaline pumping, but now I'm coming down hard.

I keep awake long enough to check in with Simone. She decided to shoot some air holes into the doors of the containers so they wouldn't have to risk cracking them open when the air got low. Hopefully the other two containers did the same. I used the scope on my FAL earlier to see that Arthur, Eleanor, Randy, and Randy's son, Joshua, are on the other stacked containers. I could have sworn I only saw three people climb up there earlier. I must have looked away too soon. I should have thought to put radios in all of the root cellars and on the stacked containers where we are. If it wasn't for Simone's quick thinking, I wouldn't even be able to talk to her.

Thinking about the screams from earlier, I'm wondering if we lost people, or if they were just screams of fear. I really shouldn't dwell on what may or may not be losses right now. This ordeal isn't over yet, and I have to try and get some sleep.

I wish we had thought to put tents up here to help block the wind. I guess none of us expected such a large number of infected to hit us at once, especially in the winter. I know I was wrong on both counts. I totally thought the snow and cold would freeze them solid, or kill them off. Hell, I thought they would have dropped dead from dehydration or starvation by now. I barely had a thought about them wandering the countryside in some type of mass exodus during winter. I mean, what the hell is this crowd? Did waves of these things head in all directions from Medford, or was it really the music in the woods pulling them this way? If someone is behind this, how would we find them if we survive?

I don't know if I'll ever have an answer to any of these questions.

*

It's morning now. My face feels frozen, and I have to take off my hat and shake snow from it. There was just a light dusting of snow last night. My arms and legs are stiff, and there isn't an inch of me that is warm. The light is just coming up, and the shadows of these monsters are still pressing up against our container from all directions. There is enough time to wipe the sleep from my eyes and eat something before there will be enough light to start shooting at these things again.

It sounds like there are fewer of them this morning, but my ears could just be adjusted to the sound now. Then again, maybe a bunch wandered off in boredom last night, or in continued pursuit of whatever they originally came this way for. I'm glad we let the horses and other animals we had out of the barns and stables before the horde got here. I hope some of the animals will survive and make their way back here if we can make it safe.

*

Two hours have gone by since the morning shooting resumed, and I use my rifle scope to look over at the other group since I don't hear them firing anymore. They must have run out of ammo, because I can see that they are still alive. Even with the dirt hills that surrounded these containers, I was concerned that the containers would still get crushed and collapse from the pressure of so many bodies. I'm so grateful that they didn't.

We are down to just over six bricks of .22lr ammo, so just over 3000 rounds. But we only have one functional gun remaining. One of the 10/22's had a bad round explode in the chamber, and we don't have any cleaning supplies to knock out the stuck round and shell. Fortunately no more infected have been pouring onto the property. We are looking at about one thousand infected still trying to get at us or the other container.

The radio squelches, and I pick it up. "Eddie, are you still there?"

"I'm here, Simone. What's going on?"

"Hi, Eddie," she says softly. "I'm not sure how many of those things you killed, but they piled up in front of our doors. We tried shooting more holes at the top of the container, but no light or air came through, so they must be piled at least that high."

"Okay, Simone. There are about a thousand more infected out here, and Arthur is already out of ammunition. Just try to stay calm and keep everyone else calm too. I'll get you out of there as fast as I can. I'll need to get to the tractor to clear the bodies from your container door, so I have to have most of them dead before I can do that. Do you think you have another hour of air?"

"Yes, I think so. We aren't gasping yet. I'll let you know if it gets really bad."

"I love you Simone."

"I love you too."

I look at the other three on the container with me, and we all shake our heads at the new bad news. *Damn it,* I think. *I'm not going to survive this flood of destruction just to lose my wife and kids to a lack of oxygen.* I also don't know how the other two shelters are doing. They could be in just as bad or maybe worse shape for air. I need to get off of this tower.

*

There are now about thirty loose infected that are aimlessly wandering in the yard. Knowing that they can't get to us, they have lost interest in trying, and seem to be just hanging around like vagrants in a blood soaked, body filled park. To my luck the larger number of the still living infected, maybe a couple hundred, are trapped around the base of the other stacked containers. We have killed all the infected that are in the trench surrounding the containers we are on and have been aiming beyond the wall of bodies to kill the rest of them, so I have somewhere to escape too. Hopefully, my frozen and stiff muscles will still move me faster than the infected.

I would love to have a gun on me, but I won't be able to aim the 10/22 while I'm running. My best bet of making it, is to have one of the other guys up here cover me with the rifle, while I run for the tractor. I walk to the edge and lower the ladder into the bloody pit below us. I take a few deep breaths to help build my resolve, finally climb over the side, and step down the ladder. With my first step off the ladder's bottom rung, I step on an arm, which rolls off the body it is laying on. I lose my balance and fall onto the pile of corpses at the bottom, and quickly scramble back up, afraid I will get pulled down by the arm that I think moved by itself.

I look around, but nothing down here is moving on its own except for me. I have a huge wall of bodies that I need to get over now, so I grab the ladder away from the container, and push it so it falls up against the wall of stacked death to begin my climb.

We are all truly alone now. The guys on my container will have a dangerous fall onto loose piles of uneven partly frozen bodies if they want to get down without a ladder. I know in movies people used to be able to make amazing jumps and falls without getting hurt, but in the real world, landing on an uneven surface can easily break an ankle. Arthur, on the other container, is completely trapped with no ammo and a pit full of infected around him. And the people in the containers might all have their doors buried by landslides of blood soaked human cadavers. If I die on this run there is a good chance everyone else dies as well.

I don't see any of the infected walking near me once I get to the top of the ladder and body wall, although some are writhing or twitching on the ground here and there. Even within the wall there are some heads or appendages that are still moving, trapped underneath the bodies of the dead, and unable to work themselves free. I am only able to carefully crawl the first fifty yards of my *run* to the tractor. My attempts to walk the distance were met with abject failure. The bodies don't start to thin out until that far out for me to get a solid footing on real ground.

Even with the human remains not piled three to four high, there is barely a bare space of ground to walk on. I still have to step on top of dead bodies almost all the way off the field. Each step brings a disgusting sound. For the frozen solid bodies, a brittle cracking followed by my foot sinking in a few inches as my weight collapses the ribs. More rare this far out from the freshly shot is a soft squish or a gurgling rasp as the weight of my foot pushes the air from the lungs of the person I trample on. Thankfully, the land around the houses, stable, barn, and outbuildings are mostly clear of bodies. The infected were drawn to our chosen field of battle, so fewer shots had to be made out this way.

I step around the corner of the stable, where the tractor is located, and nearly run into a putrid mass of flesh that turns to reach for me. There are eight of the infected between me and the tractor. More start stumbling out of the stable to join in their new pursuit of my uninfected blood. I turn toward the house and nearly get pulled down by the first infected I saw that manages to grab my jacket at the neck. I lunge myself forward to break free and pull him off balance instead. He falls on his face behind me as I start my run away from the new crowd, yelling loudly as I go, hoping to pull them all out into the open air to be shot at.

THE LAST BLADE OF GRASS

I'm lucky the fingers of these things have lost dexterity in the cold. They can't usually do any manipulation with their hands, but once they grab someone, they rarely let go without breaking their fingers or cutting off their arm.

I make it to the house and slam the door closed behind me. At least here I have a chance, and I realize I should have thought about running here originally. Now I can grab some guns and more ammo. I open the wall cabinet in the entry hall and grab out another AR-15, my five-seven, which I haven't used since we left the store, along with six loaded magazines for each.

I'm switching holsters on my belt for the FN when I get another call from Simone. "Eddie, it's getting bad in here. It's a lot harder to breathe, and I'm worried about the kids and your mom. I need you to get the door open soon."

"I'll get it done, Simone. I'm just inside the house now getting more guns and ammo. There was a bunch of the infected in the stable that came out when I first tried for the tractor. I'll get you some air soon, I promise."

There are too many banging on the front door for me to try opening it, so I go through the back door, and walk around the side till I see the crowd gathered there. There looks to be forty infected scattered between the stable and the front door, with eight or ten lying dead on that path from my saviors still on the container tower I left. I start shooting at the crowd right by the door while others keep falling from 10/22 shots. One and a half minutes later, and about the same number of magazines, the immediate crowd is down; either completely dead or giving their final twitches.

I run to the tractor, and shoot three more that come out of the stable, before I'm able to climb on. I sling the rifle over my back, draw my five-seven, and start up the old tractor, which gives me a grateful loud rumble at getting to start work again. If we didn't need to clear the rubble from the burned down shed, I wouldn't have a hope of getting this thing started in time. It took us a full day without the infected attacking to get it running for that job last week.

The tractors rumble brings the last few un-entangled infected out of the stable toward me, but I've already got it rolling roughly toward the spot that Simone's shelter is supposed to be, so I just turn in the seat, and shoot them down while I bump and roll over the bodies in my path.

I hit my first two obvious snags once I reach the leading thick edge of corpses in the field. First, I can't see any sign of the shelter's entrance. I can see the hole of the second shelter's ramp fifty yards away and can somewhat make out where this one is supposed to be under the wall of bodies based on that.

The second problem is I didn't bring the radio with me. I set it down after I spoke with Simone in the house and forgot to pick it back up. I can't contact Simone to tell her where I am or find out if they can hear the tractor when I get close. It might be possible for the tractor to break through the shipping container roof if I drive over it, but with the amount of bodies out here, I'll have to move slowly anyway so I can watch what shows up under me.

When I first push the plow into the pile of bodies and lift the scoop, I vomit over the side of the tractor. The sound of each of the snapping bones as I push in with the bucket causes me to shiver, but when the smell hits me, I lose it. The odor that smacks me in the face is what sends me retching over the side. The bodies as they rip open release a cloud of gas that smells like a sewer filled with two week old rotting meat. The normal stench of the infected is bad enough without opening them up. They are, after all, still living bodies, so even with slowed metabolisms they continue to excrete waste. All of which collects in and drips down the legs of the pants they were wearing when they became infected.

Thankfully, it only takes fifteen minutes and twenty scoops of bodies for me to find the leading edge of the ramp going to the buried storage container. I had to stop several times to shoot an infected that was trying to climb onto the tractor with me. Some of the few hundred remaining infected have been climbing out of the pit surrounding Arthur's stacked container fortress and coming after me. Five more scoops later and I can see the bullet holes at the top of the container doors appear. At least there is some air getting it there now.

"Simone!" I yell, but don't get a response, so I keep clearing the bodies from the entrance. I have to shoot seven more infected and clear two more scoops of bodies from the entryway before I can jump down from the tractor and check on the condition of everyone inside. I'm greeted with smiling faces when I finally pull away the last of the bodies and get the doors open.

"I'm sorry I couldn't respond," Simone says weakly while leaning against a stack of food storage buckets. "I could barely catch my breath and couldn't get enough air to yell back to you."

"It's all right, Simone. I'm going to check on the kids and everyone else, okay?" Everyone in the container is weak or lightheaded from the lack of oxygen, and my mom is still gasping desperately for air, even with the doors open. Amelia and Benjamin are the only ones not moving when I get to them. I shake them both lightly, and they open their eyes.

Amelia starts to cry, and so do I. The enormity of what we've been through in less than twenty-four hours is hitting me hard and brings me to my knees as it all starts swirling through my mind.

Brian and Melissa shooting at the entrance brings me back to reality, this isn't over yet. Several people inside start to scream, not knowing that the main attack is over. I step quickly back to the entrance while trying to reassure everyone by saying, "Most of them are dead, but there are still a few hundred around Arthur's set of stacked containers, and possibly more scattered in outbuildings, barns, or the stable."

"Everyone needs to grab their guns and head out to help clear the property. I'm not going to close the doors behind us, so I need someone to guard the entrance, and someone to stay in here with the kids."

Hannah says, "Dad, I want to go."

"So do I!" says Olivia.

"I would let you, but I need you to stay in here and keep your brother and sisters safe."

"I don't think I can go out," says Karen Chapman before she throws up into a bucket. "I'm just too nauseous from the lack of air and the smell"

Brian also falls to one knee at the entrance. He's a big guy, so the lack of air probably hit him harder than everyone with smaller lungs. "I can stay with Karen and your kids if you want?" Brian offers.

"Eddie, I need to stay here as well," Simone says. "Your mom is sixty-seven, and the lack of air hit her hard."

I walk back to my mom, who is still taking short gasping breaths. "Mama, I have to finish clearing the property. I'll be back soon."

She touches my hand and nods.

Walking back to the front I look at Hannah and Olivia, and tell them, "It's really bad out there. It's worse than anything we've seen before."

Hannah looks at me, and says, "I can handle it."

Olivia just says, "I need to learn. Like you keep telling us, this is how the world is now."

"Okay, you two grab your guns and some magazines, but if it's too much, then you come back in here."

I announce to everyone heading out with me, "There will be infected coming over a hill of bodies surrounding the stack of containers that Arthur and his group are on, and there will be crawlers and stragglers everywhere. Don't go into any buildings alone, and keep looking around so nothing can sneak up on you. Also, everybody watch your step, there are bodies and blood everywhere. If you fall on the wrong thing and get cut, you might get infected.

"I have to clear bodies from the other two root cellars doors. Melissa, are you coming out, or are you staying with Brian, in the container?"

"I'm coming out."

"Then I would like you to climb on the tractor to shoot for me, so I can focus on clearing bodies. Let's go."

The second root cellar shelter is in better shape than the one Simone was in. It is farther away from the stacked container towers where we were shooting from, so it didn't get completely buried. However, even with the extra distance, there are bodies piled halfway up the entrance. It's blocked enough to prevent those inside from opening up to get out, but not enough to block the air holes shot into the doors.

"Looks like they had the same idea as you guys did," I say to Melissa while pointing to the top of the doors. "They shot in some air holes." Before lowering the scoop, I turn to her, and say, "Melissa, this part gets really bad. You should hop down and keep watch from a distance while I clear these bodies."

She nods before climbing off of the tractor, with one hand covering her mouth. Brian's wife is a tough lady and a great shooter. That is why I wanted her watching my back on this thing. Under normal circumstances she would have soldiered on and told me to just get to work, but I can tell she is already getting sick from our short trip over bodies to get here. The same nauseous chill runs through my body as I pick up each scoop of partly frozen cadavers from in front of the doors. At least I don't throw up this time. The smell and sounds are just as sickening, but now I am prepared for them, which helps a little.

There are occasional gunshots going off by the first shelter I opened up. One or two shots a minute and no new infected showing up from beyond the property. This is the winning stage. All we have to do now is finish off the last of these things and then deal with burning their bodies. With the bulk of the living infected still trapped in the gulley around Arthur's stacked containers, the only worry at this point is someone getting the disease by being careless or clumsy.

I can't believe we won. I can't believe we survived this attack. There were too many, far too many for us to have come out of this alive. But here we are. Melissa and I pull the last few bodies away from the entrance. I open the door and come face to face with Conner, squinting and blinking at the light, but holding his gun ready to fight. His son Jake is next to him, ready for battle as well.

I smile at their enthusiasm and say in a tired yet elated tone, "Most of them are dead guys, but we do still have a bunch left to kill."

"Is everyone all right?" Samantha asks coming out behind her husband and son. "We heard screaming just when we had to we close the doors yesterday."

"I think everyone is all right, but I still need to open up the next shelter. Look, it's pretty bad out here, so keep the kids inside."

"We didn't have any kids in this shelter," Samantha replies.

Rebecca, Jason, and their daughter Rachel come out right behind them and run off in the direction of the third shelter.

"Where is Christopher?" I ask Samantha as I climb onto the tractor. Melissa climbs on next to me.

"Christopher would have been here, but they let him stay with Matt and Heather so he could play with his cousins, since they are all about the same age," Samantha yells up to me as I get the tractor into first and start moving to catch up to the Andersons.

Samantha grabs hold, steps onto the side of the tractor, and continues filling me in. "They have been freaking out all night while we were in there, worried about their son. If it wasn't for the bodies piled by the doors, they would have opened them when it was dark to sneak out and check on him."

"Why didn't they stay in their shelter with him? Why are they even here without him?" I yell in confusion.

"Remember, Bethany wasn't feeling well, and Tiffany was taking care of Madison and Olivia for her. So they switched shelters with Bethany and her kids. They let Christopher stay with his cousins."

"And they did this while we were under attack?" I say not understanding how they could all be so careless.

"No, they decided right away when we first came out here yesterday, while we were still setting up for the attack. No one knew it would be such a large group of these things coming here."

Just like the other shelters, there are bodies littered all over the ground near it. The initial firing line which started at the fence and led to the shelter doors dropped over two thousand bodies between all of the shooters. These shelters, or root cellars as they were originally purposed, were some of the first things placed in the field when we moved here. The stacked containers that I was shooting from were put in six months later when I started letting people rent the property for survival training.

The first shelter that Simone was in is the closest to the stacked containers with an entrance facing west. That is why it got completely buried in bodies from the shooting. As the infected fell dead from our tower defense, they would roll or slide back off the hill they were climbing, and pile up on the entrance ramp going down to the doors, and eventually over the whole shelter.

The second shelter is farther away from the container towers, and the entrance faces south. That combination kept too many falling bodies from reaching the entrance to bury it. The third shelter sits the furthest away from the stacked containers and its entry ramp faces east, the direction we are headed. So while I drive the tractor past Rebecca, Jason and Rachel I know I don't have to worry about the third container getting buried and I can see there is no huge pile of bodies nearby. As long as they shot holes in the doors, they would have plenty of air if they needed it. They weren't buried by bodies.

The third shelter is the closest to the fence line, however, which makes them the first group that would have had to secure themselves inside from the onslaught. That is the thought that is making my heart sink and my stomach tighten as I drive closer. When the screaming started yesterday, I was still outside fighting, but it started a short time before Conner and Samantha had to close their shelter doors. The third shelter should have already been closed up by that time.

Sporadic gunshots continue to ring out in the distance as I drive past the buried shelter and finally the edge of the down ramp comes into view. I drive past the ramp and turn left, stopping the tractor twenty feet away, and look into the dark shelter with its doors propped open.

I watch Samantha step off the tractor. She slowly lets go with her arm floating behind her as if it is still holding on. Melissa leans over the wheel and starts crying. Tears start to stream down my face as well. In three running strides Rebecca will be at the edge of the shelter entrance and will see the emptiness that should contain our friends, family, and her son. Two running strides left and Rebecca sees our reaction, she sees the sadness and loss on our faces. One running stride remaining and Rebecca slows down with a jolt. Her step makes that harder hit of a body still in motion, but trying to stop. She knows what she is going to see. She knows she has to see it but doesn't want to at the same time.

She screams.

The emotion released in the cry Rebecca lets loose breaks my will. Jason and Rachel fall to the ground with Rebecca as they catch up, holding onto each other, and venting their pain to the sky with their broken sobbing moans. I feel their loss, not just in hearing the pained sobbing, but it is our shared pain. We have all been a close family over these three months, since the first day the disease hit. We haven't lost a person before today, and now we lost a whole group. We lost several families; Randy and Patricia Langford have lost the most.

The loved ones we lost from this shelter are:

Christopher Anderson, age 8, son of Jason and Rebecca Anderson, and brother of Rachel.

Bethany Murphy, age 29, and her daughters, Madison, age 5, and Olivia, age 3.

Tiffany Langford, age 35, her twins, Steven and Lauren, age 13, and her daughter, Grace, age 9. Wife and children of Joshua Langford, daughter in law and grandchildren of Randy and Patricia Langford—both men are still trapped on the second stacked storage towers.

Matthew Langford, age 37. His wife, Heather Langford, age 34, and their sons, Andrew, age 10, and Anthony, age 8. They are the son, daughter-in-law, and grandchildren of Randy and Patricia Langford.

Conner is slowly walking up from the second shelter supporting Patricia Langford as she makes her way to where we are. Patricia is the mother and grandmother of many of the people lost. She was walking confidently behind her daughter Rebecca, but also nearly collapsed when she first heard her daughter scream.

"Does anyone have a flashlight?" I ask as I walk up to the container's entrance. I pull up the neck of my shirt and wipe the tears from my face with the only unsoiled portion of clothing at my disposal. Conner's son, Jake, walks up behind me and hands me the light from his pistol.

There is still complete cloud cover blocking out the sun, giving the day a dull gray look. The dark tunnel of the shelter isn't inviting. I hesitate to walk in for a few seconds. I'm no longer afraid of facing the infected. I have killed enough of them to wash away the remorse over taking a life. I am deathly afraid of walking in there and seeing one of the many people that we all knew and loved turned into one of these things, however.

Still, I take the first step, followed by another and before I realize it, find myself facing the back of the empty storage container. No one is in here. I shake my head clear, thankful that I didn't have to see any of them, and put them down. Looking at the details of the place now, I see blood everywhere. Not the thicker blackened blood that comes out of those that have been infected for a long while, but bright red that is from the newly bitten. Still, there are no bodies here, even though the story is the same as if there were.

I walk back out and shake my head at anyone that is looking. "No one is inside. No bodies either."

The crying just continues. I want to take a break and allow myself and others time to deal with this loss, but I know I can't, so I call everyone nearby back into action. "There is still a big crowd surrounding Arthur's stacked containers. We're going to have to kill them from up high," I say to whoever is listening.

At this point I feel like giving up. I had that stupid feeling of success just a few minutes ago. Thankful that I survived, grateful that *we* survived, and now I wonder what have we survived for? A third of our group is gone from one attack when we have lived so well for so long. And the worst part is that we lost a big part of our future. We lost seven of the thirteen children ages 12 and under.

Simone runs toward me around the group of mourners sobbing by the ramp. She is crying also and stops directly in front of me. "Eddie, you need to come quick. Your mother is dying."

CHAPTER EIGHT
GOOD IS GONE

I was numb for the rest of the day. Just like everyone else, I went through the motions necessary to kill off the remaining infected, and get Arthur and his group off of their stacked containers. I was running on empty even before my mom died. Apparently, the prolonged lack of oxygen was too much for her, and her heart must have given out. Once she died, I pretty much shut off all emotions at that point. The tears stopped, my expressions went blank, and I just went through the steps necessary to finish the day.

Once we killed the final infected around the second stacked containers, Arthur and Randy had to help lower Joshua Langford off the containers to us. He is in a shock induced coma or just checked out of the world due to his loss. They all knew before any of us that the people in the third container had been overrun by the infected. Joshua was shooting next to his wife by the third shelter when it fell.

Somehow they got overrun by the infected and weren't able to shut the shelter doors. Joshua isn't able to speak yet so we can't find out exactly what happened, but we know it wasn't the hinges. I was afraid that the doors on their storage container might have gotten stuck or frozen in place, but when I grabbed them after checking inside for bodies, they swung freely. That was also one of the preparations everyone did while we were setting up for the attack, to check if the doors would move and lock closed.

Arthur told us he originally thought Joshua was dead too, because he wasn't at their container when they arrived, and the infected were close behind them. They were getting ready to pull up the ladder when he ran through the group of approaching infected and climbed up. He managed to make it through without getting bitten, but once he was safe with the three of them, he just sat down in a catatonic state and has been like that since yesterday.

Joshua just sat looking out into the attacking crowd as his wife and children were put out of their diseased state, along with all the of other infected. Arthur and Randy had to see their infected loved ones who should have been protected in the steel walls underground and put them out of their misery. An act I'm not sure I would have had the strength to do.

We are all gathered in the living room of the main house now. We have cleared the property and all of the buildings of the mobile infected for now. There are some infected still alive, but trapped under too many bodies to move. We'll deal with them when we clear those specific areas. For now, we have to decide what we're all going to do.

This gathering isn't like the first night of the fall. Everyone then was happy to see each other, and while everyone knew there was trouble on the horizon, it wasn't an immediate threat, more like a distant rumble of trouble that could be ignored. Right now no one wants to meet anyone else's gaze.

"So what now?" Daniel, the former sheriff's deputy asks.

I look around the group and see their eyes all gazing back to me. I want my moment to mourn like they do, but it is my property, and I can't just throw off my responsibility. "We live or we die," I say plainly. "That has always been our choice," I continue. "We knew what was going on in the world with this thing and that the odds were always stacked against us. While we weren't all related to the ones we lost, the close relationships that we have built over the last few months made us all part of each other's families in a way. And it feels as if all of the children we've lost were my own, as if they were our own.

"A part of me wants to curl up in bed, go to sleep, and never wake up again. But my opportunity to do that passed with this horde. I fought the overwhelming numbers we faced because I want to live. Even with the pain and loss that I feel, I still want to live, and I'm sure everyone here wants to continue living as well."

It isn't a cheering or happy moment, but a few people nod almost imperceptibly or purse their lips in a determined agreement with the idea that they want to live as well.

"The next few days will be more difficult, both physically and emotionally than any we have faced in our lives. We have to clear the bodies from the land. Many are already frozen in place with these temperatures which will add an additional problem to the clean-up effort, and if it warms up, they will begin to rot. We won't be able to stay here if the bodies remain. I can use the tractor to move them into burning piles, but we will have to sort through them all one at a time to look for our missing, so that we can give them proper burials."

"There must be fifteen thousand bodies out there!" Dianne Blount says.

"I don't care!" I yell, snapping back at her. "I'm sorry, Dianne." I take a deep breath with my eyes closed, and continue, "I think we should find the bodies of the missing, but it is a nearly impossible physical task. Can anyone give me suggestions on what we do about the loved ones we lost?"

Patricia Langford stands up with tears streaming down her face. "I'm not going to lose anyone else. I know all of you loved those that were lost, but it was my son and grandchildren that died out there. I raised them and loved them their whole lives. I want to find them to give them our respects, but I do not want to lose anyone else. If we start handling that many bodies, somebody will get infected. There will be a scratch or a cut and we could lose everything. We could lose everyone. I want to give them a proper burial more than anything I've ever desired, but I need the rest of my family to survive."

Everyone remains silent, and Patricia sits back down next to Randy, who pulls her into an embrace.

Katy Chapman, Donald's eleven year old daughter speaks up, "They are all someone's loved ones, aren't they?"

I nod and look at her, and through watery eyes, Karen answers her daughter. "You're right, Katy. Everyone out there had someone who loved them. We should have a service for all of the lost, those that we knew, and those that we didn't, once we have cleared the land."

"But they tried to kill us," Hannah says in a hateful tone that no twelve year old should have. She and Steven liked each other and did almost everything together that they could. Now he is dead, and the property is full of the bodies of former people that did it.

"They didn't know what they were doing, Hannah," I offer. "These infected people should be feared and avoided. Killed because we need to survive, but they are no different than wolves, lions, or sharks. It's fine to hate what they do, but please try to remember that they were once people just like us, trying to survive, and didn't have a choice in coming here."

"Why did they come here?" Conner asks.

"I have an idea, but don't like what it means for us. Yesterday Hannah said she heard music again, which is what alerted us another attack might be coming. Right, Hannah?"

"It was faint, but it was music, playing in the distance somewhere out in the forest. Steven and I were riding into the woods toward it when we saw the infected coming."

I look at Daniel and nod. Everyone else looks at our exchange with questioning expressions.

"If you all remember, Daniel suspected after the second attack that someone might be driving the infected toward us," I say.

Daniel finishes the explanation for everyone. "Someone is using music in the woods to draw the infected toward us. Someone is staging these attacks. There was probably music or something else we didn't hear that drew the first attack here as well. My guess is, someone wants this land and the supplies, and is more than willing to kill us all to get it."

"So now we have two enemies?" Donald asks.

"Now I have someone to hate," Hannah replies coldly.

While I don't like hearing her say it, I know exactly what she means. I am filled with rage right now, but don't want to show it and encourage Hannah or the others in letting their emotions get the best of them. This attack has changed Hannah. I just need to teach her to use it to her advantage.

I want to correct her or try to bring her back to the loving and kind girl that she once was, but Jake intercedes first and not in the way I would like, when he says, "Now we all have someone to hate."

All of the older adults are looking around at each other concerned, while everyone in their 20s and younger are nodding in agreement with Hannah and Jake. The world has changed, and the young are changing with it, while the rest of us are locked into the old world that we once knew.

"Hate can be a dangerous thing," I offer. Hannah looks at me with an almost pitying expression on her face, as if I just don't understand what we are facing now.

I start talking to Hannah, but address all of the younger people in our group that are boiling over with anger. "Hannah, listen. You can feel what you want, but like everything I've ever tried to teach you, you have to be in control. If we ever find out who did this to us, you can let your hate make you rush into a fight with them which could get you and everyone else killed, or you can use it to organize your attack so none of them get away.

"I understand this isn't our world anymore, this is your world, the world of the young, but the rules for dealing with living people are the same. They are dangerous because they can think, but they are cautious because they want to live."

Daniel adds, "Whoever did this knows about this place and probably knows how many people we have here. If they thought they could overpower us on their own, they would have done it, so they must not have a huge group of people."

"They have enough people to gather thousands of infected for an attack!" Daniel's girlfriend Jessica says.

"They're like cattle," Arthur replies. "It would only take a couple of people to put those numbers together in Medford. These things are attracted to sound, so it probably wouldn't take much to attract such a large group out of a city area that held over two hundred thousand people."

Two hundred thousand people in Medford! That number echoes in my head. "We need to find who did this before they send another attack. We can't take another onslaught like this—each time they've sent more."

With an eerie sense of timing Jennifer Palmer, Daniel's mother, walks into the room, and says, "Someone's coming."

Daniel's parents, Michael and Jennifer, were keeping watch together on the roof of the house while the rest of us discussed things.

"What do you mean? Did you see someone?" I ask and everyone stands up ready to run out and fight.

"No, but we hear vehicles off somewhere in the distance."

"They have to be coming here then." I say. "We haven't heard any road traffic for months, and it would be hard to hear any vehicles from the highway, it's too far away. Grab your guns and load up. If we can hear their cars, they might be close."

Hannah flips off the safety of her AR-15, pulls back the charging handle, and loads a round.

"Use your hatred, Hannah, don't let it use you. These people might think we are all dead. They sent enough infected here to finish the job. Don't just shoot at them at first sight, we should stay hidden, and let them come onto the property. We'll know when they arrive if they think we are gone by how they act."

"How?" Jake asks.

Daniel understands what I'm thinking and fills in the blanks, "If they think we are alive, they'll park outside the property, and slowly move in ready to fight. If they think we're dead, they might drive right in, only expecting to deal with whatever infected are still in the area."

"How should we do it?" Hannah asks.

"Let Daniel, Arthur, me, or Donald take the first shot. No one shoots before we do. So if we don't shoot, you don't either."

Hannah shakes her head. "I don't like it. If we don't all shoot, some of them might live, they might get away."

"Hannah, you don't get it do you? We need some of them alive."

"No way, none of those bastards are going to live!" she yells and starts to storm out of the room when I grab her.

"You're wrong and you're going to stay here to listen. All of you are going to listen! I am angry too, but those of you that agree with Hannah, you are wrong. We don't have time to discuss this, those people are heading here right now and we need to set up, but if you shoot before we do, we could all die, so you might as well just start shooting us right now."

Hannah relents reluctantly. "I'll wait for you guys to shoot, but I think you're making a mistake."

"Donald, Jake, can you and some of the other guys roll one of the pickups over by the gate? If you have time to tip over a vehicle just inside the entrance, we can keep them from driving into the open area away from the house, and also give a few people a place to hide on the south."

"We'll get on it," Donald says.

"Hannah, you go with me. We need to talk. Two big things, Hannah, first, the cars we hear could contain innocent people. We are guessing at who they are based on the attack we just had. Second, whoever shows up might have more people waiting for them out there somewhere, and we can't leave anyone out there to send another attack our way," I say as we walk to hide behind the bushes next to the house.

"So that is why we need to keep some of them alive?"

"Yes. And why you won't shoot if we don't. We need to know who is coming before we decide to just kill them. We also need someone to question, to find out the where's and why's of this situation. Now I want you to go around to everyone that was taking your side and explain why it has to be this way."

Donald, his son Joshua, and Timothy Weyland, hide by the truck that they and several others managed to get turned on its side near the entrance to the property. It looks as if the truck got knocked over by the hoard while someone was trying to escape. They are ducked down behind the truck bed and shouldn't be seen by anyone coming in, unless they drive around it.

We have people behind all the windows in the house and have a few people scattered in groups of two in various outbuildings. Daniel, Conner, and Arthur are with me. Hannah returns from her task of explanation and nods at me before taking her position behind us.

"Where are they?" Conner asks. "If they were coming here they should already be here by now, shouldn't they?"

"We don't know what the roads are like," Daniel replies. "There could be snow drifts, fallen branches or trees, and maybe even some of the infected that they sent after us still out on the road."

*

Two pickup trucks make the turn down the lane and slowly drive up to the entrance. They stop not too far from the fallen gate, and several people from the bed of each truck hop out as we continue to silently watch from our hiding spots. If they would look closely at the house and fence with binoculars or a scope, it's possible they would see some of us, but fortunately they are too fixated with the road and gate.

"They couldn't have driven over this gate lying here," a man says loudly to his buddies. "And look at that truck on its side. They probably tried to run for it and got caught."

Several of the men cheer, and another says, "Looks like your plan finally worked Chad! We got 'em!"

The passenger of the lead truck opens his door and stands in the doorway to talk. "Move that damn gate so we can drive in, you morons. And maybe we should see if any supplies are left before we go celebrating any victory."

So we know these are the people that tried to kill us and where their leader is. The trick is capturing some of them without losing anybody. They have fifteen guys with them. Three in the first truck cab, and two in the second cab, with five men that were in each truck bed. Four of the men from the back of the first truck moved the fallen gate out of the way and are walking along side the truck as it drives in. The last man in the back is someone that needs to be shot first. He is standing in the bed holding his rifle and seems more aware of his surroundings than everyone else. He is the dangerous one of their group.

They stop their trucks a little past the house and about twenty yards away from us. All of them get out of their vehicles, except for the man still standing in the truck bed. He is eyeing the house and our hiding spot. Only the three guys behind the overturned truck are to the south of these men, the rest of us are to the north, so I'm hoping that those three will take the first shots, and right when I think it, the first shots ring out.

It feels like Donald, Josh, and Tim read my mind with the timing of their shooting. They couldn't really aim from their position, but they still knocked one man down. The rest of our invaders take cover behind their trucks with their backs facing us and start unloading on the overturned truck.

The truck bed shooter erupts in red blossoms and falls over as several of us choose to shoot him first. Eight of the remaining men are also shot to death when they turn with their guns to see who is shooting at them from behind. That leaves five of the bastards that have the intelligence to put their hands up since they know they are surrounded. The men that we let live for now are three from the cab of the first truck and two from the second. The man on the south side of the truck that got shot by Donald's group is screaming in pain.

"Daniel you're up," I tell him, since he's the former sheriff's deputy.

"Put your guns down slowly, and put your hands on your head!" he calls out. "If you fail to comply you will be shot." They all comply.

"Now each of you walk backward ten steps and drop down to your knees."

I painfully get off my own knees, hating my aging body, but glad that I'm still alive, and walk up to the men we captured. Everyone else from around house and behind our turned over truck comes out to see who did this to us.

"Chad," I say and shake my head. "I guess I should have killed you instead of turning you away that first day." He is shaking and has wet his pants. Next to Chad is the man that was giving orders to everyone. I want to speak to their boss, but the wounded man's yelling is too much to ignore. "Bring that injured guy over here!" I yell, and Donald and Tim carry him by the arms over to us.

"Are you the one in charge of this group?" I ask while pointing at the man calling the shots earlier.

All I get back is a sarcastic, "Yeah why?" with a sneer on his face.

I motion to Donald and Tim to bring over the wounded man and set him down on his knees facing his boss. He has been shot in the stomach and arm, and is in a tremendous amount of pain. I step behind this wounded man and stare at the boss in the eyes, while holding his man upright by the hair. I draw my knife with my right hand and slice the man's throat so his blood sprays on the boss' face.

"I don't like your sarcasm," I say and drive my knife down through the boss' intertwined fingers and into his skull, killing him.

My group is shocked so much by what I've done that they don't react as one of the captured men jumps up screaming and starts running away. I swivel my gun on its sling and shoot the man three times in the back as he tries to make his escape. And turn back to the remaining three captives. "You bastards have killed some very good people on my ranch, and I will make sure you pay for what you have done. The three of you won't get off as easy as the rest of your friends here."

I say that last part with complete and fierce sincerity, because I mean it. These three will not just die, they will suffer. I will make them beg for death before I am through with them for what they have done. And not just for the people that they killed, but for what they did to Hannah and to Jake and all of the other young people we have here on the ranch. They made my daughter feel genuine hate, and from her hate arises my vengeance.

"Take this one to the stable and tie him up so he is standing," I say pointing to Chad, the former reporter. "And take these two over by the bodies. Tie them up, lay them down, and bury them with the dead."

"You can't just bury us alive!" one of them yells and tries to get up. Arthur kicks him in the back and knocks him down.

"Keep their heads free so they can breathe, but make sure enough bodies are on them to make breathing difficult. I'm going to ask the three of you some questions, and the person that I feel is the most helpful I will set free. The other two will be tortured indefinitely."

I look at Arthur, and tell him, "Get it done." And the men are dragged off to their assigned locations by six of our people, while I step over to the former boss, and work my knife free from his skull.

"Eddie. What are you doing?" Rachel asks, shaking with tears streaming from her eyes. "I'm scared."

I look at her and can't help but give an intense stare that makes her step back away from me. "What, Rachel? What did you expect?" I snap at her and look around at everyone else. "Less than thirty minutes ago you were cheering with my twelve year old daughter that all of these people should be killed. I heard you say none of them should live, just like Hannah did. Did you think we would let them choose how they died or maybe give them a lethal injection? They made this a war, and war is supposed to be ugly. This is what it means to kill. Killing is violent, cruel, and heartless, and none of you should cheer the killing of other people, but when people need to die, you better be ready to do it.

"I'm sorry if my choosing not to waste any more of our precious bullets on these scumbags offended you in some way, but they needed to die and the three we captured need to speak. We have to find out where their base of operations is and if there are any more of them out there. For us to find that out, these men need to know that I am willing to do anything to them in order to get the answers that I want. Killing their buddies the way I did helped me get closer to what I need. I am not going to play nice and risk the lives of anyone on my land! So you people need to understand, I will torture and kill anyone I have too to make sure we have no more outside threats."

Simone walks up to me and takes my hand, pulling me toward the house. "Let's get you cleaned up a bit, Eddie," she says, following with a smile and a nod.

*

I wash off the blood from my face and hands, and change my shirt. I'm still angry. I look at myself in the mirror and just stare at the lines of hate and pain on my face. I don't want to let anything go, and worse, I don't think I should. My mother is dead. A bunch of good people and innocent children are dead because of these guys, and I want them to suffer. I don't want them to have a quick end and have everything over for them.

"Are you okay?" Simone asks from behind me.

"No."

She just stands and waits.

"I'm not going to just scare them. I'm going to make them suffer. Even if I get the answers I need, they are going to feel pain like they never knew was possible. All of our people are going to see me as a monster, Simone. They'll see me as a monster because that's what I am now. I know what I want to do to them, and it feels good thinking about it. I look forward to seeing and hearing those men in pain."

"You're keeping us alive, Eddie. Everyone knows that and if anyone disagrees with how you do it then they can leave." She pauses a moment before adding, "Honestly, I think most of them would do the same if given the chance."

My wife has always been unusually understanding of things. I don't think I would have gone as far with the survival supplies and even the store if she didn't encourage me. Whenever I would start to think that I am being just a bit too paranoid about this collapse scenario, or that disaster plan, she would get me going again. It's like she always knows what to say to keep me on the path I am heading. I remember several times after personal inventories and telling her the immense amount of guns and ammunition we had stockpiled, she asked me if we had enough, and she wasn't being sarcastic like most wives would be. She always thought we should have more food, guns, ammo, and medical supplies. And today when I say I am about to go too far, she looks at me, and says, "You will never be able to hurt them enough for what they have done Eddie... but I want you to try."

*

Walking through the living room, most of the group is sitting down in silence. Several are asleep. It will take weeks for all of us to recover from the emotional drain we've been through so far. Eleanor stands up as I approach, and I stop walking, expecting to hear some plea for compassion or saving my own humanity.

"Arthur left and wanted me to tell you where everyone is," she says. "Conner and Samantha are taking turns running the tractor and have started clearing bodies to a pile at the east fence. Arthur is out with them helping to stand guard and keep an eye out for any of our people's bodies. If we can find them during the clean-up, we will bury them. Donald, and his son, Joshua, are keeping watch over the two men covered by bodies in the yard. Jake and Hannah are keeping watch over the man tied up in the stable. And Brian and Melissa are on the roof again keeping watch and listening for anyone or anything else. They will let us know if any infected come back to the property."

"Thank you, Eleanor," I say relieved for not having to argue with her, and she sits down as I take a step.

"Eddie?" The voice is Patricia Langford's, and I stop and drop my head before turning around.

"Eddie. We all know you have to get answers from these people. Just don't lose yourself while you do it. They will be judged for what they have done once they die."

"Patricia...." I stop and take a deep breath. "It is very difficult for me to be respectful toward you right now, and you do deserve respect and compassion even without the loss you are dealing with. I am an Atheist, you know this. There is no afterlife, there is no forgiveness. And no punishment or judgment takes place after people die. There is no higher purpose to the deaths that occurred here today, ours or theirs. The only retribution these men will face is what I put them through. When they die, their suffering and their joy will all be over, just like those people we lost."

"But you have to believe in something, Eddie. Why else would you want so desperately to live?"

"I want to live because life is all that I have. You religious people don't seem to understand what life means to an Atheist. Life is more beautiful and precious for an Atheist because we have only one. You, you think you will go to heaven. That this life is just a trial run and something better exists than what is here. I know this is my only existence, so I cherish it, and want it to last forever. I wonder why people like you want to live when you think there is something better than this."

"There has to be something better than this," Rebecca Anderson says holding onto her daughter Rachel.

"For me there isn't. It is just this, but even this disaster of a world is better than not existing. Even with the pain of loss, there is still life to cling to. I have my wife and kids. You have your husband and daughter. In a way we all lost everything we thought we couldn't live without, but if you look around, we still have everything and everyone around us that make life worth living, if only for one more day. All I need is a blade of grass," I say and look at Simone before walking out the door.

"What did he mean with the grass, Simone?" Patricia asks.

"It's just something Eddie used to say when we were talking about people with depression or those that try to commit suicide. I always thought it was a bit silly, but I guess he really means it. He would say, "All I need as a reason to live is to have one blade of grass growing somewhere in the world. That's enough to sustain him."

*

On my way to the stable I stop at the shed next to the house and grab a few items; a fishing tackle box, a tool box, and my cordless drill. As soon as I step into the stable and Chad sees me, he starts whimpering and whining about how he is sorry and was forced into staging the attacks.

I stop in front of him and put down my tools without saying a word. He is tied to one of the stalls with his arms and legs spread in the shape of the letter 'X.' I don't want to look directly at him. Not because I am ashamed of what I am about to do, but because I fear that my rage will make me just kill him.

I look at Jake and Hannah, who have been guarding him. "You two may want to stand outside," is all I say. It isn't an order or a demand, but I'm sure they understand my meaning that this will be ugly.

I open up the tool box and pull out a heavy duty wire cutter. The kind with two curved blades that make a hole the right size to wrap around a basic electric cable that runs through the average house. The hole on this cutter is also the same size as the average man's fingers. Chad doesn't like the look I have on my face while I examine them and starts sputtering and crying.

I'll need the cutter later, but what I want now is a small box of drill bits for my cordless drill. I grab the drill bit box, remove the 3/32 bit, and put it into my drill. I squeeze the drill trigger to make sure it is still charged, and it screams to life. So does Chad. He is screaming his head off, and I'm at least ten feet away from him.

I walk up to him with the drill in my left hand and punch him in the face several times. He finally shuts up long enough for me to speak.

"Olivia Murphy, age three."

"What? Who's that?"

"Olivia Murphy, age three," I say again, and then crouch and pull off his left shoe and sock. Even though his leg is tied tight at the ankle, I kneel on his foot so it can't move. Taking the drill, I place the bit at the center of the toenail on his big toe.

He is screaming and bucking with his hips trying to knock me away from his foot, but I won't budge. I squeeze the trigger, and the drill whines to life, boring a hole through the nail, flesh, and bone of this asshole's big toe. The scream he emits gives me a warm feeling, like a blush after getting caught looking at a pretty girl. The sound of his agony makes me feel good.

I stand up and look behind me. Hannah and Jake are still here. "Grab that rope over there, and tie him down better. Tie him tight at his waist so he can't move around so much." Jake gets the rope and starts securing Chad's waist while I talk to Hannah.

"Are you sure you want to stay? It's going to get worse."

"They were my friends too. Steven and I were close, and Nana. He's getting what he deserves."

I nod and know I should feel ashamed of myself for allowing my twelve year old to witness this, but instead, feel proud that she is strong enough to deal with it. I was upset that Hannah was so furious with these people. She has always had a short fuse. She's very emotional and can get deeply angry over little things, and won't let whatever issue it is go. Now I know she gets it from me. I know I should rise above this, and be the better man, especially in front of her. I can't stop. I mean, I can, if I choose to, but I don't want to stop.

I've been the good guy my whole life, always obeying the laws, and following rules. I used to fume at how criminals and the true bad guys in life always got off too easy. I used to say at my gun shop, "criminals don't belong in jail, they belong in the graveyard." The criminals won't get away with hurting people anymore. In this world they will pay, and I get to be the man that makes sure they get more than their fair share of punishment.

It takes me half an hour to go through the thirteen names of our dead. I drill all of Chad's toes and three of the fingers on his left hand, and say nothing more to him than the name and age of each person that died before drilling each digit. Twice I had to slap him awake, because he passed out from the pain.

During his torture session, there was a rotation of our people walking by the stable entrance with a few staying to watch for a while. I'm not sure who or how many came, only that Jake and Hannah chose to stay the whole time, and remained close to what I was doing.

"Are you awake?" I say and slap Chad in the face one more time.

"Yes, yes please. I'm awake. Please stop! Please."

"I'm going to start asking you questions, Chad, and if you don't answer me, or if I don't like the answer you give, I will start making this painful for you."

He actually chuckles a bit in disbelief when he hears me say that last part.

"What? Don't you think this has been painful for me?" he says with desperation.

"Do you remember the morning I turned you away from my store?" Chad just nods.

"Do you remember what I said to you, Chad? I told you I would shoot you and tell the sheriff you were bitten, and you knew when I said it that I was telling the truth."

"I remember."

"I grab his chin and lift his head so he has to look into my eyes. I drilled one hole in you for each person that you killed on my ranch, and I promise you that whatever you felt while I drilled you was nothing compared to the pain I will make you feel if I don't like what I hear. Do you believe me?"

He says, *Yes,* and tries to nod his head, but can't until I finally let go.

"Okay, then. Let's get started." I put a small hay bale in front of Chad and sit on it. "How many more people are in your group besides those that came today?"

"Four..." He hesitates, "Well, actually, five."

I shake my head and grab the wire cutters and a rag. He is yelling, "Wait! Wait! Wait!" when I cram the rag in his mouth and start cutting.

I snip his pinky finger off of his right hand in three chunks, one snip at each knuckle.

I wait for his screaming and crying to subside before remove his gag and talk to him again. "It is important that I get the right answers from you, Chad. If you hesitate I will assume you are lying or trying to hide something, and you will lose more fingers and toes. Please take the time to think about your answers before spitting them out.

"Now how many more people are there in your group besides those that came today?"

Poor Chad looks terrible. His face is covered in sweat, tears, blood and his left eyebrow is slightly swollen. He is shaking and crying while he talks. "I was trying to tell you. We have four men, but there is a woman that they captured and are holding."

"They captured?"

"Yes, yes, they captured her, but we as a group have been holding her."

"Why didn't the other four men come with your group today?"

"Gerald, our boss or leader, he didn't want them along. They were loyal to Lloyd since they came in with him, and Gerald thought Lloyd might try something once we captured this place."

"More specifics, Chad. I don't know any of these people."

"Lloyd wanted the top spot, and Gerald knew it. Lloyd was in our truck and was standing up in the back when we drove in. Gerald thought

Lloyd and his men would try to kill him once we captured this place, so he made Lloyds men stay at our base."

"When do Lloyd's men expect your group to return? Or are you expecting them to show up here at some point?"

"We're supposed to return there tomorrow. We didn't know how many infected we'd have to clear out of here before we could check for supplies and didn't want to travel back at night. We took the only running vehicles we had, and those four guys were completely drunk when we left earlier today, so they wouldn't be able to make it here even if they wanted to."

"Is there anything else I should know about your group and its base?"

"I'll tell you how to get there—"

I raise my hand and cut him off. "One of you will show me how to get there. Is there anything else I need to know?"

"We have lots of guns and ammo. I mean, we brought a lot with us in the trucks because we thought… well we sent about twenty-five thousand of those things here—"

I slap him again. "Get back on track, what about the guns?"

"Our base is the sheriff's office. We have all of the guns and ammo they had in their little armory. Lots of riot gear, shotguns, rifles handguns and ammo, but also weird stuff like grenades, night vision scopes, all kinds of stuff. I found some transfer documents that a bunch of this stuff was Homeland Security allocations. We don't have much food or water, though, and the city just has too many of those things for us to stay."

"And so you told them about my ranch, didn't you?" I can't help but punch him several more times in the face.

"Hannah, Jake? Can you two tell whoever is watching the other two prisoners to bring one of them here to the stable? It's time to verify this imbecile's story."

"I can go myself," Hannah says.

"I don't want anyone walking around out there alone. Even I shouldn't have come here by myself. There is still the occasional gunshot out there taking out an infected, the grounds aren't secure, and won't be until we clear the land and mend the fences." She nods and they both walk out.

I called him an imbecile. I know it isn't much of an insult to the average person, but this guy was a newspaper reporter, and from what I remember, completely full of himself. That word combined with his current situation might hurt him almost as much as what I've done to him physically.

I shove the rag I have back into his mouth and wait for the next captive to arrive for questioning.

Donald and Joshua bring the next guy in, and he reeks of the guts and corpses that were piled on top of him. "Take a good look at what happened to Chad's hands and feet. I want you to take these and hang on to them for him, okay?" I say and show him the three pieces of Chad's pinky before shoving them in the new guy's pants pocket.

The guy looks nervous but so far is completely silent. There is a far greater reaction from Donald and his son to what I've done. They seem completely mortified, but Donald still whispers to me, "This guy was so terrified of being under those bodies that I think he may be in shock."

"Tie him up across from Chad here so he can look at him while we talk," I say and I pick up the drill and rev the motor a couple times to make my point. His eyes open wide so I know he's paying attention, but still doesn't say anything.

Donald and Joshua leave after they tie this new guy up, and after I put an empty feed bag over Chad's head, I move my hay bale over to sit in front of the new guy. "You are covered in infected blood right now, so I can't do the same type of questioning with you as I did with Chad. As you saw, I drilled a few holes in his fingers and toes, and removed his finger for him. But until we get you cleaned off, I can't afford you getting infected, so I'll have to drill you somewhere that doesn't have any blood on it yet. Do you know where that might be?"

He shakes his head no.

"Your mouth," I reply with a smile. "If you don't give me the answers I want, or if they don't match what Chad said, then I will start drilling into your teeth. Trust me when I say there is a good reason dentists use injections to numb the mouth. Drilling into the root of a healthy tooth will be quite painful. So my first question is, Are there any people in your group beside those that came here today?"

I'm not sure what particular brand of stupid this guy is, but for me personally, if I had walked into a room where someone was missing a finger and had holes drilled in him all over the place, I would have been more forthcoming with any answers I gave. This guy just looks at me and instead if giving me a firm answer like he knows he's telling the truth, he asks me, "None?" as if he is trying to guess the state capitol for a teacher in school.

So, I force his mouth open with a horse bit, and tie it in place behind his head. I shiver a bit as I drill into one of the upper molars on his left side. The smell of burning tooth reminds me of that horrible odor while sitting in a dentist chair. He yanks his head away screaming and my drill bit jumps around in his mouth, cutting up his gums. I stop and tie his head back to the post and finish drilling through until I know I've hit the root, because blood comes out and the pitch of his scream changes.

He answers every question after I drill his first tooth, and apparently, Chad was telling the truth. I think this man got the worst treatment so far. After he answered all of my questions, I re-secured his head, and quickly drilled into thirteen more teeth after telling him his victims' names and ages, like I did with Chad.

CHAPTER NINE
FINISHING THE JOB

I don't bother questioning the third man. I just have Donald and Joshua bring him into the stable and tied up next to the other two prisoners. He has enough fear put into him from the other men tearfully explaining what I did to them that he won't be a problem if I need to question him. And if he is a problem, I'll just torture him as well. For now, though, I think we should act on what I've found out so far.

"Donald, could you and Joshua please tell Arthur, Conner, and Samantha to come to the main house? We all have something to decide. Hannah, Jake, come on back with me. These three aren't going anywhere," I say and point to the three limp headed captives tied to the stalls.

*

Back at the house after getting cleaned up yet again, I am facing the whole group, excluding Hannah and Jake, who took the watch position on the roof for Brian and Melissa.

I head right into my explanation of what I found. "There are four more of them out there holding up at the Sheriff's office, if the information I got is accurate. They also have one woman that they captured and are…keeping her there against her will. Those four men aren't expecting the group that attacked us to return until tomorrow and are supposed to be totally drunk right now, or at least they were five hours ago, when this group left their base to come here."

"How can you be sure they aren't lying? I've heard people will say anything when they're being tortured," Rebecca says derisively.

Ignoring her tone, I nod, and say, "You're right that people will say anything to make torture stop, but the two I questioned gave the exact same details separately. So they are probably telling the truth, unless they coordinated a fake story before they arrived, which is unlikely. I want to go into Medford with a good sized force and kill or capture the last four of these guys, and I want to go in the next half hour. Does anybody have a good reason to wait or not go at all?"

Rebecca's daughter, Rachel, asks, "If you go, someone might die, right?"

"Yes," I say and nod. "Anything can happen on a trip like this. We haven't been off this ranch since the first week this all started. These men have been surviving out there in the city with the infected, so anyone that goes has to understand these men are a real threat."

"Well, I don't think we should risk losing anyone else," Rachel says.

Patricia, Randy's wife, walks over to Rachel, and sits down next to her on the couch. "Sweetie, that's why someone has to go. If those men stay out there, they will do everything they can to kill all of us."

Patricia looks at me, and says, "Eddie, you could have come in here and told us all what we were going to do instead of asking us, and we would have done it out of fear. But you asked what we think and I know you didn't get lost. I trust you to take care of this and keep the rest of our families safe."

"Thank you, Patricia. I can't do it alone, though."

*

The drive to Medford is quiet so far. We are driving the two trucks our attackers brought and one of our own, a Chevy Suburban that seats nine. When we return to the ranch tomorrow, some of us will probably have to deal with sitting in the cold truck beds if we capture or rescue anyone. Of course, maybe there will be extra room if we lose anyone in a firefight.

I'm surprised at the number of women that have come with us. Of the fifteen people in our group, five are women, and Ashley Dixon is the most surprising member. She says the infected scare the hell out of her, but she can't sit back and let regular people threaten us or abuse some poor woman they are holding captive. Her sister's boyfriend, Daniel Palmer, was an obvious participant due to his being a sheriff's deputy, and the attackers being based in the smaller sheriff's office.

The other four women are all coming with their significant others, but I suspect their reasoning is much the same as Ashley's. Hell, it's the same as what we are all thinking. Mindless infected attackers are one thing, but a thinking enemy out there that wants us dead, is heavily armed and captures women to beat and rape, is another story altogether.

Our worst enemy and greatest threat has always been our fellow humans. I know it's a naïve idea to believe that a man-eating apocalypse would unite humanity and end the infighting. I guess with the number of guns and amount of ammo I stockpiled, and the distant location of my ranch, I never truly believed people would pull together. Still, there was always a small lingering hope that more would pull together than pull apart. At least we are doing our part.

The lack of destruction on the roadway is surprising. In a way, I imagine that is a hopeful sign that most of the people that escaped Medford had the gas in their cars to make it somewhere, so they didn't stall in lanes to cause accidents. I still doubt that many people had a place to go or the means to get there if they wanted. The economy was just too bad the last few years before the fall, and the news blackout that last day really doomed a lot of people to an unnecessary death. If only the alert system had given people a warning of what was happening. Or if the internet and phones were still working...that's a lot of ifs once again. I guess it doesn't matter at this point.

So far the road into the city is scattered with only the occasional abandoned vehicle and one wrecked car. It looks like it landed on the side of this lane after overturning from the other side. No other cars are near it, so it might have been someone that was bitten, and made a hasty escape in their car before the infection turned them. We don't stop to see if there is still a body inside. Tied up in the bed of the first truck is the third prisoner that I haven't interrogated. He's the only one that is physically capable of guiding us to his "hide-out" since he escaped my torture so far.

We all know where the sheriff's office is, and Daniel knows where everything is stashed if the men staying there haven't found it all yet, but there is still a problem in getting there. The guy we brought with us is named Jordan. He says the streets in the city are packed with wrecked cars and there are certain areas where it's easier to avoid the infected than others. He also told us Highway 62 in front of the sheriff's office is a parking lot. His group walked all of the supplies to the trucks when they came after us, so he'll take us to the warehouse on East Vilas Road where they normally park their running vehicles and bug-out supplies.

The highway is starting to get clogged as we get closer to a small town called Central Point, on the outskirts of Medford. We stop and remove Jordan's gag to ask him which way we should go.

"We have to take exit thirty-five and head north on Blackwell. Take a right on Kirtland and follow it to Table Rock Road. Table Rock will take us to Vilas Road, and we'll go to the warehouse. Then we have to walk to the sheriff's office from there."

Daniel nods. "The roads are all the right direction to get us there." Then turns to Jordan, and says, "If we run into an ambush, or problems on the way there, you'll die before your friends can finish us off."

He fearfully shakes his head, "None of our guys are out there, and there aren't any other groups in this area either. This route is the way we came because the roads are the clearest, and the area barely has any infected left since we gathered them to..." Jordan leaves the left unsaid, and we gag him again to continue on our way.

We gathered a little bit of history from Jordan and Chad about their attack plans before we left on this trip. Chad developed how to attack my ranch. He was captured by the group at the sheriff's office two weeks after the outbreak, and they kept him alive because he told them about the ranch and all of the survival supplies we have there.

Struggling to survive in Medford, the people there realized the infected are drawn to noise above all other things, and that is what Chad used. To stage the final attack against us, they drove cars slowly around the Central Point area leading them to a staging area where some type of bait was used to keep the infected from wandering away.

Jordan told us that usually the bait was an animal tied to a roof or on some type of tower. However, they used humans as bait the last few days before the attack. They used people they had captured and tied to branches in trees to draw the infected in and hold them there. A few nights before the attack, the men had set up radios in the woods leading toward the ranch. They wired in pressure switches to turn the radios off when an infected steps on it. Once the radio shut off, the infected would hear the next radio in the distance, and travel toward it. It was quite a creative plan, even though it was designed to kill all of us.

Chad figured they had about 25,000 to 30,000 infected grouped together when they started the last run. He noticed they moved a lot slower and stayed bunched up due to the cold temperatures, but still thought the immense number of bodies he sent after us would finish the job. He should have been right. Only my extreme ammo stockpiling and unusual property setup allowed most of us to survive. I can't express how difficult it was not to bludgeon Chad to death as he described how he organized the assault.

The route we are taking is mostly farmland which turns into industrial area as we drive down Vilas Road. There are burned out houses here and there, and wrecked or abandoned cars along the way. Sadly, it looks reminiscent of many disaster or horror movies that were made prior to the collapse. The two things that differ markedly are the feeling and the smell. The feeling I have while looking out the window, at the forsaken landscape drifting past, is what movies and books tried to portray but could never quite accomplish. It's the feeling of personal loss and emptiness that the detached storylines and visuals could never convey.

This place was our home, the houses that we are passing had families that we interacted with in stores and at parks. They were people that I yelled at in my mind while driving behind them on the road. The rotting bodies stuck in wrecked vehicles or in a house's front yard are the friends and neighbors we'll never get to meet. There is a feeling of loss that is both real and unreal, like attending the funeral of a person you know is gone, but think will still show up one day.

The smells are another entity altogether. The lingering odor of smoke as we pass burned houses is familiar enough. It reminds me of brush fires or a farmer burning a pile of trees and rubbish on their land. It is the stench of bodies that makes the drive the most unsettling and is the furthest departure from what books and film were able to represent.

The foul aroma is different than the usual decaying animal road kill that was present before the fall, how, I'm not exactly sure. It might be that the bodies are larger like deer and never get picked up and disposed of by county road crews. Part of the difference may just be in my head, knowing that they are human remains that I smell. Either way, the stink or rather the stenches, help cement in my mind that the world is not the same in a way any earlier media could ever portray.

We pull into the staging area our attackers' group used and park the trucks. The warehouse they keep some of their supplies in is on Industry Drive, next to an auto salvage yard. Timothy and Dianne, along with Donald and Daniel, go into the warehouse to clear it. Jason Anderson and I take our captive, Jordan, in after them to verify where all of the supplies they stockpiled are. While the warehouse is cleared, Jordan tells us that the main doors to the sheriff's building have all been blocked to prevent easy entry from the outside. The only way in will be the back door and that is only if his partners didn't block it for the night already.

The warehouse is empty, or at least human and infected free, just like Jordan said it would be. I still don't trust him to get us into the sheriff's office without trying to give away our approach and want to leave him behind. If we could afford to leave guards with him, he would be staying here, but he'll have to make the walk with us, so I've prepared an insurance device to make sure he doesn't try to run.

I stand in front of Jordan and explain what I'm going to do with him. I speak to him in a soft condescending tone. "Hobbling your legs would only slow all of us down, and we need you to be able to avoid any infected or other dangers we might encounter. To solve this problem, I brought some trapping wire." I smile and hold up the wire for him to inspect.

"This wire is what I use for snares, and I set it up with this nice handle for one of our people to hold, and this loop goes over your head like this." And I drape the snare wire over his head. "If you try to run or make any effort to contact your remaining group, what this loop will do is tighten down to the size of a silver dollar. It will cut through your neck—effectively severing your head. Do you understand?" I ask, and he nods with eyes wide with fear. "We're going to leave your gag tied in place for the walk, so if you need to tell us anything, just stop and motion to the person holding your leash."

We make a straight march across the empty fields behind the sheriff's office to the backdoor. There is snow on the ground, and a cold dry wind blowing from north to south. We spread out behind the rear of the building, tying Jordan to a large white fuel tank at the back of the lot. To our fortune, or misfortune, while we are all staged and ready to head into the building to kill the four remaining members of this group, a man starts backing out of the rear doorway, not seeing that we are out here. He is using his back to push the door open, and I'm sure I'm wrong in my assessment, but it looks like he is helping the woman that they are holding captive out as well.

Randy and Joshua Langford are to the right of the door, and Michael and Megan Palmer are to the left, with the rest of us spread out in a fan shape behind the first four. We all raise our guns and aim at the man making his exit.

Megan Palmer, standing the closest to him, puts her gun to the side of his head, and says, "Let her go, you son-of-a-bitch!"

The man freezes in place but doesn't release his victim. "I can't let her go, she'll fall," he says.

"What did you do to her?"

"I didn't... I'm not with the men here. I came to rescue her," he says, pleadingly.

I don't want to trust his words, but his actions seem to be telling the truth. He is carefully holding the unconscious woman up rather than dragging her someplace. "Secure that man and help the woman," I say, and we separate the two and all move away from the door.

"Talk quick!" I say to the stranger as half a dozen guns are pointed at him.

"Are you with the men here?" he asks.

"No we aren't, now talk! Who are you, and what were you doing with that woman?"

"My name is Greg Munoz. I came here to rescue her, her name is Jessica. I killed two men inside, and there are two more that were passed out, so I tied them up."

I bring Jordan over, and he says he's never seen this guy before, so we send most of our group into the building with Greg in the lead to show us where the men he claims he killed and tied up are. True to his word, two men are bound, and two are dead; one from his throat being cut, and the other with a knife sticking out of his chest.

We all head into the building and begin securing it for nightfall. The two men that Greg tied up are retied more securely, and Jordan is tied up with them. The woman that Greg claims is named Jessica is unconscious and looks like she was severely beaten. Melissa and Megan are using some of the water we brought to clean up Jessica's face, and they have placed her in one of their sleeping bags to keep her warm. There isn't anything more we can do for her other than try to keep her comfortable and hope that she wakes up.

Greg asks us what we are doing here, and we tell him the story of the attack on the ranch, and our plan to kill the remaining men here and to hopefully rescue the woman they held captive. Greg tells us his story once we finish with ours.

"I ran into two girls about a month ago, Jessica, and Lilly. I was searching for food and saw them running from some of the sick people. They were being followed by only three of them so I thought the girls could escape, but they got trapped in a backyard. It is dangerous to help people, especially when you are by yourself like I am, but I couldn't let them get attacked, so I ran up behind the sick ones and knocked them down with my stick." Greg has a large yellow crowbar that he calls his stick. "I didn't say anything to them then, I just nodded at them, and walked away. I was still afraid they might hurt me. It was two of them and only one of me, and they are young. The young people seem to be the most dangerous.

"I continued looking for food and noticed that they were following me. They were keeping their distance and just watched what I did. After a few hours, I collected enough food from the houses in the area. I collected more this time because I thought these girls would need something to eat as well, and it isn't safe to go out collecting every day, so my cart was pretty full. They followed me back to the street where I was staying, so I decided to talk to them. I told them there was no one on this street, and if they weren't going to hurt me they could take any house they wanted, except the one I was staying in. They didn't say anything, so I just put some of the food I had on the sidewalk for them and went to my house. I couldn't sleep that night. I kept thinking those girls were going to break in and kill me, or bring back some friends to do it.

"For two weeks they stayed in the house across from mine, and I would collect food and water and leave some for them outside their door. Jessica finally decided to speak to me. They were just as afraid of me as

I was of them, maybe more so because I'm a man, and they had lots of troubles with men since the sickness spread. I didn't ask what happened, and she didn't say, but you could tell that they had been hurt and were barely surviving when I found them. We did all right for a while, with me gathering supplies, and them keeping watch for strangers and the sick ones.

"We started hearing cars and trucks driving around two weeks ago and thought hopefully someone might be putting the world back together. We finally saw the men that were driving around when they came through our street. Once we saw them we knew something was wrong. They were driving slowly with music playing loudly and getting lots of the sick people to follow them. Getting rid of the sick ones is great, but the looks on the men's faces let us know they weren't good men. They just seemed evil.

"One of them must have seen us looking through the window at them, because they came back looking for us later. Six days ago I went out to collect more supplies. When I came back, Lilly told me the men had come, and they had taken Jessica. Jessica made Lilly hide in the attic and gave herself up to the men so they wouldn't find Lilly as well. Lilly is only sixteen.

"The next day, I hid on the roof of a taller house, with binoculars, and watched for the driving men. I would see them drive and then run closer to where they were. I was being careless not watching for the sick ones and would have been killed if those men didn't clear the area of them. I just wanted to get Jessica back. She was a good neighbor, and Lilly needs her.

"I saw they were staying here in the sheriff's building, but they had too many men. There was nothing I could do for Jessica with so many men keeping her, and I didn't know if she was still alive. I was hopeful, though, and stayed the night in that building across the field.

"This morning I watched a large group of the men walking out the back and carrying lots of guns and bags with them. A few of them were staying by the building, but I could hear they were yelling at each other and sounded drunk. I knew this was my best chance to get Jessica, but I had to wait until the drinking men went back inside, or they would see me leave the building I was hiding in. I'm ashamed to say it took me another two hours after the last man went inside for me to build up my courage to go to the back door and go in.

"They were all passed out when I entered the building. I still didn't know where Jessica was, but I knew these men had taken her, so I slashed the first man's throat. The second man started to shift when I approached him, and I jammed my knife into his chest. I was terrified, but he didn't even open his eyes. I couldn't pull my knife back out of his chest because I was shaking so bad at that point. And then I saw Jessica. She was lying on the floor, by the wall over there," he says, pointing, "She was curled up and bloody, but she was still awake."

"She looked up and saw me walking toward her, but then she passed out. I quickly tied up the last two men so they couldn't chase us if they woke up, and then started carrying her out the back door. That is when I thought you were his group returning and ready to kill me. When that girl with you told me to put Jessica down, the first thing I thought was, how could she help men like these capture and torture other women? I'm glad that you weren't the returning group of men."

"I'm glad we didn't just shoot you before hearing what was going on," I say.

"So Lilly is out there still, and you've been gone for several days?" Ashley asks. "I mean, I'm nineteen and can't imagine being on my own in this world. How could you leave her there when she's only sixteen?"

"I couldn't bring her with me," Greg says. "I didn't expect to come back to her. I thought the best I could do was free Jessica and hold these men off long enough for she and Lilly to get away. I didn't really have time to plan anything. I just told her to wait for Jessica to come back and be ready to fight or run if the men return.

"Is there any way some of you could help me bring Jessica back to our houses? I would like to get back home and let Lilly know that we are okay."

"We can't move her," says Melissa. "She can't be moved until she wakes up, and we can ask her about her injuries."

"But I can't stay here, what if some of the men come back?" he asks, clearly afraid that he is trapped.

"Greg, you are free to go if you want. I don't want you to think we are holding you here. My wife is a nurse, however, and I would like to take Jessica back to our place to make sure she recovers from her injuries."

"No, you can't take her away! Lilly needs her," he shouts and stands up.

"Greg, it will be Jessica's choice, not mine," I say trying to reassure him. "We will wait here, at least some of us, until Jessica wakes up and we can find out what she wants to do. If she wants to return to her house by yours, she will be free to do so, and we'll make sure she makes it there. We will give you and the two ladies supplies to help you try and survive. I would hope that you, Lilly, and Jessica would all choose to return to the ranch with us, though."

Greg steps back. Uncertainty etched on his face. I can see a glimpse of how difficult things must have been out here for the last three months. Any act of kindness is looked upon with suspicion, as though it is a trap of some sort. So I call him on it to try and bring the issue to the surface.

"It isn't a trap, Greg. It isn't a trick question, and I'm not trying to tempt you with something that isn't real. The ranch isn't as secure as it was a few days ago, but we survived a massive attack. Once we clear the land, rebuild and reinforce the fences, we will be fairly secure, both from the infected and from outside attackers. We have food, water, guns, and ammunition. Women have nothing to fear from the men that are there, as you can see by the five women that came with us. They are fed, armed, and trained just as every man is. Just as you, Jessica, and Lilly will be if you come to live with us. And even if you only come for a short time to rest and heal, you will be free to go anytime you want."

"You're serious, aren't you?"

"Yes, I am."

"I can leave right now?"

"Yes, but you should take supplies with you if you go."

"And I can return to you with Lilly?"

"Yes, and you can come to the ranch with us if you want."

"I want to let Lilly know that I'm all right and that I found Jessica, but I don't think she will come back here with me. I'm listening to you say there is a safe place to go and that we can trust you, but even I am having a hard time accepting it. Lilly will never believe me. She only spoke to me the first time to tell me Jessica was taken."

"I could go with you," Ashley says, surprising everyone, not just Greg. "I know you all probably think I'm being naïve, wanting to go off with a stranger, but we all believe him or he'd be tied up right now. I think I can help convince Lilly that it is safe to come back."

"Oh no, I couldn't ask you to come with me. I mean, it would help convince Lilly, but it still isn't safe out there."

Dianne, Melissa, and Megan all agree with Ashley and say they want to go as well. Dianne adds, "We haven't had to face survival on our own the way you have out here, but we can shoot and have fought the infected, the sick ones. I think we'll be able to protect ourselves, especially as a group."

Greg looks at the four women, smiles, and then sits back down. "If you are coming with me then we can wait until tomorrow. We won't be able to make it back here from the houses before nightfall on foot."

"Is it that far?" Michael asks, clearly concerned for his wife's wellbeing.

"No, it isn't far. Twenty, maybe thirty minutes if we walked straight there, but you have to walk slow these days, and keep watching for the sick ones."

"We have over an hour of daylight left. Why don't we go now?" Ashley says.

"It will probably take longer than a few minutes to convince Lilly to come here, and they may have supplies they need to pack," I say. "I don't think we should split the group up for the night in a strange place, and send you off with someone that we just met and only think he is telling the truth, but don't know."

Jessica solves the dilemma for us when she wakes up during our conversation. She first sees Samantha looking down at her, and then Melissa, and Megan. She slowly sits up with an uncertain expression on her face mixed with pain when she touches her swollen left eye. Greg walks up and kneels in front of her, and she lunges at him, grabbing him in a fierce hug. "Where's Lilly?" she asks and looks around.

"She's at the house, still. I left looking for you the day after those men took you."

"We have to go get her. Please! I don't know who you people are, but we have to go get her. I can't let anything else happen to her." She tries to get up, but the movement causes her to vomit.

Samantha helps her lay back down, and talks to her, "You have a concussion, Jessica. You won't be able to walk there in this condition."

"Don't worry, Jessica," Greg says, grabbing her hand. "I'm going right now to get her. I'll bring her back here in the morning. You get some rest."

*

Throughout the night we split off in different shifts. Some do guard duty, others gather all the remaining supplies to be transported back to the ranch, and all of us worry about the four women that went with Greg.

I'm not completely sure why it was important for the women to go without any of our men or their husbands, but everyone could sense that's how it had to be. They needed to know that they could do it, and we needed to know that we could let them and still survive. Sending some men with the group wouldn't have stopped Lilly from trusting Greg, but it would have caused the women to doubt that we trust them to handle themselves. We rely on each other to survive, so we can't afford to have that type of doubt seep into anyone's minds.

Early the next morning our four departed women return with Greg and Lilly. Everyone is happy to be reunited, but none more than Lilly and Jessica. It is nice to witness such genuine happiness in such a screwed up world.

"There's more than a blade of grass today, huh, Eddie?" Randy asks me, looking at the reunions.

"Yes, much more than a blade, Randy, much more," I say and smile.

*

After returning to the ranch we found out there was an attack by one of the infected. None of our people were injured, though. An infected wandered into the stable where Chad and the now toothless prisoner were tied up. We forgot to leave guards posted there, and when Simone walked in to check on them with Hannah, they found the man with the drilled teeth had been ripped open and gutted. There was only one infected carrying out the attack and had left his first victim once he died to start chewing on Chad's bloody hand, which was now a bloody stump.

Simone killed the uninvited dinner guest and left Chad tied where he was. Since we found Kim in Rogue River, we have all wondered what the process is for someone that doesn't turn right away, and Chad is just the person we were looking for. She said he started a fever six hours after first being bitten, just like Kim, and the fever lasted almost a full hour and then disappeared. After the fever he regained consciousness and didn't seem to be infected. He was weak and disoriented, but could speak, and didn't seem to want to attack anyone any more than he usually did. This new information gives us a small bit of good news that some people are immune to the illness. Unfortunately, without medical testing facilities, the only way we can find out if we are immune is to be bitten.

Greg, Jessica, and Lilly all chose to come to our ranch. They are staying long enough for Jessica to heal and regain her strength, and then they plan on going back to survive on their own. I would like them to stay and hope they end up liking things here. Besides them all being genuinely likable, we have a shared kinship since we were all injured by the same group of men. If they don't stay, at least helping them makes me feel like we are accomplishing something from the mess Chad and his group brought on us. And we'll be able to give them plenty of weapons to defend themselves as well.

Our new supplies have been sorted, and we have gained a great deal of defensive capability with the guns and ammunition recovered from the sheriff's office. The grenades are the most shocking part of the stockpiles, though. Daniel and I have just finished looking over everything, and I have to ask him, "Why the grenades? What could you possibly need them for in dealing with the public?"

"We didn't request them. They came in with some of the other supplies the week before the attack. Homeland Security sent them to us and probably every police station in the country. Our offices were getting taken over, and were going to be used as regional headquarters if things got really bad. They knew martial law was coming, just like that old memo said. All we could do was store the stuff they sent us, we couldn't send it back."

"You think every police station received the same type of stuff?" I ask, shaking my head.

Daniel nods, and replies, "The bigger the department or area the more stuff they would have gotten, I imagine."

It's not a comforting thought that people like the gang Chad was with have access to weapons like this, but then again, that means we do as well. I think we'll have to try for the Medford and Central Point police buildings one of these days.

*

Chad is about to die. He survived my torture yesterday and the inadvertent attack by an infected. His three remaining buddies are tied up in the stable here next to him. I want to say that he will die a painful death and suffer greatly but his reaction to the infection appears to be what was originally intended with the Zeus drug. He no longer feels pain, his body barely bleeds when I cut or stab him, and his feeling of weakness after the fever is more accurately described as a general body numbness to resist reacting to trauma. So I am putting a spike in his head now that I realize nothing I do to hurt him from this point on will matter.

I wanted him to suffer, I wanted my rage and his pain to continue, but now his dead body is dangling like a discarded marionette by the ropes holding his arms in place. As much as I want to continue being angry at these other three, it just isn't there. I am worn out, and most of my anger at Chad was my regret at being a decent person on the first day and letting him live. His death on that day would have prevented all three of the attacks we've endured so far.

I turn to Simone and shake my head with a frustrated expression on my face. She's standing guard by the door, making sure no more unwanted infected people wander in while I deal with these guys. "I don't think I have it in me anymore, Simone. I'm just going to kill them and get it over with."

"Do you think that's what they would do?"

I just shrug my shoulders at her question. I'm exhausted. I barely slept last night in the police station. As much as I wanted to, I was too much on edge from everything that had happened. My body was ready for sleep, but my brain refused to shut down long enough for me to get it.

"If they had captured us on the ranch, do you think they would just kill you, or do you think they would keep you alive and make you watch whatever they did to us? What they would do to me or to our daughters?"

"I get it Simone, I do. I know what they are capable of, but I don't think I should keep doing it. I was really enjoying making Chad and the others suffer, but now..."

"But now it makes you feel dirty, right?"

"Yes."

"Eddie, who do you think this is going to benefit? I mean, if you continue torturing them, what will it do?"

"It will make them suffer."

"And who will know about the suffering these men endured at your hands? Will you leave any of them alive to go out as a warning to others?"

"No. None of these men are going to leave here alive. No one will know that I tortured them."

"You can't think of anyone, Eddie?"

I shake my head no, not knowing where she is leading me in this conversation.

"Our people will know what you did. If you continue torturing these men, then our people will know that even when we had our ranch secure, you tortured and eventually killed these men for no reason other than your desire to see them suffer for what they did."

"So you think I should stop as well?"

"No Eddie, I think you should continue," she says firmly while nodding her head.

She steps closer to me and speaks in a whisper to tell me what she means. "Not everyone will stay on this ranch. Eventually, someone will move away when things start to quiet down, and before that there will be trips for supplies. Every one of our people that survive will eventually come in contact with other people on the outside. If you want to keep us safe and this ranch secure, then when any of our people talk with people on the outside, they have to be absolutely certain that to come here and cause problems for us will not just result in their death, but in something far worse."

I'm starting to see where she is guiding me but the odd expression on my face is enough for her to know I still don't completely understand.

"Everyone here already sees you as a fair man, Eddie. These people trust you and rightly so. Being fair or decent doesn't keep you alive in a world like this, however. The people on our ranch need to know that others should fear you. You need to torture those men until they die. You need to do it slowly, and you need to look like you are enjoying it for anyone that comes to watch or asks about it later. If our people believe you are capable of being a monster, then they will have no problems in the future telling people they encounter about it, and that will help keep our family safe."

"You're an amazing woman, Simone. Thank you for always keeping me on the right path."

*

I've spent the last three days torturing our three remaining prisoners. They started begging me to kill them yesterday, but I kept on going, and actually got into a rhythm with things. After the first day of torturing them, I returned to the house, showered, and then stared at the ceiling for the rest of the night. I felt dirty and rightly so. What I was doing now was cruel, and I have never been cruel without intention before. Even the torture I performed right after the attack I could personally justify as needing to get information, it was to help us survive, but what I was doing now was different. I stared at the ceiling all night without sleep, wondering what I was doing, and couldn't come up with a reason.

The torture yesterday went easier. I was exhausted and numb. I really didn't care how much they begged, even though they increased their pitiful pleas for mercy. I started getting creative as well. I started smashing fingers and toes with hammers to make large blood blisters, which I would then drill. It caused them more pain. I raised their legs on supports and slammed the soles of their feet with a baseball bat. That one I saw in a movie when I was younger. Last night I was able to sleep. I slept well.

Today I was looking for ways to punish them specifically for raping Jessica and other women they had captured and killed. What I did was a brilliant yet simple idea that made me personally cringe when did it the first few times. I bent the men naked over a table with their legs spread and played ping pong with their testicles. I started with just light taps, the ones that hurt, but you can recover from after some deep breathing and a few minutes. By the end I was smacking them full swing, and all three men had bloody swollen scrotums that were probably more mush than testicle.

Joshua Langford has stayed in the stable with me while I have been torturing the men. He had avoided coming anywhere near the men we captured until this morning. He said he felt the men should suffer for what they did and knew he would kill them on sight if he came earlier.

I still haven't found out what happened to his family or how his group was overrun before they could get to the shelter. No one has wanted to bring it up with him yet. Even Jason and Rebecca have given him his space, even though they must desperately want to know what happened to their son Christopher. I imagine he will probably tell us all tonight, with the events going on today.

It is funeral day. The group found the bodies of little eight year old Christopher, the thirteen year old twins, Steven, and Lauren, and thirty seven year old, Matthew. We are going to bury my mother at the same time.

"It's time," Simone says to Joshua and me from the entrance. I put down the cutters I just picked up and head out the door with Joshua, to attend the funeral.

*

We are all in a different mood now that the funeral is over. Joshua decided not to return here with me, but eight other people came with me instead. Hannah is back, and I am also joined by Randy, Arthur and Eleanor, Rebecca and Jason, Jessica and Lilly. I don't bother giving them a warning of what is too come. They all know what I have been doing, and it is their choice to stay or leave.

I spend my time with rudimentary torture, alternating from one man to the next. With each action, I think of the bodies we just placed in the ground. I snip off a piece of toe with a thought of my mom. Remove a finger with thoughts of Christopher. I work slowly and methodically to ensure that each man is cognizant enough to know what is coming and remains conscious through each procedure.

They don't bother begging for mercy anymore. They just scream and cry from the pain and none of it bothers me now. Torturing these men feels like a dirty chore rather than a grotesque violation of morality. It is like scrubbing the toilet or picking up dog poop in the yard. It is something I have to do, and I hate these men all the more that I have to do it.

I say I have to do it because I know there is a larger reason behind what I'm doing, and it isn't because my wife said I should. The easier it is for me to torture them, and the better I become at making them suffer, the closer I get to understanding why it must be done. The meaning is floating there just beyond my grasp, but I will have it soon.

My cutters and drill have seen a busy day. None of the three men have any remaining fingers, toes, or teeth, now. Their hands and feet end in burnt stumps of cauterized flesh. Their mouths are nothing but bloody gums from where I used pliers to slowly extricate their teeth. Pulling the teeth was all I had left to do since I already drilled a hole through each one.

*

Today is the fourth day since I returned to the ranch from Medford with our prisoners. I haven't helped with anything on the farm. There is probably another five days' worth of tractor running to pick up and pile the bodies for burning, but I have my own task to do. I am walking to the stable now, and I am finally looking forward to my day. The first two days were difficult to make it through, even though they did get easier as I went. Yesterday was tolerable but still not a job I could say I liked or wanted to do, but today I am looking forward to hurting these men. I've given up trying to find justification for what I'm doing. I thought I was on some cusp of higher meaning yesterday, but realize now, that I just want to hurt them because I can.

Simone is walking next to me, and I reach out to hold her hand while we go.

"How are you doing, Eddie?" she asks me.

I stop and look at her, and realize I haven't spoken to anyone for days, not even Simone. No hellos, no goodbyes. No words at the funeral and no responses to questions. I've just been doing my thing in the stable. I haven't comforted my kids or reassured them even though I have held them in my arms.

"I'm actually doing pretty good, Simone," I say in response. "I feel good, and believe it or not, I am actually looking forward to today."

She looks at me with a bit of concern, and asks, "You're looking forward to hurting those men?"

I nod, and say, "Yes. It is the strangest thing, but I'm really good at it, and I'm looking forward to making them cry, and I have no reason for it. Something just feels right about it at this point."

"And what if these men didn't do anything to us?" she asks.

I just look at her with a question written all over my face, not understanding what she means.

"Do you think you would enjoy hurting those men if they weren't the ones that sent the infected here? What if they were just some people that wandered onto our land?"

I think about it for a few seconds. "No, I don't think I would enjoy it… but then again, I'm not so sure. Anyone that comes here is a potential threat if they leave, so it would depend on the feeling I get from them."

"So you would still need a reason?" she asks.

"No, I could do this to anyone if I thought it would help us somehow, but I would need a reason to enjoy it. I know these are bad guys. They may not deserve what I'm putting them through, but killing them lets them off, and keeping them as fed prisoners is like giving them a time out. I'm enjoying making them suffer."

"You should kill them now, Eddie," she says, nodding her head.

I think, *No, I don't want to,* and start shaking my head at her. "Why?" I start raising my voice as I question her. "Four days ago, you said I should make them suffer until they die. Now you want me to just kill them and let them off? Why should I?" I yell in her face, making Simone step back from me, with a look of fear on her face.

"You have learned how to be cruel," she says softly with tears in her eyes.

"What are you talking about?" I say more calmly but with a great deal of confusion.

"Eddie, you were soft...too kind. You have always been a good man, and the people in this world will kill us all if you continue to be the man you have always been. I've never been afraid of you in all of our years together, until just now. I wanted you to torture those men so you would learn to be as rotten and vindictive as the people we will encounter. One day you will face men like these, but they will be men that haven't done anything to us yet. You have to know in your heart what you will do to them or they won't see it in your eyes. What they see in your eyes is what will keep us all alive."

Simone walks off crying.

I never thought of myself as soft before. I guess it is true that I always looked to fairness above all else. I know there isn't fairness in the world, but I did my best to be even handed, and just in the things that I did. She's right. That isn't going to work in this new world. Society isn't going to rebuild itself in our lifetimes with the numbers of humans that are now lost. I need to consider a more selfish path and learn to fight for more than our fair share.

I walk into the stable and say good morning to each of the men before I cut their throats.

CHAPTER TEN
REBUILDING AND EXPLORING

After killing the last three of our attackers, I rejoined the group, and once again became a productive person on my own land. It was a hard time for all of us dealing with everything that was lost. Over the next week we found the bodies of the rest of our lost members. We buried them in four separate funeral services. Each time it dug deeper into the wounds we hoped would be healing soon. Too much had happened in such a short time for any of us to understand how to deal with it properly. It took two weeks to remove all of the infected bodies from the ranch and burn them.

It wasn't until a month later, in the middle of March, that all of the work we were doing started to feel like it had any purpose. The winter temperatures stayed below freezing throughout that month, which probably did the most to keep the group intact. A good number of our people would have moved off the ranch, trying to make it on their own during that time, due to the general hopelessness felt by everyone. The unusual cold forced us to continue working together. My behavior torturing those men in the stable played a big part in the feelings of unease everyone was dealing with. No one was quite sure if they could trust me at first. Even Simone avoided me for three more days after I finally killed the men.

She apologized for evading me afterward, but told me even though she pushed me into the state I was in, she didn't expect me to change so much. I really frightened her and everyone else for that matter. Well, almost everyone else. The kids and teenagers didn't seem to mind what I'd become. In fact, I spent most of that month with them as if I was a part of their new world more than part of the old one.

Once we reached the turning point in March, and regained the sense of cohesion, we had also made it back to regular maintenance mode. We decided to move the fences farther out from the buildings to increase our defensive perimeter. We finished that large project while we also repaired or shored up the barn, stable, and other outbuildings where they needed work. There was even a stray day of good weather where the sun was shining and the temperature almost reached sixty. That day we all decided it was time to start travelling in groups off of the ranch to resupply, and look for anything, or anyone, that might help us survive.

Getting to leave the ranch, I think, was the final turning point. It helped all of us realize there was still the possibility of having a life in this world. None of us had realized how much we all felt like prisoners on the ranch. Trapped here by an infected army of guards that would eat us if we stepped out of line.

We had to go, if not for the peace of mind, then for the supplies we were running low on. Running the tractor constantly for two weeks drained the large gas tank I have on the farm. Our generators keep the electricity on. That is a luxury I know most survivors don't have. Greg told us how difficult it was for him to survive before joining us, and I don't want the same struggles at the ranch.

There were several important things that we needed to accomplish in our trips out of our safety zone. We were good on guns and ammo, but still needed to attempt a trip to Medford's police departments and to the larger Sheriff's office off of Mistletoe and 8th, to scavenge anything left there. We also needed to check on friends and acquaintances that might have survived the upheaval on their own. The final thing we desperately needed was radios. I had stockpiled a bunch of short wave radios, walky-talky type things, but no Ham systems that would allow us to communicate with other survivors around the country and the world.

Once we made it off the ranch, we happily discovered a world that was safer than we had imagined. Notably free from danger even compared to that first trip, when we had travelled to Medford and saved Jessica. The extreme low temperatures continued after the large attack, and they combined with strong sustained winds that we were only partially protected from by the surrounding woods and hills. That combination with the non-arrival of spring in March was finally freezing the infected solid.

On one trip during the last week of March, we drove to check on Billy Underwood at his property. Billy was one of my prepping customers and would get into heated debates with me about the existence of God. Unfortunately, Billy and his people didn't survive the outbreak, which means Jessie Corrigan is most likely dead as well. Jessie was one of the four customers that arrived at my store on the day of the outbreak and was supposed to join the group on Billy's ranch.

We did get quite a vision on the drive to Billy's property. His land and the area surrounding it were dotted with human statues. Most of them were standing in various poses of frozen motion, but some had fallen over from where they had frozen while taking a step and weren't stable enough to remain upright.

Billy's land was close to Medford, in the northeast, which is probably the reason for it being overrun. Of course, Billy did mention that most of the people he was taking in were senior citizens from around his place, so it just may be that they didn't have enough capable bodies to mount the proper defenses. His land is also open ranch land, without the forest to block the winds like at my place, so I'm sure the combination of the cold temperatures and freezing wind is what froze all of the infected on his land while in motion.

We did have to shoot many of the infected that were still somewhat animated, but they were moving so slowly it was like shooting at mounted targets. We had no fear of being overrun or surprised by any of them.

I found the Ham radio equipment I needed at Billy's place, and over two days and several trips, we returned to his place to pick up all of his leftover supplies. Fortunately, Donald was able to get his big rig running, or we would have taken a lot longer making the trips with the smaller pickups.

The apparent die-off of the infected and the lack of mobility on those remaining alive prompted another point of joy for everyone at the ranch. We were all able to return to our pre-disaster homes and pick up personal items that we wanted. The first few days of April were marked by photo album sharing and family remembrance. We shared stories of those we know we lost, and those we hope are still safe. There weren't many things left for Simone and I to recover from the house we had the store attached to. The place was ripped to shreds by people trying to find survival supplies after we left. Fortunately, we kept all of our important things, like documents and pictures, at the ranch, and only wanted to get the remaining photos from the walls.

On one of our outings, Michael, our resident EMT, suggested we bring one of the frozen infected back to the ranch and thaw it out. He was concerned that the petrified ones might thaw out and come back to life like some insects will. We did four different tests, and each one proved that once the infected are frozen solid, they are truly dead. I was happy, as I'm sure everyone else was as well, that whoever created Zeus didn't make the infected impervious to the cold.

The temperatures have finally started regularly getting into the fifties and sixties. This is still a problem though since we should be averaging the mid-seventies for temperatures by now. We also recorded that the weather got progressively colder from December through April, almost as if the winter was not only prolonged, but shifted its coldest days by almost two months.

Even though the weather was horrible it helped us out a great deal. If spring had hit when it was supposed to, we would not have made the scavenging runs to all of the police departments. We discovered two weeks ago that once the weather did warm up during the day, that the remaining infected returned to their normal walking pace.

In April, since it had not warmed up yet, we were able to scavenge the Medford police departments, the main sheriff's office, and the Central Point police department. As much as I am a fan of stockpiling necessities, the amount of arms and ammunition we retrieved from those three locations is staggering, and borderline obscene. It makes me smile when I think about it, and as much as we have, I would personally love to have more.

The National Guard Armory was toast. It looked like that place had been hit in the early days of the disease. Until our group came through, no one had been to the police departments, because of the huge numbers of infected in and around them. We were the first group to search those places while the infected were still as slow as snails—because they were partly frozen. It would be a much scarier proposition trying to go into one of those buildings today with the warmer weather.

The infected in the streets and open areas are almost all dead and will fall to the ground and rot in this warmer weather. Some of the infected inside the buildings we entered were frozen solid as well, but most were insulated enough to survive. That means any open doorways or broken windows will allow the housed infected to now walk free.

Even with the returned threat of the defrosted infected everywhere, if we didn't retrieve the guns and supplies from Medford yet, I would still try to get them. We have what we need for defense on the ranch, but I don't want any more groups like those guys Chad was with getting this stuff.

It took a while for the Ham radio to be hooked up and for someone to figure out how to use it. Donald and Randy have been running the radio and have spoken with people around the country, and a few around the world. I know they have contacted people in England, Germany, Canada, Greece, and someone in Brazil. It is the same situation everywhere. Most of the population is dead, and those that are left are barely holding on, both by starving and not having defensible locations to stay.

I feel the most empathy for the plight of the people in Europe. Without easy access to firearms like most of the locations in the U.S.

had, they had survival by hand to hand contact from the beginning. I imagine the same situation played out in all of our country's anti-gun states and urban centers. Having high populations of unarmed people to fight hand to hand against a disease ridden violent enemy is not a recipe for survival.

At least the deep winter freeze we've had here seems to be all over the northern hemisphere, and the big die off of the infected is happening even as far south as Greece. If the next few winters repeat their long runs and stay as cold as they did this past season, then the long term implications of growing food, and keeping warm are not good at all. So much for the dire warnings of "global warming" destroying life on the planet. I think the climatologists of the 1970s were right in their prediction of a coming ice age. They were just off by several decades.

For the last two weeks all exploratory trips off the ranch have been on foot or by bicycle. Having the numbers of infected down to reasonably safe levels and the warmer weather made us decide to conserve whatever fuel we could for next winter. There are plenty of abandoned vehicles to siphon gas from for stockpiling, but the fuel will only stay fresh for a finite amount of time, even with the stabilizer we are adding to it. There won't be any more oil or gas exploration in our lifetimes and probably no refining either.

Another reason we don't take vehicles as often anymore is because we don't want to alert anyone to our location by having regular vehicle traffic coming and going from the ranch. The trucks also draw out more infected than silently going by on a bike. We aren't able to carry as many supplies, but the return trips with vehicles end up just as slow since we need to clear the roads of the infected that were drawn out when we passed by earlier.

The survivors of the world will be travelling mostly on foot or bicycle until the entire infected population has died off. Travelling by horse attracts too many infected, and when gathering supplies, guards are needed to stay with the horses to keep them from getting attacked. We found that out the hard way with the two remaining horses we have that returned to the farm after we were overrun.

On the last two trips we took this week, Simone and I have taken all of our kids with us. The first time we went on just a day trip, but the second trip was an overnight stay. We are trying to learn how the world is now, as well as teach the kids how to survive in it at the same time. Our plan is to take a three to five day trip on our bikes into Central Point. There are some businesses there that we want to check out that could have some items that would make life a bit more convenient for us. Central Point is also a great place to go with our kids, not just because it is between us and Medford, but because it was largely cleared out of the freely mobile infected by Chad and his group when they prepared the attack on our ranch.

The place I really want to see if it is still stocked, is an archery shop the phone book shows is on Pine Street in Central Point. If we can clear out a fully stocked archery store we won't have to worry so much about the noise all of our firearms make. Also, our kids and the other young people will need to learn archery to survive in their future. Without modern manufacturing, the world will eventually run out of bullets, primers, powder, and the shells necessary to make them on our home presses. Our children's and grandchildren's lives will most likely be one of defense with assorted swords, clubs, and bows.

If the weather remains as good as it is right now, we will leave in two days with our bikes, trailers, kids, and guns to check on that shop in Central Point.

CHAPTER ELEVEN
THE AFTERMATH

Pain. That's what I feel. Maybe not so much pain as it is a sharp tingle. My whole body feels like stepping on a foot that has fallen asleep, but in a less agonizing way. The fever took a huge toll on my body, but I can feel that I am still me. At least I haven't paid the ultimate toll this time.

I'll need to get Simone's attention to get me out of these restraints. I hope she's in here. "Himoa. Himoa?" I'm trying to say her name, but with this wood bit in my mouth, Himoa is all I can get out. "Himoa, Aah ooh Eaah?" She must be here because I can vaguely feel a hand start to grip mine. Her voice is calming as she speaks to me, like a length of rope pulling me to safety after being trapped in a deep and dark cave.

"There you are. You must not be feeling very good, Eddie Your hand is still really warm."

I love her face staring down at me. It's expressing such a mixture of concern and relief.

"You're still talking, so I'll assume you haven't turned. I'm going to remove your gag and see how well you are, okay?"

I can only grunt in reply.

The gag feels great coming out, except for my tongue sticking to it a bit. My mouth is really dry from being locked open, and I can now feel the stiffness of my jaw. I guess it's all over. I don't feel like biting her and my thoughts seem clear. I wonder how long I've been out. "Simone, I need some water, please."

She drops a little in my mouth with a large soup spoon, and says, "Just a little now or you'll choke while you're tied down. I'm going to check your temperature, and if it's good, I'll give you the rabbit test."

The rabbit test is a simple "what will you bite" test we figured on giving anyone we had to tie down after being bitten. What we do is place a live rabbit over the mouth of the infected person, in this case, me. If I bite the rabbit, then I have changed. We take extra precautions like this before untying someone just in case changes to the symptoms or outcomes in the disease occur. In this case, I was bitten by a runner that had extra mobility, so we don't know if that is a result in a change in the disease or just a change in how that former person reacted to the illness.

I have a thermometer in my armpit checking the level of my fever, and I ask how long I have been out. "Eighty-seven minutes," she says. "And you peaked at one hundred three degrees."

This is good news. It takes a far higher temperature to actually cause brain damage, especially the type associated with this disease. What is a little more disconcerting to me is that the rabbit that Simone is holding has reminded me that I am very hungry. But while the fur is running against my mouth, I have no interest in biting it. I just want to get something normal to eat, maybe some stew.

I happily declare, "That means I pass, right? Can you unshackle me now? I am seriously stiff from the fever and being locked down in one position like this." But Simone doesn't reply. "Simone? Can you loosen the straps please?"

She replies in a coy manner, "Give me a second, Eddie. I'm deciding whether I should use your immobilized state and celebrate by taking advantage of you."

I laugh, and reply while she removes my head strap and the restraining box, "You don't have to worry about me resisting, Simone. I'm not sure how well I could perform, though, feeling like I do."

Simone smiles, un-does the rest of my straps, and then helps me sit up. I ease my legs over the side and sit there as she leans in and gives me a strong yet tender hug.

She gives a little shudder, and says, "I thought I lost you again. You have to stop doing that, Eddie."

"Believe me, Simone, I know what you mean. We should have never been in this position in the first place. We let our guards down at that shoe store. I shouldn't have had everyone just watching me and the two infected we had a visual on. We'll be more careful next time. It's a good lesson for all of us to have learned."

She nods while she steps back, "I know it's that also, but we were exhausted as well. It's too difficult for us to go on these trips with all the kids by ourselves. Just like here at the house, we need a rotating shift of lookouts when we go out. We need to have more people with us when we go."

"Or we should rethink taking them with us. I mean, I know we both agreed and thought it was a good idea to teach them what is going on, but now that there are runners, everything has changed."

"That was one man, Eddie. Who knows what his circumstances were when he changed? That doesn't mean there are more of them out there!"

"There are more out there, Simone, there always are. And that isn't the worst part. The worst part is what he is capable of."

"I know! I know. He can run and move his hands. I don't want to talk about this right now," she says.

"No, Simone, it's not that, and we need to talk about it while it's still reasonably fresh in our minds. I think that runner was tracking the two slower infected, following them to see what they would turn up. Or worse, it was using them as bait."

"Oh, come on. You're just upset by the fact that we were surprised."

"Yes and no, Simone. We were surprised, but think about how it happened. We were away from the ranch for five days and barely saw any of the infected. There were plenty of bodies everywhere, so we know a lot of them have died off, either from the cold or maybe starvation. So there are barely any left freely walking out where we were, and yet two infected happen to show up following us and they are followed by a new type, a runner. It can't be coincidence."

Simone closes her eyes, shakes her head, and says, "It's the cold."

"What?"

"The winter, it has to be the cold weather," she starts explaining to me. "The fever is what damages the brain and destroys fine motor skills and higher cognitive functions. Anyone that has become infected during this past winter or during extreme cold could have had the effects of the fever minimized. They might not just be able to run and use their hands, Eddie. They might be able to think like us, to strategize."

"That would help explain the whole attack at the shoe store. If those infected were following our scent and the runner was following them, it waited for us to get separated. Once I was distracted by fighting the other two infected, it came in for the kill. There will be more of them out there, and if they can hunt us by stealth and run, it opens up a whole new world of danger for us. Just a few of them could wipe out the remaining groups of people on the planet."

My mind starts racing again on what needs to be done. We have to let everyone in our group know, get on the radio, and tell anyone we can contact about the threat of runners and the cold. Everyone will have to go out in groups, the bigger the better.

That is the key to survival throughout the ages. More people, a larger group. Defense in numbers is always the preferred way if possible. The tough part these days is finding people you can trust with your family. Which reminds me, "Simone, were is everybody? Why are Greg, Jessica, and Lilly the only ones here? What has been going on?"

Simone takes a deep breath, and says, "First, get cleaned up. Get into the house and take a shower. I have some clothes in our room that I set out for you to change into if things turned out as they have. While you're doing that, I'll go let Greg and the others know that your fever broke, you're alive and normal, well, as normal as ever." She smiles at me and sticks out her tongue before quickly continuing, "It's still early, only about eight or eight thirty p.m., so it would be a good time for everyone to sit down together. We can find out what happened here and vice versa."

She gives me another long hug and just looks into my eyes before turning and walking out the door. I leave and head to the house.

*

While I wash the grit of the road off of me, I realize I am also washing off the blood of the guy I killed when I got here. I am pissed more than ashamed that I had to kill him. He was acting crazy, and I wanted my family to be safe at home. No one will stand between my family and their safety without that person or me dying. That's just how it is now. No call to the police to remove an intruder these days. I don't know what I feel about Mike, Craig's son, or his sick wife. I guess I'll figure out what to feel after I meet with them. Hopefully it doesn't end up being a revenge shoot out.

*

Everyone is in the living room when I arrive, except for Mike's mom. She must be pretty sick to still be laid up. Mike appears to be a young teenager, 14 or 15 years old. He has that awkward teenager look where his body parts just don't seem to match up yet. He looks angry and depressed, sitting on one of the two couches next to Lilly and Hannah. He glances at me briefly, and then looks away without any noticeable change to his expression. Either he doesn't know who I am and that I killed his father, or is a great poker player.

Simone hands me a glass of water and a plate with some bread, tomatoes, and a few sausages from our canning supplies. We sit next to each other on one of the two loveseats. I'm surprised to see Randy and Patricia Langford here, as well as Donald's daughter, Katy. I thought only Greg, Jessica, and Lilly were still at the ranch. I nod to them, and they smile back in return but no words are exchanged between us. I start gobbling up the sausages and tomatoes.

Greg starts talking, "Mike, this is Eddie Keeper, the owner of this property and house we are in. He will have to tell you what happened between your father and himself, since I only walked outside right before… well, right before your father was shot."

I guess it is my turn to speak already. I look at Greg, and ask, "Usually when someone returns from outside, we give a rundown of what happened and what we brought back, has any of that happened while I was strapped down?"

"No," Greg replies. "We all kept to ourselves once you got back. Jessica and I were tending to Maria before that and returned to her when you went to the medical shed."

Simone fills in, "I had Hannah watch you for an hour after your fever hit, while I came in here to check on Maria, and get the kids something to eat and give them something to do. They're watching a movie in the back room where Maria is so they can tell us if she wakes up. I'll bring them in here when we have Mike tell us his family's story."

I nod, and ask, "You checked on the mom? Good, is she very sick?" I can tell by Simone's expression it is bad.

Simone looks over at Mike, and then back at me. "I checked her over, and like I explained to Mike, it is clear that his mother has severe internal injuries. Subcutaneous hemorrhaging is apparent in her abdominal and chest area. I can give her an injection for the pain when she wakes up, but can't give her any oral medication, because I don't know what the damage in her abdomen is and don't want to stress or further damage her digestive tract if it is injured. She is on a basic saltwater IV drip to help replenish her fluids. She had passed out right before I entered her room, so she couldn't tell me anything about her injuries. Mike will need to fill everyone in on what happened to his mom."

Mike sighs and lifts his head, but doesn't look at anyone directly. He looks exhausted, has red eyes from crying, and fresh tears welling up as he starts speaking. "It was my dad. He didn't mean to hurt her. I mean, it was an accident, but it was still his fault. We were walking toward Medford from Grants Pass and had been on the road for about two weeks already. We were stopping a lot, looking around, and scavenging for food and stuff we needed along the way. If we were going to be outside at nightfall, we climbed up trees, and tied ourselves in to sleep."

"We thought it would be better to wake up to the infected crowded below us than wake up with them chewing on us. Two mornings ago, my mom woke up earlier than my dad and tried to wake him up, but he freaked out. He was totally disoriented and kicked at her, knocking her out of the tree. It was a big oak, and she wasn't strapped in anymore. She just fell. She only hit one branch near the bottom, that's how she got hurt."

He sobs a little and sniffs before wiping his eyes and continuing. "My dad is a bit strange now. He always needed medication before things fell apart, for anxiety, I think, and now he can't get his medicine and he just freaks out sometimes. We started carrying her, just right down the center of Interstate 5 for a few hours. When it got too hard for us to carry her. I left my dad with my mom hidden in some trees and went off to find some help. I had walked about an hour when I ran into your group. They were heading toward Rogue River, so I went back along the road with them until I got to my parents. Tim and Dianne came here with us, to show us how to find the ranch but mostly to help us carry my mom. They had a deer cart that we carried her here in. We arrived this morning, and mom has been in a lot of pain. She keeps passing out. That's pretty much it."

"I think I'm going to check on my mom for a little while," Mike says through tears, gets up, and leaves.

Poor kid, it seems like he has lost both parents, unless Simone can figure some way to fix up Maria. But internal injury is tricky, even for an experienced surgeon. How do you know where to cut and operate or if you repaired all of the spots hemorrhaging?

After Mike is out of the room, I talk to Greg. "I don't see Timothy or Dianne. Are they still here? In fact, I would like to find out why everyone left."

Greg shakes his head, and begins, "They left this morning after they dropped Mike and his parents off. They headed back out to catch up to Arthur's group. Everyone is headed into Grants Pass to look for Emily, Samantha's and Conner's daughter."

Simone and I give a surprised look to each other, and then back to Greg for him to continue.

"We had two young girls show up a couple days ago. They said they had escaped a bad bunch of guys in Grants Pass that had cleared out the Wal-Mart there and made it their base or headquarters. From what the girls said, the group in control there had removed the infected from the area around the store. They also keep a bunch of the infected penned up behind fences and other enclosures around the area to the west. Kind-of like an infected perimeter guard. They will moan and alert the Wal-Mart crew if anyone gets too close.

"The men there are also scouting the area around the store and bringing in anyone they come across, but mostly women. The girls, Julie and Ava, were with a man named, Scott, originally, when they were approached by the Wal-Mart crew. They, according to the girls, they told Scott that he can walk away and live, or he could try to interfere and get shot, but that the girls would be coming back to Wal-Mart with them.

Julie and Ava said they agreed to go with these guys to Wal-Mart so their friend Scott wouldn't get hurt. Once the girls had crossed over to where the men were, the men shot Scott anyway." He sighs and shakes his head again. "They tied up the girls' hands, took them back to the Wal-Mart, and raped them off and on for the last two weeks before they escaped."

"So how did the girls find this place?" I ask.

Greg responds with a surprising, "Samantha's daughter, Emily, told them where it was! That is why everyone left. Emily is locked up with those bastards at the Wal-Mart and apparently remembered how to get here from the one time she came with her parents two years ago."

"She didn't know her parents would be here, but remembered you and your wife were survivalists, or something, and that you might be able to help her and the other girls that are trapped. Julie is sixteen and Ava is seventeen. Their escape idea was Emily's, but she sent those two young girls out instead of her. They said Emily chose them since they were the youngest at the Wal-Mart that had the skills and mindset to be able to make the trip alone."

"Damn," is all I can reply. "So our people are heading out to assault the Wal-Mart crew and try to rescue Samantha's daughter and the other girls? What did they take with them?"

"They took enough ammo to kill all those men and the infected around them three or four times over. They have about a dozen of the gasoline bombs and took a dozen extra glass canning jars to fill from vehicle gas tanks as they get closer to their target. They have most of the grenades, and all of them have body armor. They only took enough food to last about two days, though. That's about it."

Surprised, I ask, "No medical supplies?"

"Oh yes, they took their basic first aid kits with them, and one of your field surgical kits. We all figured they should be able to find more medical supplies if they need them in Grants Pass, either at the Wal-Mart, or other pharmacies and shops. And Eddie, you'll be happy to know that in spite of their bickering, Samantha put Arthur in charge of the group. She is retired Air force and he's a Marine, and you know how they rib each other all the time, but she said she will give him what she thinks is their best strategy, but the actual plan and call to action lies with him. She told us all straight up that she was too emotionally involved in getting her daughter back to lead everyone safely through what they had to do. She wasn't certain she could be within sight of her girl and still keep her mind on the group as a whole. Personally, I think just that thought process proves she would keep everyone safe. What about you?"

Smiling, I say, "Of course she could take care of everyone, Greg. Arthur, and everyone else, including me, know that. The reason she said that is because she doesn't want to be responsible for them. Not during her daughter's rescue. She is probably going to go Rambo on that gang and wants Arthur to keep everyone else safe and in line."

Changing the subject, I turn to look at Randy and Patricia. "I have to ask. Where were you when we came back earlier? I was making a lot of noise out there with my talking and figured someone would come out and diffuse the situation. We thought the ranch had been overtaken by someone when we returned and no one we knew was in sight. And I was more concerned over it when no one came out."

"We heard someone yelling out there and thought the worst," Randy replies, showing he is a bit ashamed.

Patricia continues for him, "We were afraid that the men from Wal-Mart had shown up here, and so we took Katy into the attic to hide. We didn't know that Greg couldn't hear you. We thought he was already dealing with whatever was going on outside."

"I'm sorry," Randy offers.

Randy had a bad winter and isn't doing that well anymore. After losing so many from his family during the big attack, he seemed to age another ten years. His health continued to deteriorate, and then he caught the flu. The fish antibiotics we stockpiled helped him through the illness, but he didn't truly start to recover until he found out his daughter, Rebecca, was pregnant. Even now he hasn't regained his strength, and Patricia needs to help him around.

Mike walks back in, and while he sits down, simply says, "She's still sleeping," referring to his mother.

I'll need to tell him what happened with his father, but first, I have to find out what Greg is going to do. "Greg? Jessica? Are you two and Lilly planning on heading out after them?"

Greg shrugs his shoulders in a question, and Jessica speaks up, "Greg might, but Lilly and I aren't going to go. At first, the whole idea of getting back at those men and saving the girls was thrilling. It felt like a chance for us good guys to right a wrong. But all day, Lilly and I have been discussing our own struggles and run-ins with men just like them. The problems we had until we ran into Greg and then made it here. I'm ready, even Lilly is ready to defend against, even go out and challenge hordes of the infected, and take back our world. But I'm not ready to go into battle against regular men yet. I'm not ready to take the chance that they will win and make me their slave. I think I would freeze when I need to act."

Lilly drops her head and starts to cry, then gets up and leaves the room. Jessica gets up and says she will make sure Lilly is all right.

Mike was silently watching the exchange, and when the two women are out of the room for a bit, he says, "I don't get it. How can they not want to go out and help those other girls? Even if they have a fear of men like that, shouldn't their sense of revenge or compassion for other women like themselves help override their fears?"

I look at Greg, and say, "I think you should tell him Lilly's story. Mike, it might help you understand where she is at right now."

Greg starts to tell a brief version of how he came to meet Lilly. "Lilly had things rough out there. I mean, I understand this is a war, and everyone is having a difficult time trying to survive, but she just turned seventeen a few weeks ago, and her story is a nightmare within this nightmare. She was kept as a prisoner by men exactly like this Wal-Mart gang. She had survived the first few weeks of the outbreak with her mom, dad, and a neighbor named Franklin, in Franklin's house. While their supplies were dwindling, they thought they could still hang on. Finally, an approaching fire that was consuming the neighborhood forced them out of the house. She said her mom was killed by an infected a week later.

"They had to uproot every few days because of scarce resources in that particular location, and just entered the living room of a new house, when her mom was attacked. Her mom was bitten on the neck and passed out quickly from the blood loss. They covered her wound and kept pressure on it, but she started turning almost immediately. Lilly's mom opened her eyes and stared at them, and they all jumped back. As soon as her mother started to shift her weight to begin turning over, they all ran out of that house, and closed the door behind them.

"A few days after her mother was infected, Franklin killed her father. It was an argument over sending her father out to get more supplies, but she knows it was about Franklin wanting to spend *time* with her. Her father felt that was the case as well, and made the mistake of turning his back on Franklin to tell Lilly to get her backpack, so they could leave.

"She said the whole scene was in slow motion after that, and hearing her describe it is chilling. She saw the baseball bat arch down toward her father's head, heard the terrible cracking sound of impact, and saw a look of sadness on her father's face. She said her dad looked angry until the bat hit, then his eyes looked directly into hers, and his face changed to sadness. Not shock or pain, just a look of sadness, as if the last thought he had was that he knew he hadn't protected his little girl.

"After her father was killed, Franklin kept Lilly as his sex slave and punching bag. He kept her for himself until they happened to run into another man whom Franklin had known before the collapse, and then they shared her. She had little hope for escape but through death. She escaped them only when they began to kill each other. Franklin must have been bitten in one of their encounters, but hid the bite from his partner and her. He was a slow turner. That night, Franklin turned, and when Lilly was being raped by this other man, Franklin came in behind them and bit the man on the back. She escaped while they fought.

"She survived on her own by just scavenging and had avoided everyone she had seen until she saw Jessica. Jessica was the first woman Lilly had encountered on her own. She followed Jessica and only came out to her after following and observing her for two days and making sure that she wasn't with a man. Jessica and Lilly found and entrusted me much the same way.

"We arrived here five months-ago after Eddie and his group saved us from another group of men that had captured Jessica." Greg pauses as he thinks how to explain the rest. "Lilly is having a difficult time adjusting to being here. She knows it is secure here, but also understands that no place is truly safe anymore. And she will have trust issues with men probably for the rest of her life. You're fourteen, Mike, and you have your own difficult things that you are dealing with right now. Just try to understand that we all take the problems and horrors of this life differently. We aren't equal in how we deal with stuff, is what I mean. Does that make it any clearer?"

"Yeah, I guess so. I can understand why she's afraid to face men. I just figured her anger at them would be stronger," Mike says.

Now it is my turn to tell Mike about why I shot his father. "Mike. Lilly has had six months to work through what happened to her in her mind. She is passed the initial anger stage where she wants to just get revenge and will come back to it in time. The fact that she sat on the sofa next to you as a strange male is amazing and to me means she is stronger than ever.

"You, however, are going to have to deal with some of your problems now. I need to talk to you about why I shot your father. Simone, can you bring the kids in here if they aren't asleep?" We all sit in silence until Simone returns carrying Benjamin, followed by Olivia, and Hannah. "Amelia and William are sleeping," Simone says.

Once everyone is sitting down, I start telling Mike about how we approached the house, and our concerns over some type of takeover. How we circled the house and my approach to his father. I gave him every detail I could remember about my actions and his father's as well. I finish the story by saying, "So I am ultimately responsible for your father's death."

Hannah pipes in, "But I shot him as well."

Great! I think. *My child's honesty could draw the wrath of a vengeful stranger.*

"Yes, Hannah. You shot him as well, but he wouldn't have survived my initial shot anyway. Not with our current medical abilities. And you shot him to defend your father. I shot him to defend myself. Your action is more justifiable."

Greg then exclaims, "I would like to add that while I was only there for a few seconds, no shots were fired until your father grabbed Eddie's gun."

Mike has been silent and attentive throughout the telling of his father's death, nodding occasionally.

"Mike, here is the deal, and it probably won't sound too good, but it's all that I got. You can stay with us as long as you need if you want, but only as long as you aren't a threat to me or my family.

"I know your mother is hurt badly and unfortunately it seems like she won't be getting better. You are welcome to stay here until you find a better place to survive or a more appealing one. We will treat you like an equal, but might also expect more of you in return. Everyone here has to do something to help secure the place, or clean, or grow food, at least something.

"You and I will have our times when you will hate me if you stay, and I'll need you to just talk to me about it so we can work through it. I don't want any festering anger toward me building up in you, all right? I've probably said enough for now, is there anything you want to say or ask?"

We are all quiet as we wait for Mike to digest what he has heard and process it into everything else he has to deal with. "I'm not sure how I feel," Mike starts. "I mean, I know I should feel terrible that my dad is dead. I should hate you for killing him. No matter why you did it. I just feel kind of numb right now. I'm still angry with my dad for what happened to mom, so I guess that has something to do with it. I know you guys think my mom won't make it, but I'm not ready to give up on her yet. I don't know what I want to do, but I think that choice will be up to her when she gets better."

I think to myself, *We'll have to deal with this later then.*

I ask, "Is there anything else someone wants to say to Mike or find out from me?" We are all quiet until Simone tells Mike he should go in and sit with his mother. She hands Benjamin to me and heads to put Amelia and William to bed. Mike follows her out of the room.

I turn back to face Greg. "Greg, I want to talk about Samantha and Arthur again. How many men did these girls say were at Wal-Mart?"

Greg frowns, "About forty."

"Forty? I can't believe it!"

Greg nods at the look of surprise on my face.

"The girls' said thirty maybe forty, which to me means forty maybe more. They know for certain that they counted thirty different faces and were pretty sure there were other men there that didn't come near the section they were barricaded in. The girls, including Emily, had heard other men's voices that they didn't recognize from their *visitors* or their guards. So, apparently there are some men there that aren't into raping the girls, that's a positive."

I just grunt, and add, "Unless there is another section where they keep boys locked up for the others."

Greg shakes his head, and says, "I thought that too and mentioned it to Julie and Ava, but they told me about two of the other girls that had their brothers with them when they were captured by the roving patrols. They said their brothers were too young to be effective fighters, but they would have been attractive to any guy that was into that. Those girls' brothers are being held in a different part of the Wal-Mart, and they get to see each other occasionally. One of the men said it keeps the girls motivated to be accommodating during the visits to know something might happen to a family member. And according to the girls' brothers, nothing has been done to them."

I just shake my head. "Greg, I don't like it. I bet the girls' told their brothers the same thing. That nothing was happening to them. Is there anything else that they said that sounded strange, like there might be other people there? Being held captive, I mean?"

"Well," Greg says slowly with distaste, "they play music as a distraction. The men take them to the bathrooms together at different times, and when they do, they play music on a radio. But the music is turned on at the opposite side of the store, where the girls' brothers are being held. They play the music to keep one group from hearing what is happening to the other, or so they can't hear the men's movements, or the occasional comment.

"Julie mentioned she thinks she knows when the other captives are being taken to the bathroom, because the radio is turned on in front of the girls' barricade. And they know when some of the girls are going to get raped because they turn on three radios. One at the front of the store by the bathrooms, where they take the girls to rape them, and one by each barricade to make sure no one can hear anything but the music.

"The only other thing is that, they are using some type of walkie-talkie when they are out on patrol."

I nod silently and think for a while, trying to absorb everything. "Did Samantha or Arthur take a radio with them, or did you arrange to meet them at a specific place and time?"

"They said they would stage their main area at the cemetery to the east of Wal-Mart. There is some tree cover there. They have those GMRS radios from here, but we didn't arrange any specific time to meet up or call each other."

Simone walks back in and sits down next to me. Benjamin climbs out of my lap and into hers.

"What did I miss?" she asks.

"Well, I have an idea on how we can help free Emily and the other people that are being held there. Unless Arthur and Samantha have figured out a way to do it and are on their way back already, but I doubt it.

"Greg says there are supposed to be forty men there, possibly more. More people than just the girls are being held hostage, and the groups are being held separately. There isn't a way for Arthur and those people to blast their way through so many armed men and survive. And even if they did manage to live through the assault, there is no guarantee that the hostages would. The kind of fight necessary to win against that number of people in a building the size of Wal-Mart would likely kill everyone inside. Plus, those assholes holding everyone would probably kill the hostages anyway, just to make sure the truth about what they were doing died with their victims."

Simone looks concerned, and asks, "So what do you think we can do? If it is so hopeless for Arthur, Conner, and the entire group from our ranch, then what can we do that won't just get us killed as well?"

"We can bluff," I say with a shrug and a smile. "The good news is these guys have cleared out the area around the Wal-Mart. To what extent, we don't know, but if they are sending out patrols with only three or four men, then they aren't too scared of coming in contact with an infected group. The bad news is Grants Pass had a population of thirty thousand people, so if these guys have been able to clear out the infected that survived the freeze, then they are too bad ass to do anything about directly. And even if they are a bunch of losers, they have at least forty men, to our what, twenty-five people?"

"Then how can you seriously consider going, Eddie? We just got back ourselves, and you nearly died! Heading out after them is a death sentence going up against so many men, and let's not forget the infected runners!"

"I think they may have figured out a way to trick the infected, maybe even the runners. Greg says the girls gave a description of infected being kept in fenced enclosures around Wal-Mart's perimeter. Quite possibly, if any wandering infected sees these other ones just standing there, they might assume there are no humans or animals to eat in the area.

"These guys may be bastards, but there are some smart or creative bastards among them. With this tactic, they can keep their home base relatively attack free, and venture out to slowly kill off the local infected population. That is what I think is more likely than their having finished off the entire Grants Pass population in these past eight months.

"As for the bluff, if our people haven't attacked yet, or made their presence known to the Wal-Mart group, we might make it work. We can use several boxes of those laser pointers that we have to tape about three to each person's gun and spread out around the entrance to the store. We will need at least two people covering the back, but the sides and front can be covered by the rest of our group spread out. If we have twenty guns, we can tape three lasers to each of them. That will give the impression of at least sixty snipers taking aim at the place.

"The real bluff will be in letting these guys think they are eavesdropping on our conversation and make it sound like we have a large attack force surrounding the area. This is all with the presumption that their group is monitoring radio traffic and that Samantha and Arthur have found out which band they communicate on. If we do a good job with our acting then we can pull off a good enough ruse to get them out without a fight. If not, then we aren't really any worse off than we already are."

Simone touches my arm, and quietly asks, "What about the kids, Eddie? Do you think just you and I will go?"

I nod.

She asks, "If you think it is so bad after what we have been through to have to leave the kids here, then why would we get involved?"

I'm surprised that she is asking me this. Simone has been my anchor the whole time we have been married and amazingly strong when I am floundering about. I guess my near death experience has hit her harder than I imagined. Still, we have worked our marriage always from a point of direct honesty, so I can't play nice to save her feelings.

"Simone, it's probably that bad, or worse. This isn't one of the silly action movies we have on the shelf, where we can run in there outnumbered two to one and expect to save everybody, and keep ourselves alive. I would guess we have a twenty percent chance of pulling this off, maybe just five percent to save the people inside. The odds are one percent or less to do it without at least one person on our side dying.

"If we have to fight, then it will probably be quite a firefight with us having to retreat, and escape their capture. That is why we can't have the kids with us. If we need to run, we will literally be running for our lives to get out of there. We can't move slowly and watch out for the hidden infected, we will have to move quickly, and hope we avoid all of the runners and slower infected that will be attracted to the sound of gunshots. Hannah could make it with us, but she needs to be here to take care of the others if we don't or can't make it back.

"The other bad thing about this, is if any of us gets caught and tortured, or even if Emily gets tortured, eventually these guys might find out where this property is. That is also why we need to get involved, Simone. These men have made a stronghold for themselves and will continue to expand the area they control. We may be out in the mountains and the woods here, but it's only about two hours to Grants Pass by bicycle, and half an hour by car if they had one running.

"We can't let men like that be the restart to civilization in the area. The longer they stay intact there, the more people like them they will add to their numbers, and the stronger they will become. They are a threat to us already, as much as if not more than the infected. If it looks like we have to fight them, then I'll use the gas bombs to burn them out."

Greg stands up and starts pacing back and forth, and says, "I didn't put all the numbers together like you. What do we do here at the ranch if those men beat all of you?"

"If they make it through all of us, there won't be that many of them left. You have a lot of buildings to hide in and plenty of guns and ammo to finish anyone off that comes along."

Greg asks, "When do you think you will leave, in the morning?"

I shake my head, "No, not that long, probably in a few hours. I need get some rest, I still feel disoriented from the fever, and Simone hasn't slept at all since this morning."

"Yesterday morning," Simone corrects me, since it is just after midnight.

"Why don't you go to bed right now, Simone? I would like to leave in three hours so we can get there in the early morning before the Wal-Mart group is likely to send out patrols. Greg and I will get the bikes and supplies ready, and I should be able to get two hours of sleep as well," I say.

She nods and carries a sleeping Benjamin to her room.

Greg asks, "What do you want to take with you?"

I stand and think for a moment. "I think we should get all of the bikes ready, or at least the ones I'm not taking, get them ready tomorrow to make a hasty escape to the far side of the property. If anyone shows up after we are gone that you don't recognize, you need to shoot them on sight. We will not send any of the hostages here without an escort, so if someone shows up, man or woman, assume the worst and shoot them, okay?"

I can see Greg hesitate so I need to make it clear to him what is at stake. "Listen to me, Greg. If those men find their way here, they aren't just going to move in and share this house with you. And they won't just kill you either. They will rape everyone and keep them as their slaves just like they are doing at the store. If I make it through this and return here to find someone inside this fence that I don't know or didn't send, I will shoot them, and then I will shoot you, do you understand?"

Greg chuckles.

I smile at him even though I mean what I say. "I'm glad to see you relax a little Greg, but I am serious." And I motion for him to look at Patricia, who gives him a look, and a nod that makes him stiffen up and turn back to face me.

"I have never left my kids where I cannot personally protect them, and if I feel you have compromised their safety in any way, I will make you pay. You know what I am capable of, so you do understand where I am coming from, right?"

Greg nods, and says, "Yes, I understand. You don't have to worry about it. I'll make sure Jessica and Lilly know what might be coming. You can count on them to make sure no one gets in here to hurt the children." He pauses, and then ads, "What do you need me to do?"

"Are all the bikes still loaded?" I ask, and he nods. "Then I need you to take the supplies and stack them by the house. I am going to get what I think we need for this trip and pile it by the front door. I have less to do, so when I am finished, I'll help you unload, and then get the new supplies loaded up. Sound good?"

"Actually Eddie, I think I'll just unload your and Simone's bikes, and then help you with the supplies. I can finish unloading everything else after we get your bikes loaded and you get to bed."

I nod in reply, and we head out to get things done.

What a crazy life this is. I'm so stiff I can barely walk, and I get to make a two hour bike ride through an infected land in the middle of the night to face overwhelming odds in battle. How wonderful.

I write out a checklist of what I think we should take: Zip-tie handcuffs, night vision goggles, two-way radios, boxes of laser pointers, electrical tape, trauma kits, regular med kit, guns, ammo, and some food and water. Perhaps a Bradley armored vehicle would go nicely with this plan. Where can I find one of those about now?

*

I just finished getting all the supplies out by the bikes with Greg, and he is loading them up for me so I can get some more sleep. We didn't talk much, just questions of, "Where is this?" and, "How much do you want of that?" Greg and I both know the odds of this turning out well are minimal. I will have to figure out how to put a tremendous amount of fear into these guys at Wal-Mart in order to get the hostages out without a fight. Maybe some kind of idea will hit me after I sleep or on the bike ride down there.

As I climb into the bed, I can't help but smile with delight at how soft it feels, even through the numbness. My body has spent a week on the road and in various states of physical abuse at the hands of the infected. I don't feel pain since I am still heavily infected with the parasite, but my body still interprets and sends comforting feelings like this soft bed, and for that I am truly grateful. I wonder what those people that turn feel, do they feel comfort, or is that as lost as pain is to them? As I quickly drift off, I contemplate the horrors that people must experience after they turn, but before the fever wipes out their human mind.

CHAPTER TWELVE
THE TRIP TO WAL-MART

"Eddie. Eddie. You need to wake up."
I hear a voice echoing in the distance, and it takes a few seconds looking around to register Simone standing in the doorway calling to me. "Eddie, it's time for us to go," Simone says. It takes some effort to get up due to the continued stiffness in my body. I am a thankful again that I cannot feel the pain that should accompany such tense muscles as I get out of bed.

"I'm up, Simone. I'll meet you outside in just a minute." She gives me a smile and a small wave and disappears back into the hall. I love my wife. She is a good woman. Good enough to put up with me and strong enough to keep me in check. If she felt this trip wasn't something we should do, she would have told me, and I would have listened. We work well together that way, I mean listening to each other. She has never been the type of woman that asks me how her butt looks in certain pants, and I have never been one to lie about what I see, so she hasn't encouraged me to lie, and I haven't felt a need to.

As I walk down the hall to head downstairs, I look into the kids' room and smile at their lumpy forms under the blankets. It bothers me to leave them here while Simone and I head out, but we have never specifically looked for a fight before. We have always tried concealment and stealth to avoid any issues with regular people. Even the infected we haven't intentionally sought out yet, just taking them out as we encounter them.

What really bothers me now is realizing that this far into the end of the world, hiding out is no longer going to help us survive. More and more we are going to have to seek out trouble and try to stamp it out before it is strong enough to seek us out. That goes for the infected as well as human kind. The runner that tackled and bit me must have been following the two slower infected, and was staying hidden. It was employing its own sneaking strategy and using the slow infected to flush out a human, like me, to sink its teeth into. I just hope we don't have any radioactive infected people from the East start showing up here.

My thoughts come to an abrupt end as I step out of the door and see four bicycles loaded and six people waiting for me. Simone, Hannah, and Mike are standing by the bikes. Greg and Lilly are just off to the side talking with them.

"Who wants to fill me in?" I ask as I walk up to my bike.

Simone replies, "Hannah thinks she would be more help as an extra rifle than sitting here as a babysitter. Mike... Mike's mother passed away in her sleep a short while after we went to bed. I told him I am not comfortable with him staying at the ranch when we are leaving our other kids behind. He isn't sure that he wants to come with us, but I'm not willing to have him stay here right now."

I look Hannah in the eyes to question her coming along, and then back at Simone. "Okay," is all I can say.

"Mike, you understand my wife's reasoning, right?"

"Yes, Mr. Keeper. I do."

"If you come with us, you can go your own way any time you want all right, but you won't be able to return here without us. You don't have to deal with these guys at Wal-Mart, even if you make it all the way there with us, okay?" I ask. He just nods. I also feel better with him coming along than leaving him here with our smaller children. "I'm sorry about your mother, Mike."

Lilly and Greg just stand there looking at all of us. He has his arm around Lilly's shoulder in a protective hug. I survey the group and wish we had a bunch of ex-military people on the ranch with us. It would sure help right now... My mind drifts off with that last thought, and I know what we can do. I've figured out our bluff.

"Simone, Greg, come with me. We need to get the military uniforms from the bunk house attic."

When we return, we start loading the boots and uniforms into the trailers, where there is some space left. "Lilly," I start, "I have a pretty good idea how we're going to handle the guys at Wal-Mart when we get there, and I'm feeling pretty confident now that my idea might work. The thing is there is a good chance that we will be bringing a bunch of people back here once this is done. The women aren't the only ones being held captive, and there may be other people with the bad guys that may be coming here as well.

"I won't let any of the men that have been involved in the rapes or murders survive this ordeal, but there might be others who have roles that are questionable, they might not have participated in anything but let the others do what they were doing just so they themselves could have a safe place to stay. Are you getting what I'm driving at, Lilly?" I ask.

Lilly shakes her head, and says forcefully, "I don't think you should bring anyone back here but the hostages. Only the people we can absolutely trust."

"I have to agree with her," says Greg.

I nod, and reply, "Look, I know what you're saying, and I agree. I will do my best to make sure no one involved in the rapes makes it here. What I mean is, some might slip through, and it will be up to all of us to figure out when they arrive if someone shouldn't stay here, okay?

"We should also remember what Jessica told us about the girl that was killed in front of her. She feels guilty that she didn't step in, didn't fight to protect that girl, but we all know that she would have ended up dead as well, or at least badly beaten. There was no way for her to overcome those three men and stop what was happening. In a perfect world, sure, you fight and cry for help, but in this one, sometimes people have to make horrible decisions to survive.

"Jessica survived and quite possibly there are other people at that Wal-Mart that have been doing the same thing." I look at both of them in the eyes and know they understand what I am thinking. "I promise you both, that if I am able to bring anyone back, none of them will be the rapists or killers, and I will let the hostages tell us who they are."

Lilly steps away from Greg, stops two steps in front of me, and asks, "And what if all the hostages are dead?"

"Then everyone else will die too." I smile while I say it. I know it isn't the appropriate thing to do, and it must make me look a little evil as I reply to her question, but it makes me feel good to think about killing all of those bastards. I look at Greg, "We have a good chance of pulling this off if Arthur and Samantha haven't made contact with the Wal-Mart group yet. Wish us luck?"

Sarcastically, Greg replies, "How about, break a leg?" We both smile at each other, shake hands and I walk around and sit on my bike.

"Mike, we are going to be riding at a good pace, not racing, but not a leisurely speed either. Simone and I will alternate between being the lead and rear bike since we have the night vision goggles. There is enough light out here to ride safely in the middle of the road, but we still need to look out for obstacles—like branches—or perhaps an infected that's out for a stroll. We're all responsible for each other while together. If you need to stop or rest, hoot like an owl. And don't try and push yourself too hard. If you need a break or an easier pace, let us know. We will all need to rest as well at some point. If you see possible danger, bark like a dog and point but don't stop, the person in the rear will look with their goggles.

"Reactions to danger from the side and rear will come from the rear rider. The calls we give are simple like, *Bikes stop, shoot left* or *Bikes faster, infected at r*ear. Got it so far?"

He nods.

"Okay, so never pass the lead bike unless a switch or rear infected has been called. When we switch from front to rear, a switch is called out, and the front rider speeds out ahead of everyone, stops and looks behind at the group as they come up to pass. The rear rider speeds up to get in front, the stopped driver hops on, and catches up after everyone has passed them.

"Still following me?"

He nods again.

"It is pretty much the same scenario with a rear infected call, except the stopped bike in the lead would shoot the pursuing infected. That's about it I think, any questions?"

Mike says, "Um yes, why don't we just call out, *I need a break,* or *I see danger,* instead of hooting and barking?"

"First, because Simone and I need to look around with our goggles, to check everything out. There may be people and not the infected out there. If a sound is going to travel to potential bad guys besides the infected, I want it to be animal sounds, not voices. Second, it's just more fun that way."

Simone and I put on our goggles, and the four of us roll our bikes with their saddle packs and trailers out the gate, where we hop on and ride to the road. We ride for fifty minutes in the cool night air before we take our first break. It is just after 3 a.m., and we are on Wards Creek Road about forty minutes ride away from the east edge of Rogue River.

It's nice to have those goggles off my head. It is bizarre to see the world as a bright green, fuzzy landscape. And the lack of depth perception definitely takes getting used to when riding on a bike.

The only issue we ran into so far was a tree that had fallen onto the road. We stopped and checked the area to make sure it wasn't a trap or bandit stop, but it looked like it was just time for this tree to come down. The ground had been eroded from a small stream, and the whole root base had ripped up out of the ground. It was just dumb luck that it happened in between Arthur's group coming through and ours.

"How are you doing, Mike?" I ask.

"I'm doing all right," he says, casually. "It actually feels really good to be out here. Like I am finally doing something positive and not just running."

Even though the night sky is dim, I can see him drop his head slightly, as if he is embarrassed. "Mike, there is nothing wrong with being happy that you're alive. The whole point in this struggle is to survive."

He just nods.

Simone and I look at the map to confirm where I think we are and let Hannah and Mike know the plan.

"We have another forty-five minutes to make it to the edge of Rogue River," I say. "Once we get there we'll have to walk the bikes along the edge of town and be much more careful."

Simone adds, "We also have about fifteen minutes left on this road before we start coming to houses right off the road. We will have to ride a little slower and be prepared to really peddle hard to get out of the way if anyone or anything is hanging out by the houses. At this hour it's much more likely a thing, so really keep an eye out. The good news is, we have been this way several times and have already cleared out the locals that were outside by their old houses.

"Let's all get going and remember, if we stop to shoot an infected, step off and away from your bike. If there are more of these runners out there, and they are following a slower infected, you don't want to get tangled in your bike if you need to move quickly."

*

We bike for another thirty minutes before I pull our group to a stop. There is a line of houses just off the road to the right, about three hundred yards ahead of us. I can hear the moan from an infected coming from up there. We can all hear it now that we've stopped, moaning, and a dull banging.

Mike asks, "What do we do?"

"This is going to slow us down, but we need to clear this spot. If we let that thing keep moaning, it will eventually attract others, if there aren't others already on the way. Plus, it found something alive that it can't get to. We have to make sure it isn't a person that's trapped.

"Hannah and Mike, I want you two to climb up a tree. Each on a different one, I don't want you both getting trapped in the same place. It's too dark for you to walk around these trees and bushes without night vision. A runner could be on top of you before you could shiver."

"Can they see in the dark better than we can?" Mike asks.

I shrug in the dark, aware that he can't see my response. "Not that I'm aware of, but we aren't going to take any chances. The runners are smart. I think they can lay traps and stay concealed. If I was a runner, I would be hiding behind a bush waiting to see if any tasty flesh walks up to deal with this moaning infected down the road."

"Enough talking, boys," Simone chides. "Mike. Hannah. Do what he said, get in a tree. Eddie, let's get going, I want to get back on those bikes as quick as we can."

I nod, grab my baseball bat off the bike and we move toward the sound, but at opposite angles. We split into a V shape where the sound is at the 12 o'clock. Simone is heading at 11 o'clock out into the road, and I am at 1 o'clock heading toward the houses. I'm scanning left and right, taking a few steps, stop and listen, then move again. Simone is doing the same, and we are both keeping each other in view. Once we are about twenty-five yards apart, Simone signals to me to change direction, and we both head directly toward the sound. The banging is coming from a fifth wheel trailer parked in a driveway about seventy yards in front of us. The larger problem is the banging is coming from the opposite side than we are on, probably where the door is.

As we work our way forward, I keep re-living that runner's tackle. Every time a breeze blows through the branches around me, it makes me think I'm about to get hit by the real life boogeyman. I need to pull it together. My little psych out job is just going to get me or Simone killed. Okay, that did it. I focus on Simone, and it brings me back.

Just twenty more yards to go, but I have a hedge I need to get past without making any noise. I am right next to the house, and the hedge runs from the road right up to some rose bushes next to the wall. Who the hell plants a hedge like this? They wouldn't even be able to walk around their house if they wanted to.

Simone is looking at me and shrugs with her hands out, in a, *what is taking you so long,* gesture. I just hold my hand out in a stop signal and decide to start squeezing through the hedge with my back against the rose bushes. I give little sideways pushes and try to time them with the infected banging on the fifth wheel door. Unfortunately, this infected wasn't a musician in its former life, because it can't keep a beat for shit. I'm only halfway through when it skips a beat and hears me, or at least it gets distracted by something. The banging and moaning stop, and I can almost feel its gaze curve around the back edge of the trailer to lock right on me. Luckily, the meal in the trailer is a bigger draw than I am, and the uneven pummeling of the trailer continues.

I force my way through in the first two beats of the uneven melody being played around the corner and ready the bat as I walk to the edge. I have to walk past the open front door of the house in order to reach the trailer. As I side step past the opening, I look inside to make sure no surprise visitor is waiting for me, and see keys dangling in the door. It looks like someone wasn't expecting there to be anyone at home, or at least not expecting infected when they opened the door.

When I look around the side, I'm reminded of the real devastating part of this disease. It isn't one infected but two. Two older creatures are taking their turn weakly pounding on the door of the trailer. They must have been in their late sixties and just relaxing at home in their night clothes when they were turned. Whoever came to check on them is probably hiding in the trailer, unable or unwilling to end the lives of someone they once knew or loved.

The person in the trailer has been trapped in there for quite some time. The two older people have their arms and foreheads bloody from their relentless attempts to get at the fresh meat they know is locked inside. I figure I will be able to take both of them with the bat. Since they don't have the strength to break open the cheap door they put on trailers, then they won't be able to overpower me.

My learning curve in what these things are capable of always seems to be one huge step behind what it should be. With my first crunching step out from the back of the trailer, both of the infected heads snap in my direction.

Shit. Shit. Shit! These aren't regular infected. I just gave my position away to two runners. Simone and the dark night are the only things that save me from my latest mistake. From her location on the opposite side of the road, these two couldn't hear her. She moved farther down the road so she could have an angled firing position, instead of being directly opposite from me as I came around the trailer.

When their heads snapped toward the sound of my foot on the gravel, they couldn't see me in the darkness, and since my surprise at their fast movement is keeping me locked in place, no movement gives my position away.

Simone shoots and blows out the brains of the man onto the side of the fifth wheel, giving it a grotesque new paint job. The old lady snaps around to the sound of Simone's gun, and I step forward quickly, raising my bat over my head as I go. These damn runners are freaking me out. Her hearing must be exceptional, and the unnatural jerky quickness of her movements sends a chill up my spine as I bring my bat down. She turns again toward me before impact. My bat just bounces off the left side of her head but hits with a heavy *crack* on her shoulder, knocking her down. I swing the bat down on her head two more times as she is trying to get back up and reach for me. It finally caves in and ends her fight. My skin is crawling.

Simone runs across the road toward me, and says, "Gun, Gun. Eddie get your gun ready." I think my lack of sleep and that fever are really starting to affect my actions. I know better than just standing here in unfamiliar territory after a gun has been fired. If there are any other infected here that can get to us, they will definitely come to the noise we just made.

"These were more runners, Simone. Did you see how they were moving when they heard me?" These were the only other runners I have encountered, but I am right about there being more of them. Also, they had quick movements like jerky puppets on a string. It's as if this parasite couldn't get complete control over the bodies.

Simone and I step back to back and move out into the middle of the road. It will be easier to see or hear an infected approaching out in the open than if we're standing next to a huge trailer.

Simone says, "I'm sorry I shot him, Eddie. It was just so creepy the way they were moving. Why do these things keep changing?"

I'm just shaking my head back and forth, and a shiver runs up my spine again while contemplating the question. I half-heartedly say, "Maybe everyone behaves differently when they change?" I know that isn't the case though. We saw enough of how these things behave to know this is something new. We haven't seen or heard from anyone else about the infected running or about fast jerky movements and dexterity.

One runner was chance. Two more runners and them being together means they are changing. Hopefully our knowledge about what's out here can stay just slightly ahead of the changes to this damn parasite, or we're doomed.

We scan the area for a few minutes before I finally say, "I don't think any new infected will show up after the racket those two were making. Any more in the area would have already been here by now. Let's check if someone is alive in that trailer. I think you should say hello, Simone. People respond better to unknown women than unknown men."

Simone agrees, and we walk over to the trailer. I pull the bodies of the runners slightly off to the side so we can reach the door. I'm starting to feel bad for this older couple again. Now that they are silent and still, I again picture them as they must have been in life. They were probably happy and enjoying retirement. I step back to the trailer, and Simone knocks on the door.

"Hello? Is there someone in there?" Simone asks.

The fifth wheel shifts slightly, and I can hear someone moving to the door.

A man's voice calls out, "Who's out there, is it safe?"

I figure it is my turn to talk, "Hello, my name is Eddie, and my wife Simone is here with me."

"Hello," Simone says again. "We've stopped the two... infected people that were trying to get to you. We aren't a threat to you if you aren't a threat to us. Are you okay, and do you need any help?"

The man inside asks, "Are my parents dead?"

This makes me nervous because it could go in many different directions and few of them pleasant. These were the man's parents, and no matter what they became, it is a hard thing to deal with. In the early weeks of the outbreak there were lots of healthy people killing other healthy people in revenge for a murdered family member. Of course, the family member killed was always infected, but people couldn't see it that way. They refused to acknowledge what was happening to their loved ones. The compassion people have for their own family is one of the things that helped this disease spread so rapidly. It only takes one hidden infected person in an apartment to take out a whole building full of people. Hell, even today, even with me at times I have a hard time saying that these things are no longer thinking people. I understand completely why people have a hard time changing their understanding of reality.

I breathe in deep, and reply, "If these two elderly people were your parents, then yes, they are dead. I'm sorry for your loss, mister. What's your name? Are you hurt?" The door cracks open and a man looks out with a questioning expression on his face.

"We are wearing night vision goggles since you can barely see us," I add.

Finally the man starts talking, "My name is Ruben. This is my parents' house. I'm...I think I'm okay. But..." Ruben hesitates and looks back into the fifth wheel. "Well, my wife has been bitten." Tears start to roll from Ruben's eyes.

"How long ago was she bitten?" Simone asks.

Ruben replies that he isn't exactly sure. "We got here about ten p.m. from what I can figure, and she was bitten as soon as we opened the door."

"That's about five hours," I say. "I'm assuming she hasn't turned?"

Very quickly he adds, "No, no she isn't one of them....yet." His tears start flowing again.

"Did you know some people are immune Ruben?" I ask. Obviously, he doesn't the way his head pops up. "Look, can we come in for a second, so we can turn on a light and see each other and talk?"

We all step into the fifth wheel. Simone and I take off our goggles and turn on a flashlight, which is enough light to illuminate the hall of the trailer.

"This is my wife, Maria," Ruben says, and then continues to his wife, "Did you hear what they said, Mel? Some people are immune! That's probably you, why you haven't changed yet."

You can see a sad smile of disbelief on her face, and then she lowers her head, and says, "These people just told you that so you would let them in here, Ruben. No one is immune, and they know they have to kill me before I kill you."

Ruben quickly turns toward Simone and me with a look of worry on his face. Before Ruben can start fighting us out of the trailer, I say, "Maria, It's true. I'm immune. I was bitten on my arm yesterday."

She lifts her head as she starts crying, and through the sobs, says, "Don't lie to me! I know what I will become. We've seen it with everyone we know that was bitten."

I roll up my sleeve, undo the bandage, and show them the bite mark. Once they see this, a new round of tears flows from both of them. I know the feeling they are having. When I woke up from my bite and wasn't infected, it was like I had just been born. Nothing is as beautiful or exhilarating as facing certain death and emerging unscathed on the other side. Well, relatively unscathed.

"Simone, I think you should explain to Ruben and Maria what they are going to be facing with the fever, and I will go back and get Hannah and Mike, okay?" Simone agrees and I step out of the trailer and put my goggles back on. As I walk back to the trees up the road, I can't help but think about what Ruben was doing. He was just waiting for his wife to turn and let her bite him. She wasn't tied up, and they know people change. Of course, maybe he doesn't have any rope in there and was just stuck between the active infected outside and his wife as a potential infected inside. Either way, it's a horrible way to spend five hours, thinking that the woman you love will die in your arms.

I scan around one more time before I call out "Marco." "Polo," I hear in return. "Hannah. Mike. It's okay to come down. Hannah, your mom is talking to some survivors up ahead in a trailer. There were two infected, they were the man's parents and had pinned them down in the trailer. That is what you heard your mother shoot at." I lift up my goggles and shine a light at the trees to help them climb down.

They walk up to me, and Mike asks, "Marco Polo?"

"Well, yeah. Can you think of a better way to let someone know you aren't infected when you're walking up on them?"

"No, actually, it's really smart. I get it. And it's totally non-threatening,"

"Okay guys, let's grab the bikes, and get down to the trailer so we can head out."

"I'll be right there. I just need to use the bathroom," Mike says.

"We'll wait, but if you get stuck somewhere again like a tree, you should probably go while you're up there or you'll just make yourself miserable."

Hannah and I get to the bikes, and I put Mike's bike on top of my trailer. "Hannah, I'm glad you came with us, but I need you to know that there isn't a very good chance of this ending well. We're going against some pretty bad guys, and they outnumber us by about two or three to one. If we end up having to fight them, some or all of us will die. I'll need you to get back to the ranch and your brothers and sisters as quick as you can if fighting starts, okay? Do not stay to help if I tell you to go. Do you understand?"

"I understand, but I'll make my own decision on how things are going."

"You know, Hannah, I would feel more comfortable if you would just lie to me sometimes and agree to do what I say. Why you had to inherit both your mom's and my independence streak I just don't understand."

"I'm back," Mike says. "All right, Mike, you grab Simone's bike."

As we walk down the road, Mike asks, "Are the people you found coming with us?"

"No, the man's wife has been bitten, but it looks like she might be immune like me. She got attacked about five hours ago, so she'll be going through the fever soon. We'll check on them on the way back if we make it."

"You sound pretty pessimistic for someone that has survived this long in an apocalypse," Mike offers.

I give a sad nod and start explaining my views to Mike as we approach the trailers. "Mike, I never really liked the negative aspects of humanity. People can be very good, kind, and giving in the best and worst of circumstances. But the opposite is true as well. Some people live to be vicious, and this new world is a world that the most dangerous people can thrive in." I pause, and add, "In a way, I am one of those vicious people, but I have standards.

"I had a gun shop before things collapsed and have always been into guns. Not for hunting or target shooting, my main reason for owning guns was defense. I know what shitty things thinking humans are capable of doing to each other, and it was my intent to arm as many innocent people as possible. I used to tell people, "Criminals don't belong in jail, they belong in the graveyard." I stop the bike, and call out to Simone, "Simone, we're ready to go."

Mike asks, "So how are you one of those vicious people?"

I look at Mike directly, and say, "Now there are no rules for anyone, Mike. Before the collapse, I was constrained by the law and morals, just like every other honest person was. We were at the mercy of criminals that couldn't care less about our rights, our health and safety, and they especially couldn't care less about obeying laws.

"How can you stop a criminal that will kill you the first chance they get, when the law can't touch them until they act? All you could do then was arm yourself with a gun and hope that you had it with you when the bastard criminal decides to come and kill or rob you. And the worst part about it is you never really knew who the criminal was, or when, or even if, they were going to attack."

"I don't get it," Mike says. "If someone was threatening you, wouldn't you know who that is?"

I shake my head at him in the dark, and reply, "How would you know? I'm not really talking about specific threats, Mike. I'm talking about the thousands of crimes—rape, robbery, and murders that occurred every day while civilization was still intact. All the police, sheriffs, jails, and prisons were needed for a reason, right?

"There were people that were dangerous around us every day. Lots of people lived their lives oblivious to the threat, and I would often meet them in my shop after they had been robbed. If they thought to buy a gun before they were robbed or attacked, they would have saved themselves the anguish that the criminals put them through.

"Anyway, now I can be just as vicious as the bastards that we are heading to kill. I can walk in to that Wal-Mart and kill every one of those murderous pricks in any way I choose, and there will be no police officer coming to my door to find out why I did what I did. The only problem I have now is I still have a conscience and the bad guys still don't. They won't hesitate to hurt or kill us, and our hesitation to hurt them puts us at a double disadvantage against their numbers.

"Look Mike, I don't mean to sound so pessimistic, and I definitely don't want you three to think we are just riding to our deaths. That's not what I'm trying to relay. We have a great chance of getting every hostage out of the store safely, but it all depends on three critical things. First, we can't engage in a firefight with them. If we fight them as equals, gun against gun, we will lose. There is no tactical high ground in the area, and they will have the cover of the store."

Mike adds, "I guess they have all of the supplies in the store to use as well."

"Exactly!" I say. "We can't outlast them in a siege either because of those supplies. Our food and ammo will run out before theirs. They also have hostages that they can just start killing. They'll know that is why we are there as soon as they see the two girls that escaped on our side."

Mike, Simone, and Hannah nod their understanding, and I continue, "The second thing we need to win is to convince these guys that they are facing an overwhelming force. They need to think that they are the outnumbered group and that we are trained soldiers of the U.S. Military.

Some of the things we brought, like the laser pointers, are going to be used to make each gun seem like three or four guns."

"And the last thing we need to convince these guys of is that they will not be punished for what they've been doing."

Mike and Hannah give a sour look at each other, and I stop them before they start to protest. "I said we will make them *think* they will not be punished, I never said they won't be. I'll give you the details with everyone else when we catch up to Arthur and Samantha. If they have already engaged these guys in a fight, then my plan is irrelevant."

Ruben steps out of the trailer door, and I walk back to him.

He asks, "Do you folks have to leave right away? I could use some help with my wife if you've been through this before."

I shake my head. "Sorry Ruben, there's something important we have to do. Some people we know are being held by someone. Don't worry too much about your wife, there really isn't anything you can do to help her through the fever, other than tie her arms and legs up and put something in her mouth to keep her from biting her tongue. Basically treat her like she's going into a severe seizure. Then let her sleep it off to regain her strength.

"Are you planning on staying here for a while?"

"Yes."

"Okay, Ruben. If things go well, we will come back this way in a few days, and check on you." I shake hands with him, return to my bike, and we begin the last leg of our journey to the edge of Rogue River.

The night is quiet once again. No banging or unusual noises. Once we arrive at the edge of the town, we dismount, and huddle for a quick breakdown of our plan. "We need to make it around this place without drawing any infected out. Greg said the girls came right down Interstate 5 and there aren't many cars on the road." I pull out the map of Rogue River and point where we'll head. "So this cemetery next to us puts us here. We go around this curve on Wards Creek Road, down this little stretch of River Rd, and across Classick Dr. That will take us right up the I-5 on-ramp off of Depot Street on the map here. That should have us bypass most of Rogue River and get us onto I-5 in just under a mile. Let's walk slow, keep your ears open, and we should be fine."

Simone asks, "Eddie, should we try to contact Arthur and Samantha on the radios before we get going? We might not be able to stop right away after we make it to the freeway if we've attracted any attention."

"Actually, no, and for the very reason that we might run into problems going through here. We need to know what our situation is and when we will arrive before we contact them. That means being on the other side of Rogue River. Once we are on I-5, we only have seven miles to go, so another forty or fifty minutes with no major obstacles. Once we contact Arthur however, there is a good chance that the group at Wal-Mart will be listening since they have radios too, so we can't say we're not sure when we'll arrive."

"You think they will be listening at this hour?" Simone asks

"I would if I were them. They are a big group, and have hurt a lot of people, which should make them paranoid enough to keep track of radio traffic for incoming reprisals or challenges.

Simone shakes her head in disgust, the kids remain quiet, and we begin our walk through this ghost town. Simone is in the lead and takes us in a wide arch around a few cars with infected locked inside, and I pull up the rear. The infected that didn't freeze should all be truly dead by now from a lack of food and water, but we've noticed on our trips that some of the bodies start moving and moaning when we walk close enough to cars for them to see or hear us. There must be some sort of suspended animation process with this disease to keep the body alive for so long. Hopefully this sickness doesn't morph into a true undead scenario. It is bad enough having technical zombies without having to deal with the dead walking as well.

CHAPTER THIRTEEN
THE DECEPTION

"It's time for us to try and contact the others," I say as we all pull to a stop next to each other. "Mike, are you sure you want to get into this with us?"

He nods.

"Can I ask you why?"

He says plainly, "You haven't killed me. For the last eight months almost everyone my parents and I encountered would shoot at us, try to stab us, or threaten us in some way. You did kill my father and you all have guns and knives, but I haven't felt this safe since we had to leave our house. I know I'm only fourteen, but I understand what's going on, and you could have killed me at any time by now if you wanted. I don't know if I'll stay with you, but I like feeling safe and the idea of getting back at some of the bad guys out there."

"Okay," I reply and nod. "I'm going to trust you with something important, then. I would prefer it said by a man, so I need your male voice.

"I want you to make the initial contact with Arthur for us. I have what you need to say written here, so just practice it a few times until it sounds like something you do all the time. Try and make it sound official. What I'm going for is that we are the military coming into town."

I hand Mike the note I'm holding. "I don't expect this conversation to go on long and hopefully the gang at Wal-Mart will be listening in, this is all for their benefit."

After a couple minutes Mike says he thinks he is ready, so I turn on the radio, key it twice to send static over the line, and hand it over to

Mike, who reads, "Captain Langford, Captain Langford, I have battalion commander, Colonel Keeper on the line over."

Mike stops reading, and I give him a nod and grab the radio. "Hopefully Arthur decides to play along." Twenty seconds go by with no response. I hand the radio back to Mike and have him send the message again.

I look at Simone, with concern, and have a million thoughts running through my head. This was always a long shot. Arthur could have fought the bandits already and could be dead or captured. If he and his group are doing okay, he could still easily say something that gives away that we aren't the military. I wish I had gotten a solid survival group together before everything fell apart.

Finally, we hear the radio squelch, and, "Colonel Keeper, this is Captain Langford. The line is not secure. Repeat, the line is not secure. Over"

I grab the radio back from Mike and begin my hopeful deception. "Captain Langford, this is Colonel Keeper. Radio not secure acknowledged. It can't be helped. Scrambling equipment received damage from an EMP attack. The mission has changed. Repeat, the mission has changed. I am inbound with another company. I will combine the two companies into battalion strength and take command. ETA twenty minutes. Acknowledge. Over."

"ETA twenty minutes, and you will be taking command, acknowledged."

"Mission change from assault to relocation. Repeat, assault is cancelled. Take no aggressive action and have all snipers stand down. Defensive rules of engagement only. Acknowledge receipt. Over."

"Acknowledge receipt, Colonel. Take no aggressive action and have snipers stand down. Defensive ROE only. Over."

"Captain, have Lieutenants Krenshaw, Weyland, and Blount available for full briefing upon my arrival. Let your men know, no exits or escapes from the Wal-Mart are to be tolerated, but no casualties desired. Suppressive fire to keep them from running only. Keep them in place until I arrive and can communicate with their faction leader. Colonel Keeper, out."

"Acknowledge receipt, Colonel. Captain Langford, out."

Simone, Hannah and Mike are all looking at me with confused expressions on their faces. "I'll fill you guys in when we arrive at the cemetery and speak with Arthur and his group." I shut off the small light, and we get on our bikes to continue our ride to the edge of Grants Pass.

*

"What's this business about military designations?" Arthur asks as he and some of his group walks up to the four of us, with our bikes.

"Hello, Arthur. Hello, Samantha," I say and nod to Conner and Jake.

"Greg obviously filled us in on what you guys are up to, and I thought there might be a way to get these guys out of Wal-Mart without a fight. I wasn't sure if the men holding the hostages would be able to pick up our transmission, so I started my plan like that."

"Oh they heard it, all right," Samantha says angrily. "They had no idea we were here until you broadcast on the radio. Right after your call, they put four snipers on the roof, and had guys looking out each of the main and emergency doors."

Arthur adds, "Luckily, we had our people already surrounding the place and watching, so each of those guys saw some of us with guns and popped their heads back inside right away. They haven't taken any shots at us even though I know the roof guys have had some eyes on us occasionally, so for now, they are waiting to see what's going on."

"Samantha, I know you have the most riding on this being successful. My plan in short is to pretend we are the military and are here with an overwhelming force. We need to get everything rolling within the next thirty minutes so those guys in the store don't decide to just start shooting. If two of you could bring everyone here that doesn't need to watch the store's exits, I could explain what my idea is in detail, and we can decide if everyone thinks it is a workable plan.

"I have some assorted worn fatigues we should change into. Only enough for ten of us so Arthur and Samantha should have a set. Then just pick six others besides Simone and I who would look like they belong in a uniform, and have them change into them."

"We still don't know what this is about," Samantha says.

"I know, I know. I'm sorry. We only got about three hours of sleep and way more exercise on bikes than I am used too. My brain is a bit fuzzy right now. I'm thinking we can avoid fighting altogether, but I'd rather tell everyone at once, okay? Please, just give me the five or ten minutes while they gather here and get changed."

*

Everyone is assembled around me, and I can see quite a few agitated faces among the group, probably due to my blowing their element of surprise.

"All right, it's a crazy plan, and like anything, might or might not work. If it does, then it will prevent a gun battle with these guys. If not, then we're really not worse off than before—even with our losing the element of surprise.

"Based on what Greg told me about their numbers, if we fight them, most of us could die or be taken prisoner, and no one inside will be freed. We can't lay siege and wait them out, because they have a store full of supplies and hostages that they can execute if we don't leave. So I thought a bluff would be good." I look around quickly to see that everyone is following me, and then continue, "Arthur? Are the numbers that the girls told Greg accurate?"

"We're not sure," he replies. "They haven't sent out any patrols since we have been here and have only sent a few people around the outside of the building. In total we saw about ten different faces. I don't have a reason to think they are wrong," he says while looking over at the two young girls in the group.

"Honestly Eddie, we couldn't figure out a way to take these guys on with the numbers we have and their secured position."

I nod in acknowledgment and look at Julie and Ava. "Okay, so if we go by the numbers you know are there, they have about forty men inside, maybe fifty. We have how many?"

"We have twenty-five, so with you four, we have twenty-nine," Arthur says looking quizzically that Mike is here with us. "This better be a good bluff. What did you bring to pull it off?"

"I brought boxes of laser pointers and electrical tape. Each person should get three laser pointers and tape them to their rifles to make the bad guys think there are three shooters for every one of us. Maybe even attach some to sticks. This will, of course, just be our sniper team. I'll be telling them that we have a force of three hundred plus men and women, and we are clearing areas and gathering survivors. Whoever has the taped lasers, make sure the snipers on the roof don't get eyes on the taped up guns, or the whole ruse will fall apart. I will try to convince them that they need to release their prisoners or we will lay waste to the store and kill everyone inside."

"And then what?" Samantha just stares at me with blazing eyes.

"Samantha, do you want your daughter back?" I ask. She just stares at me with pain in her eyes, and I understand why she is so angry.

"You think she is already dead, don't you?" Samantha lowers her head and starts to cry.

I continue, "You think that after she helped those girls escape, they killed her, and you just want to go in there guns blazing and kill everyone in sight. Maybe even get yourself taken out in the process so you don't have to deal with this pain anymore. Well, I'm not going to lie and tell you everything will be fine. You may be right. They may have killed her, and I am truly sorry if they did, but we don't know either way. What we do know is there are still other people in there. Other innocent people that deserve being helped and can be because of your daughter. They can be rescued if we play this smart and try to convince the hostage takers that they will get away free."

"You want to let them go free?" Samantha says nearly yelling. "We have to kill those scumbags!"

"I said we have to make them think they will get away free, Samantha. I have no intention of letting a threat to our group survive. Just try to calm down and see the bigger picture, please. Emily sent these two girls out in her place to get help for everyone. She didn't send them so they could bring in a firing squad to get everyone killed. If I can get the hostages out of there without a shot being fired, then I damn well will do it, and you will fall in line and help us do it or stay out of the way. All of our lives are on the line in this."

Her expression isn't changing as fast as I want to show me that she understands, so I need to bring it home for her. "Samantha, you were right in letting Arthur run this rescue up until this point. You are too emotionally wrapped up in the outcome to be patient enough to see it through. I think it would be better if you don't stay for the rest of my plan. Go get something to eat or just relax somewhere, but my plan might work better if you don't get the final details."

After Samantha leaves, I finish filling in the specifics of my plan, and everyone agrees with it or doesn't have a better idea.

"Is there anything I should know that you guys found out since you arrived? Anything that will help or hurt what the plan is?"

Arthur speaks up, "We don't know any more than Julie and Ava do. Their leader is called Stockton. They number in the forty to fifty range and they are listening to multiple radio frequencies. They are using channel eight to speak with each other. At least, that is the channel their shooters on the roof are using."

"Okay," I say acknowledging Arthur. "There are two very important things all of you need to know from our end. First of all, I've been bitten." There is a look of shock on each of their faces. "I was bitten yesterday at about noon and had a fever start at six p.m. When it was over, I got up, and was fine." Most of the people are looking at me like I'm telling some kind of joke. "I can see by your faces that you don't believe me, but it's true, I was bitten here on my arm under this bandage. The bite broke the skin. I was bleeding and I didn't turn."

"Second thing, the infected have runners now. Have you seen any?" This news got strong looks of fear staring back at me, so it is apparently new news.

"The infected person I was attacked by was running and knocked me down while I was taking out two regular walking infected. It blindsided me with a tackle at a full run. I stabbed it in the mouth with my knife, it sat up, grabbed my knife with its hands, and pulled it out."

A few grunts and whispers of that's not possible spread through the group.

Arthur speaks up, and says, "We actually haven't seen any infected in the area, but then we have put most of our attention on the building. I was thinking that these guys just cleared out this area really well, but maybe that isn't the reason for no sightings."

"I saw a few people running in the distance earlier," Joshua Langford says. "I assumed because they were moving fast that it was just scared survivors, but it could have been these things."

"I know we haven't seen or heard about anything like this so far, but trust me when I say it was an infected and not a psycho or drugger. I'm hoping it was the cold temperatures of the winter that kept the fever from burning out the motor skills of those people that turned. If it wasn't the cold, then we could be seeing a change to the way the disease affects people, or an evolutionary step by those that were infected a while ago. Whatever the reason for them, there have been at least three, the one runner that tackled me, and two more which we encountered an hour ago on our ride down here. There will be more."

"What the hell else are we going to have to deal with?" Ava says to Julie as an aside, but loud enough for us all to hear it.

"Unfortunately, it gets worse. From what we could figure out about how my attack happened, it seems like the runner was stalking us, and waited for one of us to get separated and distracted before it attacked. We have to make sure everyone out there is doubled up with one person always watching the rear. Don't let anyone or anything sneak up on you out there. And don't trust that the infected will be slow and you can just occasionally check behind you.

"Okay, let's get everyone in place. I'll contact these bastards in ten minutes for a face to face. I want Samantha and one other person in fatigues to come with me."

*

I key the radio and start the deception that will hopefully save our lives and those of the captives inside. "This is Colonel Keeper speaking to the men holding prisoners in Wal-Mart. I want to speak with Stockton."

Only a second passes before we hear, "This is Stockton. What do you want?"

Yes. I've got him, I think to myself. *He was hanging on to the radio waiting for my call.* "Stockton, I want to speak with you directly and make you and your men an offer you won't want to refuse."

"That's fine by me, Colonel. You come on in and we can discuss it."

"I will not be adding myself to the prisoners you currently have. You come out the front with two men, I will approach with two of my people, and I will lay out the offer. We will leave the radio keyed on while I give you the details so all of your men inside can listen in as well."

"I'm thinking I like it in the store. I don't see a reason to come out and talk."

"I was informed that you were the man that made the decisions for your group. If you aren't, then send out someone who is. I don't care. I have a deal to offer you and your men, and you will accept it or you can stay and burn with the store once we set it ablaze."

After ten seconds, he comes back saying, "You wouldn't burn down the store with all of these supplies and people in it."

"I have already done it twice, Stockton. We have encountered groups like yours before when we weren't as interested in saving the uninfected as we are now. We don't need the supplies, and while untrained civilians are a burden to deal with, things have changed requiring us to consider not only the lives of your prisoners, but your own as well. If you are unwilling to come out and talk, then for the purpose of protecting the lives of my trained soldiers, I will classify all of your prisoners as dead, and will torch the building. You have two minutes to come out for discussion. If it makes you feel more confident of your position, you can come out armed."

I turn to Arthur, Samantha, and Timothy. "Okay, Arthur, you're obviously still in charge if we get killed. Just do whatever you think will save the most people. Samantha and Tim, you'll come with me, and whatever you do, just stick with the military theme."

"They're coming out Eddie," Arthur says.

"Right. Let's get those people freed," I say and start walking to the store with Samantha and Timothy falling in a few steps behind and to either side of me.

We approach the three men from the store. They are standing about 25 yards away from the entrance, and all three look like regular people. Not the leather clad and mustache wearing violent looking sort I was expecting. "Which one of you is Stockton?"

"I am."

For some reason I thought he would be some huge bully looking fellow that is used to pushing people around with his size. This guy must keep his people together some other way, maybe simple manipulation, maybe cold and calculating fear. Good. This is another bit of luck. A thinking thug will give my offer real consideration and understand the consequences beyond simple aggression and force.

I walk right up to him, and say, "Is your radio on so your men can hear what we say?"

"No, not yet," he says as he reaches back to one of his men for his handset.

"Hang on a minute, Stockton. Before we talk, I don't want the people in your holding areas hearing what we discuss. I want you to have your men turn on the stereos in the store that you use to keep the prisoners from hearing each other."

He gives me a look of curiosity, and then makes the call to his men to turn on the music by the cages. "It seems you know more about us than I thought. Why do you want the radios turned on by the cages?"

I reply in a curt tone, "Very simple, the people that you have locked up can't hear the arrangement we are making. If they get wind of it at any point then no deal. Once you hear the offer you'll probably understand the reason for the secrecy."

A man calls back on the radio saying the music is on and no one in the holding areas can hear what is going over the radios.

"Good. Now make sure your men are listening in and we can begin."

Stockton shrugs his shoulders and has a *Get on with it I'm bored* look on his face. "Let's just hear this amazing deal you think you have for us."

I pause for a second, and turn to Timothy, "Captain Weyland, make sure our people are listening in to this conversation as well."

"My fellow soldiers on the perimeter, our orders have changed. Our entire situation has changed. For the men of Wal-Mart, I will get to your deal shortly, but I must inform my men of the situation in order to ease the tension of retribution toward you that I am sure they are all feeling. Some of the details will only make sense to my men.

"As you know, your original orders had this incursion as a fire mission to wipe out the criminal gang controlling this area. The companies of my battalion were ordered to sweep through Grants Pass to clear out the remaining infected and continue with our cleansing of the Northwest Territory. These orders have ended. General Sessions is no longer in command. We are now under the command of Admiral Tucker of the U.S. Naval forces. General Sessions and the entire Eastern Division have been destroyed by what was initially considered a nuclear attack by some remaining enemy state or rogue nation, but has since been determined to be an unfortunate and ill-timed accident due to a severe loss of properly trained personnel.

"Along with fourteen thousand three hundred eighty-six of our fellow soldiers, the One hundred and two thousand civilians we had in the Southern rebuilding zone also perished. The Pacific Northwest is now our last chance. This is our last remaining opportunity as a species to regain a foothold on this planet. It is our final moment to show that we will survive anything and everything that can be thrown at us.

"To do this rebuilding we need bodies. We need uninfected survivors to not only help rebuild, but re-populate this new world. As little as some of us may like it, we need all of the people that are in this Wal-Mart to survive. Not just the prisoners but their captor's as well.

"That is why the mission has changed. The largest organized outpost of humanity left in the world has just been destroyed, and the people in this region are all that are left. We can no longer lay waste to the criminal gangs we encounter as we were ordered to and as we have wanted too up to this point. I will not lie to you, I took great satisfaction in killing the vermin that controlled South Medford and watching these types of cowardly motherfuckers burn when we cleared the north, but that will change now. We are ordered to make it change now.

"I have been instructed to offer these people an opportunity to survive if they choose, and that offer is coming now. You men that are currently controlling Wal-Mart and holding prisoners inside, today is your final day here. Captain Langford was in charge of a company of one hundred eighty-four men and women that had your area surrounded. I have since taken command of this small battalion force and have three hundred and sixty-four armed and trained soldiers with me."

"Bullshit!" Stockton yells. "You may have some people here but my men haven't seen anything. By our count, you only have ten people. You didn't even come up here with a show of force, just two people. I think you're bluffing."

I raise my left hand, and say, "Sniper team one, light 'em up." I show a self-satisfied smile to Stockton, as he and his two companions have laser dots appear all over their bodies.

"Whoa, whoa, whoa! All right, all right, I get it." Stockton and his two men are wide-eyed with their hands in the air and turning in all directions.

"I would appreciate no more interruptions until you and your men hear what my final offer is. But since we have a radio audience, tell your men what is going on."

One of Stockton's men replies shakily, "W…we have dots all over us. Lasers."

"Stockton, tell your men how many lasers are pointed at you."

"I don't know. It's too many to count."

"Good," I say and lower my hand. "Sniper team one, lights off."

Stockton and his men start to relax a little as the lights start clicking off.

"You and your men can put your hands down now. And for the record, I have five dedicated sniper teams in this battalion. As I'm sure you know in your own experience with our infected attackers, having good long range snipers is the best way to survive in this new landscape of ours.

"Now, you also understand why I am comfortable approaching you with just two other officers. I am in little danger here, not from you, or your rooftop shooters. I am here speaking with you specifically because of my orders and don't personally think you should be getting this offer. I was honestly hoping that you wouldn't be the silent thoughtful type that you have been up until now, and we could just clear you out with lead and flame." I say finally as sternly as I can, "Should I continue?"

"Yes."

"Yes what?" I yell.

"Yes, Sir," is his stammering reply, signifying that I won this alpha dog contest.

"Right, I have three hundred sixty-four people currently under my command. Another six hundred and twenty-eight will arrive this afternoon so we can begin our sweep to clear this city and find any other survivors. You and your men will be relocated to a safe area in Idaho where you are to establish a new township. If you accept the offer, you will be in control of your own territory, where you along with other men and women will have to defend your territory against the occasional infected person. We will put no military personnel in to support you.

"Do not get the impression that it will be a cake walk. The men and women we plan on sending there that you will be working with to survive are largely of the former incarcerated types such as yourselves, but yours will be the first group to arrive, and will therefore have a chance to establish your own hierarchy.

"You will be given varying degrees of survival support depending upon your varying degrees of cooperation with military and civilian persons you come into contact with. In other words, this is your opportunity for a clean slate. A true re-start of your lives and records. What was done in the past will stay in the past and only the actions of your future will determine if or for how long you survive.

"Remember that this is a numbers game, and I'm talking overall human population. If you take this offer and head to the new Idaho territory, your group and everyone in that area may still be wiped out. If it is determined by your future actions that you pose a threat to the continued existence of humanity, you will be erased. Are there any questions so far?"

"Yeah. What's the catch?" Stockton says in a slow and derogatory way. I guess he is trying to make up for his calling me sir. "I mean you've laid out quite a honey trail for us to follow, and I'm wondering where the teeth are and how much they'll hurt when the trap slams shut."

"Smart. I see why you're in charge. There's always a catch and here it is. I told you to make sure your prisoners couldn't hear this discussion because they can't know about it. If you accept the offer, you will all be tied up and secured, and your prisoners will believe that you will be punished for your crimes against them. Each of your prisoners that are able to, will write down what each of you did to them, and in some cases, yell and cry to your faces. While you are secured and your former prisoners are being debriefed, you will not harass or taunt them in any way. If any one of you lets them know that you are getting your own territory or going free, you will all die. If any of your prisoners from this point on are killed by you or your men, the deal is off, and you will die.

"If you accept this offer then you should leave the store unarmed, walk twenty-five yards into the parking lot, and sit down with your hands on your lap. Everyone must be completely unarmed. No guns, no knives, nothing that can be viewed as a weapon. Some of my men will approach you with zip ties to secure your arms. They will be accompanied by armed guards who will shoot anyone found to have a weapon on their person. And the sniper teams will be ready to kill everyone if your men attempt to overpower my men. I don't want to have to shoot my own men, but I will. So don't try and overpower them." I give him a hard look to make sure he sees that I mean what I say.

"Once all of your men are secured, my men will enter the store, and check if it is clear. If any of your men stay in the store for an ambush, the deal is off and all of you will die, so make sure everyone exits together. That is all. That is your choice."

"How do I know you'll keep your word?" Stockton asks. "What's to keep you and your men from gunning us down once we're out here? Or some of your people like that lady behind you from taking pot shots at us?"

"All you have is my word as an Officer of the United States Military that you will get the deal that I have been ordered to give you. You have to decide if my word is worth more than that of the people you are used to dealing with. As for my people, they are listening in as well, and if any of my soldiers or officers break or attempt to break this deal, then they will be sent to Idaho with you to help you establish your town. You can do what you want with them at that point."

"You don't seem to hold any loyalty toward your own men, Colonel, if you would send them off with us."

"You are mistaken, Stockton. I can confidently make that offer because I know none of my people would show such disloyalty by attacking your men and breaking this agreement. You have fifteen minutes to get together with your men and decide what you will do."

I turn and leave with Timothy and Samantha again falling in behind me. All I hear are three sets of footfalls walking off behind us, so at least we won't be shot in the back. Finally turning around the side of the little mattress store at the edge of the Wal-Mart parking lot, I let out a sigh of relief, and lean against the building for support. I feel weak. I'm already tired, and soon I'll be hitting the adrenaline low from the excitement of that encounter.

"He was looking at you quite intently, wasn't he, Samantha?" I ask. "I mean, that guy Stockton kept looking over my shoulder in your direction, and looked like a trapped rat about to get squashed. What were you doing?"

"I was just getting so angry. I mean the idea of letting them go and start their own territory. It sounds so believable the way you said it, and I couldn't help let my hatred show on my face."

"Good, that's what I was hoping for. That's why I didn't want you around when I told everyone what the plan was. I wanted you to have an honest reaction to what you were hearing. Actually, I had planned on the possibility of Timothy needing to escort you back here, and me staying out there alone. I was sure you would say something or try to kill one of them right there and then."

"I think I would have too," she replies. "But they weren't what I thought they would be. I mean, I was expecting something more, not a guy that looked like a law clerk."

*

According to Arthur, the rooftop shooters left the roof while we were walking away from our meeting with Stockton. Ten minutes later unarmed men start walking out of the store. I feel like jumping up and cheering for this win, but it isn't a win yet. Their men still need to be secured and checked thoroughly for weapons or tools that could free them.

*

I stand with Simone, Arthur, and Samantha in front of the group of men as six other ranch members search and secure our prisoners. Once everyone is finally secure, I walk up to Stockton, have him stand, and look back at his people. "I want you to check all of the faces in your gang and tell me if anyone is missing. I am going to send some of my people into the building to check that it is secure and then release your prisoners."

"Everyone is here," he says after looking around.

"I want you to check one more time, Stockton. You should know that I will ask your prisoners if any of your men are missing, or if anyone new has been added to the prisoner cages today."

Stockton looks around, and says, "No. No one is missing."

"Okay, go ahead and sit down. Once we clear the building, everyone will head back inside for the prisoner debriefing."

"Arthur, double-check our prisoners."

Arthur walks up to each one, double checks all of the zip ties, and puts pillow cases over their heads.

"Don't be too concerned over the pillow cases," I say as Arthur walks among the people covering them. "This is the best way to ensure we don't have a mob of angry people trying to rip off your heads. If they can't see which one of you abused them the most, they won't have that anger burst to the surface. We will have the victims identify you and your crimes one at a time."

As we walk away, Simone asks me, "Is that really necessary? Putting those people inside through all of that, having to see the men that abused them?"

"Yes. It is necessary for the victims, and for us, Simone. There is a strength that comes from closure. From being able to confront an attacker and know they will be punished for what they have done. If the men and women in that building don't get to accuse these people and know that their pain is being acknowledged, then we might as well leave them in there to die. Without closure, they sure as hell won't be any good to the future of humanity if they remain trapped by the abuse that they endured here. At least that's what the latest therapy studies in rape treatment showed before the collapse," I say and shrug my shoulders.

"Who are you?" Samantha says looking at me with an honestly puzzled look. "You having guns I get. Having spare military uniforms, I understand, and the survival supplies and ranch. But knowing therapy studies? That does not fit."

"Sure it does. Survival isn't just about living another day. It's about having the will to live another day when you endure something tragic. Studying psychology and learning how to cope with devastation and loss are a vital component to any survival plan. One thing that remains a constant throughout human history is the increased occurrences of rape during any major upheaval, calamity, or war. It also helped that I found studies like that useful so the things I read actually stuck with me."

*

There is a group of people hugging and crying off to our left just inside the front entrance of the store. They all just finished detailing what their captors did to them. All of the women, all four children, and a third of the men were raped. Everyone that was held captive here was beaten at least once. Many have substantial injuries. There are twenty-eight known murders to have occurred, eleven of which were people killed in the process of being captured by this group of thugs. The remaining seventeen deaths were post capture deaths; Three by gun for running, five by knife for fighting back during an assault, and nine beating deaths which the captives were forced to watch to keep them in line.

The three most recent deaths are the hardest to deal with for all of us, but especially so for Samantha, Conner, and their son Jake. The woman that helped the two girls escape from this place and led us to this scene was Emily. As a punishment and warning to the others for helping someone escape, two innocent people were pulled from the cages, one man and one woman, and they were beaten to death. The man and woman were killed for the two who escaped.

According to the woman crying in Samantha's arms right now, Emily was hit hard and knocked down when one of the men found out she helped two other girls escape. Emily died. She never got back up from the hit.

I'm sitting next to Simone at one of the checkout registers. Arthur, Timothy, and Mike are off to the side, watching the tear filled scene. Hannah is already sleeping a few feet away from us on a sleeping bag she grabbed from sporting goods.

Mike looks at us, and asks, "So what are you going to do with these guys now that the victims have all identified them?"

"We kill them. We have enough difficulties trying to survive in this world with the infected, it will get even worse now that they are running, and coordinating attacks. I don't want to let any of these people go and have them lead some type of attack on our ranch that gets some or all of us killed," I say this thinking back to Chad and turning him away the first day of the collapse.

"Arthur, I need to get some sleep, and I'm sure some of your men do as well. With the runners out there and having to get all of these new people up to speed, I don't think we are going anywhere tonight. So could you please organize everyone into shifts of guard duty and sleep?"

"Sure, Eddie. What about the supplies from the store here?"

"Right," I say trying to clear my mind. I'm already starting to drift off with the lack of sleep and the after adrenaline low I'm hitting. "Do what you can to find a truck and trailer that you can get running. Two trucks if you can find another driver besides Donald. Then organize teams to load everything we can from the store into the trucks. Just make sure that no one goes outside without at least two armed guards to watch for the infected. I don't want to lose anyone to laziness now that we survived this ruse without any losses."

"And the people we freed? They have heard some of the talk about a safe zone and also think we are a military force."

"You'll have to explain to them what's really going on out there. Tell them everything. The ranch, the runners, what we know about the disease, and that we plan on killing all of the people that weren't held captive here and why. You'll have to decide when to tell them."

"How will I know that?"

"Just give them an hour or two to grieve, and once they calm down and start to relax, they will probably start looking forward to leaving. You need to tell them before they get too involved in fantasies of a safe zone."

Arthur nods with a frown on his face. I don't blame him. Dashing people's hopes and dreams just when they think they have a new start won't be a pleasant job. I know I would pass out from exhaustion before I was able to speak with them, so I can't do it.

CHAPTER FOURTEEN
THE DISCOVERY

I wake up to Donald shaking my shoulder.

"Is something wrong?" I ask, and he shakes his head no. "Something is up with one of the people we freed. He came here with Samantha's daughter. You need to speak with him."

I look at the time and it is just after 2 p.m. Two hours of sleep. "I've had it way too easy these last couple of months," I mumble to myself.

"Too easy?" Donald questions.

"Yes. Way too easy. The last few months at the ranch were nothing like what these people have been through. We were all just shuffling around rebuilding and practicing for re-entering the world. We had plenty of sleep and enough food. We have books to read and movies to watch and aside from those attacks, only the rare appearance of an infected at our fences. Look at those people over there. Half of them look like they just got freed from a concentration camp."

"Well, technically they were," Donald adds.

"Yeah, I guess so. So what's going on?" I ask as Donald leads me to where this man I need to talk to is.

"Well, this guy that got captured with Emily is a biologist of sorts. He says he developed the Zeus drug."

I stop and look at Donald. The fog clears from my brain as his words sink in. "Are you serious? Emily was able to bring him with her?"

"Yes. You knew about him?"

"Just a little. The first day of the collapse, when I told Samantha about the General's letter and mentioned the Zeus Drug, she freaked out and hung up to call her daughter. She told me later that Emily was in the honors program of pharmaceutical biology in Portland. The guy that developed Zeus was speaking at the University. Emily's group was responsible for showing him around, making sure he didn't get lost. He's from Germany. It never seemed important to know any more since he was just another lost person in Portland that we would never see. So what does he have to say?" I finally ask.

"You can hear it all from him in a second."

I purse my lips and nod. "Let's go."

Sitting next to Samantha on the far side of the group of freed prisoners is a man who has her complete attention as he talks to her. He has an unusual face and must be the man from Germany.

"Eddie, this is the man that came here with Emily and claims to have developed the Zeus drug."

In what I think is a very slight German accent, he says, "Are you the man who was bitten and lived?"

"Yes, I am. Did you really develop this drug?" I say more angrily than I intended.

"Yes, Yes," he exclaims with his head down. "But you must hear the whole story. Please sit, and I will tell everyone how this whole thing started. My name is Erde Fleischer, and my story starts two and a half years before this plague."

Mister Fleischer has notebooks with him, in which he wrote a detailed account of how the disease was developed, so that he or others might use the information to try and fight the infected.

"It started with my studying the toxoplasmosis parasitic disease in an effort to reduce aggression in the prison population, so that they might safely return to society. After a year of study, we found that various aspects of this illness created reduced fear, reduced stimulus to pain, and reduced blood loss. The medical implications of this were astounding. I thought I found a way with this parasite to make every surgery safer and to keep more people alive after accidents and on battlefields.

"It was the potential military applications that provided me with the most funds for research, but even with the military's involvement with financial support, there was never a push to develop this into some type of weapon. It was always being studied and refined as a way to save lives by reducing blood loss and shock in surgery.

"We did studies with apes that another doctor was previously using in psychological studies, and there were no adverse side effects from them. After receiving the genetically altered parasite, they changed metabolically for one to two weeks. Meaning, they would have no pain response, limited blood loss, and reduced fear and anxiety during the period where the parasite remained active.

"We moved on to human testing with a group of soldiers in the Middle East. It was the Tiger Squadron, and they also reacted the same as the apes in the previous study. I initially recalled there was none of this wild attacking behavior that occurred during its later implementation. However, after reviewing my notes, I realized we might have seen one instance of the violence that we attributed to other causes.

"One of the soldiers who was new to the squadron tried to kill his fellow soldiers shortly after his arrival to the group. That would have coincided with his inoculation with the Zeus drug. I didn't see the correlation before because his record indicated a slightly unstable personality, and this assignment was his last chance to remain in the military. We all thought he just snapped, but in retrospect, it could have been the drug.

"After a month of testing on the Tiger Squadron, Zeus was put into mass production, and shipped around the world for implementation."

"After a month?" a woman listening interrupts to ask. "Only a month of testing and you shipped it around the world?"

"A General's letter that we grabbed from the internet said it had been tested for six months," I mention.

"For the six months of testing, records were deliberately changed in order to expedite the release of this drug. It was actually a decision by the U.N. Security Council to change the records."

I would hate to be on the receiving end of the looks and comments he receives from the group.

"Please, please, try to remember what the world was like before this plague occurred. There was mass rioting everywhere and even occurring in the U.S. Thousands of people were being killed every day, and Zeus was looked at as a way to save the lives of the doctors, nurses, and policemen that were dealing with the rioting populace. Yes, it was only one month of testing, but if it worked the way it did in trial, it would have saved thousands of lives during the rioting and millions more in the years and decades to come. I even dared to consider that longer term study of this could work toward extending human longevity..." The horrific irony of what actually happened causes Mr. Fleischer to pause, wiping the sweat from his brow before continuing.

"What I was working toward, what I saw was a world with barely any lives lost to car accidents, wars, or any other of the many ways we try to kill ourselves. I thought it would save lives. We all did. That is why it was rushed through production. The Zeus drug is a genetically altered parasite. I altered it to try and help the world, but ultimately, in our rush to use it without proper testing, I destroyed humanity."

There is a hushed silence over the group as we all absorb what we just heard.

"So what went wrong?" I ask. "Was there a problem with the quality control of the drug production? Some kind of contamination"

"When I heard what was happening from Emily, contamination was my initial thought. I believed the drug was tainted somehow, but after reviewing notes, I saw something I had overlooked in the entire process. I missed the most basic item relating to Toxoplasmosis. Cats!"

"But you knew toxoplasmosis was from cats, right?"

"Yes, of course, that is why I was originally studying aggression, because of how the parasite affects mice and rats with respect to cats. But you must understand that in Europe, most people have toxoplasmosis as a result of eating raw or undercooked meats, it isn't because of association with felines. This is where my research failed. The mice and rats we studied were not affected by toxoplasmosis the way that apes or we humans are. We missed the cannibalistic reaction to the parasite because the test subjects all had strong associations with cats.

"The apes we used from the psychological study all had pet cats that they were trained to care for. The Tiger Squadron had as its mascot several cats which the soldiers interacted with regularly as a matter of group luck in combat. And I would bet that you, Mr. Keeper, are a person with a high exposure to cats as well. Am I correct?"

"Yes. I am definitely a cat person. I've always preferred them as pets. I've had dogs as pets throughout my life as well but there was always at least one cat."

"So I believe you are immune to the altered parasite from Zeus because you have been exposed to the feline variant of toxoplasmosis. Without that exposure, you would have turned just like everyone else."

"But why haven't we seen more people survive this? There are far more cat owners in the U.S. than me."

"Yes, but most of those people weren't set up to survive the way you and your people were. Unfortunately, most of the people that could have survived this disease were probably killed and consumed by those that became what you call the infected."

"Are you absolutely certain about this?"

"I cannot say I have a hundred percent certainty, but I have a way to test my hypothesis, if you will agree."

"I can only assume you mean testing the virus on people. Is that what you have in mind?"

"Yes."

"I don't think you will find any volunteers for that kind of study, Mr. Fleischer. And I will not allow any of my people to volunteer or these people who were locked up to be tested on."

"Yes, Yes, but you have your prisoners."

My mind flashes through history to what I know about World War II. The Nazis and the Japanese did horrific medical testing on their prisoners. The Nazis did tests on the Jews, homosexuals, and communists they captured. Japanese did their tests mostly on the Chinese. Then I think to my own experiments with torture on my captives in the stable.

"Mr. Keeper, please consider the implications. You are already going to kill these people for what they have done. Their deaths might help the rest of us continue to survive. We can interview the prisoners to find out if any of them have had extensive contact with cats and infect them. If they do not turn, then you have your answer of certainty."

"What about the change? What about the fact that there are runners now and they can manipulate objects?"

"To that I'm less sure, because I have not been able to observe them and was only told about them a few hours ago."

"My wife, Simone, was thinking it might have to do with the cold temperatures during winter preventing the fever from wiping out so much of the brain."

"It is possible, Mr. Keeper, but I think we can even test for that. These men that held us captive kept the infected secured in pens at the back of the building. If any are still alive, we could use one of them to test, as well as a fast moving infected if you could capture one."

"You want us to capture one of the runners? Alive?"

"Yes, if they are in fact alive, which I believe they are," Mr. Fleischer replies.

"I think we could capture one pretty easy," Conner offers. "The runners have been moving right up to the building to look for us or a way in. I bet we could grab one right at the front doors."

"You can't bring those things in here!" a man yells.

"You can't be considering testing this sickness on living people!" another one of the people from the freed group says.

"I will consider every possible way to keep people alive," I reply. "Mr. Fleischer is right about one thing. I don't plan on letting any of those people live for what happened here. They are too much of a danger to us if we let them go. They are even more dangerous than the new runners. If studying their deaths helps the rest of us live, then that is what we will do."

"So what are you then?" a former captive asks me. "Are you our new Stockton? Are you going to tell us what we have to put up with in order to survive?"

I look briefly at Arthur and Simone standing next to me, then turn back, and reply, "Not at all. I have only one voice in this group but everyone has a say in what we do. We should have a large majority, say seventy-five percent of us agree to experiment on these people, or we won't do it."

"What about killing them all? Who decided that? Because I don't remember being asked what should happen with them."

"What is your name, sir?" I ask.

"Dave. Dave Cromwell, and I've been locked up here longer than most of the others. So I've seen what these men are capable of. But I still don't think all of them should be killed just on your word alone."

"Dave, you're right. They can't all be killed just on my word alone, that is why you people filled out those notebooks to explain what each of Stockton's people did to you. So we have all of your words on what they did, and if it makes you feel better, we will have a vote to ensure that everyone agrees these people should be put to death. Then we will have another vote to see if we should experiment on them. Is that acceptable to you?"

"Do you promise to hold to the vote, even if we all vote to let them go?"

"Absolutely not!" I reply immediately. "I don't promise that. I will not let any of the men that committed rapes or beatings leave here alive, because they are a danger to my family and friends. You can have your vote to clear your conscience, but they will still die."

"That's bullshit. A vote like that is meaningless," he replies.

"What, Dave, you don't like it? Perhaps we can do it this way then. If the majority votes to allow Stockton and his men to live. When my people and I leave, we will release Stockton and his men, and leave those people that vote against executions here with them."

"How the hell is that fair?" Dave demands. "You're basically telling us to vote for their death or you will let them have us again."

I smile and nod. "I am doing no more than you, Dave. If you vote to let those men live, then my friends and family will become Stockton's next target. Can you honestly say we could let them go without fear of reprisal for capturing them and making them look stupid and weak?"

Dave has no reply, so I continue, "Here's the deal. You vote how you want, but if you think these men that held you are so trustworthy that they won't come after my group, then they should also be trustworthy enough not to take you as prisoners again. You decide if you can safely live with them and vote accordingly.

"I will consider everyone's arguments on the lives of the people that did not directly hurt anyone. However, I will not put my life or the lives of my people at risk over some notion against capital punishment, or an appeal to forgiveness being the essence of humanity. It is still a kill or be killed world out there, Mr. Cromwell, and this Stockton character is a reminder that the infected are not our only threat.

"Arthur, can you get everyone together so we can all discuss everything and take a vote? I need to get something to eat."

"Sure, Eddie. I'll let you know when we're ready."

*

I finally walk up to the group of freed prisoners surrounded by most of our people. "You all know the position we are in, right?" I look at Arthur, and he nods at me, letting me know he told them our story. "We aren't the military. We have no large force, and we have not cleared vast portions of the Northwest states. We have a small ranch in the area, and while the housing space will be crowded if you join us, you are all welcome to come. We have some supplies remaining to begin building extra houses and accommodations for you, but at first, you'll live in tents.

"Fortunately, this store has a lot of supplies remaining, and we can work to bring everything in here back to our place. Unfortunately, there will be plenty of work for everyone to do if you decide to join us. Each person has to pull their own weight, and you can help in a variety of ways—including gardening, cooking, caring for the animals, or construction and defense. Living on my ranch and the protection it provides does not include and will not include threats of violence, rape, or any other forms of degradation that you may have endured in your efforts to survive so far.

"Many of you may not be sure if you want to come, and I bet none of you are sure if you'll want to stay if you do choose to come. Hell, I may not want all of you to stay once I get to know you better. In any case, I strongly encourage you to join us even if it's only to regain your strength and spirits before you head out into the world again. One important point is that it is my ranch along with my wife, Simone, here. My wife and I have five children of our own and have included many of the early entries at our ranch into the family category. Regardless of how many people come with us, it isn't run as a total democracy, it is still my ranch and that is why I am doing most of the talking.

"At my ranch, not every situation will be one where each person gets to vote on what happens. Some things will be my way or the highway, but even in those cases, I encourage everyone to voice their ideas and concerns, so that I can make the best possible choice. I am willing to admit when I am wrong and change my mind when provided with the right alternative."

I stop for a moment to drink some water. Looking around at the new faces in the crowd, I know we won't be able to trust them all, but I have to get our numbers up at the ranch.

"All of you have been told that the infected are now running and can manipulate items with their hands. Some of the runners have been trying to open the doors to get in here, so we had to secure all the exits to prevent their entry. Please don't take the locked and barricaded doors to imply that you are anything but free. You can all come and go as you choose, providing your departure does not put the rest of us at risk. Don't just open a door and walk out, let someone know if you plan to leave so the store can be secured behind you.

"My group and I are hoping to leave for the ranch tomorrow, and have managed to find two working semi-trucks, with trailers, that we have started to fill with items from the store. For those of you that choose not to join us, you will be outfitted with as many items as you can carry that you will need for your survival, and some types of weapons will be provided for your protection.

"Even though I am offering you all a chance at a real life at my ranch, I am not always the welcoming Mr. Friendly I am being right now. My main concern is the survival of those that I care about, and if someone else's survival threatens the lives of my family or friends, I will kill them. If you doubt the sincerity of this threat, please speak with any of my people after we are done here about what I have done to those that threatened our lives in the past.

"Now, let's move on to the prisoners—your former captors and their executions. We will be voting on whether or not they should be put to death and also on if we should do certain experiments on them to understand how the disease has changed." I look at a notebook while continuing to speak to them. "I understand that there are forty-eight people that worked with Stockton—including nine women and four children under age twelve. Of those forty-eight people, seventeen did not personally participate in your abuse that you people are aware of. Of the seventeen that committed no direct crimes against you, nine have been found to be the family members of your captors, and eight were just people trying to survive—as several of them put it.

"When contemplating the question of their deaths, there is an added implication of using them for experiments. Mr. Fleischer will tell you what his plan is and why he thinks it is important."

Erde gets up in front of the people and looks much like a skeleton in skin and clothes, the way many of the others do. It causes me to shiver. These people were starving before they were captured and detained here and were barely fed after that. Before he begins, he earnestly looks around at the assembled people while leaning on a cane we retrieved from the pharmacy.

"For everything that we have endured so far, I am the man most directly responsible for all of it. I created the drug that turned our friends and loved ones into monsters. I created it with the intention of saving lives, but it became the thing that we all now fear because I overlooked one of the most basic aspects of the parasite…its relationship to felines.

"Mr. Keeper here was bitten and survived. I believe this is because he had been exposed to the *Toxoplasma* parasite through his ownership of and interaction with his pet cats. What I want to do is identify any people in Stockton's group that had cats as pets and infect them with the virus to see if they are immune the way Mr. Keeper is."

"You just want to test the people that had cats?" someone asks.

"No, not just those people. There is also the issue of slow moving versus fast moving infected, as well as finding out if you, Mr. Keeper, are contagious."

That gives me a bit of a jolt. I didn't consider the possibility that I might be able to infect someone else.

Mr. Fleischer looks around at everyone, and continues, "You should assume that if it is voted *yes* to allow experiments, that everyone in Stockton's group will be tested. I don't have a proper laboratory to do non-human testing, and we can't safely keep these men with us to wait for the proper facilities to be discovered. The quickest way to find out about the disease is to directly infect the individuals with a bite.

"If you vote to allow me to do the testing, I may find a way to protect us from becoming infected by exposing everyone to the natural *Toxoplasma* parasite. If I don't test, then we won't know if there is any way to protect ourselves, and we won't know why they are starting to move quickly and have higher cognitive function." Oblivious looks appear on several faces at his mention of cognitive function, so he explains further, "We won't know why they are now able to make plans and sneak instead of mindlessly attack."

Erde sits back down, and I give a moment to let people think, then move on with the process.

"We all know what Stockton and his people did here, so if there are no objections, I would like to go immediately to a vote on if they should live or die, and if they should be test subjects before they die. After that, we will vote on the seventeen others individually.

"If there are any questions or concerns let's hear them now." The crowd is still and silent.

"Arthur, check with our people on the roof."

We had to leave several guards on the roof, and they are listening to what is happening on radios. No one is watching Stockton's men, but we have a small group that periodically goes back to check on them.

"The guards up top are good to go," Arthur says.

"Okay, every person should take a paper and write three things; life or death, test or no test, and your name, and then bring it up and put it in the box. This vote is for the thirty-one people—including Stockton—that had committed direct violence against those of you that were held captive. We'll get the votes of the guards on the roof once we have everyone else's vote. Any missing vote or a vote without a name will be counted as *yes* on death and testing."

*

The voting goes quickly with only two *No* votes on the death issue. The issue of experimenting on them was also surprisingly decided by a large majority, only four said no to that.

The next part is going to be more contentious, I'm sure. It may not be the same world as it was a year ago, but we are still the people that used to live in it. What we do now will have implications for how the world will be, at least for our group of survivors. But I will need to argue against any opposition to make sure everyone stays safe."

Everyone is quiet, and while some may be uncomfortable with having to vote on others' fates, everyone seems satisfied with the outcome of the first vote. Time to get the discussion started.

"I think of how lucky my people and I are to have pulled off our trick to free you people. I know all of us could be dead or wish we were dead by now if things ended differently. Those people we have secured back there that weren't directly involved in your suffering, I don't want to let them live. I would execute all of them and would only allow those that were held captive to go free."

A woman from the freed prisoner group speaks up with a physically weakened but defiant voice. "We can't do that! We can't choose to kill those people if they didn't harm us. It is our choice to make. You and your people weren't here, so you shouldn't have a vote in it."

Some of the people with her nod in agreement and express various statements like, "That's not who we are," and, "We can't become evil like them and kill people without reason."

I let them express their concerns to everyone before continuing. "My family, the people that came here to rescue you, risked their lives to do so. It is dumb luck that the people that captured you and tortured you fell for our plan. And you have to understand that they did not let you free out of some sense of remorse or regret over what they had done. They gave up because they believed they were going to get away with everything they did, with absolutely no punishment. They believed their choice was fight and die or walk free with no punishment. You meant nothing to them in their decision."

"But the ones that didn't hurt us weren't a part of that," another woman says interrupting me.

I calmly reply, "Do any of you really believe those people had nothing to do with what you went through here? They helped with patrols, they helped with guard duty, and they helped keep watch on the roof. For all you know, those people that you think didn't hurt you let Stockton and his men know when someone was approaching this store so they could add to their list of victims. It is a great sentiment that you want to move on with your lives and let them go, but why were they left alone while you were starved and tortured? Do any of you have an answer for that?"

This time, Dave, the man from earlier, speaks up, "We don't know what they did to be left alone, but we can't punish them for that. It's not who we are. It isn't what we stand for as a people. It isn't what we want to become." He turns to face the crowd, and continues, "I'm Dave. All of the captives know me. I've been here for two months, maybe more. I was in one of the first groups of people captured by these guys, and I've seen everything they've done. You have voted to punish those that committed the crimes against us, and I accept the vote's outcome—even while I disagree with it. They hurt us, and you believe that makes us justified in hurting them in return. I understand that. Punishing those that never hurt us just because they might commit crimes in the future makes no sense at all."

"And what crimes are you referring to, Dave?" I ask and leave the question hanging.

"We all know what these men did to you folks was wrong, but calling it a crime implies that there is a law against it, right? What law is there, Dave? Can anyone tell me what law there is...? The last time I checked there was no police force. No military. No government or constitution. If you truly want to rely on the laws that existed before the disease spread, then my people and I have to leave you here and free Stockton and his men."

I continue to talk through the gasps and concerned looks. "You and I all know I don't have any legal authority to capture and hold people just because they committed crimes. In fact, if you want to get technical, my people and I are illegally acting as vigilantes. We are currently guilty of kidnapping, impersonating the U.S. military, and threatening bodily harm with deadly weapons.

"Do you people want us to let those that helped Stockton and his people free? Then we can return to our ranch so everyone can await the proper response from authorities, or should we stand together as the decent people we know we all are and deal with the threats we now face in the only manner we have available? The world has changed. Life as we once knew it is gone and it isn't coming back."

"But it is coming back. At least it can if we work on it," Dave says forcefully. "The infected are dying out, and we can start reclaiming the world."

I shake my head slowly, wondering why these people refuse to understand what's going on. "There are runners now," I say, leaving a moment for it to sink in. "We aren't facing the same numbers of the infected, but the ones that are left are more dangerous."

Everyone starts shifting and looking at each other.

"They don't just slowly come after us anymore. They are hunting us and coordinating with each other to do it. They run fast and can use their hands to manipulate things."

"When I arrived this morning, we knew about just three, the one that attacked me yesterday and two others we killed on the way here. But today, while we were working on your release, my people were split up into smaller groups. Three different runners were seen circling the area, trying to sneak up and attack.

"What this means is the only people we can rely on are those we can turn our backs too without them stabbing us. Those people that had Stockton's protection traded your lives for their own safety, and they will do it again if given the choice."

"You don't know that!" the first woman that spoke says, with tears in her eyes. "We can't kill them. We have to trust them. They could have been us. How is what we are planning to do any different from them? We are trading their lives for our own safety."

"No," I say with an angry finality. "We don't have to trust them and it wasn't you. Did any of you agree to turn on other survivors to end your rape and torture? Did any of you agree to work with those bastards in order to keep yourselves or your family out of the cages? All of you could have done it. Why didn't you?" The group is silent. "The world is more different now than the first few months of the infection. Before these things started to run, we always had the chance to come back. All of us could have survived with the infected dying off. We could have eventually overcome the criminals and opportunists to rebuild society. But we don't have the luxury of giving people the benefit of the doubt anymore. Any threat to our survival has to be destroyed now, not just avoided.

"Voting to kill these people for our own safety will do nothing to end society. It has already ended. But voting to let these people live could be the end of the dream of the life we once lived. Letting a known threat live is no different than letting a rabid animal go because it hasn't bitten you yet. I don't want to take that chance. You have to decide amongst yourselves if it's a chance you will take."

"Can we at least have time to think about it?" another woman asks.

"I want to speak with them," Dave says. "At least give those people an opportunity to explain their situation. We have to take into account each individuals behavior and should have every one of them come forward to speak for themselves."

"That is an excellent point and something I can completely agree with you about, Dave," I say while nodding. "We will hear what they have to say for themselves before any vote is made. What we do with the four children is going to be especially difficult for us to decide on. From what I understand, they are all the children of the people that directly hurt you."

This discussion has given me a headache. If we didn't need the extra manpower so badly, I would just say *fuck it* and kill everyone that was with Stockton. I'm not the type of person to just take all of the supplies and leave the freed prisoners to fend for themselves, though, so I'll have to keep my desire for expediency in check and continue listening to their concerns. Plus I have to admit, as much as I dislike Dave, speaking with those other people should have been considered much earlier in the discussion. I'm glad he brought it up. I turn to walk to the other side of the store to get some more sleep and stop in front of Samantha.

"I'm sorry we lost Emily, Samantha," I say and walk around her.

"Eddie?" she says.

I keep walking. I just can't take anymore of anything right now.

"Are you going to be all right, Samantha?" Simone asks.

"It's my fault we're here," she says, and she drops her head and starts to cry again. "Emily is dead because of me, Simone. This is my fault."

Simone grabs Samantha in a strong hug and lets her cry onto her shoulder. "There isn't anything you could have done here, Samantha. You know it isn't your fault."

Pulling back and straightening up, Samantha looks Simone right in the eyes. "You're wrong, Simone. My daughter is dead because of me." The serious tone and stern look concerns Simone.

"About two months ago, Connor, Jake, and I were scouting at the edge of Grants Pass to check the area for infected numbers, and I spotted this group. I saw them take someone prisoner, but I didn't tell anyone about it. Even Conner and Jake didn't know what I saw. When we returned, we just said that there were some people holding up in the Wal-Mart here, but weren't positive if they were criminals. I even convinced myself after a while that they were probably good guys that were just catching someone that had attacked them."

"But why, Samantha? You knew if Emily were alive she would have to come through here to make it to our place."

More tears flow. "I never believed she was alive. It was just easier to think she was already gone than trying to live with this false hope that so many of the others have when they talk about missing family. But now I know that she is dead, and it's my fault. Erde and Emily were captured here a couple weeks after I was here. Stockton only had twenty-four people working with him back then. The rest of his group has only been here for three weeks. Everyone that died here and was raped or beaten is my fault, because I could have stopped it. Your husband would have had all of us come down here and wipe out the potential threat of these guys back then. The way he is trying to do right now.

"It was a choice I made not to say anything. I am not only responsible for Emily, but I put our entire group at risk by not telling you and Eddie about Stockton earlier. I'm sorry."

*

The rest of our group and the survivors did individual interviews with the remaining seventeen people of Stockton's gang, while I got more sleep.

"It turns out none of the complaining was necessary," Arthur says to Simone and me. "It was like you guessed, Eddie. All of them had some involvement in capturing the people. Most of them acted as lookouts, and they said they got bonuses when they spotted someone to be captured."

"They told you that?" I ask in amazement.

"Some of them did, yeah. It's amazing what people will tell you when they think they won't be punished. They would get extra food or snacks if they saw someone. But the kids were the worst part of it all."

"I know. It must have been difficult to deal with. I mean, they're just kids," I say, unaware of what he means.

"No, no. It's not what you think. I mean, we all thought the kids were going to be heartbreaking interviews, and how would we deal with putting their parents to death and expect them to understand. The problem was, the kids were horrifying. I mean, they just felt evil. They didn't care what was happening to the people in the cages. Those kids had dead eyes. We took a vote after the interviews and everyone but two people voted for them to die."

"Let me guess, Dave, and that lady?"

"You got it."

"What do you think about those two, Arthur?"

Arthur looks at Simone and me for a bit, thinking before he answers. "I don't think they should come with us. People like that seem to enjoy being problems in the lives of others. Now I hate to suggest turning away people that are in their poor physical condition, but there are a lot of new people and extra mouths to feed if we let them all come to the ranch. We should check out each of them to see who probably won't work well with our group at the ranch. I'm sure if we let them all come, some of them will eventually be told to leave for one reason or other, and that will be a bigger problem for us. Maybe even a potential threat."

"I trust your judgment, Arthur," Simone says.

"I do too. Let's deal with any problem people we can before they all find out where we live and what our security situation is like. Can you speak with all of the people we freed here to get an idea of what they're like? Anyone that seems untrustworthy—like that woman and Dave— I'll deal with before we leave. As for the rest of them, we should try to convince as many as possible to join us."

"I've spoken with a lot of them already. It won't be a problem to talk with the rest."

"It is a lot of new people to place our trust in at the ranch, Eddie," Simone says. "Are you sure we should take them all in?"

"I would prefer to only bring in people with skills we can use to better survive, but there will be more groups like Stockton's that we will have to deal with, and we need numbers. Every person we bring home from here is a potential foot soldier in any upcoming fight we have.

"Arthur, one more thing, be absolutely certain about who you think we should exclude and why. If any of them choose to stay here, that is one thing. But anyone that we won't allow to come with us to the ranch will be a potential threat, like Chad was, and I won't leave them here alive and able to track us down."

CHAPTER FIFTEEN
EXPERIMENTS

I walk over to the bakery section of the store where we are holding Stockton and his people.

"Take off the pillow cases," I say to the men guarding them, and they begin walking among the groups of prisoners—pulling the covers off of their heads. "This whole ordeal is finally over."

The prisoners of Stockton's group turn their heads toward each other, with a happy confidence that comes from not knowing my next words. I just smile with them and let them in on the bluff.

"I want you all to know that I am a man of my word. As an officer of the United States Military, I have promised you your freedom in exchange for releasing your captives peacefully. Unfortunately for you, I am not in the U.S. Military, and from what I know it no longer exists." A few puzzled looks stare back at me from the crowd at that statement, and I continue filling in this crowd, enjoying every moment of their growing unease.

"There was no nuclear detonation destroying a large group of survivors as there was no large group of survivors that we have ever heard about. And there is no Idaho territory for you to travel to. You are all going to die for your crimes."

This news, of course, stuns and angers the crowd of bound prisoners. Among the yelling and curses being yelled at me, a woman calls from the crowd, "Wait, what about me and my children? I have two kids with me. My son is only eight!"

"Yes. Your son is only eight. And he ran around this store playing with his sister while other children were being raped, tortured, and killed. We were told by your kids that they took most of the food that was supposed to go to the people you were abusing, and they ate it, or threw it out. You taught your children to be indifferent to the suffering of people. In their interviews they were considered cold, aggressive, and even evil in the way they acted and responded to questions. The way you people behaved is disgusting, and human with your traits aren't wanted or needed in this world."

"You can't kill them! They're just kids," the father of the children yells. His proclamation is particularly ridiculous considering the statements of his victims. This man is responsible for raping three of the children that were held captive here, as well as the murder of four others. His particular kind of sickness won't continue in this world through the actions of his spawn, since they won't be living through the day.

"I am perfectly willing to kill the children of monsters like you so that the evil you represent is completely dead. Besides, the information we gain from researching their deaths will possibly help the rest of humanity survive."

"We were just trying to survive! I was trying to protect them! You call me a monster? You're the monster saying you will kill my kids! You can't do this to me!"

"Everyone is trying to survive, lady. Not everyone is willing to allow the rape and abuse of innocent people in order to survive."

When we moved his people back here we had to secure them in a way to allow just a few guards to control the whole group. So we had them sit in five rows, bound their feet, and tied a line along each row so if one person managed to get up, they would have to drag everyone else with them.

Stockton is in the middle of the front row and is quiet while everyone else is struggling and yelling. In a way I think he knew this was a scam. It was just too good to be true.

Mr. Fleischer is in charge of organizing the tests, so he explains to us all what he wants to do, and what he will need from us.

"To do the testing, we have to split everyone into different groups. There are people that had exposure to cats that are the hopeful group to study. They will most likely be a long term study group since it took six hours for Mr. Keeper to reach fever stage, we should assume the same for each of them. Thirteen people had regular exposure to cats. Eight of them were probably exposed to toxoplasmosis because they changed their cats' litter. The other four we aren't sure of. This is a list of their names, pull them out first, and secure them individually by that wall over there. Please separate these four from the others," Erde says while pointing to his list, "as they have a low probability of immunity."

When Erde says to separate them, we all look at him.

"Separate them, how?" Donald asks.

Donald, Karen, and their son, Jake, are here to help with the experiments along with Conner, myself, and Simone. I have to be here because I need to see if I'm contagious, but running these experiments on living people doesn't bother me the way it might bother the others.

Hannah walks in with Mike right behind her. "I want to watch, but also help, if I can," she says. "Mike wanted to come with me."

I raise my eyebrows at his seeming attachment to Hannah and remember him sitting next to her and Lilly at the house, even though there were other seats available. I let it go for now.

"These four will most likely turn quickly once infected," Erde explains. "Once they turn, we have to do a quick test to see if they become regular or coordinated infected, say by giving them something small to hold in their hands—like a pen. Once we have our answer, we can terminate them immediately."

"Okay," I say. "Let's move the ones that will most likely become the infected quickly over by that loading door, so once we are finished and kill them, we can lift the door and roll their bodies out."

"This is so creepy," Karen says. "I mean, how we're talking about these people, and dealing with their bodies. I just never thought I would be doing anything like this."

"I don't think any of us thought our lives would end up like this," Simone says.

"We are crossing a line," I say as Erde waits. "The chills you are all feeling and the deep pit in your stomachs is what lets you know that you still care about humanity. Intentionally infecting people is wrong on many levels, but it will help to keep us alive, and that is why we have to do it."

We separate the people as we were asked and the results are as Erde expected. The four people he thought would turn did turn. They didn't have enough exposure to the regular *Toxoplasma* parasite. The nine remaining are bound and waiting for the fever to hit. Hannah is sitting by them, with a watch, and checking their temperatures every 30 minutes.

For my part in the testing, I have to do three different types of exposure trials. Some of my blood will be placed in an open wound of one person and saliva in the wound of another. I also have to physically bite someone to make sure there isn't a difference between plain saliva and something activated during a bite.

As I walk past Stockton to grab those on his left for testing, he gives me an anguished and ridiculous plea. "Why are you doing this? Why can't you just kill us?"

"Hammurabi's Code, Stockton. An eye for an eye. You tortured those people out there. I can't let you off easy by just shooting you in the head. But don't worry. I'll make sure you don't survive."

The testing goes quickly for the rest of the group. We experimented on them six at a time and none of them were immune. The bad part of the results is that all of them turned into infected that were coordinated and fast. We had some of them bitten by a slow infected and some by a fast one we captured. They all became the fast infected. We determined that they moved fast by securing their mouths and hands, putting bags over their heads so they can't see, and freeing their legs to see them move. The all could move fast.

So Simone's hypothesis about it being the cold making them fast was wrong. This means that the parasite has changed in how it affects the body.

Mr. Fleischer doesn't know how the parasite had such a quick mutation period. "Typically only viruses can change so rapidly, parasites need a much longer evolutionary period to make such a dramatic transformation," he said. "It must have something to do with my alterations to the parasite to speed up the mechanisms for stopping pain and blood loss."

The floor by the rolling door is slick with blood. A scene of disgusting and morbid comedy occurred several times over the night as one of us would slip in the red gore of brain and blood after rolling a body out.

The blood and lingering burnt gunpowder gives the air in the back room a metallic smell and taste. There is also the unpleasant odor of feces and urine that came from the fear these people had of being infected.

Most of the former captives that came into the back room to see what was going on left right away. They had seen enough violence enacted upon themselves and the world that they wanted to see no more. A few of them stayed throughout the testing, however. Their eyes were glued to the turning, and then dying bodies of the men and women that tortured them these last weeks and months.

In the morning, Mr. Fleischer turns to me before he addresses everyone. "Mr. Keeper, you are not contagious."

He then turns to everyone and says in a serious manner. "A bite from any infected person, whether they are fast or slow will result in a fast moving infected person. They still have all of the qualities of their slower counterparts—lack of blood loss, no reaction to pain, and the ability to live and even move with multiple major trauma injuries to the body. Blunt force trauma to the head is the only way to put them down, but now they are moving faster, so they will be harder targets to hit. They will also be more dangerous as they will have the ability to open doors, climb fences, and maneuver around the basic types of obstacles that have so far kept us safe from attacks."

The news about the infected is hard to take for all of us. It seems like our species just can't catch a break.

After some further discussion about the new dangers we face, I look at everyone, and say, "Today we will be finishing the loading of the trucks and heading to the ranch. I said you have your choice to come and go as you wish, but there are some of you here that I don't feel comfortable with leaving behind."

"Are you going to hold us hostage now?" Dave asks.

"No not at all. As I was saying, you are all free to go your own way right now if you choose or come to the ranch, and you can stay or leave at any time. There are those of you however, with more serious health situations that I think need more recovery time before being on your own, but the choice is still yours to make. We need to know now so that we can set you up with the appropriate supplies before leaving. The medicine, food, and sporting goods sections will be empty when my group departs, so anything one of you staying behind needs from those sections should be mentioned now."

"Why don't you leave more stuff for the people staying?" again Dave interrupts.

I really am starting to hate this guy.

"This is the most likely base camp of those staying, so they should get to keep more of the store's resources."

"Dave, I want you to shut up," I finally say.

"What…"

"I said shut up, Dave. Look, I have been playing nice, but there is something that you just don't seem to understand. Anyone that stays here is dead!"

"Do you understand that, Dave?" I say it slowly and with heavy sarcasm. "I mean, look at yourselves!" I say while pointing at the group. "You're a bunch of skeletons. You were all probably barely surviving before you were captured, and then this group starved, beat, and raped most of you into the poor physical conditions that you are today. I doubt many of you would win a fight with a squirrel right now, let alone a running infected. And I am not about to leave shelves full of precious supplies that can be used by us living people, just to make the walking dead feel better."

"I don't want you to leave it for the infected," Dave says. "I mean, leave it for anyone that wants to stay."

"The walking dead aren't the infected. The walking dead are those of you that are staying behind while we go to the ranch. That is how I see it. I give any one of you a one in ten chance of survival in the physical condition you are in. The fact that you survived the torture of your captivity speaks to your strength and will to live, but your captors also kept the infected out of here, and made sure the area stayed somewhat clear. That will be on you now.

"Throughout the day yesterday, I had my people speak to everyone in your group, and they put a list together of those individuals that will not be welcome at the ranch due to clashing or abrasive personalities, or just plain strange behavior. Those of you that choose to stay will be joining the individuals on this roster." I turn and look around behind me. "Arthur, do you have the list?"

"Yes, I'll go ahead and read it, Eddie. If that's okay with you?"

"Sure," I say and move away.

"Dave Cromwell, Phyllis Marshall, Madeline Estabrook, Preston Johnson, Cynthia Ortman, and Sheila Jackson. We have set aside supplies for you to look through and need you to check them over and tell us if there is anything specific not in there that you will need to help you survive. Anyone else that would like to remain here, please let me know in the next hour, so we can get supplies ready for you as well. Are there any questions?"

"Who made the list and why?" a woman asks. She's from the survivors group but not one of the people on the list that isn't welcome.

Arthur replies, "I made the list after speaking with each of you and asking my people what they learned about you, to discover if any of you would have excessively bad attitudes. I brought it up to Eddie yesterday that I thought Dave would cause problems at the ranch, because of the accusatory tone of his questions. He doesn't ask questions to learn anything, he asks for attention, and to be abrasive."

"And who are you at this ranch?" a man asks.

"I am the caretaker. I took care of the animals and did the gardening before everything went to hell and pretty much still do it now. We call it the ranch, but as you know from the description, it is a former horse stable that Mr. Keeper bought and converted into a survival training center."

"And Eddie had nothing to do with this?" Dave asks in a sarcastic tone.

"We aren't the bad guys, Dave," I reply. "We are just trying to survive and keep as many people alive as possible at the same time. You all know that a bad attitude can be as deadly as a bullet sometimes, and we just don't need a dick like you causing us grief. I trust the judgment of everyone at the ranch, and when it comes to the six people Arthur put on the list, you just aren't trustworthy enough to risk our lives for."

One of the women from the list starts crying and walks off. Then the whole group breaks up and goes in different directions.

Mike comes up to me as everyone is walking away, and says, "You need to put guards on those people on the list."

"You think so?"

"Yes. You just sentenced them to death, and they know it. The woman that was crying won't be an issue, but the other five looked pretty pissed. Those people are like the jocks at my old school. They enjoy being assholes, but they hate being called out on it. You just embarrassed them, and they are going to try to get back at us if they can."

I like how he says *us*. Mike is identifying himself as part of our group. "You're right Mike. They really don't have anything to lose by hurting us now. I would like you to get Hannah and some of the other kids your age to follow them closely, but there's a larger issue that you need to understand. Those people won't be coming to the farm because we think they are already potential threats. I don't let potential threats live so they can come back and harm us later. Do you understand?"

"You plan on killing them before we leave?"

"Yes."

"What about anyone that chooses to stay on their own?"

"Those people we will leave supplies for and let them go their own way. I don't want to be a dictator that kills everyone that doesn't follow me. I just want to eliminate any obvious potential threats."

"And you want me and Hannah to follow these five and…"

"No, no, I don't want you to kill them. I want you to make sure they don't hurt anyone else. Don't let them sabotage the trucks, set any fires, open doors to let the infected in, that type of thing. I will kill them when the time comes."

"And you're trusting me with this information? Why?"

"You said five of those people were going to try and get back at us. You said 'us,' including yourself in our group. I know our group isn't perfect, and my planning on killing those people is extreme, but I think you understand what the stakes for safety and survival are these days. You have to know going forward what I am capable of and what type of man I am if you choose to stay with us. You should also know that I do not consider you a threat to our safety, so if you choose to go, there will be no firing squad or even ill feelings on my end."

He looks at me for a moment, contemplating what I've said, and says, "I'll find Hannah and start watching those people." Then he walks off.

"Mike has a solid head on his shoulders," I say to Simone. "I'm amazed at how he's reacting to all of this, especially me."

Simone whispers in my ear, "He told Hannah that he had wanted to kill his father when his mom got kicked out of the tree. He wanted to but couldn't bring himself to do it. If you hadn't killed his father, I think Mike would have after his mother died."

"That's a little disturbing, but I guess I understand it."

*

"The trucks are loaded and ready to go," Donald calls from the door to the back room.

I turn to Arthur, and ask, "How many people are staying here when we leave?"

"None," he replies. "Last night when I was speaking with them, there were several that were considering going their own way. I think that talk you gave about their odds changed everyone's mind, though."

"I'm glad this whole ordeal is over. I can't wait to get back home. So how many extra people do we have?"

Arthur is about to tell me when someone yells for me from the front of the store and someone else yells, "All shooters to the store entrance."

We all run up to the front and look out the doors between the shelf barricades we had set up. At the end of the parking lot I see two large pickups and three Hummer H1s, along with about twenty well-armed men. I recognize two of the men standing front and center and realize we won't be going home any time soon. It looks like this ordeal isn't actually over, it is just beginning.

ADDENDUM
THE ROAD TO HELL

The Proposal

"Toxoplasmosis. The parasitic disease that is associated with cats, but is common in undercooked meat of pork, lamb, and venison. That is the area I propose to study," said Erde Fleischer, the German biopharmaceutical researcher, hoping to get grants for study from the Umfeld Corporation CFO and board.

The Umfeld Corporation is the most generous contributor to the research university Erde was recently hired at. His work in biopharmacy so far has all been aimed at reducing anxiety and fear related ailments from the world through medicinal creations. His current pursuit, and what could be considered his crowning achievement in helping to improve the lives of people in this world, is to find a way to remove aggression. He has expanded his work into the realm of bacterial, parasitic, and viral genomic engineering.

He continues addressing the board assembled before him. "It is my belief that through the study and testing of the effects of the Toxoplasmosis parasitic disease, and discovering and controlling the parts of its genome which exhibit the apparent calming effect it has on rodentia in respect to *Felis silvestris catus* or the common cat, we should be able to reprogram the parasites genome which will enable the treatment of extreme and disabling aggression in humans. This will enable us to potentially turn large portions of the incarcerated prison population to rehabilitated, fully functioning and trustworthy members of society. That is my proposal gentlemen." And Erde returns to his seat.

One of the board members, August Trauerfall, an unassuming man that holds considerable weight with this particular board because of his connections to Germany's and several other nations' military complexes, asks Erde the only questions for the board. "Dr. Fleischer? What I am going to ask you I have read in your proposal booklet in front of us, but I would like to hear from you concisely these few things. First, what is your projected time frame for converting your studies from mice into higher mammals? And second, what is a more precise monetary outlay you feel would be what you need to get this study on its way and to completion?"

Good, Erde thinks. I am happy to hear a question of how much money would be needed. From my experience in requesting funds for research, if no mention is made on the outlay of costs, there isn't a realistic consideration being given to a proposal. Unfortunately, I don't know anything about this Mr. Trauerfall and do not believe he has much influence with the board. At least I have never heard him referred to by the other Scientists or researchers during their grant request hearings.

"Thank you for your question, Mr. Trauerfall. If the project is able to move forward, we are looking at a two or three year time frame to reach the study of larger mammals, such as apes. The first year we are looking at an outlay of twenty-five thousand Euros or twenty-five thousand Marks, depending on whether the Euro is still in circulation when project approval occurs. This small first year outlay is due primarily to student compiling of previous studies. There is a plethora of information and studies on various rodentia and the effects of *Toxoplasma gondii* parasites. We need to use the first year to continue our compilation of all the research into how the disease affects the rodentia. Running through a small portion of these studies is what led me to my proposal."

"The second year would be an outlay of seventy-five thousand Marks to do behavioral specific testing on our own rodentia, to fine tune the information compiled by previous studies." Mr. Trauerfall is looking at me intently, but I can see none of the other board members seem particularly interested in what I am saying. Why isn't Mr. Bauer, the CFO, or Mr. Faust, the Director of the board, paying attention? They are getting restless.

"The third year will either be led by some refining testing of rodentia, costing from twenty-five thousand to fifty thousand Marks. Or it will be led directly by larger mammal studies which, due to longevity issues of the mammals involved, would run approximately two hundred fifty thousand to three hundred fifty thousand Marks."

That got everyone's attention. I could actually see several of them recoil from the amount being proposed, I need to close this. "However, the potential cost benefit if we are successful in reforming the violent and preventing incarceration recidivism could reach hundreds of millions of Marks in Germany alone per year." That got them back. I can see the smiles and head nods. Good.

"Thank you, Dr. Fleischer," says Mr. Faust. "We will contact you shortly to let you know what the board's decision is."

"Thank you, gentlemen, and good day."

Once the boardroom door closes behind Dr. Fleischer, there is a general murmur among the members, with several of them chuckling at the idealism of the proposal Fleischer had presented. "How are we to tell our members that we are spending company money to study rats and mice in the hope that we can let criminals walk the streets among them?" General laughter ensues.

It is Mr. Trauerfall that quickly silences the crowd by stating simply, "I approve funds for this study." The shocked looks turn from Trauerfall, to Mr. Faust and Mr. Bauer, both of whom were also enjoying a good laugh and simply shrugged their shoulders at the questioning looks of the others.

"Gentlemen," addresses Mr. Trauerfall. "Consider the potential military or even non-military purposes for a parasitic infection or medicine derived from it that can calm aggressive individuals. Aside from inoculations or treatments for the aggressive individuals Dr. Fleischer wishes to help, perhaps a version of this could be developed that could be used to calm rioters. Or used to drop into a war zone to render an opposing military's troops inert by making them unwilling to fight. This may or may not be a public or generally commercially viable research study, but it is a study with extreme potential to provide our company with a large financial benefit."

"Best of all, if the research looks to be heading nowhere with the rodentia, it will definitely not progress to the larger mammal stage, which is where the significant outlays of capital are required."

The Research

After one and a half years of reviewing other studies and completing his own multiple studies on the effects of toxoplasmosis on mice, rats, and rabbits, Dr. Fleischer is happy to have conclusive and corroborated evidence that the disease changes the chemical fear response in the rodentia studied to make them respond to cat signs and odors in a positive way. He is reporting his findings directly to the original board member, Mr. Trauerfell, who approved the funding for his studies.

"Mr. Trauerfell, not only did I reinforce the original findings, but with some slight modification to the parasites genetic makeup, we were already able to change the lack of aversion in the rodentia to an actively seeking out of *Felis silvestris catus* by said rodentia. As I mentioned in my earlier reports, it isn't exactly the loss of aggression that seems to be the basis for the rodent behavior but actually a loss of fear. In certain cases, we have observed the rodents lose all aggression but in most circumstances the rodents, regardless of species, fought to remain alive when the cats pounced on them and or began to eat them. They would fight until they were technically dead. But in some instances we noted no survival instincts remaining, no attempt to fight off the attack, and no returned aggression.

"I believe this will allow us to move forward in two possible directions for the remaining half of the year with further studies warranted on the rodentia. First, to pursue the pathways and genomic markers responsible for the lack of aggression. To be one hundred percent certain that the changes made to the parasite's genome are responsible for that lack of aggression. Second, to pursue the changes controlling the loss of fear response. This could also be beneficial in development of possible medications to reduce anxiety for the population, which was one of my areas of specialty before this specific undertaking.

"Of course, taking our research into two different areas would necessarily increase the cost associated with the work we are doing. So I leave it to you, Mr. Trauerfell, to decide which course you and the board members feel is more vital to pursue, or if you believe both courses might both be beneficial."

Mr. Trauerfell is a happy man today. He has been following Dr. Fleischer's research very closely and has been told that the defense ministry is particularly interested in the project, as it has multiple facets that could, "Benefit the general defense of this nation and humanity in general," as it was put. There is a large grant of funds going through the Umfeld Corporation to directly benefit Dr. Fleischer's research, but not just on the two branches he believes to be beneficial.

"Dr. Fleischer, I am pleased to tell you that we are approving not just the fear and aggression portion of your research as two viable programs, but a third as well."

This had not occurred to Erde to even ask for it. He knew there were many parts of his research into this one simple disease that had the potential to be a financial gain to the company in the pursuit of new medicines and treatments. But companies are usually more cautious to pursue one course at a time, to ensure not too much capital is lost on any one venture. Caution with capital outlays is especially prevalent in these days with the economy slowing again. Almost too excitedly, Erde asks, "Which other direction did you want me to study?"

"The loss of a pain response, Dr. Fleischer. Your reports indicated that with the rodentia there was a lack of pain response while they were being consumed by the cats, as well as in the live dissections. Not just with the cases that had a loss of aggression. But it seemed in your report to suggest that the rodents were able to fight and remain alive long after they had lost several limbs. Also in certain cases it was reported that a lack of blood loss and no vocal response occurred when the limbs were lost. I'm sure you can imagine how beneficial any medical treatment would be if it prevented blood loss, or pain, or even the response to pain. Take for example simple surgery. If something we could develop were able to replace modern anesthetics. Something simpler, more effective with potentially fewer side effects. It could re-revolutionize modern medicine."

And, August thinks, *beyond our companies benefit in the medical market, if we could combine a lack of fear, lack of pain response, lack of blood loss into a package for the military, we could potentially never lose another life in war and all become billionaires in the process.*

"Because your research is looking so promising, you will be taking over building C and the rest of this building as well for your research, Dr. Fleischer."

To this Erde is truly surprised. He knows the various forms of flu research being done in the next building over have been quite successful for the company as well. But he doesn't interrupt Mr. Trauerfell.

"Dr. Schwartz and his research assistants are being absorbed under you. His research was not progressing with as positive a potential outcome as yours, so we felt to prevent a disruption in continuity, it would be best if we could absorb him into your work rather than move you to a larger facility. He will actually be receiving an increase in his benefits package to assist with the disappointment we are sure he will feel at the loss of his own research. Please let us know if there is any animosity or difficulty in working with Dr. Schwartz, as we want your research to proceed without any molestation or interruption. Do you have any questions for me or for the rest of the board?"

"No sir. And thank you."

Preliminary Results and Direction Change

Four months later, the projects are ready to move onto larger mammal testing. Dr. Fleischer is addressing the full board of the Umfeld Corp. plus one new member once again to explain his findings. The board is all smiles this day but none as self-assured as Mr. Trauerfell.

"As you can see by the graphs I have just shown you and in the reports provided. We have been able to modify or re-write the genetic markers of this particular parasite to control the rodentia in ways even I thought would not be possible in such a short time. It was my colleague, Dr. Schwartz, who recommended we focus our efforts on removing the genetic markers that seem to interfere with the parasite's natural disposition to control behavioral aspects of its hosts. Once we did this the research unfolded at the tremendous pace you see before you. Of course I must add that had this board not provided such an unprecedented amount of support for our research, we might not have arrived at this point for several more years. So thank you for your current and ongoing support in this project."

The board's director, Mr. Faust, is the first gentleman with questions today. Mr. Trauerfell is well versed in the research and knows every facet of possibility with where it is headed, but only let on to a few of the more tantalizingly profitable ones to the rest of the board.

"I understand you were able to have the mice in separate tests—display no fear to the cats, express no measurable pain when being dissected, and remove aggression, essentially the fight response from these mice? Is that right?"

"Yes, Mr. Faust, we were. As well as those effects we also observed a lack of blood loss due to extreme vasoconstrictions. And we were also able to mix the results in various combinations with each other. We have several cases in which our veterinary surgeon performed almost total dissections after the fear, pain, and blood loss mechanisms were altered by the parasite, and he was able to re-attach the limbs and organs after the dissection to have the rabbits continue to live.

"This is truly remarkable in the realm of medicine because any surgery is a traumatic event on a body which can potentially lead to death. But to be able to remove virtually all organs and limbs and have the brain survive unharmed is simply unheard of. In fact, the rabbits are still alive now, and the first surgical procedure was just over three weeks ago. The only losses occurred when injury occurred to the brain."

Colonel Bernhardt Herrmann of the German military defense forces, the new face within the board, introduces himself and leads the questions in a new direction. "As you can imagine Doctor, my interests in your work are for battlefield application. We have minimized our battlefield losses greatly in recent decades, primarily by increasing medical availability response time. Shock due to trauma and blood loss remains the major killer of our men, so any research that can help in this area we are obviously interested in. What is the response time of the altered parasite, from initial introduction to production of the desired bodily reaction changes? If we were to give this to soldiers, would we need to inoculate them some time before injury, or would we possibly be able to administer on site injections in order to say staunch the flow of blood from injuries?"

Dr. Fleischer nods his approval to the question, and then responds, "Colonel Herrmann, we have increased the application response time again by altering the parasitic genome allowing for effects from the parasite to be realized in five to ten minutes time. This is, of course, only in the studies we have performed on rodentia and have yet to perform the tests on larger mammals, such as monkeys and apes. If the effects timing remains constant once crossed over to the primates then it would essentially be your decision if the maximum time of ten minutes is low enough to still save lives.

"There may be other differences and outcomes that have not yet been realized that will also affect the determination on time to inoculate. We must move on to the primate studies to make any concrete realizations on human interaction effectiveness," Dr. Fleischer states.

"When will you be able to start primate trials?" Colonel Herrmann asks.

"Once funds are approved for the research, I can apply to the primate research facility for the next available group or groups of primates. It will take six to nine months after primate lot approval for the primates to be old enough for research. So if things go smoothly, I should have no trouble starting that research in a year's time."

Colonel Herrmann doesn't like that timeframe, and the scowl on his face shows it. He turns to Mr. Trauerfell, and says, "You told me he could get moving on it in a month! We have the world economies collapsing and increasing unrest—"

Mr. Trauerfell just smiles and holds a hand up to Colonel Herrmann to get him to stop. "Yes, yes. Dr. Fleischer is not aware that the funds for the research have already been approved and a group of primates had been ordered for research two months ago." He turns to Dr. Fleischer, and continues, "In addition to that, we have reassigned the primates from Dr. Engel's psychological research over to you to begin testing immediately.

"Dr. Engel has a group of forty primates in which he is studying the primate caring responses to various cats and kittens that are the primates' pets. Your research is more vital for our corporation to bring into completion, not only for the financial wellbeing of our investors, but also for the urgent global situation which we all find ourselves in right now. You can begin research tomorrow in building D. You will be moving your research over there as it has the proper holding facilities for the larger mammals you will be studying."

On to Human Trials

"Dr. Fleischer, can you tell us the results of your studies before the fire occurred?" Mr. Faust asks.

"Yes. Fortunately we kept all of our research data in building C, so none of it was lost in yesterday's tragic fire. The results of the primate testing are identical to the results done with the rodentia testing. We observed the same combination of lack of blood loss, loss of pain response, lack of measurable fear and increased resistance to death with extreme dissection.

"All of our tests were performed with the original group of primates that were transferred from Dr. Engel's psychological testing program. We had just received two days ago the new group of primates that were ordered six months ago. Testing was supposed to begin yesterday, but I am unaware that any tests were able to be accomplished due to the fire."

Colonel Herrmann asks, "Where does this put us in timelines for testing?"

"I think the primate testing is essentially completed, Colonel Herrmann. If any anomalies or unusual responses had shown up in the primates, as opposed to the rodentia, then I would recommend ordering another group of primates, which would take another six months. I would then need to train more lab personnel to replace all those lost in the fire, so another three months after the primates arrive.

"With the solid data that we have already compiled, I recommend we move on to small group human trial testing. Perhaps, if you wish, a small group of soldiers in the field that could benefit the most from the drug we produce with this parasite."

"I do have a group of men in mind," Colonel Herrmann responds. "The Tiger Squadron with NATO forces in Moldova. They have seen some of the heaviest fighting against the Russian troops in southern Ukraine. What do you intend to call this drug?"

"I call it, Zeus."

THE END

 SEVERED**PRESS**

f facebook.com/severedpress

twitter.com/severedpress

CHECK OUT OTHER GREAT ZOMBIE NOVELS

Z BURBIA
by Jake Bible

Whispering Pines is a classic, quiet, private American subdivision on the edge of Asheville, NC, set in the pristine Blue Ridge Mountains. Which is good since the zombie apocalypse has come to Western North Carolina and really put suburban living to the test!

Surrounded by a sea of the undead, the residents of Whispering Pines have adapted their bucolic life of block parties to scavenging parties, common area groundskeeping to immediate area warfare, neighborhood beautification to neighborhood fortification.

But, even in the best of times, suburban living has its ups and downs what with nosy neighbors, a strict Home Owners' Association, and a property management company that believes the words "strict interpretation" are holy words when applied to the HOA covenants. Now with the zombie apocalypse upon them even those innocuous, daily irritations quickly become dramatic struggles for personal identity, family security, and straight up survival.

ZOMBIE RULES
by David Achord

Zach Gunderson's life sucked and then the zombie apocalypse began.

Rick, an aging Vietnam veteran, alcoholic, and prepper, convinces Zach that the apocalypse is on the horizon. The two of them take refuge at a remote farm. As the zombie plague rages, they face a terrifying fight for survival.

They soon learn however that the walking dead are not the only monsters.

SEVERED**PRESS**

f facebook.com/severedpress
🐦 twitter.com/severedpress

CHECK OUT OTHER GREAT ZOMBIE NOVELS

900 MILES
by S. Johnathan Davis

John is a killer, but that wasn't his day job before the Apocalypse.

In a harrowing 900 mile race against time to get to his wife just as the dead begin to rise, John, a business man trapped in New York, soon learns that the zombies are the least of his worries, as he sees first-hand the horror of what man is capable of with no rules, no consequences and death at every turn.

Teaming up with an ex-army pilot named Kyle, they escape New York only to stumble across a man who says that he has the key to a rumored underground stronghold called Avalon..... Will they find safety? Will they make it to Johns wife before it's too late?

Get ready to follow John and Kyle in this fast paced thriller that mixes zombie horror with gladiator style arena action!

WHITE FLAG OF THE DEAD
by Joseph Talluto

Millions died when the Enillo Virus swept the earth. Millions more were lost when the victims of the plague refused to stay dead, instead rising to slaughter and feed on those left alive. For survivors like John Talon and his son Jake, they are faced with a choice: Do they submit to the dead, raising the white flag of surrender? Or do they find the will to fight, to try and hang on to the last shreds or humanity?

CHECK OUT OTHER GREAT ZOMBIE NOVELS

VACCINATION
by Phillip Tomasso

What if the H7N9 vaccination wasn't just a preventative mea-
sure against swine flu?
It seemed like the flu came out of nowhere and yet, in no time
at all the government manufactured a vaccination. Were lab
workers diligent, or could the virus itself have been man-made?
Chase McKinney works as a dispatcher at 9-1-1. Taking emergency calls, it becomes immediately obvious that the entire city is
infected with the walking dead. His first goal is to reach and save
his two children.
Could the walls built by the U.S.A. to keep out illegal aliens, and
the fact the Mexican government could not afford to vaccinate
their citizens against the flu, make the southern border the only
plausible destination for safety?

ZOMBIE, INC
by Chris Dougherty

"WELCOME! To Zombie, Inc. The United Five State Republic's
leading manufacturer of zombie defense systems! In business
since 2027, Zombie, Inc. puts YOU first. YOUR safety is our
MAIN GOAL! Our many home defense options - from Ze
Fence® to Ze Popper® to Ze Shed® - fit every need and
every budget. Use Scan Code "TELL ME MORE!" for your
FREE, in-home*, no obligation consultation! *Schedule your
appointment with the confidence that you will NEVER HAVE
TO LEAVE YOUR HOME! It isn't safe out there and we know it
better than most! Our sales staff is FULLY TRAINED to handle
any and all adversarial encounters with the living and the
undead". Twenty-five years after the deadly plague, the United
Five State Republic's most successful company, Zombie, Inc.,
is in trouble. Will a simple case of dwindling supply and lessen-
ing demand be the end of them or will Zombie, Inc. find a way,
however unpalatable, to survive?

www.ingramcontent.com/pod-product-compliance
Lightning Source LLC
Chambersburg PA
CBHW022215170626
46807CB00005B/2376